THE MAN WITH A THOUSAND FACES

Lex Noteboom studied modern history at the University of Amsterdam. After his studies, he worked in advertising for some time before quitting his job and pursuing his dream of becoming an author. He decided to write an audio drama podcast that he would publish himself. After finishing the script for the sci-fi thriller *The Deca Tapes*, Lex produced and scored the show on a shoestring budget from his bedroom. It went on to win multiple awards – including the Lovie Award, the biggest award for digital creativity in Europe – and landed Lex a book deal with one of the leading Dutch publishing houses. His debut thriller, *The Man with a Thousand Faces*, made waves in the Netherlands by landing multiple nominations and wins for various awards, and was named Book of the Year by the country's most widely read newspaper.

THE MAN WITH A THOUSAND FACES

LEX NOTEBOOM

Translated from the Dutch by Ida Blom

ORION

Originally published by A.W. Bruna Uitgevers, Amsterdam, The Netherlands

First published in Great Britain in 2025 by Orion Fiction,
an imprint of The Orion Publishing Group Ltd.
Carmelite House, 50 Victoria Embankment
London EC4Y 0DZ

An Hachette UK Company

The authorised representative in the EEA is Hachette Ireland,
8 Castlecourt Centre, Dublin 15, D15 XTP3,
Ireland (email: info@hbgi.ie)

1 3 5 7 9 10 8 6 4 2

A CIP catalogue record for this book is
available from the British Library.

ISBN (Hardback) 9781 3987 2181 4
ISBN (Trade Paperback) 9781 3987 2182 1
ISBN (Ebook) 9781 3987 2184 5
ISBN (Audio) 9781 3987 2185 2

Typeset at The Spartan Press Ltd,
Lymington, Hants

Printed in Great Britain by Clays Ltd,
Elcograf S.p.A.

www.orionbooks.co.uk

For D, E and M

In war, truth is the first casualty.

Aeschylus

Borders are arbitrary, and countries do not exist. The only thing that unites a people is their story.

Petar Lechkov

The West wants the Cold War to be over, and that's why we pretend Kazichia does not exist.

Anderson Holt

Prologue

I wait in the bedroom because I know she will only come in here after putting her daughter to bed, finishing her wine, and locking the doors. I look at the folded pink pyjamas. When she is done downstairs, she will come to the bedroom, take the pyjamas from the bed, and put them on. Only then will she go to the bathroom.

She always does everything in the same order. Every night is the same.

I read in a scientific article that humans do almost everything unconsciously. We only really think about five per cent of our decisions – if I understood correctly. If that's true, then all of us are soldiers; we are only allowed to make decisions if something doesn't happen according to plan.

Downstairs, the floors creak. I follow the sound through the living room, to the kitchen island. There it stops. I hear glass on marble. She drinks one or two glasses of red wine while watching TV. For some reason, she won't put the empty glass in the dishwasher until tomorrow. A few seconds later, she drinks some water and then walks to the hallway.

Same routine every time.

Every night is the same.

Until tonight.

Tonight, a man wearing a balaclava is sitting in her bedroom. After tonight, opening a door will never be the same.

Again, creaking downstairs. The sound moves through the hallway to the front door. One by one, the lights are switched off.

My breathing is too superficial. I rub my hands on my trousers. It doesn't help, because I'm wearing gloves.

The plastic curtain cords rattle in their pulleys.

Should I get out my gun? Or is the fact that I'm in her bedroom enough to scare her? I hope she won't scream. Most people don't scream. Most people shriek and then freeze. They wait. But sometimes, someone lets out an uncontrollable cry. Then you have to hit them. You tap them as if you're waking them up and then they'll shut up. But not too hard, because then the screaming will last longer.

The floor creaks again; she's going to the toilet. The fan turns on and pulls the air through the wall behind me, up to the roof. The wall is buzzing, and so are my ears.

I close my eyes and breathe in and out. When I open my eyes, I look around the dark room. It's spacious, and every corner has something in it: little chairs, tables, cabinets. The more expensive the house, the more useless stuff it contains. The carpet is nice and soft, I have to give her that. I can feel it through my socks.

The toilet flushes and the fan is turned off. I stand up very slowly and look at the bedroom door, framed by cracks of yellow light from the hallway. I try to get my breathing under control, but I can't. The ringing in my ears gets louder. Maybe I snorted a bit too much. Normally I don't take over five milligrams of Moda. Why did I do more today? Why didn't I just do what I always do?

Stumbling in the hallway, then up the stairs.

Fourteen steps.

Slowly, I walk towards the bedroom door. The soft carpet reminds me of a night in Warsaw that I spent hiding under the bed of a Polish businessman. I needed to poison the man in his sleep, but the potion didn't work. The client gave me a plastic tube and a pipette, and I asked what type of poison it contained. 'The less you know, the more useful you are,' he said. They always say stuff like that. I'm only allowed to think for myself when something doesn't go according to plan. And so, I lay under that hotel bed all night, listening to the old sleeping Pole. Waiting for him to die. But the man had a wonderful sleep, and I ended up having to kill him with his head pillow before the sun rose. The only comfort during that long fucking night was the soft carpet under the bed.

Footsteps on the landing. She will go and check on her daughter now. Her daughter is always asleep, but she checks anyway.

I snap the holster open. I hope she won't scream. If she screams, her daughter wakes up, and then we have to take care of that before I can get to my questions. Most people don't scream, though.

A few weeks ago, I read that dogs can smell the past; when they walk into a room, they know exactly where people have walked and sat. Their sense of smell goes back for days, even. Dogs know that people keep repeating their movements like they're stuck. They can predict our future.

The floor in the hallway is creaking again, so her daughter is asleep.

She's coming to the bedroom.

She's so close now that I can hear her breathing. I can hear the fabric from her sleeves as they brush against her waist. She's talking to herself. Very softly.

I bend down and forward, so that I can step in if she starts screaming. Most people don't scream, though. Most people wait for what will happen, completely frozen.

'Who are you?!' That's her version of the short shriek before she stiffens.

'Sit down,' I say softly, and I point to the white chair that she drapes her clothes on every evening.

She nods but doesn't listen. She's standing still and staring at me.

'Who are you?'

Her voice trembles.

'Sit down,' I say again, 'I'm not going to hurt you.' I talk as quietly as possible, but my voice trembles a little, too.

She looks through the open door into the hallway. In the direction of her daughter's bedroom. That's how long it takes before you don't just think about yourself, but also about your child.

3

Everyone thinks about themselves first; I've seen it happen many times.

'If we're quiet, she won't wake up,' I say.

She nods again.

'Take a seat on the chair behind you.'

She scuffles backwards without losing sight of me. In her right hand, she has her smartphone. I don't lose sight of that.

'What do you want?' Her whole body looks tense. In two days, she will have sore thighs and her jaw will be stiff.

'You want money?' she asks. Her eyes shoot to the door, and back to me. 'I don't have cash. But I can go to an ATM for you.'

I shake my head and take a step forward to close the bedroom door. 'I just want to talk, that's all.'

The room gets dark again.

'Put your phone on the ground, next to the chair.'

She nods and puts the phone down. 'I do have some jewellery,' she says. 'Jewels.' She sweeps her hair back, over her shoulder. Why would she do that? Maybe she's trying to make herself less attractive; maybe she's afraid that I'm here to rape her, and that's why I'm in the bedroom.

When I go and sit down on the edge of the bed, her legs relax a little.

'I want to talk to you about your past life,' I say.

'My what?'

'I want to talk to you about your life before coming to America.'

She folds her arms in front of her chest. 'I don't know what you mean.'

'You know exactly what I mean.'

'Who are you?'

The balaclava is starting to get itchy. Sweat on my forehead is getting the fabric wet, and now my skin is irritated. And my ears are ringing.

'Why did you give yourself a new name?' I ask.

She takes a deep breath and sinks into the chair.

'Why did you give yourself and your child a new name? In your passport, it says 'Noëlla', but your name is Michelle. And you didn't grow up in France, but in the Netherlands.'

4

She asks how I know all this.

That's strange. Most people insist they have no idea what I'm talking about. But not her. This woman immediately admits that I know the truth.

'I've been searching for answers for a while,' I say.

'Are you the man who ascended from the ice?' she asks.

I'm not sure if I should answer that. I should have snorted less Moda.

'Yes, it was you. You were out on the frozen lake, waiting for us.' She looks at my hands, but the burn marks she's looking for are hidden by gloves.

'All I want is answers to my questions,' I say. 'If I get those, I'll never come back, ever.'

She's not nodding anymore. She's thinking.

'If I get answers, I won't hurt your daughter,' I try.

Immediately her eyes shoot back to my face. 'What do you want to know?' she asks.

'Who did I work for? Who was my commander?'

'What do you mean?'

She knows what I mean.

I start talking louder. 'My question is very simple: Who did I work for? Who assigned those kidnappings and executions? The rebels? The CIA? The government?'

She shakes her head. 'Do you really think the world is that simple? Like a football game between two teams?' She slides back in her chair, her arms folded.

'There must be one person who set up the operation?' My voice trembles. 'The more research I try doing, the more confusing it gets.'

'I understand why you came here,' she says and crosses her legs. 'This is about Kazichia. You want to know what the goal of your mission was. Why you were there.'

Now I'm the one nodding. 'I want to know why an innocent woman had to die. I want to know if all that misery served a purpose.'

'I wasn't as important as you think. I don't have all the answers.'

'You're part of the Lechkov family, of course you're important.'

5

The floor creaks. Her eyes dart to the door. Is that her daughter? Is she awake?

We sit opposite each other in the dark bedroom, in silence. She watches the door, I watch her. The white in her eye lights up in the dark.

'Tell me the truth,' I whisper. 'I've had enough of all the lies. Tell me the truth, and I'll spare you both. Who is the Man with a Thousand Faces? And how did he gain so much influence?'

She swallows. 'I didn't know. I didn't know about the war with the rebels or the Man with a Thousand Faces. All I did was try to escape. All I wanted was to get my kids home.'

I stand up and pull my gun from its holster under my coat. She dives forward, but I push her back into her chair and press the barrel against her forehead.

'Please,' she whispers and looks up. Her eyes well up with tears. 'If you shoot me, you definitely won't get any answers.'

'That's true.' I press the gun to her thigh.

She stretches her arms out in front of her. 'I'm telling you the truth, I swear. I flew to Stolia for a funeral. That was my first visit to Kazichia, and we were supposed to stay for a few days. I got stuck there. I was a prisoner.' She lowers her arms and takes a deep breath. 'We're both looking for answers. We both want to understand what happened. Maybe we can help each other.'

'You know *exactly* what happened.'

'If only. Why do you think I'm living here? Under a different name? I do lie about everything. My whole life is a lie. I did not grow up in Paris, I didn't work for an IT company, and I didn't lose my husband Gabriël to cancer because Gabriël never existed. I lie about everything because I have to hide.' She leans forward, and her wet eyes glisten like glass. 'All I want is safety. That's why I'm here. I'm not part of the Lechkov family anymore. I'm scared of those people. I wish I had never met them.'

I press the gun to her head again. 'I might as well shoot you, then. You're useless to me.'

'We can help each other,' she repeats and points to the bed. 'Sit down again. Ask me something else. Maybe I know the answer. Sit down.'

I do as she tells me.

'We met out on a frozen lake. In that lake, there's a secret island – an island that's not in the atlas. And on that island, there's a house. Did you go in there?'

She nods.

'Did you go down to the basement?'

'Yes,' she says. 'It's like a recording studio; there are four cameras and a chair in the middle, and the walls are painted green.'

'In that basement, an innocent woman was filmed and tortured, for hours. I want to know why the Lechkov family did that. And I want to know what that basement has to do with the Man with a Thousand Faces.'

She looks at the door and then smiles at me. A slight smile.

'Why are you smiling?'

'I don't know exactly what they did to that woman. I don't know what happened on that island, but together with you I can find out.' She gets up. 'We want the same thing. We want answers. People who want the same thing don't have to point guns at each other. I have an open bottle of wine left downstairs, but maybe you knew that.'

'Yes. I did.'

'Let's go to the kitchen so my daughter doesn't wake up and have a glass of wine while we find out what happened. I'll tell my story, and you tell yours. We'll cover everything that happened in Kazichia, from beginning to end. Together we will find out the truth. Together, we can expose the Man with a Thousand Faces.'

Before I respond, she starts towards the door. I watch her leave the room like I'm not even here anymore. Before she disappears, she turns round. 'Come on, we can talk. But be quiet in the hallway.'

I nod and do what she says.

I. The Last Lechkov

1

The grey metallic BMW 7 series stops on the east side of Schiphol, by the gate for the private hangars. A smiling customs officer walks over to the car in big steps and takes three passports from the driver. While he hurries back to his station to check passenger records, it gets quiet inside the car.

The first passport the man opens belongs to Michelle Verdier Lechkova, born on 7th June 1986 in Zutphen. Michelle is in the back seat of the car. She is quiet because she feels like throwing up. During her first pregnancy, she was fine, but this time round, she's tired, grumpy, and nauseous. Every little hurdle seems impossible to overcome, which is why she called their favourite resort in Dubai the day before arriving; she needs sun and a pool, stat. And the villa of the resort turned out to be available. 'How lucky,' she told the resort manager, and she read out her credit card number. But Michelle knew that it was not a question of luck. The manager covered the phone with his hand and told his co-worker that the villa needed to become available immediately. 'The guests that are there now need to be moved to a suite,' he said. 'Think of an excuse. It's for Mrs *Lechkov*.' Michelle pretended not to hear them, but 'Lechkov' sounded more like a warning than a last name.

The military policeman has entered Michelle's information and opens the second passport. The document belongs to Alexa Lechkova, three years old, born in Amsterdam. The girl sits beside her mother in the car and stares out the window holding her stuffed dog. Alexa is quiet too, but for an entirely different reason;

her parents were fighting before they started driving. Alexa doesn't understand what her parents were talking about but can tell that the silence in the car is tense. It feels like something is about to happen. But what? She stares out the window at the flags behind the hangars, which are being pulled this way and that by the gusts of wind.

When Alexa's information has been entered, the military policeman opens up the last document. The passport photo shows a man with a rough face, a broad nose, and soft eyes. Daniel Petar Lechkov, born in 1982 in the former Soviet state of Kazichia. But the passport is Dutch. Daniel is sitting next to the driver and quietly texting. He is trying to reach his family because something strange has happened; that morning he had fourteen missed calls from his mother – his mother, who normally never calls. On the off chance that she wants to talk to him, she lets him know through one of her assistants. Even when his father had collapsed on the steps of the Kazichian parliament, Daniel received a text with a request for a call.

And now fourteen missed calls . . .

Daniel wanted to delay the trip to Dubai immediately. Fourteen missed calls, fourteen reasons to worry. But Michelle dismissed it as a malfunction or a mistake. That angered him. He didn't think she should prioritise a few days of holiday time over his family's wellbeing – *their* family's wellbeing. Michelle said that he wasn't understanding enough. She needed rest, did he not get that? Because Alexa was visibly shaken by their discussion, he restrained himself. But he was still worried, and on the way to Schiphol he had tried to reach his mother or his uncle. Nobody responded. And he couldn't find anything about his country of birth on any of the international news sites.

Not yet.

Because over three thousand kilometres east, just outside the capital city of Kazichia, something happened that night that would make international headlines. Between a badly maintained two-lane road and the narrow Kazichian shoreline lay the wreck of a Rolls-Royce. The road was scattered with glass and showed dark red streaks of oil and blood. On the side of the wreck, a hole was sawed to free the driver. But when the firemen pulled the man from the car, and one of them started performing CPR on him along the grey-blue surf, it was already too late. The victim had passed away. The fireman stopped, and when he leaned back, he took a good look at the deceased man's face. He jumped back in shock.

'Lechkov!' he shouted to the paramedics running out to the beach. 'It's President Lechkov!'

The name sounded like a warning.

The military policeman returns the passports to the driver and breaks the silence in the car. 'Have a great holiday, Mr and Mrs Lechkov.' Nobody responds. The gate opens, and while the car enters the grounds of Schiphol, the smile on the man's face disappears. 'Lechkov,' he mumbles to himself while trudging back to his station, and that second time, it sounds more like a curse word than a name.

A few dozen metres away, the BMW stops by the Lechkovs' private jet. Daniel helps Michelle get out of the car and tells her that she can board the jet – he'll take Alexa and get the bags through security. Grateful, she hoists herself up the steps of the plane, and while the flight attendant welcomes her, she promises herself to make peace. It's not fair to push Daniel away when he's talking about his family, especially when he's worried. She likes to pretend her last name is just as powerful as any other name, but she knows that just isn't true.

Daniel has lifted Alexa from the car, but when he feels his phone vibrate in his pocket, he sets her down and pulls out the device.

'Tsvali,' a woman's voice says. 'Are you there?'

'Mum?'

'It's Vigo.'

Daniel looks at the plane and sees his wife behind one of the windows, closing her eyes.

'Daniel, do you hear me?' Maika Lechkova asks. 'You need to get back to the family now. Your brother is dead.'

13

2

The laptop is old and the file is big, so the system needs to let the memory buffer fill up before the video starts. After a few moments of silence, a chair appears on the dusty screen. A wooden chair in front of a green wall. Nothing else.

The resolution of the recording is high: you can see tiny scratches in the wood of the armrests and dust particles floating through the air right by the lens.

The microphone is highly sensitive: you can hear all sorts of background noises. Something hums or hisses – studio lights or a fan – and people are discussing something quietly. The voices are far away and hard to understand. They speak a foreign language.

In the bottom at the right of the screen there's a code visible, which ends in three zeroes:

ANTD = >> 000

Someone starts talking, his voice booming through the sensitive microphone.

'Madam, could you come here and sit on that chair? Then we can check if everything works as it should.'

'Where did that American soldier go?' a woman's voice asks.

The man sighs. 'He will come and get you afterwards. No worries.'

To the left, a woman walks into the frame, dressed in a black robe. The sleeves cover her hands, and embroidered in the fabric

14

are countless white symbols. She looks like a pagan priest. When the woman makes it to the chair, the code in the corner of the screen starts going up fast. It stops at one hundred.

ANTD = >> 100

A different male voice sounds, this one further away. 'He recognises her immediately,' he says. 'That's a good sign.'

It's unclear what the man means by this.

The woman in the black robe turns to the camera and asks, while looking into the lens, 'Do you want me to sit?'

She has big, dark brown eyes and a black plait on her shoulder. Her face is delicate, but she has thick pink marks on her left cheek that demand attention.

'Please,' the man close to the camera says. 'We will need to turn the chair a few times, but for now, you'll look into this camera.'

The woman takes a seat, looks to her right, and then down. She seems to be unsure if she should stay there.

'You have brought an impressive amount of equipment,' she says, and she looks to her right again — maybe towards the door she entered through. 'I did not expect you'd need this much technology for a TV interview.'

When she turns her face, the scars on her neck are visible, leading down to her collar. They look like scratches from a bear's claw.

'Look straight into the camera and move as little as possible. Thank you.'

The woman straightens her back and looks into the lens. She is in her early forties, maybe a little older, and there's no fear in her eyes; mostly, she seems annoyed.

'Don't move, madam.'

The man further away says something, but he's hard to understand.

'Madam, is it possible for you to remove your tunic? What are you wearing underneath?'

'I can remove it if you want,' she says, but she doesn't move.

'Madam?'

She nods and stands up. By holding up her right arm, her sleeve falls, and her hand is free. With a hard tug, she pulls the black fabric over her head. Now she's only wearing a tight white T-shirt.

'Is this better?' she asks, putting the robe away.

She is short and thin. Her left sleeve hangs loosely over her shoulder, and the end is tied; she only has one arm.

'Much better, thank you. If you sit down again and look straight into the camera, we can try again.'

The woman feels under her armrest. 'This chair has shackles.'

'Could you sit still and look straight into the camera?'

'Why does this chair have shackles? Are you planning to chain me up if I don't cooperate?'

The man laughs. 'If you prefer, I'll have my colleague find you a different chair.'

The one-armed woman shakes her head. 'Ask your questions. It's time to start.'

'Could you briefly introduce yourself?'

'Are you with CNN? You don't sound American.'

'Could you introduce yourself?' the man repeats.

The woman rubs the scars on her neck and looks at the ground. The video quality is so high that you can see flakes of dandruff in her hair.

'Okay,' she says. 'I'm known as Nairi. I live in the mountains of Akhlos, a part of the Caucasus that you'll find in the country Kazichia in the encyclopaedia. But the border of that country is drawn by people who don't have the right to have such powerful ink.'

'You're the leader of the Jada resistance.'

'I prefer to call it a revolt.' She looks to her right for a moment. 'My people, the Jada, have guarded the true border for centuries. The border of our independent country. But we are being oppressed by the oligarchs in the Mardoe Khador, led by the Lechkov family.'

Some paper rustles. The man standing close by is holding notes or instructions.

'Maybe I should go ahead and ask you the question that everyone has been meaning to ask,' he says, while the rustling gets louder. 'Are you the rebel leader that calls themself "the Man with a Thousand Faces"?'

The rustling stops.

The woman smiles for the first time, a pretty smile. 'Absolutely not.'

'You would have named yourself "the Woman with a Thousand Faces", correct?'

'No, the name is fitting. I understand the reference to that awful statue in the capital. I get why he calls himself that.'

'So you sympathise with him.'

'As I told you earlier, I don't have a clue who or what he is. But if the shreds of rumours I've heard contain any truth, we are striving for the same thing. The same skulls.'

'Which skulls?'

'All skulls with the last name of Lechkov. All of the family's heads should be put on spikes, instead of them lying on pillows, filled with the down of *our* geese.'

'So you're inciting violence.'

'I'm not a terrorist, but I don't disapprove of the actions of the Man with a Thousand Faces. Unfortunately, there is nothing left but violence. The talking stage is behind us. Very far behind us.'

'So now it's come to putting heads on spikes? The new Middle Ages.'

'Absolutely.' The woman leans forward onto her one arm and retracts her upper lip like a guard dog. 'Starting with the head of the last-born son: Daniel Lechkov.'

While the woman starts explaining what she would do to Daniel Lechkov, the code in the bottom right of the screen shifts. The number goes down from one hundred to ninety-nine, without any indication of what just happened. Without an explanation of why it just got one step closer to zero.

ANTD = >> 99

3

The private jet sinks through the clouds and starts descending. First, dark green mountains with white peaks appear. Then the coastline, along grey-blue water. Even from far away, you can tell that the sea is freezing. The last cloud plumes disappear, revealing a city like a blot of ink on a napkin, a few kilometres from the coast. Light grey on the outside, with long, winding branches of two-lane roads and high-rise buildings. Towards the city centre, the blot gets darker and more concentrated until the very middle, which looks black. The ink has seeped in and dried; nothing can be rewritten.

The plane lands, and Michelle can hardly believe they're there. Kazichia, the country she pretended didn't exist for all these years. As if it was some abstract place that could only be a source of money. The plane meets the landing strip, and she can feel the wheels hit the asphalt concrete, and the earth underneath it – Kazichian earth. Now there is no denying it anymore. It exists.

Another thing that can't be denied is Vigo Lechkov's death. The president of the Democratic Republic of Kazichia was killed, and on paper, his brother, her husband, is the rightful heir. Michelle has never studied the country's politics that extensively, but she knows the name 'Democratic Republic' is ridiculous. Blood determines the highest appointment of the country, not the people. There are elections, but the results are determined beforehand. So, if Daniel hadn't built a life in the Netherlands with her, he would now ascend the throne. Her Daniel – the scientist, the computer nerd – is entitled to an entire country. It feels surreal. But when she looks at him, even that can't be denied anymore. During the four-hour flight, he seems to have lost a few kilos. His cheeks are hollow. His grey-blue eyes look dull, like they have lost colour.

What are we doing here? she thinks. *Why didn't Alexa and I stay home?*

When Daniel told her on the plane that morning that his twin brother had died in a car crash, she had one thought: I'm here for you. Naturally, she would join him for his brother's funeral, even though his family scared her. Naturally, they needed to stay together and grieve. The plane was rerouted from Dubai to Stolia – better known in the West as Kazichia City – and within thirty minutes, they received permission to take off. But when Amsterdam had shrunk to a grey dot from her window, she started hesitating. She asked Daniel: was it wise to bring Alexa and her unborn sibling to such a turbulent country? He reassured her that nothing would happen; his mother said it was safe. And the civil war took place in the East, between minorities. In the capital, it was quiet.

'But the funeral will be tense, right?' she asked. 'Things will change in the country. And people will expect something from you. You're the heir; the last Lechkov.'

'Yes and no. I am indeed the last male Lechkov, but that's all. I will tell them they can't count on me. And you're right, that will be difficult. Especially with my mother, who will do everything in her power to change my mind.'

'Are you dreading that talk?'

Daniel shook his head. 'No. If she expects me to drop everything and come back, she shouldn't have sent me away.'

'But what will happen if you refuse the presidency? Does the government have a plan?'

'One of the other families will try to take my place. There will be chaos, I assume. But they will have to figure that out amongst themselves, Michelle, we have nothing to do with that. Anyway, I don't want to think about that now. My brother just died.'

She nodded but felt uneasy for the rest of the flight. And now that they have landed, that unease has turned into anxiety.

19

A ground stewardess waits for them at the private gate. As soon as the family leaves their jet, the blonde woman leads their way. Hurry up, says her body language. They walk through a myriad of narrow hallways to avoid the terminal. Michelle doesn't need to show her passport anywhere, and while she is used to getting priority everywhere, the way they are being coached through Vorta Airport feels more like a necessity than a luxury – as if standing still would be dangerous. The thought occurs to her that someone might be watching the airport. Maybe they'd want to know if Daniel has landed. Whoever 'they' is.

When they leave the airport through the sliding door of the diplomat's exit into the cold air, a row of black, armoured Mercedes four-wheel drives awaits them. Next to every car, a soldier is holding a machine gun, their faces scrunched into a frown.

The men salute only Daniel, as if Michelle and Alexa don't exist. Their luggage gets loaded into cars, and they take off before getting the chance to settle into their seats. Alexa jolts awake in her car seat, and Michelle has to grab onto the door so she doesn't go flying.

Anxiety makes way for fear.

'Why are we in such a hurry, Daniel? Do they expect trouble?'

He rests his hand on her leg and smiles reassuringly.

'Don't worry, nothing is wrong. They drove me around like that as a child every day. I went to my friend Leonid's birthday party with flashing lights. All the neighbours came outside to watch. I almost died; I was so embarrassed.'

'Couldn't your mother make an exception for you back then?'

'When I asked her to turn off the flashing lights, she said I shouldn't be too modest. Lechkovs can't afford to be modest. I had no idea what she meant by that; I just didn't want to be gawked at.'

She can tell that Daniel is not just grieving his brother's death, it's also painful to be back. He is dreading coming home. And however bad she feels for him, it mostly comforts her. The faster they can return to Amsterdam, the better.

*

The convoy drives through the streets of Stolia, and after a few minutes, Michelle can relax. She studies the capital they rage through, surprised by its strangeness. Of course, she has always known that Daniel came from a different country with a different culture, but only now does she truly see the difference between East and West. The suburbs are modern, but neglected; tall grey flats, abandoned car parks with groups of people hanging around. It looks unsafe. When they drive into the city, the roads get wider, and the architecture is Stalinist. In the middle of the giant, empty roundabouts they have placed statues of workers with strong jaws and farmer wives with wide hips. But the Soviet slogans on the tall government buildings are hardly legible anymore, McDonald's restaurants colour the side streets red and yellow, and they pass the *swoosh* of a Nike store. It is as if they are driving through history, through the rings of a tree.

After three roundabouts the cars hit a ridiculously wide, empty road, heading to the city centre. She sees the ninth-century city wall, and behind it winding alleys and even older buildings, the central ring of the stump. She has seen this centre before: it comes up when you look for the city on Google. The most important landmark is a statue of a traditional Kazichian soldier towering over the prolapsed town gate.

While they pass under the soldier, Michelle presses her face to the window to look at him. His legs are wide apart, he has his hands on his back and the weapon of Kazichia on his chest. But the strange thing is that there is nothing beneath his thick head of curly hair: no ears, no nose, no mouth.

'He's kind of scary in real life,' she says.

'The Man with a Thousand Faces,' Daniel says. 'My grandpa had it placed there to honour the Kazichians who freed the country from Ottoman oppression. He stands for all those soldiers who could only have won with the power of many. That's why he is faceless.'

'But that makes him elusive.'

'I think so too. I do like the idea. The new nation of Kazichia needs a story to become a real country. But that statue is not the way.'

21

'If your grandfather had it built, then the Man with a Thousand Faces must be younger than he seems.'

'Yes, the statue is supposed to look like it's been here since we became independent. But the inside is made of steel and concrete.'

The five Mercedes race through the city gate and ancient pastel-coloured buildings pass by Michelle's window.

'It's beautiful here,' she says.

'This is the nicest part of Stolia. There are restaurants, tea shops, and an underground market. If we have time, we'll walk around.'

He forces a smile, but she can see his pain.

'We'll get through this together,' she says.

'Thank you for coming with me.'

She squeezes his hand gently, while her other hand clings to the car handle like a trapped animal.

Through the windscreen, Daniel points at a hill in the middle of the city centre. An old, dark brown fort lies submerged in the rocks.

'Is that the Neza fort?' she asks.

'Yes, and the hill is called Arschta Sk'ami. The Chair of God.'

'The Chair of God?'

Daniel laughs. 'The Arabs called it that. Long before grandpa seized power.'

'Even your megalomaniac family wouldn't go that far.'

He lets go of her hand. 'Plenty of insanity, here.'

'And you lived on the Chair of God? That's the house from your childhood photos?'

'On top of the hill, behind that gate, lies the Mardoe Khador. That means "the House of the Highest Law" or "the High House".'

'From which the country is governed.'

'Yes.'

'And your family has the most influence in the Mardoe Khador?'

'*Our* family. And yes, as of yet. My grandpa had the Mardoe Khador built, and since then, the Lechkovs have had the most influence. So, the question now is what happens when they don't appoint a new president.'

The cars enter a tall gate, with barbed wire and cameras. They end up on a dirt road and start to climb the hill. Michelle sees a giant Russian-style villa looming, with five wings that grasp the Chair of God, like fingers. A building that exudes power. The Mardoe Khador. She can hardly fathom that Daniel grew up here and wonders what would have happened if Daniel's mother hadn't sent him away. What would have become of him? *Who* would he have become?

The convoy stops next to a bombastic-looking fountain. The front doors of the High House open, and a small woman appears; Maika Lechkova, mother of the nation and her mother-in-law. Michelle sees the small woman standing there and forces herself to count to ten. Everything about her mother-in-law, even the tiniest things, offends her. The way she puts out her cigarette in an ashtray held by a staff member, as if that thing can't be placed on a table. The way she has to waddle to the car, as she has her trouser suit tailored a few sizes too small, even though she is getting fatter. But Michelle knows she needs to get over that.

She just lost her son. However insufferable she is, these people are your family, and they need you.

Daniel gets out and greets his mother in Kazichian. Michelle can tell by his voice that he is about to cry. When she walks to the other side of the car to get Alexa, who has fallen asleep again, out of her car seat, Maika grabs her shoulders. Michelle holds her breath. The old woman smells like the fruity tobacco of her Merit cigarettes. For Daniel, that smell is nostalgic – he told Michelle once that he smuggled packs of Merit to his room in boarding school to burn them without taking a single hit as if they were sticks of incense, to fade away his loneliness – but for pregnant Michelle, it's hard to imagine the smell bringing comfort. Her nausea is getting worse, but she forces herself to embrace her mother-in-law.

'I cannot imagine what you must be going through, Mother,' she says slowly, in English. 'We are here for you.'

'Grandma iPad?' Sleepily, Alexa looks at the grandmother she has only ever seen on FaceTime.

Maika pecks her granddaughter on the cheek and points Michelle to a window in the big building. 'We prepared a private apartment for you. You will be taken care of here. It's a pity that winter is coming, but you'll see how gorgeous this country is once the sun comes out in a few months.'

Michelle looks at her mother-in-law in surprise. 'In a few months?'

'Yes, springtime in Kazichia is beautiful.'

'Um, Mother, that's very kind, but we won't stay for that long, unfortunately. After the funeral, we'll have to get back. But maybe you would like to come to Amsterdam? You could stay with us for a few nights. We redid the guest room.'

Maika looks at her but doesn't respond. She turns round to her son and says something in Kazichian. She sounds angry.

'What is it?' Michelle asks Daniel. 'Did I do something wrong?'

'Let's not mention our return trip.' His voice sounds curt. 'My mother just lost her eldest son.'

Is he scolding me? Michelle thinks. *Should I have lied about staying?*

Daniel turns round and is about to follow his mother to the house when a car comes racing up the hill, its brakes screeching as it halts next to the family. The door swings open, and a tall, dark Kazichian man gets out of the car. Michelle recognises him immediately from family photos. General Radko Lechkov, Secretary of Defence and commander-in-chief of the Kazichian army. Daniel's uncle. The military man, tall as a tree, reminds her of an American football player, but Daniel has told her once that a sensitive soul hides behind his intimidating appearance.

'*Tsval'a!*' the man shouts. In two steps he is with them and holds Daniel's face between his enormous hands. Tenderly, the military man kisses his nephew's forehead.

'Uncle Radko, let me introduce you to my wife Michelle,' Daniel says when he manages to wriggle himself out of his uncle's firm grip.

The man turns round to Michelle and kisses her cheeks as if they've known each other for years. 'Welcome to Kazichia, Mikaella Lechkova.' He turns back to Daniel.

'We are going to make this right. You do know that, Daniel? We are going to make this right, as much as we can.'

'What do you mean? Vigo's accident? How can we make up for an accident?'

Confused, Daniel looks at his mother, and Michelle can see he's startled. Radko wants to explain, but Maika stops him.

'*Chumad!*' she says fiercely.

Daniel asks what is wrong in English.

'*Chumad'i sule! O'tu abscha var?!*' Maika continues. She sounds grim.

Michelle wants to ask if she's done something wrong, but the conversation turns into a heated argument, and she turns Alexa away from the commotion. Now and then, Radko's baritone voice interrupts the two quarrellers as if trying to calm the situation, but it doesn't seem to have any effect. After a few minutes, Maika suddenly walks to the front door.

Michelle pulls Daniel's sleeve. 'What was that all about? Was that about Vigo's accident?'

He smiles. 'No, it was about our stay here. I asked if they had a cot prepared for Alexa. So that she can go right to bed.'

She gives him a puzzled look. 'A cot? You fought over a cot?'

'I don't want to go to sleep,' Alexa says, unconvinced of her own words.

Daniel bends down and kisses his daughter. Then he gets up and looks Michelle right in the eye. 'Something went wrong, but it's all been taken care of,' he says. 'Don't you worry.'

4

The one-armed woman they call Nairi shifts in her chair.

'Stay seated, please,' a male voice says.

The woman arches her back. 'I'm not a doll. Ask your next questions while I relieve my joints.'

'Maybe you could give us some background on Kazichia. Most Westerners hardly know the country, if at all.'

The woman rubs her eyes. 'Can I have some water?'

'I'll send someone for water. In the meantime, look straight into the camera and answer my question. The longer you look straight into the camera, the sooner we're done here.'

'You'd think my answers determine whether we're done, not the position of my body. But that's not how it works at CNN?'

It's quiet. Someone is typing. The keyboard sounds like rain drumming on a window.

'All right, I'll tell you about Kazichia,' she says.

While the woman starts talking, the code at the bottom of the screen changes.

ANTD = >> 98

'There are two countries named Kazichia. The true Kazichia is centuries old, and the largest part of that small country was inhabited by all sorts of clans and tribes of my people, the Aschjadazians. Or the Jada, for short. The *current* Kazichia is a country taken over by oligarchs who oppress my people systemically.' The woman's neck breaks out in hives, and she starts talking faster and faster.

'But nobody is willing to save our children. Just as Yemen is cast aside, despite all its horrors, Kazichia seems to have been erased from the world map. Forgotten by the whole world.'

'Perhaps you could give us some concrete context?' the man asks. 'And please, look . . .'

'Yeah, yeah, I'll look into the camera. And I'll tell you about this country. Am I getting water or what?'

'It's coming.'

The woman shifts again and looks into the camera. 'The story of the modern Kazichia is the story of Petar Lechkov. In the capital, he is seen as a god, but my people call those kinds of people parasites.'

'Tell us about him, please.'

'That's what I'm doing. During Stalin's reign of terror, Petar was born in a peasant village. West of old Kazichia, by the Black Sea. He made it to the communist party's leadership in Moscow – I'm not sure how. Not out of conviction, anyway. "The most successful capitalists sit at the head of the communist table", is an aphorism you might have heard. That's Petar Lechkov's.

'Anyway, he used his position in the party to take over one of the seven big banks and became a bank director. When the Soviet Union imploded, the Russian government made all sorts of arbitrary attempts to introduce a free market – as if that's a matter of policy. The big state companies were sold in auctions, and everyone was meant to get a fair shot at buying shares. But of course, that didn't happen, because people like Petar Lechkov saw an opportunity. He wanted to gain control over the Kazichian mining industry because he knew the Akhlos mountains have not just coal, but lithium, too. So, he made sure that his bank organised that state company's auction. And you guessed it, he was the only one who showed up to bid on the mining industry in the Akhlos.'

'How did he manage to do that?' the man asks.

'Petar made friends in the Russian underworld during Yeltsin's reign. And he used those sketchy men to threaten anyone who wanted to bid on the Kazichian mining industry. Nobody dared come to the auction because they were afraid their children would be murdered. So, Petar organised the auction and was the only one who came to bid. Within a few minutes, he had bought the entire mining industry of the country.' The woman raises her index finger. 'For one American dollar.'

A hand appears with a glass of water, and she drinks it in one gulp.

During her monologue, the code at the bottom of the screen has come two steps closer to zero.

ANTD = >> 96

When the glass is empty, she continues. 'So, Petar Lechkov buys – just like almost all Russian oligarchs – his imperium ready-made from the Soviet Union. But that's not enough for him. He wants independence from the Kremlin. And rightly so; if Yeltsin becomes ill and an economic crisis ensues, many of his fellow Russian robber barons will lose their power and most of their capital.

'But not Petar. Petar had a megalomaniacal plan to become independent. Together with three other powerful families, a group of former KGB spies, and two divisions of the Russian army, he returned to Kazichia. Back to his country of birth. He entered the capital with tanks and planted his flag in the Seat of God. Simple as that. No shots fired, no victims. Not only did he control the mining industry, he had power over the entire country surrounding the mines. You can't make this stuff up. There was just so much chaos and anxiety that the Kazichians were grateful for him. He told them who was in charge and what they had to do to become a modern country. He brought them clarity.'

The woman shakes her head, and the rash on her neck grows.

'But that still wasn't enough for him,' she continues. 'Conquering old Kazichia was so easy that he got even bolder. Petar casually moved the border up to the Caspian Sea. My people suddenly lived in the same country as the Neza clans in the East. And naturally, conflict ensued. At the same time, Abkhazia and Georgia tried to recover their lost territories, but Petar guarded the new borders with his modern Russian army. Nobody had the military or economic power to do anything. And between all the other former Soviet states in chaos, nobody noticed that he redesigned the map to his liking.'

'The international community just let it happen?'

'The international community was celebrating; the Cold War was over, and the Caucasus was relatively quiet.'

The man coughs. 'Maybe we can focus on present-day Kazichia.' Some paper rustles. 'You're stating that the Lechkovs still have absolute power. But the country is much more democratic now. Presidential elections are happening, so the people decide who leads the High House.'

'The Lechkovs always come out on top. By ninety-five per cent or more.'

'But there's a parliament and opposition. Three political parties are participating in the election. And the most popular party gets to appoint a premier to lead the parliament. This year, premier Penka Rosca was elected: the first and only female premier in the region.'

'Is this what you want to discuss? Is this what CNN wants to discuss?' The woman looks to her right. 'Of course Kazichia isn't democratic. It's as democratic as Syria, or Hungary. The presidential elections are predetermined, and those three political parties are the same party behind the scenes. I don't have to tell the people that. What exactly is the aim of this conversation? I thought we would talk about the Jada revolt.'

'You are overestimating how much people know about this country, madam. We need to give them some background information, so the audience understands what you're revolting against. Tell us about the High House. What is that?'

The code has not shifted for a few minutes, and it seems to upset the man – he is under time pressure.

The one-armed woman sniffs. 'The Mardoe Khador, or the High House, is the epicentre of power. Three families control it.'

'Introduce us to the three families of the High House, please.'

'Apparently, I'm a schoolteacher now,' she mumbles. 'All right, if this is what you want. The Lechkov family is the most powerful group within the High House. The oldest male Lechkov is head of the High House and is always elected president of the country.

In fact, the president of Kazichia is more like a king; he has complete control. And the head of the Lechkov family is automatically the CEO of Lechkov Industria, the money machine destroying the Akhlos mountains with mining. After the Lechkovs, the Karzarovs are the most powerful family of the Mardoe Khador, Lev Karzarov leading them. The Karzarovs run all sorts of transport and infrastructure in Kazichia and Russia: airports, trains, seaports – all kinds of hubs. Also, Karzarov has ties to Gazprom and the Kremlin. The third family is Yanev, and they control the energy sector. That big thermal power plant outside the capital is theirs, for example. The head of that family, Igor Yanev, is the director of the OMRA, the Kazichian intelligence service. Those people make entire families disappear. Those are the people leading the work camps, which our friends and loved ones get sent to without any reason.'

'If those three families control Kazichia, why is there a parliament?'

'The international community pressured the Mardoe Khador. As a precondition for joining international institutes like the United Nations and the World Trade Organisation, they had to reform their government. The High House founded all these democratic institutes, but in reality, those didn't have any power. The parliament is led by a so-called democratically elected premier, but she's a puppet too. She is there to serve the Lechkov family and to rein in "the Twenty".'

'What's that?'

'Not what, but who. Mixed in with all the imposters and puppets, twenty ministers in the parliament actually have a say. The twenty most powerful industrialists, outside of the High House families. The Twenty want more political power and apply pressure through the parliament. There is an internal power struggle between the parliament and the High House.'

'Why did the High House admit those men to the parliament?'

'When the High House instated a parliament, a few powerful businessmen demanded minister spots. Boris Lechkov, the president back then, didn't see that as a problem. They were symbolic positions – the whole parliament was symbolic. Boris thought they would be happy with just the titles, but by combining their power, the parliament was suddenly an institute with control. Boris hadn't anticipated that. A big mistake, because as a consequence, the Lechkov family still has to fight them off. How ironic that a sham parliament has turned into a weapon against oligarchs.

'However, my point is that the parliament is in no way a democratic forum. It may seem that way from the outside, but from within, it's a clubhouse for powerful men. Just like all the other institutes in our country. If you ask the ministers what party they belong to, there is a great chance they would misspeak.'

'That's enough, thank you.'

The woman looks up. 'What do you mean? I'm not done yet.'

'Just a moment, I have to check on something. Look into the camera while you wait.' It sounds like the man is standing up and discussing something with someone else.

Bewildered, the woman stays in her seat. 'What is this?' she asks.

'I ask the questions,' the man says. 'Look straight into the camera and talk about Inima.'

The man doesn't say please anymore.

'I'm not following.'

'Madam, I'm sorry for pressuring you, but I just heard that we are not making enough progress. It's very important that you sit still, look straight into the camera, and answer my questions. Time is ticking. Tell me about your hometown. Now.'

'Time is ticking?' The one-armed woman doesn't try to smile anymore. She has stopped hiding her suspicion of the interviewer. 'Time is ticking for whom? For what? What are you trying to do here?'

ANTD = >> 95

5

In a coffin plastered white, surrounded by gold-framed drawings of saints – selected by the patriarch himself – lies Vigo Lechkov. Daniel and Maika, brother and mother of the deceased, stand at his feet. They both solemnly hold their hands behind their backs as if the service had started already.

'They say all twins have a supernatural bond.' Daniel's voice sounds fragile in the cold space. 'That they are always connected.'

'Did you know something was wrong?'

He nods. 'I had a dream last night that someone killed me. Somebody put some type of insect in my water to make me choke. I took a sip and could feel the critter wriggle in my throat. When I jolted awake, I had fourteen missed calls from you.'

'You had a unique bond, and now he is gone. You should have visited more often. He missed you; he said that a lot.'

Daniel makes a choking sound.

'You chose to stay away,' Maika says before he can react. 'Nobody stopped you from coming home.'

Daniel shakes his head but doesn't get into it. 'How did the accident happen, Mother?'

'He was crushed between a truck and a concrete crash barrier. That thing came from the left on a T-junction and was speeding.'

'Did he die instantly?'

'No.' She sighs and looks up for a moment. 'He lost consciousness while the firemen sawed him out of the wreckage. He had been stuck for two hours. And all that time, he felt everything.

32

I saw pictures. The blood was everywhere.' She swallows hard. 'I can never sleep again.'

Daniel squints. 'Vigo drove the heaviest Rolls-Royce ever produced. That thing is basically a tank, right?'

'How am I supposed to know? The truck was speeding and hit him on the side. And now I'm never going to see him again.'

The words are so heavy that her voice breaks.

Daniel stands awkwardly beside his mother while she cries — like he is waiting for someone to finish sneezing.

'Why did Michelle say you're going back to Amsterdam after the funeral?' Maika asks, drying her cheeks with a linen handkerchief.

'Because we live there, Mother.'

'Because you live there?' She almost spits her words. 'Daniel, you do understand that you are now the eldest son; the most important man in this country? Everything depends on you.'

'And I'm sure you understand I can't simply abandon my life in Amsterdam? Alexa needs to get taken to daycare, Michelle has her work, and I own a company. Our life is in the Netherlands.'

'Stop the charade. You're not that foolish.'

Daniel raises his hands. 'I'm expected to drop everything I've built, to come back like nothing happened?'

'Everything *you* built?' Maika scoffs. 'Who do you think you are?'

'You pushed me away, Mother, banished me. And now you expect me to return? I don't know this house, and I certainly don't know this country.'

'Pushed away? Banished? Don't be so dramatic. We had to think of the bloodline, you spoiled brat.'

'The bloodline?'

'Yes! Of course! And behold!' She hits her flat hand on the side of the coffin. 'The ultimate proof that we were right.'

'Mother, control yourself.'

'Don't you understand, Daniel Petar Lechkov? If you leave, I might as well jump from the highest building in Kazichia. Is that what you want?'

That makes him go quiet.

'We're under attack, Daniel. Your brother was killed. You do understand that?'

He opens his mouth, but nothing comes out.

'You didn't really think it was an accident, did you?' Maika continues. 'They killed your brother on that highway. My eldest son. You knew, Daniel, you even had a dream about it. They lured him out of the city and killed him.'

'Who are "they"?' he asks quietly.

'That's the question. The Kremlin is the most obvious answer. But don't forget Lev Karzarov or that snake Igor Yanev.'

'Karzarov? Yanev?' Daniel leans forward and puts his hands on his mother's shoulders. 'Are you becoming paranoid?'

She shoves him aside and finds her cigarette case.

'You're talking about the families that have founded this country with us. Karzarov, Yanev, and Lechkov make up the Mardoe Khador *together*.'

'Don't be so naive, boy. They're all sharks, they can smell our blood. They know we're weak. Your father is dead, your grand-father is confused, and your mother is not a real Lechkov.' She takes a drag and points to the horizon from the high narrow windows. 'And in the meantime, our mine workers extract more and more coal and lithium from the Akhlos mountains. We are richer than we have ever been, and weaker than ever. Do you think our friends will remain friendly? Of course not. Radko and I know exactly how long alliances last in this country.'

'But you can't turn our families against each other. You need each other. Now more than ever.'

'You?' Maika blows out smoke over her son's coffin, white smoke. 'You're not a child anymore, Daniel. You mustn't forget that there were four families once. In this house, fights are always being fought. And now it's your turn to fight.'

He resolutely walks to the door, stops, and hesitantly holds on to the doorknob. 'You cannot expect me to give up my life.' His voice sounds fragile. 'It's too dangerous for my family here. I don't want to take Vigo's place, I can't do that to Michelle, and I can't do that to myself. After the funeral, I'm flying home.'

'Home? With your private jet, my boy? Filled with kerosine? Back to your house on the canal and your Porsche?'

He looks at the golden doorknob in his hand.

'Back to your academic career that doesn't pay a living wage. To your own little company, which costs more money than it generates? You say you built something, and I'm curious what you mean by that because up until this moment, Grandpa has paid for your lifestyle unconditionally. Well, that ends here. The old man has been declared mentally incompetent, and from now on, I decide what happens to our resources. And I think you should work for your money.'

'I can't go back, Mother. I'm a different man now. I belong in the West.'

His mother laughs. 'You had a jet-setting life in Europe, many people from this region have that. But trust me, you aren't Westerners. You reaped the fruits of our labour, that's different, but playtime is over. Our enemies are ready to attack, Daniel. They will hang your grandfather and your mother on the highest tree, like Nazis. And our money will disappear faster than you ever thought possible.'

'You trapped us,' he says quietly, and looks at the doorknob again. In the gold leaf, three symbols have been engraved: the crests of the three families he grew up with. The families that rule the country. Once there were different doorknobs, with four crests.

'You decided to come home, Daniel. Despite your dream about an assassination. Do you know why? Because you belong here. You are meant to sit at the head of the table, and deep in your heart that's what you want, or you would have stayed away.'

'I asked you if it was safe to bring Michelle and Alexa. Alexa is three.'

'They're safer here than anywhere else in the world. That's what I told you, and it's the truth. Especially after what happened.'

He lets go of the knob and turns round to the coffin.

'I'm here to say goodbye to my brother,' he says, 'and that's all.'

'Not all important decisions in life happen by choice,' Maika mumbles. 'Your grandfather has always said that.'

6

The first time that Michelle met her in-laws was two years ago in New York. Before that, the Lechkovs were just voices on the phone or names in an article. They didn't attend the wedding or Daniel's PhD defense at the university, and they had never met Alexa. When Michelle asked, Daniel explained they kept their distance to protect them. He said there was no other way, but she could see he was hurt. She thought it was better this way — Kazichia should be far away, literally and figuratively. She had no interest in speaking to members of the most powerful family from the Caucasus while looking for ripe avocados at the supermarket. And when one of her girlfriends had read something on the internet and asked difficult questions, she could truthfully say that Daniel hardly ever spoke to them. It was better this way. And she assumed this was how it would remain.

But then Boris Lechkov collapsed on the steps of the parliament building: a heart attack brought about by cigars, alcohol and work stress. It took a few hours before Daniel could reach his mother, and by the time he did, his father had passed away. He asked when he could come, but Maika told him to stay away. She thought it was too dangerous because their family's position was insecure, and Vigo still had to prove himself as the new president. They would send him a DVD of the funeral. Daniel covered the phone with his hand and told her what happened.

Michelle couldn't believe it. She thought he would protest — she would never let anything or anyone prevent her from going to her father's funeral — but nothing was further from the truth. He agreed on one condition – he demanded to see Vigo. Confronted with death, the bond with his twin brother proved the strongest. And Maika agreed.

A few weeks after the funeral, they would meet in New York, where Vigo and his American wife, Harper, lived. Lev Karzarov, one of Daniel's 'uncles' was supposed to be in America for a medical checkup, so it would be like a family reunion. A secretive reunion, because no one was allowed to know that the Lechkov twins would be in the same room. Maika hired a middleman to rent a penthouse, and they scheduled who would enter the building at what time so nobody would be seen together. Michelle and Daniel had to pretend they were on a work trip. Vigo and his wife promised to get to the penthouse inconspicuously.

Michelle didn't like it. The precautions made her nervous. She was scared that Daniel would get sucked into Kazichia, that he would become a public figure. He promised her that nothing could happen. Nobody knew of the plan; they would all use private jets. And it was a one-off meeting; after that, everything would return to normal. Their life would continue just as before Boris died.

'Believe me,' he said, and she did.

When the lift doors of the apartment complex in the Upper East Side opened, Michelle saw a gigantic loft stretched in front of her with six-metre ceilings and glass walls looking out over Central Park. Daniel walked her to a tall, bony woman and a short, somewhat corpulent man, standing next to a girl in a wheelchair. The woman came over to Michelle and kissed her cheeks.

'My name is Nia Lechkova Karzarova. How wonderful to finally meet you. I'm Boris's sister. Or *was* his sister. This is our daughter, Katja.'

Michelle waved at the girl in the chair, who hardly reacted.

'I'm so sorry about your brother, Madam Karzarova,' she said. 'I've heard so much about you.'

'Call me Aunt Nia. You must be nervous, but we're all family here.'

She hugged the woman and felt nothing but bones and muscles under the flowy dress.

Aunt Nia introduced her to Uncle Lev, Lev Karzarov, her husband and head of the second family in Kazichia. Lev stood a few feet from his daughter, looking out at the East River absently.

'We're seeing our specialist later,' Nia said. 'There are lots of medical developments in America, so we come back every year to have Katja examined.'

'My wife has incredible perseverance,' Lev said, facing the river. 'Sometimes against her better judgement.'

'When it's your child, giving up is not an option. Right? And what a treat we can be here for the twin brothers reuniting.'

'I wouldn't call it a treat,' Lev sighed. 'While we're here, a change of power is happening in our country. It's a critical phase.' He watched Daniel walk to the bar. 'Vigo should be in Kazichia. Just like us. And Daniel should hide in Amsterdam until this has all blown over.'

Nia shook her head apologetically at Michelle. 'Time for some red wine.'

As Michelle followed Nia, she heard the lift doors open. Looking sideways, she felt her body stiffen. She had seen photos of Vigo, but only now that he approached her in person could she see his resemblance to Daniel. The expression, the way he walked, the way he rubbed his hands over his face: Vigo and Daniel were identical. It was surreal, and when he came and stood next to her, Michelle could hardly breathe. She tried introducing herself politely. She tried to laugh at Harper's jokes and listen to Vigo's stories about his brother, and after a few minutes, it seemed to go a little better. But then Maika arrived.

It was the first time she met her mother-in-law. The old woman told her she had learnt how to do video calls and wanted to meet Alexa through her iPad. Michelle tried to sound excited talking about her daughter but felt as though she was out of oxygen. Kazichia came close now. Too close. What would have happened if she had fallen for Vigo instead of Daniel? Or if Daniel had been the only son? Would she be living in Kazichia now? Or would she not have fallen for Daniel if he was the next heir? But what was her marriage based on, then? What was her love based on? Was it just convenience?

And what happens if Vigo is a terrible president? she thought. *Or if the family is under attack? Will Daniel and I be in danger?*

When they finally made it outside, Daniel asked if it had been okay. She looked at him and saw *that* face: President Vigo Lechkov's face. The face that raised a lot of uncomfortable questions.

She tried to quell the panic. *When we're home, this feeling will subside,* she told herself. *You're tired from travelling, and you miss your daughter. When we're home, things will go back to normal.*

But the face followed her to the Netherlands. Not just attached to Daniel, but everywhere she went. The press had somehow found out about the sensitive change of power in the Caucasus. Several news outlets posted Vigo's face; he was mentioned on the evening news and a late-night talk show. There was no escaping it.

Michelle asked Daniel if he was worried that people would confuse him for the president of Kazichia. He dismissed her. He said it would be just a few days until they move on to the next story.

'This will blow over,' he said. 'Believe me.'

She wanted to believe him, but when Vigo was officially 'elected' the Lechkov family received much more attention. Michelle walked across Spui Square in the centre of Amsterdam and saw Vigo everywhere. The new issue of *Forbes*, with Vigo's face on the cover, was all over newsstands. *The new emperor of the coal mines*, it said. Vigo Lechkov. She could tell they were mocking him, and his name – *her* name. She walked on quickly, hoping she wouldn't run into anyone.

Later that month she took her sister Fleur to the street art museum Moco because Fleur liked Banksy so much. The artist was having a presentation of some new works that morning, and Fleur was curious to see what he had come up with. One of the works was a long, black party garland hanging over the other artworks. Her sister didn't even notice it, she was studying the floor plan. But Michelle saw the sign immediately: *JUST ANOTHER LECHKOV PARTY.* She looked up in shock. The garland consisted of a collection of men in suits, connected by their arms, their stomachs covered by the endless sentence: *Long live the king is dead long live the king is dead long live . . .*

She put her sunglasses on, raised the collar of her coat and walked over to the sign with background information on the work. It said:

The suited men represent the bloodline of the Lechkov Family, which reigns over Kazichia like it's a monarchy, despite the Kazichian parliament and elections. As if it's their holy birthright to suppress and exploit. After Boris Lechkov's passing, Banksy hung this garland in the capital, honouring the crowning of Vigo, the eldest Lechkov son. He hadn't been appointed yet, but the artist decided to decorate the town beforehand because everyone knew what the election results would be. The decorations were confiscated immediately by the OMRA (intelligence service), and two people were arrested.

When she had read the sign, Michelle grabbed her sister's arm and pulled her outside. She had to leave. Fleur asked what was wrong, but she didn't reply. She didn't want to explain because she knew what Fleur would say: 'You chose to marry a Lechkov. You should have known this.'

Later that day, she and Daniel were at their favourite Italian place on Prinseneiland. He asked how the museum was, and she finally asked the question running through her head.

'What happens if Vigo dies?'

Daniel put his glass down. 'What do you mean? Why would he die?'

'He won't, of course. But just imagine. Are there protocols in place? Have you discussed it?'

'Don't worry, I belong here. Together with you two. It hurts to admit this, but in New York I could feel that Vigo and I had drifted apart. My mother has managed to turn twin brothers into strangers. There is nothing left in Kazichia for me.'

'I'm sorry to hear that. I want you to have a bond with your brother, but I have to ask. You never know what happens in a country like that. Everything works differently there, doesn't it? Isn't it like a royal family? All they care about is bloodline.'

'Vigo will remain president. From when he was eight, he has been prepared for this role.'

'So you're not worried about what might happen?'

'Nothing will happen. He is where he is supposed to be, just like me. Luckily, they don't need me there because my life is with you.' He leaned forward and covered her hands with his. 'We will never go there, Michelle. Believe me.'

7

Carrying fifteen kilos of toddler on her shoulder, Michelle climbs the wooden stairs that revolve around the chandelier in the foyer of the High House. She had hoped that Daniel would walk them to their room so she could ask him what his uncle meant when they were standing by the fountain. And so he could carry Alexa, because her hips are sore. But Maika wanted to take her son to see Vigo's coffin, and Michelle didn't dare to argue. Moreover, she didn't want to tell her mother-in-law she is pregnant.

She continues through an endless hallway on the second floor, decorated with oil portraits. Suddenly, one of the high doors opens, and a woman appears in the cold light of the chandeliers.

'Harper? Is that you?'

The woman standing there is a ghostly version of the Harper she met in New York: her hair is messy, her face is grey, and she is wearing a tank top and tight tracksuit bottoms that show how skinny she's got.

'Michelle?' Nervously, she looks down the hall. 'Why did you come here?'

Michelle sticks out her free arm to embrace her sister-in-law and offer her condolences for her husband's death. She can smell booze and cigarettes.

'Why are you here?' the American asks again. 'Why did you bring your daughter?'

'Daniel and I came for the funeral. We want to be there for you.'

'Don't you think it's better to go home? Just to be sure? For your daughter?'

'Calm down, Harper, we're here for you too.' She puts her hand on the woman's shoulder, who pushes it away.

'I don't want you to be here for me. It's not safe here. As soon as Vigo is underground, I'm gone. I'm not staying for another minute.'

'I understand, and don't worry. Daniel checked with his mother whether it was safe for us, and it's okay.'

'Maika said that? Well, then it must be fine,' Harper says sarcastically.

'What do you mean?'

'Are you moving to Kazichia? Is Daniel here to succeed his brother?'

Unsure if she can answer that, Michelle awkwardly shakes her head.

'Then you should never have come here. The throne is empty, and two families would do anything for that spot. It's a power vacuum: I paid enough attention in history class to know those don't get resolved peacefully.'

'What do you think will happen?'

'No idea, but if I were you, if I had a young daughter, I would have stayed far, far away from this hill. In this house, there is so much money and power up for grabs, Michelle, it changes people. Even the people you thought you knew.'

8

After Michelle has put Alexa to bed, she starts looking for Daniel. She needs to speak to him. When she gets downstairs, she wanders through the many hallways of the High House without seeing anyone, but then she hears muffled voices and the clinking of cups and saucers. The sound leads her to a large room filled with people. A man in a wheelchair sits by a fireplace, and on the other side, a group of men shrouded in cigarette smoke. Is Daniel amongst them, the heir at the centre of political attention? But what is he to them; the future president who will lead the country in times of crisis, or an outsider obstructing the power change?

Ignoring the nauseating smell of greasy Georgian dumplings and tobacco, she works her way through the crowd. With every step, hands and friendly smiling faces appear. In the middle of the room, it's not Daniel she finds, but his mother. Now that her eldest son is gone, Maika is suddenly at the centre of power. Radko is standing next to her and hits someone's shoulder, spontaneously but too roughly.

When Michelle tries to find her way back, Lev Karzarov suddenly appears before her. He looks different from the way he looked in New York. His thick, black hair is slicked back, his tie is straight, and he carries a green binder under his arm. Just like the other men in the room, he wears a tailored suit in a dark, even colour, and a pin of the Kazichian flag on his chest. In the Mardoe Khador, he's not the father of a disabled girl but a statesman with authority.

'Good to see you again, Michelle,' he says, kissing her cheek.

'Hi Uncle Lev, do you happen to know where Daniel is?'

'He is right there. Is your daughter here? Alexa?' He looks past the people down the hall as if the girl is about to enter the room. 'Is she upstairs?'

'She's asleep,' Michelle answers, surprised by his interest. 'She's tired from travelling.'

Karzarov nods and stares down the hall again.

'My condolences on Vigo's death,' she says to break the silence.

'It's awful. But it's wonderful you could be here so soon. When will you ship your things from Amsterdam?'

'Our things? We're going home after the funeral.'

'Oh.' He frowns.

'Is my husband here?' she asks again.

'He's back there, talking to the premier.'

She stands on her tip-toes and sees Daniel lean against the panelling. He looks at the people around him, overwhelmed. She smiles apologetically and slips through dark blue and grey business suits.

'We need to talk,' she whispers in Daniel's ear, motioning for him to follow her.

He takes a deep breath, obviously relieved that she's here. 'What's up?'

'I just ran into Harper. She's very worried about us. She thinks we're in danger. Do you think she's right?'

He stares at the floor, and she can tell he's hesitant.

'What's going on?' she asks. 'Talk to me, Daniel.'

'Okay, but don't freak out. My mother suspects foul play with Vigo's death.'

'What do you mean?'

He stares at her but says nothing.

'Daniel? Was he . . . murdered?' she whispers.

He nods.

The nausea is instantly gone. 'Then we leave for the airport right now. We're packing our bags and leaving. I don't even want to know what happened.'

'There's no need, Michelle.' He gestures for her to stay calm and comes closer. 'Nothing will happen, truly. We don't even know if she's right. We'll go to the funeral, and in a few days, we'll be home again. We need to be careful, that's all.'

'But why the hell would we take that risk? Why don't we leave straight away?'

'Because he's my brother, Michelle. I want to bury him.' He looks at the people behind him. 'You need to understand it's not easy to leave my family behind. If you or I get on that plane and leave, everyone will know I'm not succeeding Vigo. Things will turn into chaos here.'

'And how is that our concern?'

'I want to give the families time to come up with a different plan. The High House needs to prepare for the end of the Lechkov empire.'

'But you said that's not our responsibility? That it's their battle, not yours?'

Silence.

'Something else is bothering you,' she says and caresses his cheek with her hand. 'Tell me.'

'If we leave, my mother will take our income away. We'll have nothing left.'

She removes her hand. 'What do you mean? She can do that?'

'We'll be fine. I just need some time to talk to her. But if we leave right now, we'll make her angry.'

'And when she's angry, she can take our money?'

'It's not our money.' Daniel looks at the fireplace and the old man sitting in his wheelchair. 'Officially, it's my grandpa's money. But his Korsakov has got so bad that my mother is in charge. We can't get around her anymore.'

'Safety before money, Daniel.'

'Of course. But safety *and* money would be ideal.'

She thinks of Alexa's private school. Their family homes. She thinks of her career and how much she enjoys that work because she could quit at any moment. She feels free. Or she felt free anyway before she found out Maika controlled her life.

Daniel rubs his face like he does when he's stressed.

Michelle grabs his hands and pulls him towards her.

'If you can prevent the money from disappearing, we'll stay for a few days. If you can release us from your mother, you should – I want to be free from this house. But I don't want to take any risks at all. Our safety comes first.'

He nods. 'We'll go to the funeral. I'll make sure my mother leaves us alone, and I'll talk to the families so they can prepare for when I leave. Then we get on our flight. Before you know it, we're home.'

She looks into his grey-blue eyes – the same blue as the cold sea of his birth country.

'Believe me,' he says.

And she wants to.

9

In the days leading up to the funeral, Michelle tries to support her in-laws, but they won't let her. She goes to Harper's room twice a day, knocking on her door, but Harper never comes out. When Michelle listens by the door, the room is quiet. She tries to see Maika, but the old lady is at her office all day – probably having meetings about the country's future. The other families appear and disappear down hallways or get into their cars and drive off. The Mardoe Khador is like a maze of doors, none of which she may open.

When she walks around the house with Daniel, people come out. Suddenly, she is allowed to explore the different wings. There, she sees how different they all are. The Karzarov domain is elitist and bombastic, with crystal chandeliers, giant ornaments and marble tops. The Yanev wing is modern, with designer furniture and tight plastered walls. Only the presidential wing and the Lechkov chambers have been kept in their original Mardoe Khador style: wooden floors, wooden panelling, Persian red carpets stretch down the hallways, oil portraits on the walls, and a large fireplace in every room. Not quite regal, but almost.

Daniel says the three families have grown apart since he was young. The private chambers used to be in the same two wings, and the offices and conference rooms in the other three. Only the central part of the house has remained the same – where ministers and other civil servants have their offices and conference rooms. While they walk through that part of the house, Michelle sees the staff staring at Daniel.

'They're looking at you as if they see a ghost,' she says.

'And they do,' Daniel says with pity in his voice. 'They see the ghost of the murdered president.'

The day before the funeral, Daniel works hard on his eulogy. He doesn't want any visits from politicians or other powerful men coming to try and charm him. Even his mother isn't allowed to stop by. Michelle can tell not only is he trying to say goodbye, he is trying to take his distance. He is getting ready to leave the house.

While he writes, she walks to the living room to call her parents. Her relationship with her father has been strained for years, but she needs to let them know what is happening. They might see Vigo's funeral on the news and their granddaughter in Stolia without them knowing about it. She can't do that to them.

Her mother picks up. She can tell by Michelle's voice something is wrong.

'Everything is okay, Mum, don't worry. But we're not on holiday. We're in Kazichia.'

'Wait, I'll get your father,' her mother says. She leaves the phone on the countertop.

Her mother always gets Luc when she is scared she won't be able to follow. Or when she thinks she'll get too emotional. 'Why are you there?' her father asks fiercely. 'Is it because of Vigo's accident? I saw it on the news. Isn't it dangerous for Daniel to be there? And for you two?'

While Michelle comforts her parents, she looks through the open living room door at the wooden gates of the mezzanine. From below she hears the footsteps of people she can't see, having conversations in a language she can't understand.

10

Sophie, a freshly eighteen-year-old woman, looks at an old laptop. She sits in the attic under the sloping roof, the window looking out on an Oregon suburb. The sun is setting, and Sophie hasn't eaten all day, but there is no time for hunger. She found a video file. A secret file. A woman with only one arm is interviewed while a code changes. Sophie has had lingering questions for years. Questions about Kazichia. She is hoping the video can answer some of them. But after watching for a few hours, she is none the wiser. She still doesn't know what the code stands for, or why the woman was placed in that chair.

Getting impatient, she moves the mouse to make the time bar appear. To her surprise, she is at less than five per cent – maybe less than one per cent. Sophie fast-forwards the video, and the one-armed woman sways quickly from side to side. Sometimes, the woman disappears for a bit and reappears suddenly. How long must she have sat in that chair, answering questions?

While Sophie fast-forwards, she watches the strange numbers at the bottom of the screen to see if they represent minutes or hours. But they change quickly sometimes, while other times they remain static.

She plays the video at normal speed.

ANTD = >> 85

The one-armed woman leans back. With her fingertips, she feels the scratches in the wooden armrest.

A man sighs, but it's a different voice. The interrogators take turns, it seems.

'Have you met the new rebel leader?'

'You mean *Asch-Iljada-Lica*?' she asks. 'The Man with a Thousand Faces?'

'Yes. Keep looking straight into the camera, please. Do you plan on working with him?'

'I want to work with everyone that can help my people. The only problem is that this man is just a rumour. And to be honest, I'm sceptical of most rumours.'

'They're too good to be true?'

'They say he will ensure we beat the capital. He's going to restore the old borders.'

The man moves some papers or instructions around, as his colleague did. 'And you don't believe that.'

'No, of course not. One man saving an entire people; where have we heard that before?'

'Hope is good, right?'

The woman slowly places her clenched fist on the scratched-up armrest. 'Our centuries-old border towns are being turned into construction sites, where parents and their children get forced to work — twelve- and thirteen-year-olds. And the longer a town is mining, the more it looks like a labour camp. A gulag. And when the Jada dare to denounce the situation, the OMRA makes them disappear from the earth. Sometimes, entire families get arrested by Igor Yanev's monsters. And the world has no idea. Nobody knows how bad it is.' The woman slams the chair. 'Hope is not enough. We need a lot more than that. Especially now that Daniel Lechkov has returned to Kazichia.' The woman has more to say, but stops because the man behind the camera is talking to someone. She leans forward. 'Hello? Are we still recording?'

'Sorry,' the male voice says distractedly. 'We're still working on the technology. Could you say, "the Man with a Thousand Faces" once or twice?'

'The technology? We've been talking for hours.'

'And please repeat the word "Neza" three times. And take your time for the double emphasis: Ne-za.'

'I'm going to the bathroom,' the woman says, standing up. 'With double emphasis: *bath-room*.'

Sophie fast-forwards the video by many hours. When she lets go of the mouse, the code has counted down further.

ANTD = >> 54

'I know this isn't an interview,' the woman says. She looks tired.

'What do you mean?' one of the men asks.

'As soon as I entered this room, I knew CNN hadn't invited us. Well, maybe I was really invited by the Americans, but you don't work for that network. You abducted me and are keeping me hostage.'

The man is quiet.

'What are we doing here? What do you want from me? Maybe I can help you reach whatever goal you have. Maybe we can help each other out.'

'If you keep cooperating, we won't hurt you.' The tone of the man's voice is unchanged, businesslike and monotone. 'If you do exactly as I say, I won't have my colleague get a knife.'

The woman's expression changes from one frame to the next, like a crack appearing in a porcelain mask.

'If needed, we'll tie you to the chair,' the monotonous voice says. 'I don't want to use knives or braces, but my assignment is to finish this conversation and get that code to zero. So that's what I'll do. Whatever is needed.'

'Why are we having this conversation? I don't understand what you want from me.' She frowns to stop the tears from welling up. 'What happens when we get to zero?'

Sophie is getting impatient: she wants to understand what the goal of the conversation is. She fast-forwards more, to the last few minutes. When she presses 'play', the image on the dusty screen shocks her.

The one-armed woman screeches like an animal, powerless.

Her hand stuck in the brace, she hangs slumped over the chair armrest.

'Almost there,' a man's voice says. 'Look up and repeat these words, then it's over. Then I'll release you.'

The woman is hunched forward and looks like she is about to die. The code is almost at zero.

ANTD = >>04

'Look over here,' the man says. 'This is the last thing you need to do. We're almost there.'

The woman lifts her head with difficulty. Her torso starts shaking. Her skin looks grey, her eyes dark.

'Akhlos,' the man says, and the woman repeats the word with a raspy voice.

'Daniel Lechkov.'

The woman repeats the name, but her head starts falling again.

'The Man with a Thousand Faces,' the man says. 'Look up, look into the camera, and repeat as I say. Do it!'

'The Man with a Thousand Faces,' the woman repeats. Her head falls again, and the code jumps to zero.

ANTD = >>00

'It worked,' the man's voice says, relieved. 'The conversation is done.'

'Are we done?' the woman asks softly.

'It w-w-worked,' someone else says. A new voice belonging to a man who stutters. 'W-w-we're done.'

The image shifts and the chair in front of the green wall is empty again. The code has disappeared. So has the woman. Dust particles float in the lens, and the chair armrests are scratched up. More scratches on the right side than on the left. After a few minutes, the screen is black: the video is over. A face reflected on the screen. Sophie's face in the attic. With a pen in her hand, she stares at the laptop. She thinks about what she just saw – what she can do with it or how she should use it. Next to the old laptop is a pile of papers with the notes she took. On the last page, she scribbled two questions and circled them. The first question: who is Daniel Lechkov? The next one: who is the Man with a Thousand Faces?

11

The night before Vigo's funeral, Lev Karzarov is in his private kitchen looking at a glass of water. In his right fist, he's hidden a plastic pipette. He takes the glass with both hands, says something to the empty kitchen, and stretches out his arm. Oily droplets appear in the water. After standing like that for a few seconds, he pours the glass into the sink and fills it with water again. He repeats his steps as if practising for a magic trick. He takes the glass, presses the pipette in his palm, offers the glass, and smiles, relaxed. Nobody is at the other end of the marble countertop, but Lev pretends to hand the water to Daniel Lechkov. He pretends to execute the second step of the plan to eliminate the Lechkov twins. The plan of the Kremlin that he is cooperating with, to guarantee a position in the new Kazichia for his family.

The pipette contains a combination of fluid benzodiazepine, sildenafil, GHB and LSD. No poison. They wouldn't get away with a second murder. Nobody would believe it was an accident. That's why Lev is practising a hit on the credibility of the last Lechkov heir. The next day, during his brother's funeral, Daniel will be found in a brothel with two underaged girls: an indirect death sentence. A deserter division of the Kazichian army is ready to invade the government buildings during Vigo's service and take the leaders of the country hostage. The clip of Daniel with the girls will go viral, and everyone will see that the future of Kazichia is no longer in safe hands with the Lechkovs. Someone else will need to bring stability to the country. The Karzarovs are the most capable and influential party for the job.

Lev believes in the plan, but his conscience bothers him. He doesn't know if Daniel and his family will survive the coup. Maybe Maika will drive it to a confrontation. And even if Daniel manages to flee the country, he will forever be known as a rapist. A paedophile. Lev knows, directly or indirectly, that he is ending Daniel's life, and he doesn't want that. He loved Petar Lechkov, who was his biggest hero. He doesn't want to endanger Petar's offspring, but he can feel his father watching him from beyond the grave. And he can feel the Kremlin has him by the balls.

And so, he takes the glass one more time to practise.

During that last rehearsal, his wife walks into the kitchen. 'Are you ready?' Nia asks, a burning cigarette between her lips.

'They brought their daughter,' he says. 'Why would Michelle take that risk?'

'You were hoping he'd be alone?'

'When I give Daniel this drink, there's no way back. We seize power, or it will turn into war. Those are the only two outcomes. And none of those options is good news for that little Dutch girl. Or her mother.'

'There hasn't been a way back for years now, Lev. The Kremlin is coming, with or without our help. By seizing power, you'll prevent Russian tanks from rolling down the streets. You'll prevent hundreds of thousands of girls from getting involved instead of one.'

'You're right,' he mumbles. 'It's just hard.'

'I know.' She kisses his cheek. 'These people are our family. But it's either this,' she flicks the ash of her cigarette into the glass, 'or an invasion.'

He sighs. 'We are putting everything on the line by staying in Kazichia and executing the plan ourselves. If we fail, Maika will ensure we get skinned alive by the OMRA. And our children will be stuck in Moscow. What will Katja do without us?'

'There is no other option. If one of us had left, Maika would have known something was off. She would have locked the city down. We can only get the Twenty on our side if we lead our soldiers to the battlefield ourselves. This is the only way. And this is the right way. We won't fail. We are going to write history.

And we've tried everything to prevent violence from happening. We told Maika, time and time again, that Vigo was not a suitable leader, a spoiled cocaine junkie. She refused to see it. And so, she's forced us to intervene.'

He nods. 'You're right.'

'Think of your kids. Be brave for them,' she says, and kisses him again. 'I'll see you in a few hours on the stairs of the parliament, Mr President.'

As his wife walks away, Lev looks at the glass. Flecks of ash spin in the water like black vultures circling a starved bison.

12

The three families have gathered for the funeral in the great hall at the front of the Mardoe Khador. Michelle has stayed near the door with Alexa; Daniel is talking to his mother, and she doesn't want to enter the snake pit without him. While she waits, she looks at the old city through the glass conservatory. The Man with a Thousand Faces stands at the bottom of the hill, his back facing her. She is nervous about the tense funeral, and for some reason, the nerves get worse watching the statue. Seen from the hill, he looks vulnerable, not impressive.

'Dad,' Alexa says.

Michelle turns round and sees Daniel walking towards her, looking defeated.

'I just heard they're expecting seven hundred guests.' Shaking his head, he buttons his blazer. 'My mother turned it into a giant state funeral last minute, even though Grandpa has always said we should never become a royal family. Politics is for the country, family affairs for the family.'

'Why is Maika doing this, then?'

'Because she wants to present me as a competent politician. Why do you think she kept asking if I wanted to give a eulogy? First, she took my chance of having a relationship with him, and now she's taking my only chance of an intimate goodbye. She's using his coffin as a press conference.'

Michelle bends over to whisper to him, 'A competent politician? You did tell her that you won't take Vigo's place, right?'

'Of course. Multiple times.' The last button of his jacket won't close, and Michelle can tell that he's angry by the shaking of his fingers.

'If you don't want to do the eulogy, or if you want to postpone it, that's your call, Daniel. You don't owe her anything.'

He puts an arm around her and tries to smile, but she can tell her words aren't helping.

'Where are we going?' Alexa asks, like she's been doing all morning.

'We're going to a church.' Michelle crouches beside her daughter. 'With all these people.'

'What's there?'

'We're going to say goodbye to Uncle Vigo there.'

Alexa thinks for a few seconds, then says, 'I don't know him. I want to go home.'

'Me too, sweetie. We'll go home in a few nights. I promise. Is that okay? Do you think you can do that?'

The girl nods.

When Michelle gets up, she sees Lev Karzarov come their way.

'Daniel, my cousins and I would like to propose a toast to Vigo, and we'd be honoured if you were there. May I invite you?' Somewhat coercively, he points to the people on the other side of the room.

Daniel answers his uncle in Kazichian and walks with him. Michelle pulls her black dress down, picks Alexa up, and follows the men. She finds that Karzarov looks anxious, and when he hands out glasses by a bar table, his hands tremble.

'What are you drinking?' she asks Daniel.

'Vodka. In Kazichia, you drink together when you celebrate and when you mourn. And when you're thirsty.'

'Is that a good idea?'

'I don't have a choice.' He takes the glass from his uncle.

'But you need to be sharp on an important day like this.'

'It would be disrespectful if I declined.'

Before she can tell him that she has a strange feeling about this, Karzarov hands her a glass, too. She shakes her head.

'I'm afraid I have to insist you drink with us.' He presses the

59

glass against her hand. 'Michelle Lechkova, drink with us in honour of Vigo, please.'

'No, thank you,' she says politely. She hasn't told her in-laws she's pregnant and wants to keep it to herself for now.

Karzarov stares at her, unsure how to respond to her rejection, then shrugs. He turns to Daniel and his cousins and makes an unintelligible toast. The drinks are downed.

The doors to the great hall open; it's time to leave for the cars. The group starts moving, and Michelle lets herself get carried along with them. She feels vulnerable amongst the Kazichian politicians and other dignitaries. Some metres ahead, she sees Karzarov's cousins take Daniel with them. She understands that he has a part to play on a day like this one, but still feels like he's abandoning her. Did he really have to leave her there? The stream of people pushes her out the door. In the driveway, Daniel stays and shakes someone's hand, and Michelle turns round to call out to him, but a man in a black suit walks up to her.

'Madam Lechkova, follow me, please. I will take you to your car. Your husband will follow us shortly.'

She objects, but there's no use. The funeral is organised like a military mission, and with Alexa on her hip, putting up a fight is difficult.

She straps her daughter into the car seat. Her companion doesn't leave her side, and only when he's sure she won't escape does he move away.

The driver starts the engine. 'Take a seat, madam. We are ready to leave for the church.'

'Wait just one second. My husband isn't here yet.'

She turns to look at the black cars but doesn't see Daniel anymore. The driver mumbles something into his walkie-talkie, and someone responds right away.

'Your husband will be riding with the other pallbearers, madam.'

'That's not right, he hasn't said anything about that. We were going to drive to the church together.'

She fixes her gaze on the row of cars slowly moving, but Daniel is nowhere to be seen.

'Madam, please, we're blocking the exit. Your husband will be right behind us. Shall we leave?'

Anxiously, she gets in the car and gives the driver permission to drive off, as if she has any say in how this day will go. The convoy slowly circles the fountain like a slithering snake, then glides down the hill. She looks through the back window, but nobody stays behind at the house. Then she gets her phone and calls Daniel. He doesn't pick up. She calls again and he still doesn't pick up.

The driver starts telling her about the new football stadium that was built right next to the church, dubbed 'the Egg' by locals. She mumbles about wishing to grieve in silence while sending Daniel a message with many exclamation marks. This time she gets a response.

I'm in a different car. We'll see each other at the Grand Church.

She curses. Why is he in a different car? How could he leave his family? Especially now, after all their conversations about Vigo's funeral and her fear that the Mardoe Khador will demand something from him? After what Harper said? How dare he leave her alone at this moment?

Thankfully, the ride is short. The convoy stops in front of the Kazichian-orthodox cathedral, a beige construction adorned with triangles, bigger and bigger, from the gold leaf spires to the doors, through which the black line of visitors enters. The driver opens the door for Michelle and points at the modernist football stadium next to the church, which, admittedly, is shaped exactly like a horizontal egg. He looks at her expectantly.

'You're right,' she says impatiently, grabbing Alexa from her car seat. 'Just like an egg.'

Hoping to lose the driver, she steps onto the pavement looking for Daniel. The cars in front of her and behind her empty quickly, and the members of the three families enter the church. But wherever she looks, she can't find him. She does see Harper. The American walks towards her and hugs her, slightly too long. Then she tries to kiss Alexa but almost trips onto the pavement.

'Walk with me?' Harper says, her words slurring. 'My husband, my lover, will be buried, and I know hardly anyone here.'

The woman smells of booze, so strongly that Michelle has a hard time keeping a straight face.

'Well, sweetie, if you don't mind, I'll wait for Daniel. Have you seen him?'

Harper looks behind her and then focuses her wobbly gaze on Michelle. 'I was in the last car. If he hasn't passed by, he must be in the church.'

'Then we will meet you there.'

Before Harper can say anything, Michelle quickly carries Alexa past the line of people. There is no time to take care of her sister-in-law now. She can support her later, but first, she needs to find Daniel.

At the church entrance, she sees Nia Karzarova talking to a member of the Yanev family. She walks up to them and asks if they have seen Daniel.

'Not since we left the Mardoe Khador,' Nia says. 'But it's so crowded. If I were you, I would go and find a seat.'

'I have to find him. I have a bad feeling.'

For some reason, Nia tries to stop her. A bony hand grabs her arm. 'Go and sit down, Michelle, everything is fine. I don't want you to worry.' For a moment, Michelle is surprised by how strong the woman is, but then she pulls away and quickly walks off. She searches around the church and tries to call Daniel for the umpteenth time. She gets his voicemail.

Where the heck are you?

'Where's Dad?' Alexa asks.

'Everything's fine, little girl. We just need to go look for him.'

Stay calm, she tells herself, *Alexa will get scared. And there's no need because everything's fine.*

While Michelle is scanning the room, Maika walks up to her, a burning cigarette in her mouth and two big guards beside her.

'Is Daniel in his seat?' she asks while the guards take her coat. She doesn't look like a mother attending her son's funeral, more like a boxer on her way to the ring, tense but belligerent.

'I don't know where he is. He wasn't in the car with us. He didn't ride with you?'

'He's probably in his seat. Let's go up to the first row. I want to get started.'

Maika leads the way, but when she halts to embrace someone, Michelle passes her and walks to the front row.

The wooden benches are empty.

Stay calm, she tells herself again. But she is everything but calm. Something is wrong. She can feel it. She knew from the beginning that travelling to Kazichia was a mistake and going to the funeral was a mistake, and now something bad has happened.

She tries to call Daniel. Listening to his voicemail, she looks around the church. At the entrance, she sees Nia leave the line of people. The woman buttons her coat and rushes outside as if she had shown up in the wrong classroom.

'He's not here?' Maika asks. She has walked up to Michelle's side and looks at the empty row of benches. 'Was he nervous about his speech?'

'Where is Daddy?' Alexa asks her grandma. 'I want to see Daddy.'

'I never asked him for anything,' Maika shakes her head. 'All I'm asking is for him to say some loving words for his twin brother. That's not a crazy thing to expect, right? A tender goodbye? It is so very important that he shows up today. For me and the country. Could you call him?'

Michelle ignores her mother-in-law and opens the location app, which can tell her where Daniel's phone is. But as the program loads, the icon stays grey; his phone has been turned off. Absorbing that information, all the anxiety of the past few days shoots through her body like electricity.

'Where is he?' Maika asks, and she pokes Michelle's shoulder. 'Hello Michelle? Where is Daniel?'

She wants to tell her that she doesn't know; that people should go and look for him. She wants to tell her that she will go back to the car, that she will take Alexa to the airport and wait for him there – if necessary, she will fly back early. But she just stands there, looking at her phone, completely frozen.

Suddenly, the sound of heavy shoes echoes against the arch of the building. Michelle looks up and sees a group of men run into the church, Radko Lechkov in front. The commander-in-chief of the Kazichian army brusquely pushes guests aside.

'Come! Now!' He points at Maika and then at Michelle and Alexa.

'Radko, what is it?' Maika asks.

'They're on their way to the church. A league of soldiers. We need to get out of here.'

His voice scares Michelle. His voice filled with fear.

'Where is Daniel?' she asks while pulling her daughter close.

'No time,' Radko says, and he motions to one of his men.

A hand presses her head forward, and she gets taken away. All she can see is the stone floor and her own shoes.

Outside the church, a hum sounds, getting louder and louder.

'Etaji!' the man escorting her says.

Instantly, she trips over a step and almost drops Alexa. They get lifted onto a stage, and from the corner of her eye she can see the lectern and the altar. A small door opens, and they end up in a narrow corridor. Behind them, in the church, she hears screaming. *The people Radko was talking about are here*, she thinks. Alexa starts crying.

Another door.

Another step.

More screams in the church.

A loud bang.

She wants to duck, but the man pulls her up and drags her along.

Was that a gunshot?

A wooden door opens, and she walks on the cobblestones – her heels clack. She's outside but barely feels the cold. High above her head, she can hear a helicopter roaring.

The man lets go of her, and when she looks up, she sees she's standing in front of a big car with blind windows.

'Get in and move over.'

She half-stumbles into the car, and as soon as she sits, she turns to Alexa so she can look into her eyes.

'Everything will be all right,' she says and pulls the seatbelt tightly around both of them.

The car speeds away from the terrain, and Michelle sees about a dozen military vehicles parked in front of the church. Soldiers walk around, armed and alert. One of them shoots their gun in the air. *A coup*, she thinks, and suddenly Michelle pictures Nia running outside. And she thinks of Lev Karzarov. The beads of sweat on his forehead, the way his hands shook when he proposed a toast. Karzarov never made it to the church. Neither did Daniel.

13

'I don't feel good,' Daniel mumbles.

He tries to get in the SUV but falls over in the back seat. Two men sit next to him and make him sit upright. A third man closes the door and sits in the passenger seat. Outside the tinted windows, Michelle and Alexa pass; they are looking for the car that will take them to the church. Daniel tries to call out, but one of the men covers his mouth with a hand. It's Lev Karzarov.

While the procession leaves for the church, Karzarov removes his hand.

'Is this a coup?' Daniel asks. His tongue lies weakly in his mouth. 'Did you give me something?'

'Yes, I'm sorry.'

'Poison?'

'No, drugs.'

'Why?'

Karzarov lights a cigarette. The heavy signet rings on his pink and ring finger rattle against the silver of his Dupont. He looks out the window and takes a long drag. 'When your genius grandfather conquered this city, he told my father that, from then on, they had started an infinite chess game. And he said that we could never stop playing because Russia would come and take our place on the board.'

'What do you want from me?'

'Your brother wasn't suitable for the presidency, and the Kremlin got nervous. I'm preventing a war by doing this. You'll think I'm a traitor, but I'm a guardian angel.'

Daniel wants to get up, but Karzarov puts his hand on his chest and pushes him back into his seat. 'I understand your frustration. But this is the only way to save all of us. Your grandfather would understand.'

The procession leaves the old city centre and turns at a round-about. While the other cars take the first exit, Daniel's car exits the procession and drives straight. He tries to look outside but can barely keep his head up. From his window, the other cars get smaller and smaller as they head to the church down the main road.

'Michelle . . . Alexa . . . ?'

'Today, we're occupying every government building. If there's no resistance, we won't need to fight, and there won't be any casualties. If the High House surrenders, everything will be fine, but if they use violence, we need to defend ourselves and this country. Basically, Maika and Radko decide on the fate of your family, not me.'

One of the men takes Daniel's phone and holds it in front of his face to unlock the smartphone. Using Google Translate, he writes a message to Michelle. Daniel stares at the man's uniform: he's a soldier with the Kazichian army.

'Where . . . to?' he asks. His tongue hangs from his mouth, and he can barely speak.

'Give in to the drugs,' Karzarov says. 'There is nothing you can do to change what is about to happen.'

The rest of the car ride is silent. They drive around a sketchy area north of the centre and stop in a narrow alleyway. Under a neon sign shaped like a woman, Daniel is pulled out of the car by two soldiers. The alley stinks of grease traps and garbage bins. Cutlery trays rattle, and kitchen staff yell at each other.

Karzarov stays in the car. 'Take him inside, we'll keep driving.'

'That wasn't the deal, Mr Karzarov,' one of the soldiers holding Daniel says. 'We were coming with you to the parliament building. We were going to stand next to you when you grabbed power.'

Before Karzarov can respond, there is a loud bang. The soldier, who, moments ago, claimed his spot in Kazichian history books, falls back against the wall. His body slides down, leaving a dark red smear of blood on the bricks.

'We're under fire!' the other soldier yells. He grabs Daniel more firmly with one hand and takes out his gun with the other.

'Get out!' Karzarov yells. 'We've been betrayed!'

The driver wants to hit the gas, but just as he is about to, a grey minivan backs into the alley. The vehicle moves so fast that the side mirrors get smashed, and between the rims and the wall, sparks fly. It halts about ten metres before them, its tyres screeching. The back doors fly open, and a unit of soldiers jumps out with weapons ready to fire. Their sleeves have a white circle with a red vertical line on them.

The soldier holding Daniel wants to throw his hands up, but a single shot is fired, and he falls to the floor with his captive. Daniel looks up at his uncle. The traitor.

Karzarov tells the driver to break his nose. Immediately, the soldier takes his rifle and smashes the back of it against his boss's face. Blood runs down Karzarov's navy suit like someone turned a tap on. He drops into the back seat and holds his face with both hands. He mutters something. A name: Katja.

The saviours with the strange logo on their sleeves circle the car, yelling at the deserters to surrender. As soon as Karzarov's men stick their hands out of the car, they are executed.

One of the soldiers helps Daniel sit up straight so he can lean against a wall. 'Are you wounded, Mr Lechkov?'

Daniel tries to respond. He wants to speak. His mouth moves very slowly, and his bottom lip shakily separates from his upper lip. But he can't.

'Thank god,' Karzarov says when one of the men helps him out of the car. 'I thought we were dead men. Who sent you?'

'General Radko Lechkov. We're here to stop the seizure of power and protect the Mardoe Khador.'

'Amazing. Is my cousin okay?'

Daniel can't keep his eyes open. His mouth trembles with effort. He is doing everything he can to speak, to say something to the loyalist soldiers, but he can't. As he loses consciousness, his uncle says, 'Save your energy, my boy. We're safe.'

14

'There they come,' Maika says. 'Get ready.'

Michelle turns round and sees two military jeeps zigzag through traffic. She grabs her daughter and tells her again everything will work out. 'We're just in a bit of a hurry.'

Bang!

A white mark appears on the rear window.

'Get down!' Maika yells, and she pulls on Michelle's dress. 'You never know if the bulletproof glass will hold!'

She unbuckles her seat belt, slides off the seat, and presses a crying Alexa between her legs. 'Where are we going?!' she yells.

'To V'kra-Neza, the old fort, there are soldiers who can protect us there.'

The car rocks back and forth violently, and Michelle can hardly hold on.

'What if the attackers are waiting for us at the fort?' Her voice is barely audible over the roaring of the engine. 'Why don't we go to the airport?'

Maika shakes her head. 'If we run now, we lose everything!'

She wants to tell her mother-in-law that they will lose everything when those men kill them, but one of the jeeps appears next to the window. She sees a soldier with a machine gun hanging out of the car's sunroof. He shouts something – probably telling them to stop – points his weapon at Maika's door and pulls the trigger. The sound is ear-shattering, and the bulletproof glass bends like a parasol in the pouring rain. Maika screams, and Michelle holds Alexa tighter.

The driver yanks his steering wheel again and again, but he can't seem to shake off the cars chasing him. Michelle squeezes herself up and sees that the jeep is now in front of them. The car has overtaken them. Maika shouts something in Kazichian, and the man in the passenger seat opens his window and takes out a gun. Before he can shoot, the car skids. One of the tyres is hit, and the car is swaying wildly. Because she is still holding Alexa, Michelle hits her head on the car door. Immediately her left ear starts ringing. She can feel blood running down her temple and her vision is blurry, but she still won't let go of the girl.

'I've got you,' she says. She feels the driver regain control of the car. 'Don't worry. I'm not letting go.'

The pain in her temple feels sharp, but she tries to remain calm.

In through your nose, out through your mouth, she tells herself.

She wants to get her heart rate down, for herself, but for her unborn baby, too.

And I've got you, little one, she thinks quietly. *I'm not letting go of you, either.*

The ringing fades, and the sound of a helicopter replaces it. She looks outside and sees they have turned into a different neighbourhood.

'Did we lose them?' she asks Maika.

The old lady nods. Because of the bullet impact, there is nothing to see from her window.

'And now?' she asks, sitting up straight.

'We follow emergency protocol. We're driving to the old city, where they'll lay out nail mats as soon as we've passed.'

'And the helicopter? Is that ours?'

'I don't think so. But we're going via the underground bazaar. They won't be able to follow us there.'

They enter the city gate. Tourists duck away just in time and the helicopter hovers over the Man with a Thousand Faces. With astonishing speed, the driver gets them through narrow alleyways, until they reach a sand-coloured little square. The car hits a gate and drives onto the busy square, towards tiled stairs. They hit a man who collapses, but they don't slow down. Only when they reach a fountain in the middle of the square, does the driver finally hit the brakes. Wheezing, Maika jumps out of the car and runs down the stairs, as fast as her stubby legs will take her, to the underground market. Michelle takes Alexa in her arms and follows her mother-in-law and the two soldiers, their weapons drawn. It's crowded in the narrow halls, and she walks behind one of the soldiers so he can clear a path through the hordes of tourists. He's been shot, he is limping. She can smell the iron tang of blood, mixed with the aroma of dried fruits and tea. She notices a dark stain on his arm.

Out of breath, Maika leads them towards a little hallway filled with tea stalls. The walls of the round space have been painted, a giant arabesque made up of oven-baked stones, swirling around Michelle like a storm of colours. She points her eyes at the floor and tries to control her breathing. Her body feels sore from exhaustion, and she is worried she'll faint.

In through your nose, out through your mouth.

'Over here!' Maika points at a wooden stall.

Michelle doesn't understand what her mother-in-law is hoping to find there, but she runs over anyway. One of the soldiers yells something at the stallholder, who gets his cash register and runs off with a clamour. The tourists have noticed the weapons and are trying to leave the market as fast as they can. At the bottom of the stairs, people push each other to get away, screaming and crying. When she gets closer to the stall, Michelle sees a door hidden in the arabesque. The tiles on the door are just a tad lighter than the rest of the wall.

Maika comes and stands next to her. 'There is a secret entrance to the fort here. We'll hide behind this stall until they open it from the other side.'

Michelle does as she's told, and crouches behind the stall, when she hears crying on the other side of the bazaar.

'They're coming,' Maika says. With two hands she pounds on the hidden door.

One of the soldiers gets his gun from his shoulder and walks towards the commotion. Carefully Michelle gets up and looks from behind the stall to see if the other soldier is still there. He's on the ground in the middle of the hall. Around his shoulder, the blood has formed a small pool on the stone floor. Startled, she hides behind the wooden divider. There is no one left to protect them. What do they do now? Wait until the soldiers find them? And then? Will they be taken captive, or executed right away?

'We're trapped,' she whispers. She can hear the desperation in her own voice.

'What?'

'We should have gone to the airport. We never should have come here, we have nowhere to go now.'

Maika looks at her with contempt. 'Didn't I tell you we'd lose everything?'

'I don't care! This is your war, not ours. I'm not going to sit around and wait for them to find us. Alexa and I can disappear with all these tourists and make our way home.'

'And Daniel, are you abandoning him?!'

'Daniel would want us to be safe.' She wants to get up, but Maika pulls her down.

'Are you mad? This isn't just about you or me, Michelle.'

'Let me go!'

'Think of your child!' Maika pulls her dress even harder.

'That's what I'm doing!'

'Michelle, please think this through. The people that are trying to take the High House will make sure that no Lechkov can ever seize the throne. Now or in the future. They won't stop until they find you. And until they find *her*. Until they kill the last Lechkov.'

'You've lost your mind. This little Dutch girl has nothing to do with this miserable situation.'

'She's a Lechkov,' Maika says. 'We need to protect her.'

Behind them, there is a loud crack. A cloud of sand-coloured dust whirls down as the arabesque opens. Two soldiers with white circles on their shoulders step out of the small opening. Silently, they help Maika up and lead her into a low, dark hallway. But before the old woman enters the door, she turns round to her daughter-in-law.

'You don't have a choice, Michelle Lechkova. This isn't just my fight, but yours too. And your child's.'

15

Daniel and Vigo were nine years old when, as an exception, they were allowed to play in the catacombs of the old Neza fort. It was the day after Boris Lechkov, their father, received two new titles at once: he became COO of Lechkov Industria and minister of foreign affairs of Kazichia. Petar didn't want to resign just yet, but he had started thinking of possible successors. Boris needed to be prepared for the presidency in case something happened to Petar.

After the ceremonies surrounding Boris's appointments had ended, Maika had a surprise for the twins. Because they had behaved so well, she took her boys to the tunnels under the fort, the part filled with ruinous altars and centuries-old storage rooms, inaccessible to the general public. Their arsenal of plastic guns had been brought out so they could run around for a few hours, on one condition: they weren't allowed to go near the door at the end of the tunnel.

'That door is forbidden. You're not even allowed to go near it,' Maika said. 'Promise?'

The twins promised and ran off. But after half an hour the novelty wore off, and Vigo couldn't contain himself anymore. He snuck by the sign with the skull, through the long, narrow hallway to the secret door. He tried pulling the big lever, but it wouldn't budge.

Daniel stayed away and looked at his brother from a distance, telling him he should listen to their mother.

And still, it was he who got punished, not Vigo.

'What are you doing?' Maika asked. 'You can't touch that door!'

Daniel and Vigo didn't hear their mother approaching, and they were so startled they almost fell over. Maika had the secret door opened and grabbed Daniel by his skinny arm.

'Get in!' she yelled. 'This is what you wanted? Get in, then.'

'I don't want to,' he said quietly. 'Why do I need to go in? I didn't do anything.'

'You're going to find out the hard way. In with you!'

She pushed him into the dark corridor, and with a dull thump, the door closed. It was pitch dark, and Daniel knocked on the thick, bumpy slabs. He didn't know what was behind the forbidden door, but the skull on the sign was not a good omen. After a while, his small fists started hurting. He stopped hitting but still wouldn't turn round. Dead silent, he stayed by the door and stared at it. Sticking out of his pocket was the plastic gun from his time as a brave soldier, but now he felt warm urine running down his leg.

On the other side, Maika Lechkova smoked a cigarette. 'That's what you get,' she muttered to Vigo. 'You need to listen to your mother.'

'Can he come out now, Mummy?'

'Not yet.' She took a long drag and blew smoke into the low, stuffy corridor. 'Whose idea was it to ignore my order?'

Little Vigo looked at his feet. He was holding his plastic gun but also didn't feel like a soldier anymore.

'Well?' His mother pulled his arm. 'Was it your idea?'

The boy started nodding, but when he saw his mother's expression change, he quickly shook his head.

'Good boy.'

'Can he come out now?' he asked. 'We won't do it again.'

'Your family is different, Vigo. Your family has real secrets. Important secrets. And you will need to keep them, whatever it takes. Tunnels run through this mountain, through the whole city even, like roots under a tree. Some are new and some very old, but they all lead to this door. That door ensures that our family can get to the bunker safely. Wherever we are in the city, we can always get home. Unless someone reveals the secret of this door. Do you understand what I am trying to teach you, *tsvali*? We have more important secrets than normal people. Our secrets are worth lying and deceiving for. That's not bad, it's wise. Do you understand? There are different rules for us.'

Vigo nodded and asked if his brother could come out.

Four years after the incident in the fort, Daniel entered his mother's office. He had started growing into a slouchy teenager.

'Remember when you locked me up in the bunker?' he asked.

'The bunker?' Maika was eating from a silver plate on a silver tray, sitting at her desk. Surrounding the tray were piles of green folders, marked with the intelligence service logo.

'I asked Dad what's behind that door, and he said it's a crumple zone. A long corridor to make the explosion stop.'

'A crumple zone won't stop an explosion. The impact is broken down until nothing is left, like a wave hitting the shore. You need to be more precise with your words, Daniel.' She looked up from her plate. 'Don't you have class?'

'Why did you get angry with me when it was Vigo by the door? I wasn't doing anything. And all that was behind the door was a long corridor. There is nothing there. Why did you get so angry?'

His mother sipped from her black tea and opened a green file. 'All the city's secret corridors lead to that hallway.'

'So? You locked me in the dark for hours. Why would you do that to a small child? And you knew it was Vigo. How is that fair?'

'You were in there for a few minutes, my boy. Your brother needed to learn his lesson about family secrets. That is important for when he takes his father's place.' She put her tea down and closed the file. 'And stop that nonsense about "fairness". Fairness doesn't exist. Fairness, or justice, are things that people make up to get their way. That's the lesson you could have learned that day if you had paid attention. Your name is Lechkov, you have some hard lessons to learn, my boy. Many people want what you have and will do everything to get it.'

Twenty-three years later, when Daniel is thirty-seven, he enters the secret bunker door a second time. But this time he is on a stretcher, and this time the darkness around him is caused by

75

him losing consciousness. He is carried to the sick ward of the underground bunker and laid on a bed. The doctor checks his heart rate and reflexes and sticks a needle into his thigh.

Daniel jumps up in bed, gasping for air.

'Relax, Mr Lechkov. You're safe.' The doctor shines a light in his eyes. 'We just gave you some adrenaline and an IV with a saline solution. We also drew some blood to find out what they gave you.'

'Where am I?'

Next to Daniel stands one of the soldiers who saved him. His uniform has a white circle on it. The man salutes. 'You're in the bunker, Mr Lechkov, don't worry. I'm here to protect you.'

'What happened? I ... There were soldiers and I was in a car, but then ...'

'My name is Corporal Vyli and I'm a member of the *Krugul*.'

Daniel notices the logo on the corporal's uniform. 'The Circle?'

The soldier nods. 'The Circle is a special military unit, formed by Madam Lechkova and General Lechkov, to protect the Mardoe Khador against a coup d'etat from within.'

It takes Daniel a moment before the soldier's words sink in.

'My mother and uncle knew this would happen? They were preparing for it?'

The door flies open. 'Is he awake?'

Maika steps over the high threshold. Her short hair is tousled, her suit ripped.

'How could you act so dangerously, Daniel? I thought I'd lost both of you.' She grabs his hand and kisses his palm. 'I thought the entire country was lost.'

He pulls his hand back. 'Where are Michelle and Alexa?'

'They're next door. They are all right, don't worry. As soon as the doctor is finished, Michelle will come in.'

He sinks into his pillow. 'What the hell is going on? Did you know this would happen?'

'I told you to watch out for the other families. You let yourself get abducted and put everything in danger.'

'I *let myself what*? Are you angry with *me*?'

'Yes, of course. I told you not to trust Karzarov, didn't I?'

'Uncle Lev did this?' Slowly, images of the shooting in the alley start crystallising.

'Yes, the dog.' Maika nearly spits the words.

Daniel stares at his own feet on the other side of the hospital bed. As a boy growing up in the High House, Lev was the sounding board after fights with his mother, the longest hug before he moved to England. As a boy growing up in the Mardoe Khador, there weren't three families – Lechkov, Karzarov, and Yanev – but one family. His family.

'You knew this would happen, you knew I couldn't trust Lev, and you still let me come here. And my family, too.'

'Everyone is safe, that's all that matters. We formed the Circle so they could prevent a coup from happening, and that's exactly what they did. Karzarov had a whole division of our army behind him, which enabled him to storm the parliament and the ministries of defence and national affairs, but the Circle, and our loyal troops, saved the capital from those traitors.'

'And where is Uncle Lev?'

'It looks like he's fled the country,' Maika says, her lip raised. 'Most likely through the secret tunnels, back into the city. And then by helicopter. The borders are closed, but I think it's too late.'

'So he will get a second chance to attack?'

Before Maika can defend herself, Radko enters.

'I'm so happy to see you, Daniel. That was way too close.'

'It was,' he responds. 'The army was in on it, Uncle Radko. I was abducted by soldiers. How is this possible? Hasn't the army always been loyal to us?'

The tall commander-in-chief looks at his feet. 'They still are, but there was a small group that started an uprising from within. A few years ago, we obtained a Belarusian regiment from the OMON, as we have done before. Apparently, there were some infiltrators among them. All this time they kept quiet. Waited for this day. Most likely, they have gathered more and more people around them. That's the downside to a mercenary army: they will work for the highest price. But we hit back, and the attack was stopped.'

'The infiltrators were probably placed there by Russia,' his mother mutters. 'We suspect Karzarov is working with the Kremlin.'

At that moment, Michelle comes running into the room. She doesn't look at Radko or Maika and jumps onto Daniel's bed. He grabs her and they press their foreheads together – as if they can ground each other.

'Are you all right?'

He nods. 'Where is Alexa?'

'In the next room, with a nurse. She's shaken up, but fine otherwise. I'm going back to her in a bit. Daniel, we need . . .'

'You don't have to say anything. Can you send our pilot a message?'

Michelle nods and climbs off the bed. She leaves the room.

'What are you two talking about?' Maika asks.

'We're leaving as soon as possible,' Daniel says. 'If Russia is really working with Uncle Lev, they won't stop here. They opened the attack, and there is no way back.'

'What do you mean?' The veins in his mother's eyes look like a red river delta, filling up faster than its shores can handle.

'We're going home,' he says and quickly rips the IV needle from his hand.

'But you can't.' Maika is quiet for a moment and looks at the ground. The veins in her temples have swelled – blue deltas. Somewhere in Maika Lechkova's heart, a dam is about to burst. 'We need to show that our family is strong,' she says. 'Or they will pull all of us down.'

Radko folds his hands together. 'Daniel, please. If you leave, chaos will reign.'

'I'm sorry, I need to get my family to safety. I can't keep them here while Russia invades.'

Maika takes a step forward and grabs him. 'You *need* to stay because that is the only way to keep them away. We can protect you. And we need you to protect us.'

'Protect? You used me and my family as bait. You were willing to sacrifice me for the Mardoe Khador. As always.'

'What are you talking about? How dare you say that?'

'You brought me and my family here, knowing there would be a coup.'

Michelle enters the room again and holds up her phone. Daniel knows the jet is being prepared. He nods at his wife and then looks at Radko. 'How is the situation up there? In the High House?'

'It's safe. The coup is over,' Radko says quietly. 'But don't underestimate your position, Daniel. Your role is the most important one right now. If you leave . . .'

Daniel tries to stand up but falls back into bed. The doctor gets out of his chair immediately. 'You need to lie down, Mr Lechkov. Please. You were drugged.'

'Give me another shot of adrenaline.'

Maika huffs. 'If you leave now, we're all doomed!'

'Mother, come with us to the Netherlands. There is plenty of room on the plane. And Grandfather too, and you too, Uncle Radko. You can all come.'

'That won't solve anything. Do you think the Russians will leave you alone when you're in the West? Or all those other oligarchs who are after our lithium? Do you think they will leave you alone in Amsterdam? Don't you remember what they did to my parents? Your grandpa and grandma?'

'Lithium has nothing to do with me. I am a Dutch computer scientist, and I am going home. With or without you.' Daniel rolls up his sleeve and looks up at the doctor. 'Are you giving me the shot or should I do it myself?'

'You will have our blood on your hands,' his mother whispers. 'And when we're dead, they'll come for you. Wherever you run to. Wherever you hide your child. They will not stop until the last Lechkov has disappeared.'

16

It is total chaos at Vorta Airport. No tourist wants to stay in Kazichia for another minute after the fighting, but the Mardoe Khador has cancelled all flights and closed the borders. Maika hopes to keep Lev Karzarov in the country this way. And so, Michelle, Daniel, and Alexa drive through a crowd of angry tourists. The car is being beaten, and people are squeezed together. Michelle sees a mother holding her child up, hoping someone will make space. When they finally reach the terminal entrance, the four soldiers that came with them get out of the car first. They leave the suitcases in the car; they would only slow them down.

Michelle follows a big Kazichian soldier. Around them angry yells sound in different languages, and she tries to follow the soldier more closely. While looking at the camouflage on his back, she thinks of the chase earlier that day. The abduction in the church, the white stars in the car windows, and how she fled to the underground bazaar right behind another soldier. A soldier who bled to death after getting shot. How could it have gone so wrong, so fast?

Reaching the diplomat's entrance, the four soldiers form a human shield so the Lechkovs can enter without an intruder sneaking in. While the doors close, Michelle looks over her shoulder and sees dozens of eyes. Eyes filled with disbelief. Filled with fear. Hundreds, thousands of people, just trying to get home, trying to get their families to safety. Just like her.

But the doors close.

Walking through the terminal, it feels like they've reached a different world. The airport is deserted and dead silent. Michelle is conscious of her hearing, like coming home after a concert. All she hears is the echoes of their footsteps in the empty space, and far away, the muffled chaos from outside. In the silence, as they look at their plane through the windows of the glass terminal, she finally tells Alexa they're going home. Straight away, the girl lays her little head on Daniel's shoulder and falls asleep without saying a word. Her mother's promise is like a spell, releasing her from stress. Only when they've made it inside the plane does Michelle also give in to her exhaustion. She sees the pilot and co-pilot going down their checklist, the flight attendant bringing out bottles of water, and the ground staff removing the fuel hose, and finally lets herself believe that they're going home. It's real now. They are flying back to Amsterdam. That night, she will lie in her own bed. She will be able to hug her little sister. In the Netherlands, their troubles won't go away; she understands that, but at least they'll be back home. Back to a country where the police and the army are there to protect them, not to stage a coup.

Carefully, Daniel lays Alexa in a chair.

'I'm sorry,' he tells his sleeping daughter softly.

Michelle walks to him and grabs his hand.

'I'm sorry,' he says to her.

She lays a hand on Alexa's head and tries to swallow her tears but fails. She wants to tell him that she forgives him and that she knows why he needed to come back. And that he couldn't have known what was going on. But before she can say anything, the flight attendant coughs.

'Sir, madam, a few people here want to speak to you before we leave.'

'People from the airport?' Michelle asks.

'No,' she answers softly. 'I don't understand how they got in.'

Three figures step into the cabin: a short middle-aged woman with foggy glasses, and two muscleheads.

'Daniel Petar Lechkov? Michelle Verdier Lechkova?' The woman pushes her glasses up her nose.

'*Esti tu var?* Daniel asks. '*I pravish tuk var? Tova chasten e tvitmprivani.*'

'*Me ak stuva Andropov,*' the woman says. '*La loc aresta.*'

Michelle stands before her sleeping daughter. 'Daniel, what is happening? What are these people doing here?'

'She says she represents someone named Andropov. I suspect he's GRU,' Daniel whispers. 'The Russian military intelligence service.'

He motions for her to sit down.

The two men close the door to the cockpit so the pilots can't listen in, and send the flight attendant outside. Michelle feels all the stress returning to her body. She has panicked so much that it's starting to become a reflex.

'Daniel, is this okay?' she hears herself ask. 'Are we being taken hostage?'

The woman takes a mobile phone from her inside pocket and holds it out, like she's trying to sell the thing. A cheerful voice speaks to them from the phone, in English with a Russian accent.

'Mr Lechkov? Are you there? And Madam Lechkova?'

They don't answer.

'You're speaking with Yuri Andropov, I'm calling you from the Russian embassy in Stolia. I'm calling because it looks like you're trying to leave the country.'

'That's right,' Daniel says. 'Strike the "trying".'

His words are aggressive, but she can hear fear in his voice.

'I strongly suggest you don't,' the Russian says.

'Or else?'

Andropov laughs, it sounds awfully fake. 'Mr Lechkov, you're very direct. A wonderful trait for the future president of Kazichia. I'll be direct too; without a leader, your region is vulnerable to unrest and change. Moscow has no interest in that. We were hoping to ensure stability with Lev Karzarov, but unfortunately, your mother damaged his credibility today. So that leaves us with two options: merge the Democratic Republic of Kazichia with powerful Russia or do business with the Lechkov family. My superior prefers the first option. He has never forgiven Petar Lechkov, your grandfather, for his betrayal. But I prefer the second option, because war is always messy, and I don't like uncertainties.'

'Russia wants a friend in power,' Michelle says.

Daniel sits up. 'I cannot be that friend, Mr Andropov. I'm neutral. And I'm going home now.'

The man on the other end of the line says something in Russian, and his right-hand woman opens a file on her phone immediately. While she does, Andropov addresses Daniel and Michelle again.

'Will you please take a look at these photos, Mr Lechkov? And show them to your wife, too.'

Daniel takes the phone, and Michelle looks over his shoulder. She sees a dark green door and wisteria hanging over the brick wall.

Our dark green door. Our brick wall.

Another photo appears, and her face feels hot. Every last shred of hope is gone now. The second photo is of their bedroom: their box spring mattress, ready for their return.

'Mr Lechkov, these photos were taken a few minutes ago by friends of mine, who arrived in Amsterdam a few days ago. They tell me you have a beautiful house. The large bedroom with the adjoining bathroom is especially gorgeous. They call that 'en suite', if I'm not mistaken. My friends will be staying in that house for the foreseeable future. You don't mind, do you? They will take good care of your things.'

Michelle stares at her husband, whose face has turned red.

'Did you kill my brother?' he asks.

'So young, so tragic,' the voice from the phone says. 'Squashed by a big truck.'

'Was it you?'

'Big trucks ride on the roads around Stolia. And they ride on the highways around Amsterdam. Big trucks are everywhere. That's why it's important to be careful. Especially with a beautiful, vulnerable daughter.'

Michelle looks behind her at Alexa, who is starting to wake up.

'I got it,' Daniel says.

'Wonderful!' The Russian laughs. You will return to the Mardoe Khador now, Mr Lechkov, to tell your mother you're willing to accept the presidency. As soon as you're in that presidential chair, I will contact you to discuss the next step in our collaboration.'

'What if Alexa and I leave,' Michelle whispers.

Daniel nods. 'I'm staying here,' he tells the phone. 'I'll do as you ask. But I'm sending my family back to the Netherlands.'

'No, no, no. That's not how it works. You need to understand, Mr Lechkov, *we* make the rules, not you. One of those rules is for your lovely little family to stay together. Have a nice day and see you soon.'

The call is disconnected, and Michelle stares at the phone in Daniel's hand. The screen turns itself off and the black reflection of a face appears – a vague outline of the man she married.

'You're cancelling the flight?' the Russian asks, while she grabs her phone from Daniel's hand.

'No,' Michelle says. 'No!'

'Michelle, we . . .'

'No, Daniel! Call that man back. We need to make a deal with him. There must be something we can do. If necessary, Alexa can go home by herself, and I'll stay here. I can call my mum; she'll pick her up from Schiphol.'

'There's no use,' Daniel says and hangs his head. 'There's nothing we can do now.'

'What do you mean? Of course we can do something.' She looks up at the woman. 'What do you want? What can we do for each other?'

'Your husband understands the situation,' the Russian says and turns round, exiting the plane with the two silent men.

Michelle looks at Daniel. 'This can't be happening. What can we do? What can we give him?'

'We need to stay here. If we fly to Amsterdam now, the tanks will enter Stolia, and GRU agents will be waiting in our bedroom.'

'So we'll be stuck here for the rest of our lives? Imprisoned?'

He rubs his face. 'I'll find a way to get you home. I swear. Even if it means turning this whole country upside down. Even if I have to take power, I'll get you out of here, Michelle. But first, we need to return to the Mardoe Khador.'

II. Darkness

17

When I open my eyes, it is still dark.

I can't see anything.

I can hardly hear anything.

The four plane engines roar. I know I'm sitting in the cargo hold of a C-130 Hercules military transport plane. I recognise the sound. Not that I know that much about planes, I just know this type well. I've sat in the back of a Hercules dozens, maybe hundreds of times.

I listen to the trusty roaring and stare at the black of my eyelids. Something is starting to form in the darkness. Circles expanding and shrinking, like lungs or a heart. There is something relaxing about it. When I was a little boy, I liked sitting in the dark. In my tiny bedroom I'd turn the light off, close the curtains, and sit in the corner. In silence. It felt like I was underwater, where nobody could reach me.

But the darkness never lasts.

When my eyes started getting used to the dark and my bedroom came back, I'd turn the light on and go outside to play. Or watch TV. I would have sat in that corner all day.

But the darkness never lasts.

Someone next to me coughs a few times, so loud that it drowns out the plane engines. Because of the sound, I lose the moving circles, and memories start flooding back: I get taken from my bed in the middle of the night. I'm being put in the back of a car and driven to a military airport in Germany. While entering the gate, they gave me a blindfold and told me to wear it for the rest of the journey. Someone took my hand and guided me into the plane. Someone else gave me a bottle of water. The last thing I remember is estimating the flight time to be around five hours.

How long have I been asleep?

Shit, I was planning to stay awake. Did they put something in my water? A sedative?

I turn my neck and stretch my legs. Now that my body is waking up, I can feel that we're descending. Say we're on an eight-hour flight, then we could be flying over Niger right now or New York.

The man next to me coughs again.

I can guess why I'm wearing a blindfold; tonight, mercenaries like me have been woken up all over Europe and driven to that airport in Germany. This cargo hold is filled with blindfolded men trying to estimate how long we have been flying. Men who are not supposed to see each other's faces.

The plane tilts, and the engines start squealing; we're turning towards the landing strip.

The operation is about to begin.

I'm not nervous, I'm relieved. The man that pulled me out of bed a couple of hours ago, asked if I was willing to disappear for a while, maybe months or years, to execute a complex operation for a major client. I nodded and signed a contract. The second I let go of the pen, I was taken. Abducted. Without knowing where, or why.

It doesn't matter, I need money, and assignments like these are well-paid.

Beneath my feet, there is a high-pitched sound, probably the landing gear getting extended.

'Three minutes,' someone to the left of me calls out. He has an accent I can't place. It could be Russian or Georgian, but a little more delicate.

The darkness starts moving again – straight lines this time.

The other day I read that almost all people die in a radius of ten kilometres of the street they were born in. Or was it one hundred? Anyway, you end where you start, that was the gist, and the article made me feel claustrophobic. In the past year, I've been going further back. Back to the beginning. It felt like I had to leap back into the pit that I had used my fingertips to climb out of, all those years ago.

Caro stopped giving me assignments. She said nobody wanted to work with me after what I pulled in Yemen. That's how she phrased it: what you *pulled*.

Nonsense. How could I have prevented us from getting trapped?

I asked if I could come over anyway, but she didn't feel like it. 'We should stop doing that,' she said. 'Let's keep it professional from now on.'

Strange woman. If nobody wants to hire me, how am I supposed to keep it professional? Anyway, I didn't have a choice but to return to the gutter. To the men who always have jobs. The men that have had jobs since I was a good-for-nothing fifteen-year-old boy, before enlisting. I'm not proud of it, but I did some break-ins, threatened and robbed some people, stuff like that.

'Maybe it's time to consider getting a normal job,' Caro said when I called to beg her for an assignment. 'Maybe it's time to return to society. To resurface.'

That's what she said: resurface. Bitch. She knows I can't do that. How am I supposed to do that? What name do I choose? What passport do I bring when I register at the municipality? I haven't used my real passport in so long it expired. I don't even know where it is. Besides, I need more money than you can get working demolition. A lot more.

The plane hits something. It startles me and I grab hold of the seat. It's the landing strip. I didn't know we were this close to the ground.

How long has the flight been? I think eight hours, but I can't be sure. Maybe ten. If we've flown for eight hours, we might be back in Yemen.

I hope not.

The engines slow as the plane brakes down the runway.

Caro thinks she can get rid of me. She thinks she can turn me on and off, like a lamp. But I could ruin her entire life. She might think I'm not on to her, but I see more than most people. I'm smarter than my clients think. Her official title is 'probation officer', that is how she's finding all these mercenaries. After my military service, I got assigned a probation officer who specialised in reintegrating ex-militaries. That was Caro. But Caro didn't want to reintegrate me, she wanted to introduce me to her friends at three major private military contractors. By sheer coincidence, she knew which shady assignments were waiting for discharged specialists like me and the rest of the blindfolded men on this plane. I could destroy her; I could reveal that she uses her work to recruit soldiers. But I don't. I'm not that kind of person. It was hard to accept that I couldn't see her at night anymore – I really thought we had something beautiful growing between us – but oh well, I'll get over it.

Darkness never lasts.

'Stay put until someone gets you,' a voice says.

The plane stands still. With a warning beep and a mechanical sigh, the cargo door opens. This is the moment of truth. I'm starting to get a little nervous. What did I agree to? What am I going to do? And for whom? Has Caro helped me after all? Or did they get my name through someone else?

Someone puts his hand on my shoulder. 'Get up and come.'

What kind of accent is that?

I let the hand lead me. We exit the plane. It's cold, but not freezing. I hear people shouting at each other and focus on their dialect: hard, short.

We're in Eastern Europe, we have to be. I think the Caucasus.

'Keep looking ahead.'

The synthetic fabric of a glove moves over my forehead and removes the blindfold. I'm standing in front of a beaten-up Honda CR-V, by an empty plane hangar. Next to me is a short, broad man. Without saying a word, he pushes a phone into my chest.

'Hello?' I don't know which language to speak.

'This is your client,' a male voice says. 'After this conversation, we will never speak again. All briefings will go through a local agent, you will hear their voice as soon as I hang up.'

He sounds American. Is it the CIA? Special Operations? No,

why would the CIA hire me? Why would they go through such obscure channels?

I want to turn round to see if the rest of the passengers are regular CIA agents, but the man in front of me grabs my shoulders. 'Look ahead.'

I nod and look at the old Honda again. Someone comes carrying my stuff and throws the bags in the back seat.

The American man talks faster and faster. 'You will get more details when you need them. For now, it's better to know as little context as possible. For the coming days, you will be looking for a person of interest, someone calling themselves "the Man with a Thousand Faces". We know this person is preparing an uprising against the government. We have no idea who they are or where they get their resources.'

I ask where I am.

'In Kazichia.'

The Caucasus. Just as I thought.

'What do I do when I've located this person?'

Behind me, a car starts; one of the other specialists finishes their briefing and drives off.

'The Man with a Thousand Faces poses a danger to Kazichia. He can disturb the power balance in the country.'

Another car starts. We're getting released one by one, like racing pigeons.

'We're willing to do everything to find this figure.' The voice sounds strange now. The connection falters, and the sound is a little distorted. I hear static as if a digital storm is on the horizon. 'That's all you need to know for now. Good luck.'

The static goes quiet, and I suddenly hear a female voice with a Kazichian accent.

'Get in the car and drive to the address I'm about to give you. When you've arrived, call this number for further instructions. There is water, food, money, and a city map in the back of the car. Don't buy a phone, and don't buy a computer. You need to stay invisible.'

While the woman reads the address, I close my eyes to visualise the words and numbers. In the darkness, the signs are written out for me.

'These are the keys for the car,' the man who handed me the phone tells me. 'Are you ready to start?'

I open my eyes.

18

Night has fallen, and I am driving through Kazichia for the first time in my life. I am in the outskirts of the city, with tall flats on wide, poorly maintained roads. The closer I get to my destination, the rougher the neighbourhoods get. It reminds me of a Serbian town where I killed the wrong man once; he was in the wrong place at the wrong time. At least, as far as I know. Maybe that mistake was my real assignment – maybe it was all part of a greater plan.

I stop in front of a blackened flat. Some youths on the pavement turn quiet when they see me – they are probably selling drugs. As a soldier, you preferably don't drive up to your objective in a loud, unreliable car. Especially unarmed. But that's the way it is.

When I look through the front window, I see broken glass and abandoned washing lines. I call the number and ask for instructions. The same female voice I heard at the airport explains what needs to happen. 'Enter the flat. Take the stairs to the fifth floor, apartment 142. There is someone there, a man. We want him to tell us who the Man with a Thousand Faces is. Pressure him.'

'What are my rules of engagement?'

'Violence is permitted, but no serious injuries. Keep it clean, he needs to stay alive. Do you understand, soldier?'

'Understood. What can you tell me about him? Is he a politician? A soldier?'

The woman sighs. 'We didn't bring you here to ask questions, soldier. Call me after you speak to the man.'

The call disconnects.

Who does this woman think I am?! Could she not tell by my resumé that I'm trustworthy? That I'm a specialist who needs intel to carry out an operation? I feel anger welling up in me. Anger that flows through my knuckles like boiling water. This keeps happening lately, I keep getting these sudden moments of intense frustration, I don't know why.

I park the car round the corner from the building complex, out of sight of the drug dealers. In the back seat, I snort five milligrams of Moda, swallow a beta blocker, and drink some water. Then I enter the flat, no weapons or bulletproof vest, feeling eerie.

In the staircase, it stinks of piss and heroin. The building looks worse the higher I go. On the fourth floor, two walls have been torn down. I can look inside the apartment. Some junkies lie on a small brown mattress. A woman stares at me. I don't know if she is alive; she's not blinking, anyway.

What am I doing here? Why is this job so well paid?

The fifth floor is empty and quiet. I walk to apartment 142 and pick the lock as quietly as possible. Before opening the door, I cover my face with my balaclava. Years ago, together with a Scandinavian soldier, I chained two Arabs to a radiator, torturing them for hours. The client I was working for wanted to know who supplied their rebel group with weapons. I knew we would kill those men eventually, whatever the questioning would bring, but still, the Scandinavian insisted we wear masks.

'A mask is not just to hide your identity,' he said, 'but also for us to intimidate more effectively, being faceless. You don't see doubt or regret in our expression, or exhaustion around our eyes.'

'Do you feel doubt or regret sometimes?' I asked.

'The point is you always need to wear a mask.'

I open the door to apartment 142, and it is like stepping through a magic portal. In the middle of that drug den, someone has hidden a printing house. Or is it the newsroom for a magazine? The walls are plastered with paper: newspaper cuttings, pictures, sketches, and Post-its. In the living room, there are two big printers, rolls of paper hanging out of them like white tongues. I sneak past it and see two doors. The one to the bathroom is open, and I look inside: no one there. From under the other door, a beam of light shines. I rest my hand on the cold doorknob and listen intently. Someone is snoring. I open the door carefully and walk in. The room is filled with pamphlets in a language I can't read. In the corner of the room lies a mattress. A man is asleep, lying on his stomach. I hope he speaks English.

I stand over him and poke his back. The man shoots upright, and I grab his neck with my arm. I pull his body towards mine. He freezes, then starts hitting my underarms with his hands.

My mouth right next to his ear, I whisper: 'What can you tell me about the Man with a Thousand Faces?'

'Who?' He tries to shake his head. 'I don't know what you mean. I make pamphlets. I'm not important, I just write down ideas.'

I tackle him to the ground. He's a sinewy little guy. 'You know exactly what I mean,' I say, and stand on his hand so he doesn't move. 'All I want to hear is his real name. Who is he?'

'Please.' Submissively, he presses his forehead to the ground. 'I don't know what you mean. Is he a donor? Is he a Jada?'

I have no clue what he is talking about.

'How do the rebels keep in contact with their leader?' I ask.

The man turns round so he can look at me. 'I don't know who he is, I swear. The only leader the Jada know is a woman: Nairi. No man. No thousand faces.'

I believe him. My instinct tells me this man does not know what I am doing here. But the client told me to apply pressure. And so, I do.

Half an hour later I leave the flat. I kicked the man around the room a couple of times, pushed him against the wall, and choked him. I smashed up his things and threatened to find his family. When I mentioned his mother, he started naming names, and I remember every last one. But it was useless. I could see he was lying. The Kazichian had never heard of the Man with a Thousand Faces and was just doing what he had to do to get rid of me. And me? I was starting to wonder if I had entered the right door. We were like two actors acting out a play, not allowed to know what the plot was.

What kind of assignment is this?

19

For the next three days, I pressure people. I sneak into a chic hotel and lift a man from his bed. I pull two guys from their car and ambush a woman leaving her office building. Nobody knows what I'm looking for, nobody understands what name I want to hear, and nobody has ever heard of the Man with a Thousand Faces. I am hunting a ghost.

In a cabin in Lemnos, a village forty kilometres east of Stolia, I need to make a father talk. His two little sons are in bed. I wake them up and drag them to the living room by their arms. I prefer to leave children alone. They don't have anything to do with stuff like this. Besides, the father doesn't understand what I want from him. He says he doesn't know who the Man with a Thousand Faces is. He tells me a confusing story about a statue in the capital and mentions 'Jada' – like the sinewy pamphlet man.

'If I knew what you need, I'd give it to you,' he says. 'Nothing is worth my family's life. But I don't know anything about a human with one thousand faces.'

After a while the mother gets hysterical; she throws money and car keys at my feet. I look at her and can't help but feel ashamed. I am in a house in a strange country with a terrified family, and I have no idea what I'm doing here.

Nobody has answers.

In the early morning of the fourth day, my contact person calls. She says the questioning is done. The strange thing is, she doesn't sound disappointed. I didn't get any information from my targets, but she seems satisfied. When I apologise for not getting any information, she says it doesn't matter.

'It's more important that they heard the question.'

I don't get that. Why would my client let their enemies know what he's looking for?

Before I can ask, the woman says the second part of the operation will start now. She tells me a long set of coordinates I should drive to the next morning.

'Burn the car when you get to the old tower. You'll know when you see it.'

I don't ask what she means by that, because I know she will hang up before I can say anything.

20

Who is the Man with a Thousand Faces?

That is the question I've asked dozens of times now. That is the question with no answer. Normally I don't need answers. Normally, I do as I'm told, and get money sent to one of my foreign accounts. Simple as that.

But this operation is different.

This time, I feel something new: curiosity.

Who is the Man with a Thousand Faces, and am I with or against him? Of course, it's possible that the CIA wants to support a rebel movement to gain influence in this country. But why would they send me? They have their own insurgency specialists for that.

I try to shake off the questions and park the car in an empty parking space, in front of a building with closed curtains. In the bricks, I see holes and lines: traces of a sign.

I'm back in Stolia and this is where I will stay tonight. For the past few nights, I slept in the car, but I'm supposed to stay here until sunset. I walk in, but don't see anything. The light switches click when I press them, but it stays dark. I turn on my flashlight and see a deserted lobby. This used to be a hotel. By the lift is a folded cot, some food and a camping lamp. I drop my bags on the carpet and look around. Next to the lobby, there is a big lounge. Against the back wall of the bar hang shelves filled with liquor bottles. The fact that this hotel has not been plundered, means it's a good part of town.

I want to walk to the stairs to explore upstairs but see myself in the mirror walls. A dark figure in a room of empty chairs and tables. What is going on with me? What changed? Why does the same question keep taunting me, like a blister in my mouth?

With no plan I go outside again. To the cold town. This neighbourhood is definitely better than the area where I had to question the pamphlet-maker. The apartment buildings are just as ugly as everywhere else in Stolia but are kept well. The street lanterns next to the narrow two-lane road are working, and lots of cars are parked next to the wide pavements. It's late, and the street is quiet. That's a good sign; the neighbourhoods that I looked for work in when I was young came alive at night.

I walk a few blocks and reach a street with some night shops. Fruit is out on display, and brightly coloured words that I don't understand blink. Foreigners don't come to this part of town; I can tell by the way the smoking shop owners watch me.

Suddenly, I'm standing in front of an internet cafe. It's a narrow, deep shop, with faded turquoise walls and two AC units about to fall from the ceiling. It has four or five old grey computer screens on little tables and one man sits behind a counter staring at his laptop.

I'm supposed to keep walking. I know that. I just need to wander around a bit to calm my nerves, and then return to the deserted hotel. I just need a good night's sleep, before leaving town in the morning. That's what I'm allowed to do, so that's all I should do.

But I can't resist.

I pull the sliding door open and enter the cafe.

It smells like tobacco, and something else. Something sweet. On the floor lie white cables, seemingly not plugged into anything.

The man frowns at me and asks something in Kazichian. I point at a monitor, and he nods.

The screen makes a static sound when it turns on and the modem starts dialling up. With some effort, I change the browser language to English and google 'the Man with a Thousand Faces'. A Wikipedia article appears on the statue in the capital. That statue has something to do with the Ottomans, centuries ago. That doesn't help me. There is also a book called *The Hero with a Thousand Faces*, but that is about myths and stories. I don't find anything else. But that can't be all, can it? If he is a rebel leader, shouldn't I be able to find something on a news website, something about his uprising?

After a while, the cafe owner walks up to me. He smells of hash.

'You're not from here,' he says. 'What are you looking for?'

I tell him I'm writing an article about a man with a thousand faces, but that my research isn't going anywhere.

'You're not looking in the right places. For twenty *ivot* I will look for you on the dark web. Everything is on there. I have Tor.'

I have no idea what he means, I have no idea what Tor is, but give him the money. We walk over to his laptop at the counter, and he starts typing.

'The common man thinks he is free on the internet,' the Kazichian says, 'but we are all stuck in these capitalist prison cells that Google and Facebook built for us. And we're lucky, still, that the High House has not built a firewall around the country yet, like the Chinese.'

I nod as if I'm listening, but I am starting to regret giving him twenty *ivot*.

'The true freedom is here,' the man says, and he points at his screen. 'True freedom is only found in places with no rules, like the dark web.'

'Are you finding anything?' I ask.

'I found a forum. Look.'

'I don't understand.'

'There are not many people who speak this language. This is the language of my people: the Jada. This language is our pride and we will never give it up — even if there would be only ten people left in the whole world who understand it.'

'Who are the Jada?'

'The Jada are the original inhabitants of the Akhlos,' he says, and points outside, through the wall of his cafe. 'The mountains of Kazichia. We guard the borders of the old country.'

'What does it say?'

He leans forward to read the tiny white letters. 'This is a forum for Jada and Neza, who . . .' he looks for the right word, 'are politically active, if you know what I mean. Activists.'

'Who are the Neza?'

He shakes his head and waves. 'Crazy people, alcoholics. They're from the east, they don't belong to this country. Between our people there should be a border, it's better that way. But the Mardoe Khador erased that border and put our people to work on their land and in their mines, side by side. That's asking for trouble. The Neza suddenly start thinking they belong in the Akhlos. They start to build villages in the Jada territories. They don't belong there. They belong on the east coast, in the woods.'

'What do they say on that forum about the Man with a Thousand Faces?'

'It's a conversation between two rebels. One of them says: "Brother, you speak of hope, but our villages are being destroyed, our children arrested." The other one says: "There is more hope now than ever before. According to the village elder, the Man with a Thousand Faces has risen. Collect your courage and kiss your wife." Then the first one asks who that is. The second one says: "You don't know him? The Man with a Thousand Faces will blast the oppressor to the afterlife. Just you watch, soon, the capital city will burn like a fireplace. The Lechkovs will be the firewood." '

'Whom do you think they're talking about?' I ask.

'I've heard of him,' he says. 'But I think they're just tales.'

'What have you heard?'

'They say the Man with a Thousand Faces is summoning a rebel army. They say he has weapons and lots of money. He will launch a major attack.'

'An attack against whom?'

'Did you see the house on top of the hill? By the old fort? That's the Mardoe Khador, the High House. That's where power resides. That's where the oligarchs live. That's what keeps Kazichia in a stranglehold. My people want to burn that building to the ground, so Kazichia can become peaceful and democratic. And many think that now is the time to do it.'

'Why now?'

'Vigo Lechkov, the president, died in an accident and nobody has replaced him. Maybe his brother will take over, but people say he's not strong enough. Which means that if there was ever a time to strike, it's now. And according to these people in the forum, the Man with a Thousand Faces will do it.' The man shrugs. 'I'll see it when I believe it.'

I tell him I've heard the name 'Nairi' mentioned a few times.

'Nairi is our leader. She is a living legend. She is the first woman uniting all Jada clans to one front.' He stands up. 'She lost her arm to a grenade, my friend, and still she shot the soldier that threw the grenade. Just imagine! Who can do that? Who can bear that pain? Only Nairi. But she won't be able to get rid of the Lechkov family. She doesn't have the resources and she's not a terrorist. We need someone who can get weapons and who's not afraid to use them. If the Man with a Thousand Faces really exists, then we stand a chance. But I doubt it.'

I thank the man for his help. Walking back to the hotel I think about my assignment. There are two scenarios. Either I work for people resisting the Jada rebels in the mountains. In that case, I need to find the Man with a Thousand Faces, whoever that may be, and eliminate him. Or I work for people trying to overthrow the Lechkov family, whoever they may be. People looking to arm the resistance. In that case, I need to find the Man with a Thousand Faces and offer him my help.

Whichever side I'm on, one thing is clear: I'm here to stir up a conflict that has been brewing for years.

I'm here to create chaos.

III. Power Vacuum

21

After the failed coup of Karzarov, only one man can prevent Kazichia from crumbling. All eyes are on this man: Daniel Lechkov. But that man is asleep.

Michelle looks at that man, her husband, while driving back to the Mardoe Khador. When they had just left the airport, he tried to stay awake. Russian intelligence service agents had just threatened to kill them, so he wanted to support her. 'I am not leaving you,' he said. But Karzarov's drugs were too strong, and by the time they drove into the centre, his chin was on his chest, and drool dripped down his shirt. Seeing him like this, Michelle feels terrifyingly dependent on him. What will happen? Will war break out? Will she ever hold her parents again? Will her children be forced to grow up here, speaking a language she doesn't understand? She tells herself there is no use in assuming the worst. Together with Daniel, she will find a solution. She always does when something unexpected happens. She married him for a reason: he is an intelligent and empathetic man, a peaceful man who will do anything to get his family home. She is sure of that. But when they are back at the Mardoe Khador, she has to take a deep breath.

As the car halts, Maika Lechkova lights a cigarette in her office at the High House. She is also watching the one man on whom Kazichia's future depends. She watches him through a security camera while he gets out of the car, his knees shaking. That one man. Her youngest son. The son she doesn't understand. One moment, he seems as intelligent as his grandfather, and the next, he does the stupidest things. He lives off the Lechkov fortune, but when it is his turn to get to work, he tries to flee the country. Does he not feel any responsibility? And if he doesn't want to be a politician, why does he want to flee to the Netherlands? Didn't she tell him that the Russians would follow him? Doesn't he trust his own mother? What has she done to deserve that? Is it because she sent him to the West when he was a young boy? That was the hardest decision she ever had to make, but it was the only way to keep him out of the spotlight. It almost cost her her marriage because Boris disagreed. It was, moreover, terrible for her reputation, because in the High House people whispered about her cold heart. But she persisted. In exchange for her son's safety, she let herself get mocked. Now she looks at him, hoping he knows which role he plays in Kazichia. She is terrified the Russians will come and make her disappear, just like her parents. *Can I count on you,* tsvali? she asks him with her mind. *I have always been there for you.*

Opposite Maika, on the other end of the big wooden desk, sits Nia Lechkova Karzarova. Aunt Nia gazes at the screen too, at Daniel, and her body trembles with excitement. Lev is probably on his way to Moscow, to their children. He managed to escape. Not her. She is stuck in the High House, and it's a miracle she is still alive. Somehow, she has convinced Maika of her innocence. She is safe from the OMRA for now, but in the end, Daniel will determine her fate. Nia looks at him and tries to gauge who he has become. She remembers him as an intelligent and friendly little nephew – too softhearted, perhaps, for Kazichian politics. But she doesn't know anything about adult Daniel. So, she watches him, hoping he will believe her lies. Hoping she will get to hold her children again. Someday.

While Daniel and Michelle move into the presidential wing of the High House, the Russian Yuri Andropov looks at that one man, too. Or tries to, anyway. The Ally Specialist, as they call him at the Kremlin, has ordered his team to write a report on his new Kazichian 'friend'. The friend that is supposed to seize power so Andropov can fortify Russian influence around the Akhlos. Based on their information, there is nothing meaningful to say about his qualities as a political leader or industrialist. They know he is a driven academic. A computer scientist researching neural networks. Apart from that, they know nothing. So, what is Andropov supposed to tell his superiors? He managed to keep Daniel in the country by threatening his family, but that almost always works. Time will reveal if the youngest Lechkov will accept the presidency and what he will do with that title. Is Daniel Lechkov his brilliant grandfather's grandson, or a copy of his unhinged twin brother?

Andropov pours himself another glass of beer. He doesn't like insecurities. How can he make sure that Daniel will be a successful and obedient president?

In Langley, Virginia, insurgency specialist Jonathan Rye, Andropov's counterpart, asks himself the opposite question: how can America ensure the next president of Kazichia will fail? Because of the gigantic lithium supply, the CIA wants to get a proper foothold in the Akhlos region. And after Vigo Lechkov's death and the failed coup, there is suddenly an opportunity to weaken Russia's position. The country's entire political tapestry is hanging by a thread, and that thread is the last male Lechkov. Rye knows as little about Daniel as Andropov, so he decides to aim for the country's minorities. The Jada and the Neza have wanted to be liberated from the oligarchs and their reign of terror for many years. Will he find a way to make them stronger, now that cracks are starting to show in the High House? And would they be willing to fight against Daniel Lechkov?

Rye puts his team to work. In the following days, he gets a clearer picture of the possibilities in Kazichia. Changes are coming in the Akhlos mountains. There have been signs of an uprising, it appears a rebel army is being raised. An army, fed by rumours of a newcomer with enough manpower, weapons, and knowledge to intimidate the ruling class. The deeper the CIA team digs, the more online activity they will find on this new figure and his army.

*

Most Neza and Jada civilians don't believe the stories at first: they don't dare believe in them. But the whispers grow louder. Within a few weeks, *Asch-Iljada-Lica* is synonymous with cautious hope. 'The Man with a Thousand Faces' has risen, and nobody knows who he is, or where he came from, but more and more men pack their belongings and travel to one of the rebel camps. All of them become new soldiers wanting to march to the High House. Soldiers willing to fight. They are watching that one man, too. Daniel Lechkov. And what they see is the embodiment of evil.

22

An urgent crisis meeting is called in the Mardoe Khador. Normally, Karzarov would sit at one end of the table and a member of the Lechkov family at the other end. But after the coup, the Yanev family moved up a spot in the pecking order. The meeting is held in their wing. In Lev Karzarov's seat sits a short man with barely a gram of fat or muscle on his body: Igor Yanev. His light, thin hair, and ghostly white skin make him look almost transparent. 'A useful trait for the head of the intelligence service,' his late friend Boris used to joke.

Yanev pulls up his chair and lights a cigar to numb the tension. He feels vulnerable. If the OMRA – *his* security service – didn't see a betrayal like Karzarov's coming, what else can't they see? How long until the next attack? And how far is the Kremlin willing to go? An invasion? Karzarov planned the coup with the Kremlin, that much is clear, so what will their next move be?

Whatever happens, Yanev fears the High House stands even less of a chance against Russia than before the coup. A third of the political and managerial leaders were Karzarovs. What to do with all these family members, these ministers and directors? Political chaos might ensue. Years ago, the High House dealt with the disappearance of the fourth family, but back then Petar Lechkov was firmly seated on his figurative throne, controlling the crisis quickly. Now, that throne is empty. Even worse, the man slated for the presidency tried to flee the country.

The Chair of God wobbles and Igor Yanev takes a long drag from his cigar.

One by one the ministers trickle in for the crisis meeting. They nod at Yanev and quickly find seats. He looks at them and wonders what they're thinking. Evil tongues say he wants to grab power, and he knows that Maika believes those stories. But that is the last thing he'd want. Being the president of Kazichia is the most dangerous job in the world now, and when the coup started, he only thought one thing: I need to flee. He has about thirty-five million dollars in his foreign bank accounts, for emergencies – not enough to keep three wives and his current lifestyle, but if he could choose one wife and three of his nine children, he could live out the rest of his life in Europe in relative luxury. And it would be a good life.

But Yanev doesn't want to leave Kazichia. He doesn't want to leave behind what his father built; he doesn't want to stop playing the game of politics. That's his passion. His addiction. So, when he heard Daniel was staying in Kazichia, he decided to stay too. And when Maika got her son to come to the crisis meeting, he promised he would chair the meeting. Because everything depends on Daniel. He has to take responsibility and become president, so that Igor Yanev can get back to the best position of Kazichia; infallibly powerful, behind the scenes.

The high doors open and Maika appears. She sits down without looking at Yanev. Apparently, she still thinks she can't trust him. He finds it hard to accept how irrational she's become these past few years. Yanev is her last ally now, but instead of him, she's chosen Nia Karzarova to confide in. The woman who collaborated in the assassination of her son, most likely. It is clear to him once again that women should stay far away from politics.

After Maika sits down, she looks back at her son, who is still standing in the doorway. Daniel looks around bewildered – he looks tired.

'Daniel, how good of you to come. Sit down,' Yanev says to calm his nerves, and he gestures to his assistant to pour Daniel some coffee.

Slowly, Daniel starts moving. To everyone's surprise, he sits down on one of the empty chairs against the wall instead of at the head of the table. Those seats are meant for assistants or stenographers. Maika hisses at her son. She points at the empty seat of the former president. Daniel seems to hesitate, but then he gets up, visibly reluctantly, and shuffles towards the table. Once he has finally taken his seat, the room gets quiet. Everyone waits for the heir to open the meeting, but he unsuspectingly sips his coffee. Maika shoots her son a meaningful look, trying to get his attention, but Daniel seems unaware of his surroundings. Nobody speaks and the silence in the room starts weighing heavier until Yanev can't take it anymore.

'Right, Daniel is here. We can start. Are there urgent matters we should discuss before I read the itinerary?'

As is expected, one of the Lechkovs takes the floor immediately. But instead of Daniel or Maika, it is Radko. The commander-in-chief thinks they should change the composition of parliament, if necessary, through another 'controlled' election. He has barely finished speaking when Vadim Ivanov, minister of agriculture, objects loudly.

'Elections are dangerous,' Ivanov says. 'An opportunity for the enemy to create more chaos.'

'You're scared to lose your position,' Radko answers. 'Leave your personal politics out of it. We control the elections completely, why would they create more chaos?'

'It's no secret that your position in parliament is much weaker than that of the Karzarov family. *You* are the one scared of losing your position, Radko Lechkov. That's the only reason you want to hold elections. But as a member of the Twenty, I will never let that happen.'

A few ministers cough softly, to signal their approval. The minister of agriculture has held his position for fifteen years. Not because he is an expert on agriculture, but because he is a prominent figure within the Karzarov imperium, with many confidants in parliament.

'I want order,' Radko says. 'That is my priority.'

The old Ivanov stands up but has to place one hand on the table to keep his balance. 'General Lechkov, with all due respect, our own troops are attacking us. For the first time since this country was founded, we can't trust our own army anymore. If you want order, shouldn't that be your priority?'

Yanev notices Ivanov occasionally glancing at Daniel. He tries to estimate what the new presidential candidate thinks of him.

'One regiment is deserted, only a fraction of our forces,' Radko says, 'led by three infiltrators who have all been arrested. Igor Yanev's men are being interrogated as we speak, at OMRA's head office. Don't make a mountain out of a molehill.'

'A molehill?' The minister points at Daniel. 'Mr Lechkov was abducted and almost killed. We lost control of parliament and two ministries, and hundreds of people were taken hostage during a state funeral. A *molehill*, he calls that.'

Everyone looks at Daniel again, and Yanev watches the blood drain from his face. He finally understands what they expect of him; he needs to pass judgement.

'I'm sorry,' he stammers. 'I'm just here to listen. I'm not really up to date on everything that's going on.'

It becomes so quiet that Yanev can hear the tobacco from the many cigarettes smouldering. And as the silence drags on, his anger intensifies. If Daniel doesn't understand that he needs to save the High House, there is no hope left. And all thanks to Maika Lechkova, the woman only looking for short-term solutions. If she had kept her son at home at the time, like everyone advised her to do, all of this could have been prevented. But instead, she turned him into a foreigner. A stranger. Thanks to the mismanagement of yet another woman who thinks she's cold enough to lead a country, all of them are watching a hierarchical machine that has been ploughing on for three generations straight, come to a standstill.

More and more guests turn their heads to the other end of the table, facing Yanev. More and more people think he will take over Daniel's spot. Just as he feared.

'There is something else,' Daniel says quietly, and the heads turn back to him. 'I'm here to ask for your help. My wife and child are terrified, they are being held hostage by the Russian intelligence service. Is there anything we can offer the Kremlin in exchange for their freedom? My daughter just wants to get back home. Is there anything we can do, anything at all? Please?'

Yanev almost jumps out of his chair from shock. He can hardly believe his ears. Is this man the grandson of the great Petar Lechkov? Is Daniel Lechkov only concerned about his family, after a violent coup? Doesn't he understand that this crisis meeting is not for discussing his personal life, but to save the political order in the entire Caucasus? Maybe in all of Eastern Europe? Here, at this table, they need to save the future of hundreds of thousands of families.

Stay calm, he tells himself. *Stay friendly, or you'll scare him away.*

'Let's return to this item later on,' Maika says.

'Do we need to suspend the meeting for a few hours?' Radko asks. 'We can catch Daniel up.'

'No,' Maika says. 'There is an urgent matter we need to decide on right away.' She turns to Yanev. 'Your men locked Nia Lechkova in her chambers and confiscated her phones and computer. I demand her release.'

'Karzarov's wife? She's still in the Mardoe Khador?' one of the ministers asks in surprise.

'Yes, of course!' Maika says sharply. 'She had no idea what her husband was planning. I know her.'

Yanev shakes his head. 'I can't do that, Maika. All three of the infiltrators admitted that Nia Lechkova Karzarova was part of the conspiracy.'

'That's not trustworthy information.'

'Why not?'

'If you hit someone with a hammer for long enough, they will tell you whatever you want to hear.'

It takes Yanev a lot of effort to remain calm. 'The OMRA applies pressure if necessary, and thanks to that pressure, we found out that Nia is a threat to us. We should arrest her immediately. What if she tries to kill your other son? Think, Maika. Use your head instead of your heart. She needs to leave this house, before doing even more damage.'

'Nia has nothing to do with Vigo's death, I just know it!' Maika looks at her son. '*Tsvali*, you agree with me, right? Nia, your aunt Nia, had no idea. She couldn't have.'

This is the last straw, Yanev thinks. Maika uses her son's insecurity to save her friend. Daniel's first decisions could determine the rest of his career; she is risking everything.

'We're adjourning the meeting,' he says, before Daniel can open his mouth.

'Who made you chairman, Igor Yanev?' Maika asks. 'Nia is innocent. And we all know what your men will do to her. She won't survive!'

Yanev gets up, puts on his suede blazer, and gestures to Daniel. 'Walk with me.'

The rest of the crisis council looks at each other.

'Where are you going?' Maika asks.

'You're staying,' he says. He doesn't have time for this emotional old woman. 'Daniel and I are visiting Petar.'

23

When Yanev walks into Petar Lechkov's room, the man is sitting in his chair by the fireplace, where his reading table used to be. As always, he wears an old-fashioned double-breasted jacket with broad shoulders and two rows of big buttons, as shiny as military distinctions. Daniel sits with his grandfather and kisses his cheeks. Yanev avoids the old man as much as possible because he finds his deterioration too confronting. Besides, he is not there for Petar, but for what the old man left behind.

He crosses the spacious living room and enters the library. There are tall bookcases filled with classics – rare prints and special editions that Daniel's grandmother collected as a hobby and investment. A few shelves in the back sit behind thick, transparent slabs. Those shelves hold Petar Lechkov's diaries, hundreds of thousands of handwritten words in dozens, maybe hundreds, of notebooks. The origin story of one man and one country.

Yanev slides the plexiglass to one side and takes a blood-red notebook. On the cover, Petar drew the Lechkov family crest, a symbol that looks like it has belonged to a noble family for generations but which he created for himself. And above the crest appears the title: *The Future of the Mardoe Khador.* He takes the book and walks back to the living room, where Daniel listens to Petar's incoherent whispering.

'This is Petar's last diary,' he says. 'He wrote it right after he was diagnosed with Korsakov's syndrome, because he knew his mind was going to fade.'

Daniel frowns and asks if it is appropriate to read that.

'It's advice to us. About us. He wants us to read this.'

Yanev starts leafing through the book. He has his reservations about a man who leaves ice-cold analyses of his family and friends, but maybe it will help Daniel. He remembers the annual Christmas celebration on Lechkov Island in the Central Lakes. During those holidays, Petar went ice fishing every day and would take one of his grandsons sometimes. Daniel and Vigo were always competing for that honour. They wanted to come out as the strongest, fastest, or smartest every day. A few hours alone with Grandpa, the boys would fight to the end for that. And he remembers the day Daniel left for England. He can picture the twelve-year-old boy trembling with excitement. Leaving his twin brother behind dysregulated his nervous system, and Yanev thought little Daniel wouldn't make it. But Petar had the flight postponed and strolled the garden with his grandson for a few hours. Yanev doesn't know what Petar told Daniel then, but his words gave the boy enough strength to leave.

That's what he wants to give Daniel now: the strength to stay.

He finds the passage and presents the diary. As the president-to-be takes the book and looks at the founder of the country before reading it, Yanev gets a strange feeling in his stomach. As if he's hovering a few inches from the floor. That sensation always arises when he witnesses something that will be part of history books – when he might be a co-author of a passage, even. That is the feeling he is not ready to give up on.

Daniel looks at his grandfather for a moment, as if the old man could still give him permission and starts reading. His eyes dart across the page, and Yanev knows exactly what they see. Old Petar writes about the twins as if they accidentally split into two. As if each brother makes up half of one grandson. And Daniel is the better half. It says Vigo has the brutal force and toughness needed to lead a country. But he needs direction. Petar describes Vigo as a high-pressure hose you need to hold firmly to prevent chaos. He doesn't think Vigo is a natural leader, but his brother is.

Daniel is a highly gifted boy, no doubt about it. And he possesses a few contradictory talents that could make him a great politician.

116

He has an analytical mind, but a creative one, too. He is oppor-
tunistic when needed, but never lets go of his core values. Daniel
needs to work harder. He needs to become as strong, bold, and
cold as Vigo. If he does, Lechkov Industria and Kazichia will be
safe in his hands. Maybe even safer than in mine.

Daniel closes the book and looks at his grandfather with tears in his eyes.

'You can do this,' Yanev tells his fake cousin. 'You can save this country.'

Daniel looks at the red book. 'I feel so guilty, Uncle Igor. I want to take Michelle and Alexa home. I want to make it up to them.'

'But you understand that's impossible. Unless some extreme changes happen.'

Daniel nods.

'Then you know what to do now,' Yanev says and taps the family crest. 'Petar himself says you are capable.'

24

In the weeks after the failed coup, Yanev and Maika try their hardest to keep order in the Kazichian government. They decide to spare the rest of the Karzarovs because the power vacuum would be too great if all of them were to disappear. Besides, they don't want to provoke Russia. That's why Lev Karzarov's remaining cousins may keep managing Karzarov Transport. The High House also decided there would be no elections: the Twenty will keep their positions in parliament and the prime minister stays on. All of this to buy time. Time is needed to make Daniel change his mind so he will run for president. Then they can call for elections, which he will win.

The one thing Yanev and Maika cannot agree on is Nia. She still lives in the High House, and Yanev can't seem to convince Maika that her friend is a danger to everyone. The deserters questioned by the OMRA confessed that Karzarov's wife was part of the ploy to overthrow the regime. Why would they lie about that? What is in it for them? And how would Karzarov hide this elaborate plan from his wife all this time? Nia's story is simply not plausible, but Maika will not admit that, so Nia can keep moving through the Mardoe Khador freely, even in Daniel's family's chambers. If Karzarov wants to attempt to grab power again, or if Russia moves on to annexation, she can open the attack by killing Daniel. She can weaken the High House from the inside and open the doors for the enemy. And so, Yanev has secretly hired extra security for the Karzarov wing. He will not let her out of his sight.

He is not letting Daniel out of his sight, either. Two spies are watching him, day and night, sending Yanev constant updates. The first few days after the crisis meeting, it seems like he hasn't been able to get through to Daniel with Petar's diary. The Lechkov heir sits with his family all day, seemingly waiting until his problems get solved for him. For the second and third meetings of the crisis council, he doesn't even show up. But then something shifts. For no apparent reason, Daniel starts requesting policy documents and background research. He has meetings scheduled with policy officers who can update him on current affairs in the High House and asks the prime minister for a crash course on the strange power dynamics in the Kazichian parliament. In the short reports of his spies, Yanev reads that Daniel works day and night. With the minister of foreign affairs and a few analysts from the security service, he discusses the GRU and the CIA. He wants to understand how Russia and the United States could thwart him, and how far they would go to reach their goals. With army officials, he discusses the composition of the large Kazichian mercenary army.

Has Daniel finally accepted his fate?

Yanev is not sure how much credit he can give himself for the turnaround, but the diary of Petar seems to have been a brilliant move. He decides to give Daniel another week and ask him then if he is ready to announce elections to the public. But during those days, something changes again.

Through the many conversations he has, Daniel is informed about the dormant conflict between the Jada and the Neza, and suddenly, he focuses entirely on the rumours of a new rebel leader. Yanev has no idea why. The years of civil war between Kazichian minorities – if you can even call it that – are so insignificant that they haven't threatened the stability of the country in any way. But that week during the general council, Daniel focuses only on the new Jada alignment and their anonymous leader. He holds a monologue on someone calling himself 'the Man with a Thousand Faces', and nobody knows what he is talking about.

Maika scolds her son. 'Stop talking about those goatherders. They have never been a threat. You are embarrassing your family.'

But Daniel keeps going on about 'the terrorist that must be feared' and when Yanev tries to tell him he is focusing on the wrong things – Russia is the only real threat – it falls on deaf ears.

'You underestimate the power of a surprise attack. The Jada know that the Mardoe Khador is unstable. And we have no idea what that new rebel could do, or what he wants. His online following is massive.'

A few ministers snicker and Yanev understands their reaction. What is wrong with Daniel? Even if, by some miracle, the Jada and Neza make peace, they would never stand a chance against the Kazichian army. Even if they receive money from a foreign power, that would barely make a difference. However many mysterious names their leaders think up, it doesn't change the power relations. But instead of directing his attention at the real dangers, the president-to-be goes on and on about terrorists from the Akhlos and some man with a strange nickname.

The next morning, Yanev has a meeting with Daniel scheduled. He needs to talk to him. One final attempt to get him back on track. But his assistant can't find Daniel – he is not with his family and not in his office – and after a long search, it turns out he has a meeting with the OMRA. The security service, led by Igor Yanev. Without him knowing about it.

'What is he doing there?' he asks. 'And why was I not informed about this? Why won't he talk to me?'

'Apologies, we thought you knew,' the assistant says. 'He has been in Leonid Torelli's office for a few hours.'

25

During his childhood, Leonid Torelli was Daniel's best friend, and his only one. When they were eleven, they took their first sip of liqueur from a stolen bottle. Together, they ignored the strict house rules, sneaking down the hill past the soldiers. While everyone slept, they roamed the town centre for hours, returning home as the sun rose – nobody found out.

Daniel's world consisted of his parents, his brother Vigo, and the family's private tutor. Leonid was bullied relentlessly in primary school for his lazy eye and for being smarter than the other students – smarter than the teachers, perhaps. During lunch break, he would sit at the edge of the school playground, as far away from the next punch as possible. No wonder the lonely boys stuck together when Leonid's father started working for the Lechkov family. And for the next six years, Leonid was the only thing Daniel had that his brother didn't have; friendship from the 'outside'. A friendship that grew closer when Maika started separating the twins, to prepare for Daniel's departure. When Daniel finally left Kazichia, two weeks before his thirteenth birthday, he said goodbye to two brothers.

Twenty-four years later, Daniel stands in a grey, cramped office, under a suspended ceiling, and kisses his second brother on the cheeks.

'Old fr-friend,' Leonid stutters, 'The-there you are.'

Daniel grabs his shoulders. 'You've become the biggest spy of Kazichia, Igor Yanev's number two. I can't believe it!'

'Daniel, I feel guilty,' Leonid says, and he jerks his head to the left involuntarily. 'You were abducted in the country I'm supposed to k-keep an eye on. U-unforgivable.'

'You have nothing to apologise for. How are you?'

'G-good. My sons are healthy.'

Leonid gestures to the empty chair in front of his desk and sits down. He says he follows Daniel's career as a computer scientist closely. 'We could really use your help here,' he says, pointing at the coiled cables and two patch cabinets against the wall, wrapped in plastic.

'Are you building a server room?' Daniel asks.

Leonid laughs. 'Yanev is letting me develop the "IT department", as he calls it.' He gets a ballpoint from his breast pocket. 'This is what our people are working with now. And that won't change anytime soon.'

'How do you monitor IP and phone traffic?'

Leonid shakes his head.

'You don't monitor anything? What happens when a terrorist orders parts to build a bomb?'

'Th-then a bomb explodes.'

Daniel goes quiet.

'I've h-h-heard that you have been busy lately. Are you preparing for the presidency?'

'I want to protect my family. And the only way to do that is by knowing where the danger lies. Cyber security is the same. It's about finding attack vectors. Ever heard of those? That is what they call weak spots in a system or network that malicious parties can use. I charted the attack vectors in the High House, there are too many. Way too many.'

'L-l-like the influence of Russia?'

'That's the threat everyone is looking at.'

'Russia is the greatest threat. We know that the Kremlin has been taking over our army slowly for years. Th-that's why General Lechkov founded the Circle. The GRU invades our computers and phones, w-which is why I need to mo-modernise the intelligence service. And the pa-parliament is half Russian, that's why the High House will only appoint you as president.'

Daniel folds his arms. 'I am an attack vector myself. When I was at the airport, we got a call from someone at the embassy, some guy called Andropov. He wants me to be president and an ally of Russia. Otherwise, he will hurt my family.'

Leonid thinks for a second. 'I think I met Andropov once. Officially he is a diplomat, but we suspect he is a GRU agent. It sounds like you're stuck, old friend, between the High House and the Kremlin.'

Daniel nods impatiently. 'Another attack vector is the Karzarov family. They will do everything in their power to keep their positions in this country. They will try to attack the Mardoe Khador from the inside. And the question is if Nia Lechkova will help them with that. My mother swears she is innocent.'

'W-w-with all due respect, your mother has turned blind. Her friend is a traitor.' Leonid's head still hangs to one side, and he squints. His tics have gone from bad to worse over the years, like paths walked so many times, they've become trenches.

'I heard about your interrogation methods,' Daniel says. 'If you torture someone for long enough, he will admit to anything.'

'Read the reports; they know about Karzarov's plans. She's one of your vectors, or whatever you call it. I u-understand that it's hard surrendering your aunt to the OMRA agents, but you need to be tough. You've got no other choice.'

'All right. I'd like to see the reports.'

'W-what else did you see, Daniel?'

'There is one attack vector no one takes seriously. The most important of all. An uprising from the east, led by someone they call the Man with a Thousand Faces.'

'I heard about your warnings during the general m-meetings. But there is no reason to w-w-worry. The Jada and Neza are simple people and with r-relatively little.'

Daniel smiles. 'You sound like your boss, Leonid. You sound like Igor Yanev, who doesn't understand what I'm trying to do. It's disappointing. Are you monitoring online? Are you keeping an eye on the Jada forums, where they exchange their information?'

Leonid shakes his head.

'So you have no clue who the Man with a Thousand Faces is?'

'That's r-r-right, we know nothing about him. Why that fix-ation, Daniel? What do you propose?'

'There is a way to sideline Karzarov once and for all. There is a way to keep Russia at a distance. There is a way to beat everyone and keep my family safe. It's not easy, but it's possible.'

'I'm here to help you, old friend,' Leonid promises without stuttering. 'I'm on your side. But to be honest, this is too big. There are too many fronts to fight at, and I don't see how you could go up against the Russians. You will become their puppet; you have to accept that. And your family needs to build a life here.'

'Everyone thinks we need to defend ourselves against all the attack vectors. That is impossible. What we need to do is pit those vectors against each other. We need to have our enemies attack each other. We don't declare war on Russia, we need to do it through the Man with a Thousand Faces. He seems like our enemy, but he could save us.'

IV. Who is Daniel Lechkov?

26

In a large, quiet villa in a Portland, Oregon suburb, Sophie sits in the attic. She made coffee, fried an egg, and now sits nestled behind the old laptop she has been sifting through for days. The laptop contains the video of a woman with one arm and a strange code counting down. And a document labelled 'private'. An encrypted document she doesn't have the password for.

Sophie stares at the screen as if a password will pop up if she waits long enough. Surrounding the computer are lists with possible names, references, or number sequences that could unlock the file.

Her mother's date of birth?

The zip code of this house?

Her own date of birth?

INCORRECT PASSWORD

She flicks through photo albums in the living room, and searches the office for a safe or notebooks, but doesn't find a clue anywhere. She keeps writing down theoretical passwords, but there are too many possibilities.

The name of the street?

The house number?

A combination of both?

She has turned the sound of the laptop off because she doesn't want to hear it anymore; that short, judgemental tone when another attempt gets rejected. The sound makes her nervous because she doesn't know if there is a maximum number of tries. And when this file is gone, when it disappears behind an even more complex lock, she'll have to go back to the drawing board.

And that is the last thing she wants.

Well, the very last thing she wants is to return to campus without answers. That would be excruciating. She can't go on like this, she can't live like this. She needs to find something in that house. She needs to find something that will make her understand what happened in Kazichia.

The name of her father?

His favourite movie?

Her own name?

Her name is Sophie. And every time Sophie enters a password, she closes her eyes. She doesn't want to see the grey window disappear, making it seem like the computer will open the file. She doesn't want more false hope.

INCORRECT PASSWORD

A few nights ago, during another sleepless night, she went looking for help. Through a forum on the dark web, she found someone who called himself a hacker. He or she promised to help her. She needed to enter some commands into the old laptop – her mother's old laptop. And then she needed to copy and send a number sequence. For all she knows, she gave the hacker full access to the security system of the house – her mother's house.

'If you make a deal with a thief, don't be surprised when you get robbed,' her ethics professor had said once. That sounded wise to her at the time, but life was much simpler then. She needed to take the risk.

After a few minutes, she received a disappointing message: 'This is a quantum encryption. There is nothing you can do except enter the correct password.'

So, she keeps guessing. The name of her mother's company? The city where her mother was born? The city where she was born? She closes her eyes, and the sound is muted, but she knows what the screen says.

Last night it happened again. Right before she fell asleep, she saw memories that didn't seem hers — stolen memories. In those memories, she is a little girl, about three years old. And it's always the same scenario.

> *She is in a church, a large church, and somebody shoots. She is put into a car and the car takes off. However fast they drive, they are still getting shot at. She sees white stars in the windows.*

> *She is in an underground market; the walls are bright-coloured and a stench of terror hangs in the air. She is held by a woman — most likely her mother. Then, two soldiers appear from a hidden door in the wall. Behind the door is darkness.*

> *She stands on a frozen lake, and beneath her feet swims a shadow. Someone pushes her. She falls, hitting the back of her head on the ice. Someone yells. Shots are fired. The shots are so close by they make her ears ring.*

Those are the short flashes it starts with. Those are the fragments waking her up. That means the finale is about to begin. Irrevocably. Usually, she tries to sit up straight in bed, have a glass of water, or go for a walk. But nothing can stop it. When the strange memories start, in the end, she will see the house on the hill.

> *She sees an old town. At the gate stands a grand statue of a man without a face. She stands on the hill, by a villa — a palace, maybe. She looks out on the neighbourhoods of the old centre and chaos reigns. People run through the streets, fighting and plundering. And the big house on the mountain is on fire. Her mother is pregnant, and they need to flee. They drive off quickly, the two of them; out of their car windows she sees groups of people go mad like packs of wild dogs.*

She has tried everything: sleeping pills, party drugs, boys, girls, hypnosis, meditation, and hardcore exercising. She even saw a therapist. The therapist said the city doesn't exist. He said that the old walls surrounding the centre symbolise the wall Sophie built for herself. He said she needed to break through those walls, and the city would disappear.

So, she tried to follow that advice, but it didn't help.

It didn't help because that city *does* exist.

She saw it with her own eyes, it's not a dream vision. She was unsuspectingly watching a documentary in her dorm room, a documentary on the Cold War that was mandatory for a class on international affairs. The image jumped and there it was, that strange place, with the faceless statue. And there was the house on the hill that she saw burn down. *Kazichia City* it was called, or *Stolia*. The palace on the hill was called the *Mardoe Khador*. There could be no mistake: this is the place Sophie visits when she tries to fall asleep. All she could do was cry.

'What's going on?' her roommate asked.

But she couldn't explain. She didn't know how. All she could do was cry, and she knew she had to go looking for the source of those memories. They hadn't been stolen. Those things happened to her, a long time ago, when she was a little girl. She also knew she could stop therapy because that guy was a hack.

Sophie needed to search for answers herself. But where to begin?

The name of that place? Stolia? Or the Western name: Kazichia City?

INCORRECT PASSWORD

She asked her mother if she knew Kazichia, but she pretended she had never heard of it. So, when her mother leaves for work for a few weeks, Sophie searches the house. In the attic, underneath a loose floorboard, she finds an old laptop. A laptop with a text file marked 'Private'. Everyone has a right to privacy, but Sophie has no choice: she needs to find her mother's secrets. And so, she tries to open the file, hoping it's a diary.

While she contemplates passwords, she finds another secret file on her mother's old laptop: a video recording. In a hidden folder, she finds a large video file. The file is encrypted, but the hacker from the dark web forum says the lock is from before the quantum revolution; within two minutes the password is cracked.

The video starts playing and she sees an interrogation. A woman with one arm has to sit in a wooden chair for hours answering questions. The interview takes so long that the conversation becomes torture. The woman is tied up and threatened. She needs to keep talking, even when she is about to faint from exhaustion. Sophie has a hard time looking at it but forces herself to continue. The woman speaks a strange language, sounding a lot like the language they speak in videos about Kazichia. That can't be a coincidence.

In the end, the video only raises more questions. Why does the woman need to keep talking? Why does she need to look straight into the camera? When Sophie looks up the name 'Nairi', she sees the leader of a people called the Jada. In some articles, she is described as a hero, in others a terrorist. She gets connected to an extremist rebel group and their leader: the Man with a Thousand Faces.

Why does her mother have a video of this woman on her computer?

During the interrogation, a strange code appears on the screen. Sophie tries to enter the code as a password for the text file: ANTD=>100. She tries it with and without the numbers, but nothing works. She tries the words that the woman needs to repeat, like Jada. And she tries her name: Nairi. But nothing works.

Incorrect. Incorrect. Incorrect. The password is always fucking INCORRECT!

Sophie sits in her mother's office, in her quiet home, and she is ready to give up the search, after weeks of locking herself inside. It feels like she is digging herself into a hole of confusion, not getting any closer to the truth. Maybe she should shower, put on some make-up, and move on with her life – knowing that some questions will never be answered. Maybe she should return to campus and make up for some of the damage she did by staying away for so long.

But right before she closes the laptop, she suddenly knows.

She remembers a moment during that long interrogation that gave her a strange feeling. The feeling that she could finally navigate a little bit, as if someone far away lit a match, leading her through the fog.

Sophie returns to the text file and while she enters the password, she can feel the document will open. She doesn't know who he is or what her mother has to do with him, but still, Sophie enters his name: DANIEL.

She doesn't close her eyes. She presses 'enter' and looks at the blue bar that fills up slowly.

PASSWORD CORRECT. FILE IS BEING EXTRACTED.

27

When the file appears on the screen, Sophie sees it's a diary. That's exactly what she hoped for, and why she wanted to find the password. But now that her mother's most intimate thoughts are laid bare before her on the laptop screen, she wants to look away. She doesn't want to know what the best sex of her life was, or how disappointed she is in her daughter. Children aren't supposed to know their parents this intimately. But Sophie doesn't know how else to move forward.

The diary starts in October, almost twenty-five years ago.

13 October 2009

His name is Daniel, and I don't know much about him. But still, suddenly, life feels more beautiful. That sounds melodramatic and silly, I know. I just biked home from university and the city is even prettier, and Kim is playing loud music in her room, but her awful country music sounds wonderful now. Is this what love is? That can't be it already, right? We hardly talked. Daniel came to do a guest lecture for our class on the philosophy of law. He is only a few years older than me, very young for a lecturer. And he was a little shy, but in a charming way. I can picture him right now, like he's standing next to me. Nice dark hair, grey-blue eyes, not very tall, but broad. He had something mysterious about him. You could tell he sees the world differently. Haha, I'm being so vague.

I think he liked me too, because he kept looking away shyly when we made eye contact. He is from Eastern Europe, but his Dutch is amazing, and he speaks English very well.

I don't even remember what he was talking about. He is
a computer scientist. I'd never even heard of that course.
Together with a professor, he was getting his PhD in artificial
intelligence, something related to photos. I was not really paying
attention. All I could think about was what I would say to him
after class. But when it was over, he walked off, and I didn't
want to run after him like some groupie. That seemed a little
much. Too bad. That was Daniel. I don't even know his last
name. Oh well! At least today, everything felt more beautiful.

16 October 2009

I found Daniel. His name is Daniel Lechkov. Kim says I'm a
creepy stalker, but I don't care. There is a faculty for maths
and information sciences and that's where you can study
computer science. I just biked over there. Maybe I am a creepy
stalker, but all I can think about is Daniel. All day long.

I walked around the halls of that faculty. I felt like an idiot, he
could have been somewhere else that day. But then I saw him and
pretended it was a coincidence. We had an awkward conversation
for a while, and then I gave him my number. Pretty cool of me, I
think. He looked around the whole time and spoke very quietly,
so I don't think he's allowed to flirt with students. Who cares,
haha. All day I've had a knot in my stomach. A wonderful knot.

22 October 2009

It's six-thirty in the morning and I just got home from the
best date ever. I puked a lot. Sorry, Kim, if that woke you
up. We sat at the bar all night, just talking. About my travels
and about his family in Kazichia, where he's from. It all felt so
natural. He knew when I was being sarcastic. People usually
can't tell. He can. And he told me everything about his job. I
hope one day I'll find a job that I feel as passionately about.

During our last date, I thought it was pretty obvious that we
would go home together, but he didn't say anything when the
bar closed, so I said he should take me home. Haha. Slut. He
lives in a bizarre, gorgeous apartment on the Prinsengracht,
totally out of this world. Not what you expect from someone

working for the university. But definitely a bachelor's pad. It
was almost empty; it just had the stuff you need to survive.

He tried to be smooth, but he was very nervous. He put on
some music and dimmed the lights by clapping his hands. It was
clear he never had any girls over. Fortunately! When we had sex...

Sophie looks down. She stares at the tabletop and tries to erase the image of her mother having sex.

She concludes this Daniel was more than a boyfriend. He was one of her mother's great loves. Or maybe he still is. His first name is the password for the entire diary.

Why did her mother never tell her about him?

Was she cheating?

Sophie searches Daniel Lechkov's name in the university database. Three old research papers appear that he published with a professor named Tim Stewart. She writes down the name of the professor in her notes and scribbles: *Try to find him.*

Then she tries to read the research papers, but they're filled with maths equations. And titles like *Convolutional Neural Networks Tasked with Image Classification* aren't exactly helpful either.

From the abstracts, she concludes that Daniel built neural networks, artificial intelligence. Sophie doesn't know much about it, but she sees the term 'deepfake' a few times. Deepfakes she knows; videos in which someone appears to be doing or saying something, generated by AI. The internet must have been simple and organised back then; Sophie can't really wrap her head around it. The internet she knows, in the year 2034, is confusing and unreliable. Everyone can manipulate the truth. Everyone can generate deepfakes and synthetic voices in two clicks. Her generation assumes that everything in the digital world is a lie. Even videos of your best friends talking should be taken with a grain of salt. The NSA made 'snitches' that can be installed on your computer for free, but they rarely work.

Sophie summarises her findings in her notes: *Daniel was a computer scientist making deepfakes. My mother fell in love with him during a class in 2009.*

Then she searches 'Daniel Lechkov' using her personal search engine. More articles come up than expected. Daniel comes from a family that runs multiple companies in Eastern Europe and Russia – that's probably how he was able to afford that nice apartment in Amsterdam. He has been leading Lechkov Industria for decades and is the most influential man in Kazichia. He had a twin brother who was the president of Kazichia, until he died in a car crash. Sophie concludes that sometime during his life, Daniel turned his life around majorly, from academic in Amsterdam to magnate in the Caucasus. Sophie wonders if he had to succeed his brother after he perished.

When she tries to find out more about Daniel's life, she finds lots of inconsistent information. Someone describes him as a dangerous man who sacrificed many lives, other articles name him as the one bringing more democracy and peace to the country.

She can't fully grasp him.

After digging for a long time in the oldest, darkest corners of the internet, she finds an article by an American journalist. One Anderson Holt writes about the year 2019 when a civil war erupted in Kazichia and minorities attacked the capital city. Bombs exploded, and civilians died. And this article again mentions that rebel leader calling himself 'the Man with a Thousand Faces'.

The city appears in her mind's eye; there is fighting and chaos everywhere. And she sees that big house on the hill, burning.

Was she in the country during those fights?

She clicks back to another window. In 2019, Vigo Lechkov died, and Daniel became the legitimate leader of the Lechkov imperium. She had deduced that already, but now she knows the year: 2019, she is three years old. It says Vigo Lechkov was buried next to 'the Grand Church'. One of the strange images she sees when she tries to fall asleep is a church of some kind. Her mother is running back and forth, looking for someone. She calls out a name – it might have been 'Daniel'.

Sophie searches images of the Kazichian capital but applies the filter 'Grand Church' this time. A grainy photo of the building appears. Military jeeps stand in front of the entrance.

That's it. Sophie recognises the church.

She can feel tears welling up. Every time she's able to place one of those strange memories on the world map and on a timeline, it feels like a relief and new grief at the same time.

I was in that country in 2019, she concludes, staring at the screen. *During a coup. And I was still there when a war broke out between the government and a rebel movement from the mountains, led by a man with a thousand faces. I was in a war zone as a little girl. And that's why I have suppressed memories.*

Why would her mother drag her to a church in a faraway country? What were they doing in Kazichia? And where was her father, Gabriël? Why hadn't he come?

But the answer is right there. As if she had always known.

Could it be? she thinks. *Daniel Lechkov?*

Sophie says it out loud to the nice street behind the attic window, from her mother's empty house. No one hears her. But she needs to try out the words; she wants to hear if they sound like a lie or the new truth.

'Daniel Lechkov is my real father.'

And she knows it is true.

28

Michelle stands in the presidential wing of the High House and watches the back of her three-year-old daughter's head. Alexa is watching the smart TV that Daniel had installed for her to watch her favourite YouTube shows. She spends most of her days there, and Michelle lets her; she wants her daughter to unwind. She needs to feel safe, that is what's most important. Gunfights, terror, a chase through the city – enough to traumatise an adult, let alone a child. When they get back home, Michelle will find a good child psychologist for her. Until then, Alexa can watch as much TV as she wants.

Daniel doesn't seem to understand what happened to his daughter. Or maybe he is not letting the guilt get to him. He says everything will be fine. He says it's a matter of time. Michelle finds that hard to believe. The little girl seems calm, but what is happening below the surface, in her subconsciousness? It's not unthinkable that Michelle's decision to take her to Kazichia, will mark Alexa forever. Guilt spreads its cold wings inside her stomach. Turning away from the girl in front of the television, she walks to the bathroom.

First, we need to get home safe, she tells herself as she sits at the dressing-table. *We will have them make a treatment plan. In the meantime, keep your head cool, Michelle. Go on with your day. Daniel is working to get us out of here.*

She pulls up her T-shirt and reaches for a jar of oil, but is startled by her belly and how much it has grown. That always seems to happen in fits and starts instead of gradually. During her first pregnancy, she was fascinated by that change. But this time, she finds the transformation stifling; it is a wry reminder of how many weeks have passed in the High House. In captivity.

Just go on with your day, she tells herself again and picks up the jar of oil. But instead of turning the lid, she looks at the Kazichian label. During her first pregnancy, she tended to her belly every day. Maybe the serum didn't do anything, but she didn't have stretch marks after giving birth. And so, after finding out she was pregnant again, she got the same serum from her dermatologist and kept it in her bathroom.

The bathroom in Amsterdam.

The bathroom she can't return to.

When she told Daniel about the skincare oil, he sent one of his employees to every beauty shop in town. She bought dozens of tubes and jars but didn't find that one brand. Michelle knows she is being a brat, but she wants *that* bottle. She wants Golden Lotus, just like last time. She wants the bottle that is waiting for her to return from Dubai – like a trophy for her naïve certainty that she can always go back home. She wants that naïveté back. But that is impossible. She looks at the jar and wants to smash it against the mirror. How long will she last in the High House before losing her mind? She can't look at her daughter without feeling guilty. She can't look at her belly without feeling terrified. And she can't even look at a jar of body oil without getting so angry she wants to smash a mirror.

How long will she last?

It would be easier if Daniel had more time for her. The loneliness is getting to her. Her first pregnancy was pleasant, despite all the insecurities and discomforts, because Daniel was with her day and night. She remembers the moment her contractions started. They were lying in bed together and he put his hand on the little foot pressing against the uterine wall. He pretended to feel who their baby would be. 'It's a boy,' he said and rubbed his fingers on the moving skin, 'and he will never be a grumpy teenager, he will always be sweet and reasonable to his parents but will still grow into an independent man.'

Michelle smiled. 'Is that what you wish for your child or yourself?'

Daniel kissed her forehead and said he was proud of her. Proud of her and their baby.

Two hours later, she sat next to him in the car on the way to the hospital. She was tense but not scared because they would do it together.

Now she is locked up in a strange country and doing it all by herself. During the first few days, Daniel was with them a lot. Then he started working more and spending more time at the OMRA – whatever that is. He doesn't even sleep in their bed anymore. Now and then he will come by to shower, and she tries to talk to him. Those conversations usually make her feel even lonelier.

'How are you?' she asked that morning. 'Is a solution in sight?'

He let out a heavy sigh. 'It's not exactly a simple assignment, Michelle. I know it's taking a long time, but we don't have any allies in this country. The High House wants to keep me here because they fear a power vacuum. Because they're afraid of Russia. So, no one wants to help us. It's all on my shoulders. I need to find a way out, all by myself. And that takes time.'

Michelle couldn't imagine they were on their own. 'Why don't we call the Dutch embassy?' she asked. 'Or the French? I have two passports, I brought them both. Let me help.'

'The embassy? What will those governments do, send an extraction team to the house to abduct the family of the future head of state? Those countries would use their official channels to inquire, at most. And *we* are their official channels!'

His fierce reaction startled her. 'I'm just trying to think with you, sweetie,' she said.

'Sorry.' He took a deep breath. 'I'm not mad at you. I just feel a lot of pressure right now.'

'Shouldn't we talk to America, then? Maybe they can help us?'

'As soon as we reach out to the CIA, Russia will escalate to military action. War will break out. With one phone call, we could risk tens of thousands of lives.'

'But how will we get out of here, Daniel? What the hell can we do?'

He held her. 'I'm not sure exactly what we need to do, but I will protect you, I promise. I will get you home in the end.'

'Us,' she said. 'You will get us three home in the end.'

'Trust me,' he said and got in the shower.

One person makes the endless wait a bit more bearable: Harper. Vigo's American widow doesn't dare to leave either, and Michelle visits her for tea every afternoon. However bleak the situation, Harper always makes her laugh. A few days earlier, Michelle had been complaining about that serum she left in Amsterdam. Harper listened for a few minutes, then jumped up from the couch.

'Oh my god,' she said and pulled open a cabinet. 'They only have regular coffee beans here? I always drink kopi luwak in Manhattan.' She motioned for Alexa. 'Come on, let's go. We need to catch a cat and make coffee from its droppings before I lose my mind!'

Everyone laughed – even Alexa, who didn't understand a word.

But Harper is having a hard time too. Michelle knows she drinks too much. She can see it in her eyes and smell it on her breath. Harper has been close to her breaking point for weeks.

And that afternoon, she finally breaks.

As soon as Michelle enters Harper's apartment, Michelle can see something is wrong with the American. Her smile has disappeared, her eyes have lost their sparkle; she drank too much and slept too little.

'Michelle, listen,' she whispers as if someone is in the room with them. 'We need to get out of here.'

'What a great idea, I can't believe we hadn't thought of that,' she replies mockingly.

'We've waited for Daniel long enough. He has become one of them now.'

'One of whom?'

Harper gestures she wants to continue in the kitchen and slides the door closed behind her. 'Why are we sitting here like sheep, waiting for your husband? We want to leave, right? We need to think of a plan.'

'What can we do? All I want is to go home, but the Russian GRU agents will be waiting for us there. Daniel is working on a solution day and night. We need to trust him.'

'Michelle, the man you were sharing your life with in Amsterdam is not the one who came with you to this country. Here, he's a Lechkov.'

'Daniel is different,' Michelle says. 'He grew up in the West.'

'Vigo was different in New York, too. That's why I tried to keep him out of this country. Here he changed . . . into something else.'

'Into what?'

'Into a manipulative politician.' She pours herself a glass of water and downs it. 'You've seen dictators like Lukashenko or Maduro on the news, and taken a look at their wives, right? You've wondered how someone could stand side by side with a cruel dictator like that? We know the answer now, Michelle; you get pulled in slowly. Without realising it, you become a part of their country and their regime. They make it seem like they're the good ones. Or like there's no way out. But there is a way out. Always. We need to escape. With Alexa. We need to leave the country before it's too late, instead of waiting around like we have no power anymore.'

'Daniel isn't luring us into anything, Harper. He wants to help us escape. He wants to protect us against the tyranny.'

'You really don't see it? You really don't understand what kind of choices he is facing? Would you abandon your mother, grand-father, uncles and aunts, your cousins? Of course not. And Daniel can save them, by accepting the most powerful position in the country. The position that he was denied as a young boy. The position that was given to his brother for being a few minutes older. Do you know how appealing that position must be to him?' She sighs deeply before continuing. 'We need to get out of here, Michelle. And Daniel will not take care of that for us. In fact, he will do everything in his power to keep you right where you are, because he wants to stay here. He wants to prove himself.'

'You don't know him.'

Harper takes a seat at the kitchen table and whispers. 'I have a plan. There is a way to get out, but I couldn't live with myself if I left you here.'

'Seriously? You have a plan?'

She nods. 'It's risky, but not as risky as staying here.'

'If that's true we need to tell Daniel about it. He wants to come with us. He could probably help us.'

Harper looks down and presses her palms together as if sitting in a pew. 'Michelle, promise me you won't say anything. Swear on Alexa that you won't tell him about what we discussed here.'

'Why not? You're paranoid, Harper.'

'Paranoid? Maybe. But you're naïve. Do you know what they do to traitors? The OMRA building is not far from here. People cross the street because the basements are so badly insulated that you can hear the screams of torture when you're outside. Those screams can be heard day and night.'

'You're not listening to me: Daniel would never have you arrested. He's on our side. He's trying to think of an escape plan.'

'Daniel will do everything to protect you, but he will never return to the Netherlands. He will be the next president of Kazichia, I guarantee it. The question is what you want. Do you want to give birth to your second child in a Kazichian hospital? With soldiers by the door to protect you from an attack on the Lechkov bloodline? If that's what you want, then sit here and wait until Daniel gets into power. But if you want to go home, then you need to flee across the border. You need to come with me without saying a word to Daniel. If you wait for him, you will stay in the High House for the rest of your life.'

29

Harper is not the first one to warn Michelle about Daniel Lechkov. The night she introduced her new boyfriend to her parents, her father started asking difficult questions before dinner was even served.

'If you don't have an income of your own,' he said, 'you live off your family's money. Is that not a moral concern to you? The way that money was made, the oppression in that country? The injustice?'

Her mother entered the room with a bowl of steaming hot green beans and told Luc to go easy on Daniel. But he didn't. On the contrary, he attacked his guest for the entire evening. And by the time they got to dessert, Daniel was fed up.

'The Netherlands and Kazichia are the same,' he said. 'This welfare state your daughters safely grew up in obtained its wealth through war, oppression, and the slave trade. The Netherlands was built on exploitation too, just a few hundred years earlier than Kazichia. All the wealth in the world was built on someone else's back.'

Her father shook his head and muttered some French curse words to the pudding.

Michelle wanted to break up the fight and put her hand on Daniel's leg, but he couldn't stop himself. 'And your pension, the one you live off, receives returns on investments in the arms trade, the extraction of precious metals by modern slaves, and the drilling for fossil fuels in countries where women are oppressed.

But still, you accept that money, so that your wife can cook us a delicious meal.'

'Enough,' Michelle said. 'Let it go, please.'

Daniel held his tongue. But her father wouldn't let it go. The day after, he called her.

'Did you hear what he said, Michelle? He thinks oppression is necessary. That's what those people believe. Stay away from anything to do with the Lechkovs, my girl.'

Michelle got angry. She wanted an apology. And she wanted him to keep his nose out of her business. But he couldn't. The more serious the relationship got, the more her father resisted. Even during their wedding, right before walking his daughter down the aisle, he kept going. 'Think about what you're doing,' he whispered as the music started playing. 'I understand money is nice, but you're marrying into a hornet's nest. Listen to your father. This will be your downfall.'

'It's not about the money, Dad. And stop being dramatic.'

'I'm not being dramatic; that man is dangerous.'

'He's a scientist. He writes computer code all day,' she said and tried to hold back her tears. 'Do we need to do this *now*? Right before I'm getting married?'

'This is my last chance. I want to protect you.'

'He is the most wonderful man I've ever met. He is the love of my life.'

'*Il est le fils d'un tyran,* Michelle!' Luc Verdier shouted helplessly – so loud that all the guests could hear him.

She walked down the aisle without her father.

The second warning came from an unexpected person: Professor Tim Stewart. Tim was an important figure in Daniel's life. Because of him, he enrolled in computer sciences, and when Daniel turned out to be talented, Tim brought him to the University of Amsterdam so they could collaborate on his research.

As a strategy consultant, Michelle worked on all kinds of high-level developments in the market and complex data sets, but the work of Tim and Daniel was too abstract for her. She vaguely understood it; they researched neural networks that can make themselves smarter. And they used these networks to make 'deepfakes'. Michelle knew what deepfakes were from those apps where you swap faces with a celebrity. But the technology behind it, the codes Daniel would write all day long, were like a foreign language to her.

The two scientists became big names in their field and after years of breakthroughs they decided to start a company to put the artificial intelligence they developed to work. They called their network ERIS, named after the goddess of discord. And the goal for ERIS was not immodest: it was going to save the world. Daniel and Tim argued that it would not take long before everyone could make deepfakes. Everyone with a laptop or phone could have the president of the United States declare a war or have the CEO of a multinational talk total nonsense during a shareholders' meeting. That's why there needed to be a lie detector that was sophisticated enough to detect the truth. That lie detector was ERIS.

Trade press embraced the idea from the first press release. One of the world-leading deepfake scientists wanted to save the world from a flood of lies and confusion, together with his right-hand man. They had a flying start. But the fame had a price; Daniel had to give up his academic career. Tim demanded it. One of the two needed to focus on ERIS full time to make it a success, and because Tim had the highest tenure, 'That would be a waste,' the professor said. After much deliberation, Daniel decided to listen to his mentor and cut short his academic career. A big sacrifice, but it seemed like the right decision; the company made giant leaps. And their work on ERIS progressed much quicker than they thought possible. Things couldn't have been better.

But then Tim suddenly showed up at the door. Michelle was home by herself and asked what he was doing there. The professor walked into the living room without taking his coat off and said he wanted to talk about Daniel.

He took a seat on her chair. 'Maybe we should quit ERIS.'

'What do you mean? Things are going great with ERIS, right?'

'Yes, too well.'

'But you can't do that to Daniel. He gave up everything for this company. For you.'

'Do you think I want this? I don't have a choice. He's behaving . . . dangerously.'

'Dangerous? Daniel? Where is this coming from? Aren't you overreacting a little bit, Tim?'

'Don't underestimate the implications of our work, Michelle. ERIS could start a war.'

'I don't understand how a lie detector could be dangerous. Aren't you working on the solution to the problem?'

'You can only make the ultimate lie detector by making the best possible liar,' Tim explained. 'The neural network we're building is a "generative antagonist network". Actually, it's two networks, not one. And those two networks are each other's opponents. One of them is called the "generator", which produces an image that seems real but isn't. Tom Cruise kissing a llama, for instance. And the other one is the "discriminator", which tries to determine if the image of Tom Cruise is a deepfake or not. By constantly working against each other, the network gets better at making deepfakes, and at recognising them. You're essentially building a shield against the weapon and the weapon itself: the lie detector and the liar.'

'And you think Daniel is handling the part that makes deepfakes irresponsibly?'

'With a network as advanced as ERIS, you need to find the right moment to publish it. When you're too late, your lie detector isn't smart enough to be of use. But when you're too early, you're giving the world a more dangerous weapon than they had. Our work on ERIS progressed so quickly that we need to wait. We're so far ahead that we need to put the moral implications before the business opportunities: if we come forward with this now, we will make a lot of money but will also make matters much worse. I thought Daniel would agree with me on that.'

'What is he proposing, then?'

'When I said I wanted to postpone publishing, he got angry. He wanted to put the network to work as soon as possible, to make sure we're the first ones. He says I don't understand how much depends on the success of ERIS, for his career. This is the only thing he cares about: his own success.'

'But that's true, isn't it? That this is very important for him? His grandfather invested almost two million into the company. Daniel doesn't want to disappoint his family.'

'This is bigger than him!' Tim said it so loudly that Michelle pointed at the baby monitor to remind him of her sleeping daughter.

'I know his intentions are good, Tim. I think you just need to talk to him.'

'I've been talking to him for months, but he refuses to listen to me.' Tim leaned forward and put his hand on hers. 'Michelle, if ERIS falls into the wrong hands, it's a weapon of mass destruction. And Daniel is treating it like it's a cap gun. Will you please talk to him? These past few weeks I've seen a side of him I don't understand.'

She assures Tim he doesn't need to worry. Most likely, Daniel was just tired. The whole family was tired. Michelle's pregnancy was tough on her, and both of them worked too hard. She would book a holiday and talk to him then. She promised. Tim walked out with a grave look on his face, and Michelle called her favourite resort in Dubai. Lying by the pool, she would ask him about it. She would help Daniel to see Tim's point of view. But they never made it to the pool, because Vigo was murdered that night. And the next day, they flew to Kazichia.

30

A few days after the conversation with Harper, someone knocks on the door. It's day twenty-six in the High House and Michelle expected this day to start as all the others: by staring at Alexa's cartoons. But someone knocks, and so she ties her dressing gown and opens the door.

Before her stands a staff member, who gives her a friendly smile. He's relaying a message from Maika: does Michelle have time to have a cup of tea in Maika's private wing?

Somewhat perplexed, she stares at the man. She hasn't spoken to her mother-in-law since the day of the coup. So why now? Why this sudden attention? The man stares back questioningly and she hesitates. Then she tells him she needs to get dressed and put some make-up on, but that she'll hurry.

About half an hour later, she sits down in one of the giant armchairs in Maika's apartment and studies her mother-in-law. Is the old woman experiencing a rare moment of empathy? Is she finally offering her daughter-in-law some support? Maybe because she recently learned that Michelle is pregnant? But the tea has barely been poured before Maika starts talking about her friend Nia. She asks if Michelle will put in a word for her with Daniel. She is terrified Nia will be arrested by the OMRA and disappear from the face of the earth.

Of course it's not about us, Michelle thinks. *Of course it's completely unrealistic to think someone could be concerned about my or Alexa's wellbeing.*

Without even taking a sip of tea she gets up.

'No,' she says. 'I won't put in a word. I don't want to be a part of your power games. All I care about is going home to the Netherlands.'

She doesn't want to sound cold, but she can't bring herself to hide her true feelings. She is too pregnant and too stressed for diplomacy.

Maika puts the teapot down, shaking her head.

'Michelle, Daniel and you can't possibly return to the Netherlands. You know that, right? In order to do that safely, he needs to leave the High House stably without becoming president himself. That's impossible. The harsh truth is you can't leave here without causing a bloodbath.' She goes quiet and looks at Michelle with her head tilted. 'Does Daniel tell you what he's working on? Because as far as I can see, the one thing he works on day and night is consolidating our power. I haven't seen anything close to an escape plan.'

'Why do you think that?'

'He is modernising the security service. Together with Radko, he's vetting the army and having the civil war in the east assessed. That doesn't sound like he wants to get out as soon as possible. It sounds like he's preparing for presidency.'

Michelle looks at Maika, wanting to speak her mind, but instead she calls for Alexa and walks out of the room. She can't do it anymore. She can't hear any more theories on her husband. She doesn't know who or what to believe, but she does know that sitting and waiting in that damned High House is not an option anymore. She can't lie to her boss anymore that she's sick and read his worried messages every day. She can't hear herself tell her best friends that she has faith in Daniel. That everything will be all right. Because she has no idea if that's true. She has no idea what her husband is working on.

It's time for clarity. No, it's time for the truth. Daniel can't exclude her any longer. And so, she calls for one of the drivers.

'To the OMRA headquarters,' she tells him.

With the same questioning look on his face as the staff member that invited her to tea, the driver stares at Michelle through his rear-view mirror.

'Are you deaf? Drive. To the security service.'

The two receptionists shoot each other a panicked look: what do they do? No one is allowed to enter without an appointment. If it were anyone else, they would be arrested, but this is Daniel Lechkov's wife. And Michelle Lechkova is refusing to leave without having talked to her husband.

After ten minutes of persisting, Daniel finally comes down. In the bright fluorescent lighting Michelle sees how exhausted he is. Agitated, he points to a bench in the reception area where they can sit.

'What's going on?'

'Your mother told me we can never go home again, and that you're aware of this. She says you're preparing for presidency.'

She can tell his mind is somewhere else. 'I'm going crazy, sweetie,' she says. 'All day long I'm waiting, sitting in that house. I'm losing my mind. I need to know what your plan is to get us out of here. If there is a plan. I need to know if I can ever hug my parents again. My whole life in the Netherlands is crumbling. I need . . .'

He takes her hand and tells her it will be okay. He promises.

She doesn't want to cry in front of Alexa, but she can barely hold it together. 'Is that true?' she asks, putting her head on his shoulder. 'Do you really think it will be okay? Because I don't know anymore.'

'I have one priority, Michelle, and that is your safety. All I've been doing for days and nights is protecting you.'

'What does that mean, though? What are you working on? How will you get us home?'

Daniel lets go of her and rubs his face. 'We can't go home right now; the situation is too dire. I didn't get into this because I don't want to cause you even more stress, but an attack could come from all sides. From Russia, from America, from the rebels in the mountains and Karzarov's friends in parliament. I need to stave all of them off, so my priority isn't returning to the Netherlands. My priority is your safety.'

'But how will you go up against all those parties by yourself?'

'Leonid and I are quickly building a digital department from scratch. They work with pens and fax machines here; I'm trying to turn the OMRA into a modern institute. That way, we gain a lot more control and oversight. Besides that, we're working on...'

While Michelle listens to him, it feels like she's floating up from the couch. Her stomach turns and her legs feel tingly. *Building a digital department from scratch*, she thinks. *That's what he has been doing all this time. He is exerting control. Or as Maika put it: consolidating power.*

Leonid enters the hall. The short, cross-eyed man points at his watch and shouts something to Daniel. He pretends Michelle and Alexa are invisible.

'I need to go,' Daniel says. 'Leonid and I are working on something important.'

He wants to get up, but she pulls him back to the couch. 'Wait, please. I don't understand. Setting up a digital department for the security service. That doesn't sound like we'll go home today or tomorrow. I... I don't get it. How long will we be here?'

'I don't know when we'll go back yet. I don't know how we would get there. I understand why you feel lost. But you need to believe me when I tell you that all I'm doing is working on your safety. We'll talk tomorrow, okay?'

Without waiting for an answer, he kisses Alexa's forehead and disappears behind the lift doors.

'What are we going to do?' Alexa asks. 'What is Daddy doing?'

I don't know, Michelle thinks.

31

In the middle of the night, Michelle jolts awake. Did she hear someone yelling out? She's not sure if the voice is an echo from her dream. She turns round and sees on her phone that it's 3 a.m. Judging by the fluffed pillow, Daniel is still working. As always. She tries to fall asleep but thinks of their conversation yesterday. About his 'digital department'. That evening she told Harper what happened, and the American nearly jumped out of her skin with frustration. 'Exactly as I predicted; he will never leave this place. We need to plan our own escape. We need to get control back over our lives.'

There is more yelling. It's not a dream. It's a woman, in the High House.

She gets out of bed and sneaks in her pyjamas to the living room, through the door, to the banister overlooking the dark wing. The wooden floor creaks under her bare feet and despite her weak hips she tries to walk on her toes. She looks down and sees three or four men detain someone. A woman, but she can't see who it is. The woman lets herself get dragged across the room, like a protester at a sit-in. The group walks towards the hallway and the moonlight falling through the high, churchlike windows illuminates their faces. It's Nia Karzarova. She is being taken by a few men – probably the security services. Michelle knows this arrest was hanging in the air for weeks and was hoping it would happen fast; she doesn't want to sleep in the same house as the wife of a traitor. The woman she saw leaving the church right before the coup. But now that she hears her screaming like she's on fire, she doesn't know what to hope for. There is so much fear in Nia's voice she sounds delirious.

Someone else yells out and the screams fall silent.

Maika enters the hallway through one of the tall doors wearing her nightgown, surrounded by guards. Michelle can't hear what she says, but it's clear she's trying to save her friend. Nia stretches her neck out like an animal reaching for water. The most powerful woman of the High House waves her short arms around while giving orders to the men, but they won't let go of their prisoner. A small figure steps forward from the darkness. Michelle leans forward to be able to see him. The man stutters but sounds calm and authoritarian. That must be Leonid. It sounds like Maika says 'Igor Yanev' a few times. She probably wants to know if he gave the orders. Leonid shakes his head and says something Michelle can clearly understand. A Kazichian name: *Daneil*.

The name is like a magic spell paralysing all of them. The hall goes dead quiet, and Michelle holds her breath. Carefully she takes a step back, afraid someone will notice her. The wooden floor creaks softly.

It's Maika who breaks the silence. She whispers something to Nia. Michelle can only imagine one possible translation: I'm sorry. The woman starts yelling – no, screaming – while getting dragged out of the house. The sound echoes through the empty hallways, long after the front doors have been shut and Nia has been taken away across the driveway.

Maika stands in the hallway and lights a cigarette. In the light of the flame, Michelle sees yellow tears glisten. She considers going downstairs to console her, but instead she sneaks back to bed, lies under the covers and stares up at the ceiling, wide awake.

Daniel did this. That's all she can think about.

Naturally, he needed to arrest his aunt. He didn't have a choice. But still, Michelle can't fall back asleep after this. She thinks about Harper and what she told her about the OMRA and the torture. If Harper knows, Daniel surely knows, too.

Could Harper be right? she thinks. *And my father? Tim? Does Daniel have another side to him, a side I don't know? A face that's only showing now that we're on his native soil?*

The rest of the night she stares at the dark ceiling full of ornaments, and, studying it like a Rorschach test of shadows, tries to see the face of her husband.

32

Michelle's dating ultrasound is scheduled for the next day. She finds it hard to accept that it's taking place in Kazichia and that she can't see her own midwife. Daniel promised her she could visit the best private clinic in the country, with better midwives and doctors than in the Netherlands. But it doesn't feel like a privilege.

A helicopter from Lechkov Industria is ready for them. Daniel hasn't come home that night, and when she crosses the roof of the High House to get to the landing platform, she sees him for the first time since their conversation at the OMRA. Under the roaring rotating rotor blades, she kisses him and asks how he's doing. He says something, but she can't hear him. The helicopter lifts off and soars over the city. Since the failed coup the streets are empty and the shops closed. The only people she sees are the long lines in front of the supermarkets, where locals are wanting to stock up on provisions, fearing more violence. Because there hasn't been an election for a new president, the Kazichians don't know what will happen in the High House. After a few minutes they have left Stolia and under Michelle's feet appears an endless carpet of treetops. Daniel turns the microphone on his headset on and says he regrets their conversation. He understands that she wants more information. That she wants to know what he's working on.

'We needed to make a difficult decision,' he says. 'That's why I was so rushed and absent. I'm sorry.'

'Do you mean Nia's arrest?'

He looks at her, surprised.

'Or was I not supposed to know about that?'

'Of course you are.'

She asks if it bothers him that he surrendered his aunt to the security service.

'It was the only way. It was too dangerous to have her at the High House. She did this to herself, not me.'

'That's true, but it must have been a tough decision. Right?'

'No decision I make here has been easy.'

It sounds clinical. Distant. She doesn't get why he acts this way. Her questions are reasonable.

The helicopter tilts a little and at the foot of a snow-covered hill, a white building appears. Daniel looks out the window and repeats that they will receive excellent care there.

'Is there a chance I will have to give birth in this country, Daniel? Is that why you keep telling me how excellent the health-care is here? Because I refuse. My second child will be delivered back home, regardless.'

He tries to smile but gives up halfway. 'I can't solve this in a few days, as much as I would like to. It will take time, but I've got a plan.'

'A plan to get out of here?'

'I've considered all the options. All of them. And I believe there is only one safe way to escape. But in order to execute that plan, I'll need time. Honestly, it's not unthinkable you will have to deliver here. That's why I wanted to show you this clinic.'

'No way.'

'Michelle, I . . .'

'Let me be clear, Daniel: that's not going to happen.' Her voice sounds eerily calm, but nerves form a lump in her throat. 'If you can't get us out of here, we need to talk to Harper. She's got a plan to get away, a quick way to escape.'

While the helicopter starts descending, Daniel leans over her. 'What do you mean? What's her plan?'

She covers her stomach with two hands. 'Calm down! What's the matter with you? I don't know what her plan is, she hasn't told me yet. But maybe it will be useful to us. Why does that upset you? Harper wants to get away, just like us. She's on our side.'

157

'You mustn't listen to her, Michelle. Do you hear me? If you try to escape, you'll put yourself in danger. Do you understand? You need to wait, that's the only way. You mustn't make your own plan. I forbid you.'

'You what?!' She raises her finger and pushes him back. 'Who do you think you are? How dare you raise your voice at me? I'm not giving birth to my child in a country where fighting could break out any moment. And if that means I need to find my own way out, I will.'

The helicopter reaches the ground, and the door slides open from the outside. On the platform a blonde woman with a clipboard waits for them. She smiles uncomfortably and asks if everything is all right.

'Nee,' Michelle mumbles in Dutch while climbing out of the helicopter. 'Nothing is all right.'

After getting introduced to the director of the clinic and her new gynaecologist, Michelle lies down on an examination table in a dark room. She tries to stay polite, but her mind wanders to the unfinished fight hanging in the air.

The ultrasound technician rubs cold gel on her stomach and slowly slides the ultrasound device back and forth.

'That blinking light is the heart.' Daniel translates what the woman says and points at the screen. 'The heart is beating.'

'So, everything is okay?'

He nods.

She tries to focus on her baby, but keeps looking over at her husband. The white light of the screen paints shadows by his mouth and eyes – as if someone stands behind him, changing his expressions with their long, black fingers. *Why do you keep so much distance?* she thinks. *Why don't we solve this together, like the team we once were?*

While the technician looks for another angle to better show their baby, Daniel's phone rings. His jacket hangs over his chair and the iPhone vibrates against the wood of the backrest. Startled, he jumps up and answers immediately. On the other end of the line a man speaks so loudly that Michelle can hear there is panic.

She rolls onto her side and grabs her own phone. On her screen is a message from Harper.

Explosion in military barracks. I think war. Come back now.

'What's going on?' she asks. 'Are we under attack? Has the war started?'

He puts his hand on the phone. 'Bombs exploded, but there's no need to worry. I have it under control.'

'Did the Russians do it?'

'The rebels did it. But you need to trust me, you're safe.'

Michelle's phone buzzes again. A push notification from a news app.

Two explosions in Kazichia. Most likely terrorism.

'See, this is exactly what I mean. We need to get out of here!' She says it so loudly that it startles the technician, who quickly gets up.

'Calm down, don't jump to conclusions.'

'We're going home right now, Daniel. We're going to get Alexa and we're escaping.'

He starts putting his jacket on. 'I have it under control. Believe me. I knew this would happen; I just didn't know when. But I have it under control. Promise me you won't listen to Harper, okay? Promise me you'll wait for me in the High House.'

Before she can say anything, two security men come in and take her away. With the sticky gel from the ultrasound still on her stomach, she is led to the main entrance by the men. Outside there is a car ready for her. She sits in the back seat and immediately asks the driver if he knows what is going on. The man doesn't have much to say, just that the capital is safe and the High House too – the bombs exploded in a different part of the country.

That means Alexa and Harper are unharmed.

While the car drives off, Michelle looks up and sees the helicopter with Daniel aboard fly back to Stolia. Where would he go? To a different secure location? To the headquarters of the OMRA?

For the whole ride to Stolia she wonders what will happen. She opens news apps on her phone, but not much is known about the circumstances of the explosions. Is it war? Is it a terrorist attack?

Will airspace and borders be restricted again? When they finally reach the High House, she runs to the apartment she's called home for the past few weeks. Alexa is playing with her toys; Harper looks at the TV with watery eyes.

'The fighting has started,' Harper whispers. 'They're talking about a rebel army from the Akhlos mountains. I'm out of here. I'm getting out. You need to come with me, Michelle. You need to leave Daniel and get your kids to safety.'

Michelle stares at the screen. She sees smoke and dust and people with bloodied faces trying to get away.

'You're right,' she says. 'What's your plan?'

V. Nairi of the Jada

33

The woman's voice on the phone says the second phase of the operation will begin. I've questioned multiple people about a man with a thousand faces without getting a step further. But my contact is happy and gives me new coordinates.

With the old Honda I got at the airport I drive out of the city, towards the east. It's a long drive and the gearbox is hanging on by a thread, so I need to pull and push to keep moving. But I can't complain; I'm surrounded by Ladas barely able to move – models that look like they were produced before the Wall fell.

After two-and-a-half hours the road ends and I'm driving on a field of grass, along the edge of a dense forest. The vehicle wobbles over the field. I'm wondering if I read the map wrong, but after thirty minutes the blackened tower appears.

'Burn the car when you get to the old tower,' the voice on the phone had told me.

I poor gasoline over the Honda, light the map and throw it in the side window. When the smoke plumes rise above the treetops, I hear a helicopter far away take off.

I estimate it will reach me in about five minutes.

The tyres are exploding and there is glass flying around, so I turn away from the car and walk to the tower. The fire's shadows shoot between the thick beeches like fish, hitting the ruin like waves.

When I step inside, I see a metal spiral staircase wind up. I wonder what this building was used for. It looks like a light-house. But who would build a lighthouse on the edge of a forest?

I want to climb the stairs to see if there is a light on the roof, but the construction starts squeaking when I get on it. Instead, I sit down right in the middle of the tower on the stone floor. I close my eyes.

I feel safe in that circle – like the bottom of a well. I feel like a young boy in the dark, pretending to be underwater, where nobody can find him.

The sound of rotor blades approaches.

The louder the sound gets, the more I wish no one would come and get me. I don't want to continue this strange assignment. I want to be forgotten. I want to stay in the tower. Forever. I could live off the land and restore the lighthouse. Not that that's useful to anyone, but still, I want to. It wouldn't be part of some grand plan; it wouldn't serve any hidden purposes. I would build it because I want to. That's all.

But I have an assignment that needs to be finished and I need cash to pay my debts. So I guess the lighthouse will have to wait.

While the helicopter lands on the field, I walk outside. A woman gets out holding a big sack over her shoulder. I stick out my hand to introduce myself, but she won't even look at me. She drops the sack on the ground and asks me to check the contents. I recognise her voice from the brief phone conversations.

I try not to take her bluntness personally.

The bag contains American spec ops gear. Stunned, I take out an M4A1 assault rifle. The weapon is equipped exactly how I like it – from the way the grip is angled, to the brand of IR laser.

I ask the woman how she knows what I like to work with. And if America is our client. The uniform has American flags on it.

The woman says there is no time for chitchat, that I need to get in so we can leave.

'I have to check the weapon and zero my scope,' I say, and sit down on one knee.

'Are you deaf?' she asks. 'We're leaving *now*. We don't have time for this.'

Every soldier knows what the most common cause of a weapon malfunction is during a fight: the gunman. That is why you check and maintain your weapon yourself. That is why you zero your own scope. Every professional knows that. And yet, I sit down in the helicopter without checking my gun. Like a good dog. Like a bad soldier.

While we ascend, I feel the anger flow through my knuckles like boiling water. I look down. Under my feet, the burning car shrinks into a tiny red dot beside an endless sea of trees. I will never find that old lighthouse again.

34

'Jump. I can't get closer than this.'

The pilot tries to keep the helicopter still by a stone plateau sticking out from a hairpin bend. I can tell by his hands and feet he's doing all he can to steady the helicopter. This high up in the mountains the wind must be unpredictable and strong.

The woman opens the door and jumps out.

I tighten the gun's two-point sling and jump out after her.

Crouched, we stay on the icy rock while the helicopter takes off. I put on my hood and pull my scarf in front of my face. Once the helicopter is gone, the snow floats down quietly again. Before us a narrow mountain path winds down, disappearing in the mist. The woman has walked onto the path without saying anything. I slide my gun from my back to my chest and follow her. The snow crunches beneath my boots.

'You haven't introduced yourself yet,' I say after a few minutes.

'No.' It sounds hostile, as if I asked something inappropriate. 'That won't be necessary for the mission. I don't know your name either, soldier.'

'If I need to protect you, I need to warn you when we're in danger. So it is necessary.'

She sighs dramatically. 'Sasha.'

Why does she sound so irritated? Why does she shoot down everything I say?

'Okay Sasha, and why are we here? *Where* are we?'

'Didn't they brief you at the airport, soldier?' She pulls her gloves further over her wrists. 'This is the Sjivida Pass.

It's completely frozen down there seven months of the year. Completely inaccessible. Hence the helicopter. The last part to Inima we walk, it will take us about an hour.'

'What's in Inima? What are we doing there?'

She puts her sunglasses on. 'It's the biggest settlement of the Jada, the traditional border guards of the Akhlos. The Jada live by the Russian border and the Russians keep moving that border. That angers the Jada, but there is not much they can do. At the same time, they have been waging a civil war with the Neza, along the border in the West. The forgotten battle, they call it here. Or the invisible battle. But this conflict has calmed down in the last few months.'

'So, this group fights the Russians on one side and the Neza on the other.'

'This group, as you call them, is a people consisting of countless tribes and clans with multiple subcultures. And yes, they are fighting everyone. And they would fight the government if they could. But how do you face a modern army when your life consists of ancient rituals and homemade cheese?'

'And in the settlement we're on our way to, we'll meet the Man with a Thousand Faces?'

'Our target in Inima is a woman named Nairi. She is the leader of the Jada and we're picking her up for an interview. With the Americans. Hopefully she can tell our clients more about the Man with a Thousand Faces. And in exchange for information, she'll get airtime on CNN. That's what she wants because she hopes the CIA will notice her that way. If America is behind her, she might be able to take on the government.'

'So, we're kidnapping her for the CIA?'

Sasha stops abruptly and turns round. 'Are you deaf? We're not kidnapping anyone. They know we're coming. This is a very simple assignment.'

I nod and apologise.

This isn't simple at all. This woman is terrified, I can hear it in her voice. She's scared of what awaits us in Inima. Or she's scared of that woman Nairi. And if it's really such a simple assignment, why would she be afraid?

She is lying to me.

I look up the mountain wall. The mist is thinning out and things are emerging along the incline. They look like trees, but that's impossible at this height.

'What are those?' I point, holding the M4.

'Those are the old watchtowers of the guards. They are still being used. Closer to Inima you'll see more, some are centuries old.' She is out of breath from the thin mountain air.

'Can they see us from there? I don't have a sunshade for my scope, so I can't defend us.'

'They probably know that we're coming, but they don't have long-range weapons.'

'They're rebels in a civil war, right?'

'They're rebels without money. That's why they need the help of the CIA.'

'Was the tower where you picked me up a watchtower? I liked the building.'

'You liked it?' She smiles without looking at me. 'That tower was part of a prison. On that field used to be a huge complex that burned down during a prisoner uprising. The watchtower is all that's left.'

The way she says it bothers me. The way she shakes her head and smirks bothers me too. She likes to make a fool of me. How would she know what that tower was for? It looked very old, and I suspect she's making up a story to put me in my place.

She wants to remind me she is my superior.

'The assignment is simple,' Sasha repeats, to clarify that I need to keep my mouth shut: 'We'll take Nairi for that interview to ask her about the Man with a Thousand Faces. You protect her, if needed. You'll make sure she gets to our helicopter so we can take her to the location where we're filming her.'

'And that's it?'

'Apart from that you don't do or say anything. Seems simple enough to me.'

35

It's hard to believe that we are standing in the epicentre of the Jada. There are no fences or barricades as you would expect, so we just walk in.

We are at the lowest point, a place you don't want to be as a soldier. Everywhere I look, I see danger. Scattered over the empty hills are old, sturdy towers, with wooden ladders leaning against them. People are sitting on the flat roofs watching us. Some have weapons. Some of those are pointed at us. Around the towers are low, slated buildings with tiny windows. In the windows, I see people moving. Some have weapons. The part of the settlement we're standing in is much newer. The buildings here have multiple floors, large windows, satellite dishes, and roof tiles. Between the houses, men are crouching and waiting. They don't talk to each other. They are just watching us.

This is not good.

I should have snorted some Moda and Concerta.

Caro always said I used drugs because I didn't trust myself, but that's not true. I use drugs to push myself to my limit — that's completely different. I think she didn't like it that I always took a blue pill before we had sex. She got offended because she thought I couldn't do without it. But she misunderstood. I could do without it; I just want my body to perform optimally.

'Behind you,' Sasha whispers, and I turn round.

A big group of men is right behind us. I don't understand how I could have missed them. They are holding Russian Mosin-Nagants. If the rebels in the watchtowers have those too, and if they know how to work them, we were in much more danger walking up that mountain than my travel companion seemed to think. They might not look like modern sniper rifles, but they are most certainly dangerous long-range weapons.

I look ahead. Men are climbing down the tower, appearing from in between the houses. They are coming down the hill. A circular net of rebels starts enclosing us – like a noose getting tightened.

'Fighting is not an option,' I say and slide my rifle onto my back.

'We don't need to fight. We are here for the interview. Nairi is expecting us.' Sasha doesn't sound convinced.

Two older unarmed men greet us. They are both muscular and have battered faces. They speak a mixture of Russian and English, so I understand some of it. Sasha explains we work for CNN and have come to pick up Nairi, as agreed.

'I'll get my press pass,' she says. Her hands tremble as she unzips her coat.

The two men each hold one side of the plastic card and look at it confusedly. One of the two looks at me. At the American flag stitched onto my chest.

'Walking please with me,' he says politely in broken English – as if we aren't prisoners.

Between two old watchtowers stands a wooden house with tall glass sliding doors overlooking the village. A black figure awaits us at the door opening. While nearing the house, I forget to watch my flanks. I forget the rebels circling us. All I can do is look at the black figure. She is wearing a long robe embroidered with white symbols I don't recognise.

'Welcome to Inima,' she says. Not in that strange mixture that the rest speaks, but in fluent English.

Sasha walks ahead and asks if she has the pleasure of speaking with the legendary Nairi of the Jada.

'Here in the mountains, they call me Nairi, indeed,' the black figure says, 'but I'm not a legend, because I am not dead yet.'

She has a stunning face – much more delicate than the other Jada – but her left cheek and neck are marked with scars.

'We can still decide my part of the story before it becomes folk-lore,' she says, motioning for her men to leave. It seems like she is missing her left hand. Maybe even her entire arm. I remember the story the man in the internet cafe told me, about how even a grenade couldn't stop this woman.

One of the men behind us grabs my rifle and points at my gun. I take the magazine out of the SIG Sauer and hand it to him. He accepts the compromise. Apparently, he is unaware the chamber has a bullet. One shot won't make a difference in a gunfight, with dozens, maybe even hundreds of Jada fighters, but it's good to know how little experience these men have.

'It's an honour to be here,' Sasha says. She looks bad, pale as a ghost and trembling.

'Come in,' the woman called Nairi says. 'The village elder could feel you coming closer and wants to meet you.'

We follow her through the glass sliding doors and enter a provisionary throne room. In the centre of the room sits an old woman in an elevated wooden chair, surrounded by candles and photo frames. She is wearing a black robe, too. The fabric is so long that it hangs over the chair and reaches the ground like a black bridal veil. Behind the woman stand two long tables filled with old broadcast radios – dozens, maybe hundreds. Two young men sit with their backs to us, speaking in their strange language into the amplifiers.

The analogue static from the radios sounds like a flowing creek.

Nairi gestures at the guards by the door and sits on a stool next to the eldest one. The doors and curtains are closed, and the room gets pitch dark, except for some candlelight.

'Can this not stand the light of day?' Sasha asks, smiling nervously.

'This way all we see is your intentions,' Nairi whispers.

I can't tell if she is joking or not. Sasha seems unsure too because she stares at our host with anxious eyes. She steps forward and folds her hands together.

'My name is Eva Fletcher and I work for CNN.'

I look up in surprise.

'I'm here to take you to the studio, where we will interview you.'

'You say you work for CNN, Eva Fletcher, but judging by your accent you're from Stolia.'

'That's right. My father was British, and my mother was Kazichian. I was born here. I'm the correspondent for CNN in Kazichia. Didn't you see the report we sent you?'

'I saw the report. I recognise your face from the video.'

The old woman whispers something and Nairi leans over to her. The scars on her neck stretch out.

'Tell me, where will these recordings take place?' she asks.

'On an island in one of the Central Lakes; we have a house at our disposal. There will be security and we have prepared a comfortable room for you to stay the night.'

'That's not what I agreed on. The interview was going to take place on Jada territory.'

'Plans have changed because we couldn't find a suitable spot.'

Naira studies the woman next to me like she is trying to gauge if she is being lied to. 'Then I insist on bringing a military convoy. Twelve men.'

'I apologise, but that won't be possible. In the helicopter is room for one passenger. But we can guarantee your safety. America guarantees your safety.' She points at me.

Nairi looks at me and deliberates with the old woman next to her.

I look at the woman who said her name was Sasha, and who now calls herself Eva. Why would she lie about her name? Or is she speaking the truth now? Am I working for the Americans?

Nairi faces us again. 'If I can't bring anyone, I sadly have to cancel the interview. I'm sorry you travelled all this way for nothing.'

Sasha looks at me. The anxiety is getting too much for her. I would have liked to help her, but if she won't tell me what the plan is, I can't help her when that plan falls apart.

'Nairi, please forgive me.' Sasha takes another step forward and one of the soldiers makes a disapproving noise. 'But this is your chance.'

'What do you mean, Eva Fletcher?'

'The Mardoe Khador is highly unstable. President Vigo Lechkov is dead, and rumour has it his brother doesn't want to be in power. The Karzarov family tried to take over but failed, and the Yanev family seems passive. This is the time for the Jada to strike.'

Nairi sits up straight and looks down at us from the elevation. Her eyes are empty.

'This is the moment to show the world you're here to end the oppression,' Sasha continues. 'This is the moment to consider an allyship with America. The Man with a Thousand Faces has a rebel army on standby. With him and us, you stand a chance.'

'What do you know about him, about *Asch-Iljada-Lica*?' Nairi asks.

'Nothing. But you must know who it is. Or at least suspect someone.'

'I've heard rumours, that's all. If you came here hoping I would lead you to him, to the Man with a Thousand Faces, I have to disappoint you.'

Sasha wants to say something, but suddenly the old woman in the chair starts coughing uncontrollably. I know that cough. Deep and painful. It sounds like dark blood on white handkerchiefs, like the future humming of the refrigeration under an open casket.

Nairi rushes to the village elder and pats her back. The old woman catches her breath and whispers something in Nairi's ear.

Both of the women suddenly turn to me.

'The village elder hears the voices of our ancestors,' Nairi says. 'They're only speaking about you. Not about CNN, not about America, not about this Eva from Stolia — if that's her real name. Only you.'

I don't know what to do. From the corner of my eye, I can see that Sasha watches me as if I betrayed her somehow. My heart rate is much too high. I should have snorted Moda.

'They see your intentions,' Nairi translates the old woman's whispers. 'Your intentions are pure, but you're lost. The ancestors have nicknames for you. They call you the silent man. They call you the soldier without a name.'

'Is it true that you don't have a name?' the village elder asks. She addresses me directly, which startles me. I hadn't expected her to speak English. Her voice is low and grating.

'Was there no one to name you when you were born?'

I look into her small, beady eyes, sitting deep in her wrinkly skin, and my throat turns dry. I see the dark lake my father took us to. I am in the red tent with my sister. I see her squint her eyes as the tent unzips.

'I have a name,' I say quietly, 'but I haven't used it in so long, I'm starting to forget.'

The village elder nods and beckons Nairi. But when she leans forward to listen, the coughing starts again. The old woman jerks up and down in her chair.

'Is your village elder ill?' Sasha asks.

Nairi nods. 'Her turn to step through the next door is near, unfortunately.'

'We could take her with us. There are private clinics in the West where she can receive treatment. CNN pays. Naturally.'

Nairi frowns. 'So now there are two free spots in the helicopter, Eva from Kazichia City? I thought there was one spot.'

'There are two, no more.'

Nairi gets up abruptly.

'I've heard enough,' she says, and her black robe puffs out like a sail, then slowly falls to the ground. 'You are our guests. We will make sure you get warm meals and soft beds. Meanwhile, I will have you taken to two different residences so we can find out the truth.'

The doors open and let the daylight in. Sasha looks at me helplessly – her big eyes are trying to tell me something. The woman claiming to be a CNN correspondent probably wishes she had told me what we came here to do, and who we work for. But now it's too late.

174

36

Sasha gets taken to a room in the back of the house. When she's gone, two short Jada men take me to a wooden cabin on the steepest point of the hillside. They don't grab my arms like the other men did to my travel companion. They show me where I can sleep and where the sink is and ask if it's up to my standards. It's a little primitive, but I've survived the desert in Yemen for two weeks without food – to me, this is luxurious.

After the tour, the men stay lingering awkwardly in the doorway. In clumsy English, one of the two explains that I'm invited to dine with Nairi and the village elder that evening. They tell me a few times it's a great honour – apparently, they are worried I will decline. While I try to make it clear I will be there, the two men look at each other. They want to ask me something else but don't know how. Eventually, one of them points to the other side of the hill.

'Show us what you can do. Please.'

The other one nods. 'We have beer.'

Just outside of the village is a shooting range consisting of empty cans on boulders. There are about ten young men with a few rifles. As soon as I arrive, everyone gets quiet, except for one slightly older man. He introduces himself as Paada and asks me all kinds of questions about his Mosin in fluent English. I show him how to reload the bolt-action rifle faster using three fingers and explain why it's better to squat down before firing a long-distance shot – if you have the time. The men hang on my every word. I show

175

them why you should always zero a scope to one hundred metres, and how to use a knife for close combat. And despite their poor English, I even manage to talk about my love for chemistry for a little bit. I fold open my narcotics pouch and prepare a simple recipe for a performance-enhancing drug. The Jada thank me after every tip as if I returned their children to them.

I don't know why but it feels good to share my knowledge. Maybe I could be an instructor someday. It could also be the Jada. They are friendly and approachable guys, and I kind of feel sorry for them. They are not fighters and definitely not soldiers; they are being forced to take up arms and can use all the help they can get. They are a peaceful people.

As night falls, the men sit on the cold grass, drinking beer. I tell them I have to go – I'm having dinner with Nairi and the village elder. Paada asks if I will have lunch with him tomorrow. I thank him for the invitation and explain a helicopter will pick me up, so I won't be able to.

The men laugh. 'You'll stay here for a while, soldier. That helicopter will return to the valley tomorrow without you.'

Dinner is at Nairi's house. In the living room the throne is gone, instead there is a long folding table covered in candles. The radios against the back wall are hidden under yellowed sheets, the whispering men have gone home.

I'm seated at the head of the table, directly opposite Nairi and the village elder. On the long sides of the table sit Jada I haven't met yet. Almost no one speaks English, but now and then someone offers me a smile or a nod – they want me to feel comfortable.

The chair next to me is empty. I hope Sasha will hurry up. A man with a strange string instrument has entered the room, and I think she should be here before the music starts.

'This is our *inamorv'edi* or toastmaster,' Nairi explains. She looks right at me and the scars on her face seem to glow in the candlelight. 'Before we serve dinner he will propose a toast to our ancestors, who are guests at the dinner table every night.'

I want to ask about Sasha, about Eva Fletcher, but Nairi gestures for me to be quiet.

The toastmaster starts speaking very slowly in his unintelligible language and raises his glass to the people he sees standing behind us around the table. Nairi takes her glass and gestures for me to drink. In the cup is cold beer. Most people would be happy with that, but I don't like alcohol. I don't get why you would sedate and weaken yourself on purpose. To be polite, I take a sip. My first sip of beer in over ten years.

The toastmaster claps his hands together and takes his little three-stringed guitar out from under the table. He tunes it and starts strumming and singing. Meanwhile, a girl enters with a tray filled with bread and cups of salt. As the song plays, everyone takes a piece of bread and a cup.

I take a bite and look up. The village elder is crying – tiny glittering tears glide down her wrinkled cheeks. She talks softly to herself, looking over our heads. She is looking at the ghosts. These people are so connected to their ancestors that they can still see them after they die.

When the toastmaster finishes, he walks round the table and sits down next to me. Apparently, that is not Sasha's seat. While it feels inappropriate, I raise my voice to ask Nairi where my travel companion is.

Nairi smiles at me. 'She is safe and well, but she wasn't invited to this dinner. We want to get to know you, soldier with no name. The woman who says her name is Eva, we have known her from the moment she walked into the village.'

37

The sun has just risen, but the Jada have been awake for hours. Despite the cold, I'm standing in front of my cabin, drinking the coffee someone put out for me. A farmer walks by with two horses pulling bales of hay. He waves at me. Behind him walks a man with a giant jerrycan on his shoulder. I think they're joking about hard work and smart work. I lift my earthen mug to greet them.

While the men disappear behind the hill, I look at the buildings scattered on the mountain. Some houses have a dish on the roof, others don't even have windows. Some are made of wood and others are brand new; others are centuries old, made of slate. This is what happens when you never get rid of anything but keep finding ways to fix things; your history will surround you, like the ghosts around Nairi's table. I wish I had a history. Or that I could retrieve it. As opposed to them, I don't belong to the world I live in. I've come loose; I'm a fringe, dangling in the wind.

A few hours later I see Paada approach me. I haven't seen Sasha all morning. I am starting to wonder if she's okay. It looks like we will keep the helicopter waiting for nothing today. Paada asks me again if I will have lunch at his house. He looks at me as if he thinks I will say no. But why would I? Of course I want to.

While we walk through the village, I tell Paada I feel good in the mountains.

'Naturally,' he says. He explains that the Jada want to live as high as possible to be closer to God. 'Do you feel His warmth? It is wintertime, but not cold.'

I understand what he means, but what I feel has nothing to do with any god.

We eat a simple lunch of bread and homemade cheese, and afterwards, I play with Paada's sons. The boys laugh at my tattoos. They pull on my arms and try to smudge the ink. They are the first children I have seen since being here. Paada's wife Ambi'va explains most children sleep at school because it is a two-hour walk to get home along the steep slope of their mountain. Even the Jada, born with steel calves, don't like to take that walk twice a day. I ask if it's difficult to see their children so little. They explain the tight-knit Jada community starts at school; the children have to get along all week. The next generation grows close there. For some reason that gets me emotional.

In the West, I wouldn't have lasted ten minutes with someone else's family. Suburbs and Volvos make me want to kill myself. But these people calm me down. They are honest. Their lives are simple, and I always thought simple meant uncivilised. I thought people in less developed countries were running behind, but now I know they are ahead of us. Ahead of me. No one here is indebted to some shady criminal, and no one here gets forced to hurt people to work off their debt.

I am back at the shooting range, and the young men are angry. I was worried I had done something wrong, but it has nothing to do with me. They received word from another Jada village. Two girls were killed, fourteen-year-old twins.

Life in the Akhlos is not as simple as I thought.

Paada stands next to me and puts his hand on my shoulder. 'That part of the mountains has been taken over by Lechkov Industria,' he says, his voice raspy.

I know that name now. And it has a sulfur aftertaste.

'Those two girls got caught under a landslide of mining waste. They had done such long shifts in one of the Lechkov workcamps that they took the shortest route home, completely exhausted. Right by the waste dump. That is extremely dangerous, but they wanted to get to their beds. When sludge came down the slope, it hit them like an avalanche.'

Paada lights a cigarette.

'Two young girls choked on the shit of those greedy dogs. And if their parents would sue them, or even criticise them, they would get arrested by the OMRA. Everyone knows what happens, but nothing will change. Things will only get worse. Europe doesn't want to depend on China for their electric cars and whatever else, and the largest lithium supply, apart from Portugal, lies here,' he stomps the ground. 'So they're going to drain the entire Akhlos. And Europe will pretend they don't know under what circumstances the Jada live. You know, those lithium mines are so much worse than coal mines. They need to dig deeper and extract lithium from ore. It makes unbelievable noise, and all the houses shake until they collapse. Cattle get scared and run off. People still living in free villages give up.'

Again, Paada can't hold back his tears. The other men stare at their feet awkwardly, muttering curse words.

'Our people will disappear.'

'There must be something you can do,' I hear myself say to break the silence. 'You have weapons, you're with many.'

Paada smiles with pain in his eyes. 'We're a simple people, soldier. You saw us mess around with our old rifles. And the Mardoe Khador has the most modern army of the region.'

One of the guys says something to me, but his friend gestures for him to stop.

'*Asch-Iljada-Lica*,' Paada repeats, and he nods at his friends that it's okay. 'The Man with a Thousand Faces. They're rumours, but the Jada find hope in it.'

Upon hearing that name, I feel my heart rate rise, but I don't let on. I ask who that is, as neutrally as possible.

'Somewhere in the mountains, a Jada with lots of resources and influence seems to be forming a rebel army. The people who witnessed him working claim that everything will change. They say an attack on the capital is being prepared. A real one. They say he stands a chance against Lechkov.'

The other guys seem annoyed that Paada is sharing the secret with an outsider. They whisper at him and shake their heads.

180

'They're just rumours,' he says, first to me, then the group. 'We know as little as you do.'

'And Nairi?' I ask. 'She seems determined. And she is much more than a rumour.'

Paada squints. 'That's up to you, stranger,' he says, pressing his finger into my chest. 'If you ensure she gets support from America, she stands a chance. But if you work for those dogs, those child killers . . . if you kidnap our leader and murder her, I hope you and your family go to hell where you will be buried beneath the sludge into eternity.'

'I don't want to hinder you,' I say.

The men look at me expectantly, but I don't know what else to say.

'Is this the moment of truth?' Paada asks, breathing anxiously. 'Will you tell us what you came here to do?'

I want to say I work for America and that Nairi is safe with me. I want to be on their side, but it's not up to me.

'I don't know,' I say. 'I'm sorry. I have no idea who I work for.'

Paada puts his hand on my shoulder again and tells me it's time to go home. 'Maybe you will tell us more tomorrow.'

He is trying to de-escalate the situation, despite my silence.

I don't deserve his hand. I don't deserve his smile.

I feel small, here on this mountain.

38

I have been in bed for just a few minutes when there's a knock on the door. It's Nairi. She asks if I'm awake. I don't know why, but I lie very still, like a child hiding by not moving.

The door opens and a different woman than I expected appears. It is Nairi, but she's wearing a faded red sweater and oversized jeans. Her brown hair is in a bun. She seems much smaller, much more normal. Much more vulnerable. Her left sleeve is folded inward.

'Can I come in? I want to speak with you for a moment.'

She closes the door behind her and sits next to me on the bed. I smell earth and alcohol and a little bit of sweat. It smells nice; it smells real. Very different from Caro. I read somewhere that we choose our partners with our noses. Unconsciously, people find an immune system that complements theirs through smell. As Nairi moves closer, I wonder if I have ever been in love.

'The village elder says you have a shadow hanging over you, soldier.'

I ask what she means.

'A man keeping you in your place. Someone dead for years. Who is he? The village elder says that he baptised you when you were little. In dark water. Was it your priest?'

I shake my head. 'I never got baptised, and I'm definitely not religious.'

'But you are docile.'

'I get an assignment, I execute it. I don't ask questions.'

'Did you get an assignment from America?'

I don't know what to say. I don't know if I can lie to her. I don't know if I *want* to lie to her.

'Did you get an assignment from the CIA?'

'Possibly, but I'm not sure,' I admit. The hopeful faces of the men at the shooting range are ingrained on my retina like bright spots.

'Do you get why I'm important to these communities, soldier? For the children and their mothers in the mountain villages?' She leans closer. 'Thanks to me, they can go home again. They dare to think of standing up to the oligarchs. Did you hear about the twins? The girls who died?'

I nod.

'The misery needs to stop. The village elder says I should take the risk. She says I should get in the helicopter. Because if the CIA helps us, that will change the history of our people.'

'I never know exactly who I work for. This operation feels like a CIA insurgency operation. That would mean the Americans want to support your movement in exchange for loyalty. But I don't know for sure. I never do.'

'You don't know what purpose you serve? You don't even know if you're doing bad or good? What a strange life.' Nairi looks into the room. 'We would never treat our people that way. Everyone is our confidant. No one is the mercenary, and no one is the client. We protect the border together.'

I nod because I don't know what else to do.

'Where do you feel at home, soldier?'

'I don't know what that feels like. I've never had a home.'

'How is that possible?'

I tell her that I used to work for criminals growing up. At least, from what I can remember. That I used to sleep in brothels or illegal casinos, sometimes on the street. I tell her about my time in juvenile detention and afterwards as a soldier. That the army offered me direction and confidence but didn't make me feel at home. 'And ever since I have been working as a mercenary, I live in hotels, in military camps, in planes. Never more than a few months in the same spot.'

'It sounds like you don't have any other choice,' Nairi says.

'I'm indebted to dangerous people. I need to pay them back.'

She stands up and nods. 'I understand it seems like you can't escape this life. But know this, soldier with no name: this house is yours. If you're looking for a place to settle, you can stay here. In the mountains, with us. Here you have no debts, and you won't be a mercenary. Here you're one of the Jada, just like me.'

I look around me. 'This house? But I can't just come and live here like that?'

'Why not? You can live wherever you want. We would accept you as one of us. Think about it for a few days. We ask for loyalty, that's all.'

39

Every morning, I stand in front of the house, drink my coffee, and greet the farmer with the horse and the guy with the jerry-can. Every afternoon, I am at the shooting range with the guys. And every night I have dinner at Nairi's house. For five days I've done this. I have no idea where Sasha is. Down in the valley, the operation has probably been called off. They must think we're dead, or imprisoned. But I don't care. Every day I can stay in the mountains is worth it. I don't use drugs anymore, I don't feel pressure on my chest, and I don't feel the rage pumping through my veins. I don't feel angry at all; I feel calm. All I can think about is Nairi's offer to stay here. To live in the wooden house, become one of them. A Jada.

She comes by every night when I'm in bed and asks about my life. I tell her everything. I had never done that before; I am hearing my own story for the first time. It is a story of struggle and repression. A story of war. And she is honest, too. About the fear she feels because people are counting on her – expect miracles from her. Sometimes she wishes she could run. But she would never do that. That's not like her. We talk about the Man with a Thousand Faces, too. She doesn't know who he is, but she hopes the rumours are true. She hopes he is as bloodthirsty as people say, because she could never be that heartless. She could never plan an attack or use fear as a weapon. But she does think it is necessary – the Mardoe Khador leaves them no choice.

And it's not just us; all of Inima is buzzing with stories about the mysterious rebel leader. At the shooting range, they are speculating who he is and how he was able to rise to power so fast. One morning, two of the guys suddenly disappeared; they left for one of the secret rebel camps. The army of the Man with a Thousand Faces is growing by the day.

After seven days, I see Sasha again. She is wandering on the hill, like one of the villagers.

'There you are. I was looking for you. Have you been here all this time?' she asks.

'Yes, where else would I be?'

'What have you told them? Did you talk to that Nairi?' Her voice sounds tense.

'I haven't told them anything. I just taught them to shoot. Where were you?'

'Locked up. I thought they would torture me for information. Or worse.' Skittishly, she looks around, even though the hill is deserted.

'They would never do that.'

'You don't know that.'

'What happens now? Has the operation been called off?'

'No, they considered the possibility that Nairi wouldn't come with us straight away. The helicopter flew to the takeoff spot every day at ten to pick us up' – her eyes get more confident – 'but tomorrow morning it lands for the last time. If we're not there, we will be left to our own devices. This is our last chance. We *need* to convince Nairi somehow.'

I calmly take my last sip of coffee. 'Not before I know who our client is.'

'*What?*'

'I want to know if we're here to help these people or work against them. Tell me the truth, or I'm not convincing anyone.'

'Or *you're* not convincing anyone? Who do you think you are?!' The condescending frown is back. 'You're not here to talk, soldier. Your only care is the safety of me and our target.'

'That's right. My mission is to protect Nairi, that's what you said. What is on that island? Where are we taking her?'

186

'I work for CNN and you work for the Americans, that's the story. We have one last chance of getting out of here. And these people have one last shot at getting the CIA to support their cause.'

Is she speaking the truth? I can see the tension in her eyes. I can see that she is trying her hardest to seem confident. But that doesn't have to mean she is lying. It could also mean that there's a lot at stake.

'Tomorrow morning the helicopter comes for the last time. After that, we'll be stuck on this mountain.' She thinks that that scares me.

That evening, Nairi looks bad. Exhausted. She stands in the doorway of my bedroom and has a big bottle in her only hand.

'Take a sip, soldier. This stuff is good for your heart.' We sit on my bed. She presses the bottle against my chest.

I shake my head. 'I don't drink.'

'Most hearts are asleep, drink this and wake up.'

I want to take a small sip, but Nairi tilts the bottle, and I drink until I choke.

'Good job, let it burn.' She takes the bottle and rests her hand on my back while I catch my breath.

'I tried speaking to Eva, or whatever her name is,' I say. 'All I know is that tomorrow morning is the last chance to get in the helicopter. After that, it's not coming back.'

Nairi nods. 'Thank you. Tell me about your father.'

I look up. That took an unexpected turn.

'We've been avoiding this for days,' she says. 'Time to tell me what happened.'

I look at the wooden floorboards under my feet and take another big sip from the bottle. 'He took my sister and me on holiday,' I say, handing the bottle back to her. 'On holiday for the first time; we couldn't believe it. But the lake we drove to had no campsite. There was nothing there. And he just brought a tent and booze. No food or activities. So, we were hungry and bored, but we didn't complain. We wanted to make something out of it. We wanted to go on holiday, just like the other kids.'

'That lake is the water you got baptised in. The dark lake the ancestors saw.'

'Every morning, he gave me "swimming lessons". I needed to get tough, he always said. I needed to learn how to control my impulses. With both hands he pushed me underwater to train me. The first few times, I fought him, hitting his arms, but it was no use. That made it take much longer. After a while, I found peace in the dark, cold lake. Funnily enough, I enjoyed being underwater. I learned to accept that he would decide if I came back up in time, and surrendered to the darkness. It became a safe place.'

'What happened to the girl?'

I need to take a deep breath to make space for the words. 'On the last morning of the holiday, he took her instead of me. I wanted to stop him, but he was too strong. They were gone all day. I went to look for them, but it was a giant lake, and I was a little boy. Eventually, I waited by the tent. My father returned after dark, psychotic from the booze, and without his daughter. Without my little sister.'

'Was she still in the water?'

I don't say anything. I can picture the way she squints as the zip of the tent opens. And her brown hair floating on the water like an empty trash bag.

'What did you do?'

'I took that bottle from his hand and killed him with it.'

'And that's when you started your life without a home.'

'I hitchhiked to the city and made up a new name and a new life for myself.'

Nairi sits closer to me. 'I see you, soldier with no name. I see who you are and who you could have been. You were baptised with violence, and now you think violence is your only way back in. But it's not. You can find a home, too.'

'Where is my home?'

'Here in the mountains, if you want it to be.' She puts her hand on my face. I thought her eyes were brown, but up close they are dark green. 'There is a place for you here. A place to build something. But only if you stop accepting jobs for money and start making promises to people.'

'What do you want me to do?'

'Promise you will protect me,' she says, quickly and quietly, like the words escaped her mouth by accident. 'Promise the Jada that you will bring me back to my post here in Inima, whatever we find on that island. If you do that, you have a home here. On the Akhlos. Forever.'

Her face touches mine. She smells of mountains.

'If this interview is really with CNN, and if the Man with a Thousand Faces really brings weapons and people, then a huge uprising will begin. And with that uprising, we need people like you to defeat the families in the High House. You can help us make history. Are you willing to become a soldier of the Jada?'

I nod.

'You need to say it out loud.'

'I'm willing to become a soldier of the Jada. I will protect you.'

'Are there really only two spots in the helicopter?' she asks. She holds her mouth close to mine.

I look straight into her dark green eyes. 'Yes.'

'The remote island they're taking us to, is it a recording studio or a trap?'

'I don't know. I've never been there. All I know is I need to get you inside the helicopter safely. So that's what I will do.'

Nairi leans back and her eyes turn dark brown again. 'Then I will come with the helicopter tomorrow. With you.'

I take the bottle and take another sip. The liquor warmed my chest. My hands are cold. My knuckles haven't burned for days now.

Nairi slides nearer and puts my hand on her thigh. 'Take a deep breath, soldier with no name,' she whispers. 'After tonight you will not soon forget my name.'

While she kisses me, her words penetrate me too. It doesn't matter what is on that island, studio or prison. And it doesn't matter who my client is and what side he is on. Because debts don't exist in these mountains, so I don't need money. And so, I'm not a mercenary. I'm not part of an incomprehensible whole; I'm just one man who made a simple promise. To her: Nairi.

I'm not a soldier with no name.

I'm a soldier of the Jada.

VI. The Uprising

40

It starts with three bombings, one closely following the next.

In the situation room of the High House, General Radko looks at a giant map of Kazichia. With a pencil, an analyst of the OMRA just placed an 'X' in the north-western part of the Akhlos, near the Russian border. There was an explosion in a coal mine there. The mine workers were changing shifts when it happened, so there were no casualties. But the entrance has collapsed, and the mine is inaccessible. A mining village with no mine means everything is at a standstill. And that means 230,000 dollars in losses for Lechkov Industria. Per hour. A huge problem that needs a quick solution, but not Radko's problem, nor that of the OMRA. It must have been an accident.

The men start packing their things to leave, but then another alert comes in. A second explosion. The analyst marks the spot with an 'X' again: a hundred-and-eighty kilometres west of the mining village. Radko starts making calls. The highest commander of the Kazichian army does not panic easily – even if he does, nobody can tell – but at the second explosion, he widens his beady eyes. And when he picks up the phone to have the members of the house come together, his hand trembles. That second explosion means an attack has been launched on the country. And not just any attack. The second bomb went off in the Petar Lechkov base, the largest military complex of Kazichia, the most intricately secured terrain in the region. But Radko's hand mostly trembles because the bomb went off in the main building during the weekly staff meeting of the Kazichian army. A meeting which he usually chairs, but just this week, as an exception, he sent a replacement to the base. Lieutenant-Colonel Pjotr Lechkov. His only son.

And then a third explosion is reported. The third cross on the map is eighty kilometres west of the second one, the Karazov family's brand-new factory, right outside the city of Baghsenka. Electric buses and forklift trucks were supposed to be manufactured there soon — the preparations for the launch were in full swing. The bomb exploded in the middle of the factory hall, which partly collapsed. According to the first reports, there were no casualties, yet all six firetrucks of the western barracks in Baghsenka were sent there to prevent the fire from spreading to the storage filled with lithium-ion batteries.

As the situation room fills up with people, Radko wonders where the next bomb will hit. With his index finger, he draws an imaginary line on the map. Maybe it's a coincidence or an optical illusion, but the three attacks seem to have happened in a straight line. A track on which a train of explosions races, rushing from Jada territory onwards to the west. To the capital. The analyst puts on his glasses and looks up through the ceiling, waiting for the blow. Waiting for the bomb that will wipe out the Mardoe Khador.

41

The situation room is in a state of chaos. Members of the military leadership that weren't at the Petar Lechkov barracks have drawn up a plan that Radko Lechkov needs to authorise. In the middle of their presentation the commander-in-chief gets up and walks away while on his phone – he has been trying to reach his son for an hour but has not spoken to him yet. He walks by the minister of foreign affairs, whose one ear is on the phone with the White House, the other covered with his hand. After that, he will call the Kremlin. The White House promises to find time in the president's schedule for a short phone conversation. The Kremlin wishes them strength. Both deny any involvement.

Meanwhile, everyone argues with everyone.

'Of course, Russia was behind this,' premier Rosca says. Her long brown hair is wrapped into two tight buns. 'How else did they enter the barracks? There are Russian infiltrators in our army, and they set off a bomb.'

Igor Yanev, sitting opposite her at the long table, shakes his head. 'Why would they? Russia drove us into a corner already. Besides, the Kremlin has no interest in damaging our industry. Gazprom has close ties to Karzarov Transport.'

'It was Karzarov himself,' Maika says with a raspy voice. 'That snake is trying to scare us away again.'

Minister Ivanov gets up and asks if anyone has proof for their accusations. 'This is a witch hunt!' he says and other ministers who have remained loyal to Karzarov applaud him.

'Silence!' Igor Yanev tries. 'This is not getting us any further.'

'Am I not allowed to accuse Karzarov?' Maika asks. 'The man who had my son killed? Of course *you* would defend him, Ivanov. It's a miracle you haven't been arrested yet for questioning.'

Two Lechkov sympathisers agree immediately.

In the only calm corner of the room, Leonid and Daniel look at the only computer screen in the bunker. Alec Medva, one of the data analysts they recently hired, is furiously attempting to find out what happened. In his glasses, news articles, photos and codes are reflected. And twenty minutes later, Daniel hits the table with a flat hand.

'We have information!'

Because only a few people respond, he walks to the table and yells that he knows who is behind the attacks. Nobody stops arguing or talking on the phone, and so he walks to the front of the room and gets up on the wooden table, between two ministers. He stands there in the middle of documents and ashtrays and raises his hands.

'Silence!'

Finally, the room goes quiet.

With all eyes on him, Daniel is at a loss for words for a moment. 'We know who is behind the attacks. The attack came from the east. We are being attacked by the Jada.'

Maika and Yanev look at each other, Minister Ivanov laughs with a raspy voice.

'Are you saying a couple of cheese farmers from the mountains broke into our biggest army base?' he says.

Daniel gets off the table and signals to Leonid and Alec. The big screen turns on and the room is shrouded in a white glow. A choppy low-resolution recording appears. A stately red brick building is visible in clouds of grit. The outer wall has a gaping hole. Daniel explains it's the base, less than a minute after the attack.

'We found these symbols,' he says and points at the screen. Something is written on the wall. A logo of some kind, four or five in a row, seemingly drawn with a spray can and a stencil. It looks like a stretched-out crown with three dots under it. 'And we found this same symbol after the two other attacks.'

On the screen appear photos of a high fence, and behind it, a mine lift shrouded in clouds of dust. All the 'Strictly No Entry' signs are covered with that same crown.

'How did you get these images?' Ivanov asks. 'Did this come from a satellite?'

The data analyst looks up from his laptop in surprise.

'People uploaded their own photos,' Daniel says without turning round. 'They call that the internet, Minister Ivanov.'

Before the old man can respond, Leonid starts a video recording of the Karzarov factory. A column of smoke rises up from the factory hall, like a giant pressing his black arm into the building. Alec pauses the screen, so everyone can see that that same symbol is drawn on the access road – hastily and crooked, but unmistakable.

'Daniel, we don't have time to look at photos of graffiti right now,' Maika says. 'We need to announce the state of siege as soon as possible.'

But Daniel stoically continues. 'We have copied the symbol you're seeing and entered it into Google reverse-image search. That is a way to scour the internet for places a certain shape or photo appears in. One of the places we see this image a lot is on Jada forums. Places where rebels come together and talk about the Man with a Thousand Faces.'

Alec makes a forum appear on the screen and translates the Jada dialect. 'Brothers and sisters from the Akhlos, the Man with a Thousand Faces has risen. The fall of Lechkov has begun.'

'The Man with a Thousand Faces?' someone asks. 'The statue?'

Ivanov laughs. 'Am I hearing this right? You found a page showing the Jada are unhappy with the current government? Congratulations! Quite a find!' Many of the attendees chuckle along.

Daniel stays quiet for a moment. Frustrated, he looks at the room filled with people who don't see what he sees. Then he asks Alec to show all the search results. All the places they found the symbol. The screen starts filling up like a virus spreading in front of their eyes. They see Facebook groups where Jada rebels discuss ways to plan attacks. Discord servers where weapon distribution points get shared. And many, many photos of the base, the mine and the factory, before the bombs exploded.

'The Man with a Thousand Faces was able to recruit the largest rebel army in the history of the Jada through the internet,' Daniel explains, 'because we – the Kazichian government – don't monitor digital traffic. Because the High House is blind in the digital world.'

He wants to show a photo of the rebels setting up a military camp in the mountains, when the screen suddenly turns white. He looks at Alec, who takes his hands off the computer like the laptop is burning hot.

'Someone is breaking in.'

'A cyber attack!' Daniel runs back to the computer. 'Everyone needs to disconnect from our network. Now!'

The members of the crisis team get out their smartphones, but the devices do not respond to input anymore.

'Turn everything off!' Daniel yells at Alec.

All landlines in the situation room start ringing at the same time. Calls from parliament, the ministries and the OMRA. Everything is down. Industries. Infrastructure. All networks are under attack.

Daniel sinks into his chair. 'They've been inside for weeks. They waited for this moment.'

Igor Yanev comes and stands next to him. The head of the security service is white as a sheet. 'We are not prepared for this,' he whispers.

Daniel rubs his face. 'We need to make drastic changes. As fast as we can. I will need complete access to the security service. I mean total access to everything.'

Yanev nods. 'Tell me what you need, and you'll get it.'

Alec gets up and interrupts the conversation. He says that a video file appeared on the network. A file that was sent to all devices.

The members of the crisis team go quiet. On the large screen and all the phones laid out on the table, the black logo of the Man with a Thousand Faces appears: the crown with three circles under it.

'It's a play button,' Alec says.

Leonid hesitates. 'Should w-we click it? It might be a trap.'

'They have access already,' Daniel says. 'Just press play.'

An empty chair against a grey wall appears. The room is dark and there is a faint noise of humming or breathing. For a few seconds nothing happens, but from one frame to the next someone appears in the chair. The figure wears a black turtleneck and a balaclava with two holes for eyes. The harsh lighting makes even their eyes covered in darkness.

'We are the border guards of the Akhlos,' the figure says.

From the movements of the mask, you can tell that the mouth is moving, but the voice has been distorted. It sounds like different kinds of voices are taking turns in speaking – every word has been cut from a different sound clip, like a cut-and-paste ransom note.

'We refuse to be the goat that House Lechkov sacrifices to the gods of greed, so they can suck the mountains dry and fill their fat stomachs. Every day they want more. Because it is never enough. And it will never be enough. The Mardoe Khador is an ensconced parasite, biting down on the Chair of God so hard that no one dares to pull it out. No one, except for us. We are the Jada. We are the true men with thousands of faces – the army chasing the oppressor away. We will descend from the Akhlos to the valley, to puncture the bloated tick that is the High House. The Chair of God will be painted red, and the world will see the truth come streaming down like a waterfall of blood.'

The figure in the balaclava is silent for a moment, looking into the camera unmoved. Dust particles float through the air, reflecting the white light.

'Corrupt leaders of the High House, remember this promise: the Jada will come and get you. Today was only the beginning.'

The screen turns white again, and the crisis team stares at the emptiness in silence.

'Did the Jada just declare war on us?' Maika asks quietly.

Igor Yanev turns to one of his assistants and says he wants to contact Nairi. He wants to know what their demands are.

'We don't know if this is Nairi,' Premier Rosca says. 'Even for her this is extreme. And the face looked masculine.'

'No,' Daniel says, 'We are not contacting the Jada. I need to prepare a counterattack. Until then, no one acts. You wait for my orders. I am in control.'

Before anyone can object, he gets up and gestures at Leonid and Alec that it is time to go. On his way out he runs into Radko, who stares at the white screen of his phone.

'Did I miss anything? I was on the phone with my son, but my phone stopped working.'

42

In a few hours, Daniel has managed to set up a Jada war room in the security service building, where he coordinates the counter-offensive. The room is on the same floor as the new digital division so that he and Leonid can lead both teams at the same time.

Leonid has started setting up new networks. The hacked government networks are a lost cause, so he is having the entire digital infrastructure rebuilt. Thousands of gigabytes of data have been destroyed, but they will have to accept that loss. They are starting over, using the best security system there is. And he is ordering hundreds of new phones and laptops so all the government officials, members of the High House and leaders of the most important industries can get back to work as soon as possible.

Radko immediately increases security around all government buildings, while Daniel places an overnight order for an AI camera system from overseas. The cameras are installed by the Circle in the entire inner city and linked to the OMRA servers. Radko also mobilises the riot police and places them under military rule. At the roundabout in front of the parliament building a group of Jada is protesting, and while there are fewer than a hundred people, holding two or three banners, he is worried. There have never been public Jada or Neza protests – especially in the capital. Thus, the riot police are ready to intervene. To Radko's frustration, Daniel has ordered him to wait.

The Kazichian people are getting ever more restless. People are locking themselves up in their houses and trying to obtain weapons. Daniel lets the Kazichian news broadcaster know that he has a plan to get the situation under control and asks the people to remain calm. His mother and Radko strongly encourage him to declare elections so he can be sworn in with a grand show of force. But Daniel asks them for a few more weeks of respite.

'First, I show the country what I do with terrorists.'

Meanwhile, Igor Yanev has instructed the OMRA to find out how the rebels gained access to the best-secured locations in the country. They don't find the answer but do find out that someone stole a load of RDX from the military depot. The bombs were most likely made with this.

'So not only did they invade the base, but also the armoury,' Radko concludes ashamedly. 'The most secured building, on the most secured terrain.'

'D-do we know more about the method of the Man with a Thousand Faces?' Leonid asks.

Yanev reluctantly tells him they don't have a clue. 'Our theory is he might be getting help from outside. The only question is from whom. Maybe America? And that isn't the only problem. A lot of explosives got stolen. More than has been set off yet.'

'How much more?' Daniel asks.

'Enough for two more big bombs,' Yanev says, opening a case of cigars. 'Or one giant one.'

Nobody says anything, but the ticking of the clock on the wall seems to be getting louder and louder.

43

In Manhattan, cars and pedestrians swarm the streets. People hurry to work with full coffee cups and empty stares. Taxi drivers stick their hands out to announce they are switching lanes, whether there is room for them or not. Lifts shoot up and subways glide under the river to dispose of as much chaos as possible. The New York Stock Exchange blinks red and green, as if they can map all changes, and on the giant screens around Times Square breaking news broadcasts from CNN and Fox yell for attention, as if they can always keep a finger on the pulse.

On the eastern part of the island, along the banks of the East River, lies the headquarters of the UN. The members' flags all wave at the same height – Kazichia's flag, too. New York has never paid any attention to that country. Most Americans are probably unaware it exists. But then, three bombs go off in one day and fear arises in the Caucasus.

Jada and Neza refugees have been trying to come to Russia or Georgia for years, or cross the Black Sea to Turkey, but there have never been as many refugees at the same time as after the attacks. And never before were there Kazichians amongst them. The surrounding countries ask the UN for help; they fear chaos. Not just governments, but NGOs express their worries, too. Doctors Without Borders warns of a shortage in provisions along the Russian border. The Red Cross has started building refugee camps in Abkhazia and Georgia. And powerful companies from the region are sounding the alarm. The cyber attack not only shut down the government, but also part of the industry. Even

Karzarov Transport, the biggest transport company from Eastern Europe, was shut down for a few hours. How is that possible? And who is next?

From one day to the next, New York is talking about Kazichia. The stock exchange colours red for a few minutes, CNN and Fox News feature Stolia, and the UN calls a Security Council meeting to assess the situation.

The Kazichian ambassador Alin Pipia paces through the UN building sweating. The Mardoe Khador wants absolutely nobody spying on them and Pipia needs to prevent the Security Council from sending inspectors, or maybe even troops. Spread throughout the country are dozens, maybe hundreds, of work camps filled with Jada and Neza prisoners that absolutely don't meet the international legal norms. The OMRA's policy probably can't count on the world's approval either.

The only problem is that Kazichia is not a member of the Security Council, and therefore doesn't have the right to veto. That is why envoy Pipia scheduled an informal meeting with the United States and Russia, in the small cafeteria on the second floor. The two powerhouses are members, and he needs to convince them to vote against all types of intervention. That kind of pre-conciliation is normal course of business in the UN building. Everywhere, countries are deliberating in preparation of official meetings. The diplomats meet in the building because it is international territory; that decreases the possibility they will be recorded or overheard.

Together with his team, Pipia determined a strategy the night before the talk with America and Russia. Everything seemed under control, until he received a confusing message from the High House:

Show M and B that we are afraid of A.

M and B stands for MacKay and Bogrov, the American and Russian UN envoys he is meeting. 'A' stands for *Asch-Iljada-Lica*. In other words, Pipia needs to show his colleagues he is afraid of a Jada terrorist. Why does the High House want people to fear the Man with a Thousand Faces? And why did they give so little context? If he is unsure of what the Lechkov family is trying to do, there is a greater chance he will make an unintentional mistake.

While Pipia gets out of the lift and walks to the cafeteria, he wonders why he didn't accept the job offer from the NGO two weeks ago. The salary is good, the job dull; it sounds perfect. When he enters the small cafeteria, he sees Judy MacKay waiting for him. She is thirty minutes early. Pipia waves at her while passing empty tables, but she stares straight at him without moving a muscle. MacKay always looks angry. Her face hangs like a Bernese Mountain Dog's, with eyes almost disappearing under skin folds and a mouth pulled down by her cheeks. Pipia finds her an intimidating woman, and not just her looks. She speaks eight languages, including fluent Russian and Mandarin, and is known for walking off during important meetings if she is unhappy with the way things go. Not many members could get away with that, but nobody dares to contradict MacKay.

He has barely taken a seat when MacKay asks if he invited a third party. What she means is if he asked France to join the meeting. The French are often invited to unofficial meetings as a neutral party, but the US didn't do that this time because they think the consultation is too sensitive. Pipia didn't invite the French either, to show her that Kazichia agrees.

The American nods and asks if Kazichia knows who the Man with a Thousand Faces is. 'Your government knows something. You have a theory, at least.'

Pipia shakes his head. 'It's a mystery.'

MacKay doesn't believe him and insists. She says America would be very grateful for that information. It could yield the Kazichian government a lot.

Yes, a lot of misery, Pipia thinks. The CIA wants to know who the Man with a Thousand Faces is, so they can overthrow the High House with him.

'Is the threat legitimate?' MacKay asks. 'Is the Man with a Thousand Faces as dangerous as the press has us believe?'

Pipia remembers the message of the High House. 'Presidential candidate Lechkov doesn't know where to start,' he says. 'The

High House doesn't understand who it is or how he planned the attacks.'

'Interesting,' MacKay mutters.

At that moment, Bogrov walks in. The first time Pipia met the short Russian diplomat, he thought Bogrov was absent or distracted. But since he knows that the Russian is a chess master, he sees his glassy eyes in a different light. This man is not a dreamer, he plays several different boards at the same time.

The Russian gives MacKay a curt nod and shakes Pipia's hand. He sits down and says he is receiving disturbing messages; the High House seems to fear the Man with a Thousand Faces.

Pipia confirms it.

Bogrov nods again and turns to MacKay. The Russian and the American ask about each other's children and partners, as if the Kazichian is not even there. After a dance of pleasantries, they carefully start a conversation, both giving as little information as possible. They ask each other if their intelligence services are active in Kazichia – as if they aren't both aware of the answers.

'Barely,' MacKay says.

'Neither are we,' the Russian says.

It gets quiet for a moment. MacKay stirs her coffee, the spoon hitting the bottom of the cup like a metronome. Then MacKay asks if Russia thinks the UN should get involved.

'We need to be careful with that,' the Russian says.

'Maybe you're right,' the American says.

Again, it gets quiet.

'And what do you think about inspectors?' Bogrov asks.

'They usually can't do much,' MacKay says.

The two diplomats nod.

MacKay says she thinks the threat isn't imminent, and the chance of instability in the region is slim. The Russian agrees with her. It is unnecessary to send troops.

Pipia knows they are lying. And now he understands why he was told to glorify the rebel leader. If the CIA sees a chance to gain a foothold in the Akhlos, they want as few active parties in the region as possible. So, the fact that the Man with a Thousand Faces seems influential is reason enough to keep the United

Nations out. Russia doesn't want any interference because they infiltrated the Lechkov regime. But now that Bogrov knows that Daniel Lechkov fears the Man with a Thousand Faces, the UN definitely needs to stay out. He wants to give the High House space to wipe out the rebel army quickly and effectively – without treaties or human rights making things difficult.

And so, the result of an hour of careful questions and evasive answers is simple: both countries will advise the council to respect the sovereignty of Kazichia and not pursue further action. The next day the council will convene for a pointless meeting and a pointless vote.

MacKay lets go of the spoon and leaves without having taken a sip. The coffee spins in the cup. She says she is happy with the outcome of the consultation, even manages a smile. Pipia wants to get up too, but the Russian asks him to stay seated.

'Tell me, comrade Pipia,' Bogrov says when his American opponent is gone. 'Who is the Man with a Thousand Faces? You should know, the OMRA always does its homework. Tell me his name, and we will help you get rid of him. We send a drone and it's done.'

'I would love to tell my Russian friends, but we have no idea,' Pipia says.

'Director Yanev must have a theory? How could a Jada manage to do all this? That giant cyber attack?'

'We have no idea, truly,' Pipia repeats. 'But one thing is certain: my country has never seen a danger as great as this man.'

Bogrov nods and stares at his empty cup. His glassy look starts to focus, and Pipia realises that from then on, the Russian is only playing one chess game – against a rebel leader with no name.

44

It is early in the morning when Daniel gets up from his desk to stretch. He is at the OMRA headquarters, in a high-security part of the digital division he built with Leonid. The top members of his new team whom he recruited from all over Eastern Europe with irresistible salaries are sitting around him – they stayed up all night, too.

Daniel controls his workstation from a special terminal. His screen mirrors from all angles, except when you sit right in front of it – even someone standing next to him and looking over his shoulder only sees his own reflection. The computer itself is in the basement of the building, in a fireproof room, behind a vault door with a biometric lock. When someone tries to force the vault door or when Daniel does not log in for a week, the operating system automatically formats its own hard drive, and all data gets erased. And the encryption on the hard drive is so advanced it would take a quantum revolution to crack it.

The advantage of Daniel's way of working is that his next move always remains a secret. No one oversees the whole plan, except for him. The disadvantage is that he needs to do all the preparation himself. Only when it is time to execute part of his plan can he use the manpower that is available to him as de facto president. Until then he is on his own. No wonder his eyes are bloodshot. Next to the keyboard is a cup of cold coffee; the caffeine has lost its effect. But his fingers hit the keys undisturbed.

The door opens and Leonid steps in. It is obvious the short spy did get sleep and showered, but still, he looks exhausted, too. He reports to Daniel on the new digital infrastructure.

'Everything is o-online. We can start monitoring.'

'Thank you, dear friend. That means we are ahead of schedule.'

The main advantage of the cyber attack is that the security service got to build new networks for the government and industry, networks that they have full access to. Nobody second guessed what the OMRA was up to because they were all shocked by the attack and trusted Daniel to protect them. And now, the security service is also becoming an extremely sophisticated intelligence service. The OMRA can see everything that every civil servant, minister, employee or CEO does.

Leonid places a laptop on the desk and shows the status of their work. Daniel turns his chair to the computer and points at a shaded chain of code. 'That's where the Russians are coming in.'

Leonid nods.

The High House knew that the Kremlin had been tapping phone conversations, emails, and other communication in Kazichia – Russia could see exactly what the Kazichian government was doing. They were so far ahead in technological progress that they could get away with it. But their lead also made them act carelessly. Because now that Russia needs to break in to all the new networks, they are pulling out the big guns, without covering their tracks, exactly as Daniel had predicted. That has been the second advantage of the cyber attack; they are now not only aware of what is happening in the country but also of who is trying to invade.

'They don't expect us to be watching,' he says, 'and thus they're showing their true colours. Great job, Leonid. We are getting back control over our own country.'

Leonid coughs. Something seems to be bothering him. Daniel asks what is up.

'Speaking of t-true c-colours,' the spy says quietly. 'W-we need to discuss something else. Your wife.'

Daniel turns his chair. 'What do you mean? Did you hear anything?'

Leonid nods.

The two have been having discussions about Michelle for weeks. Daniel let slip that Michelle was behaving irrationally and impatiently, and Leonid proposed to place a listening device in the presidential wing of the High House. Only audio, he promised, no video, just for Daniel to keep his finger on the pulse. Daniel wouldn't hear of it. He saw no reason to spy on his own family. Even when Leonid insisted – he proposed using software that only started recording when certain trigger words were uttered – Daniel wouldn't budge; he stopped the conversation then and there.

But that changed when he was on his way to the clinic with Michelle in the helicopter. There, she told him Harper had an escape plan. She wanted to run. He couldn't imagine Michelle was serious, that she would be that careless. Didn't he know her? She would never kidnap their baby girl and put her in danger. Leonid said he couldn't be sure. 'You never know how someone acts under extreme p-pressure.' And so, Daniel permitted him to hack the microphone of Alexa's smart TV remote and place a camera in Harper's apartment.

After that, they never discussed it and Daniel acted like the devices hadn't been installed. But that morning, Leonid checked his software and saw that a conversation had been recorded in the presidential wing. Someone had said something that triggered the recording device. Leonid read the automatic transcript and could only draw one conclusion.

'They w-want to run.'

Daniel stares off into the distance. For seconds, a heavy silence hangs in the room, interrupted only by the soft buzzing of the servers, and the typing of their team. Then he seems to wake up. 'I don't believe it.'

'I'm very sorry, friend. There is no doubt about it.'

'I want to hear the recording.'

He opens the audio file and moves his head closer to the laptop speakers, to hear what the women are saying. He hears Harper, but her voice sounds hollow and far away. 'We need to turn off our phones,' she says. 'We need to be careful.' Then there comes Michelle. The first part of her sentence is hard to understand; the two women are probably far from the remote with the microphone. But then she moves closer. Suddenly her voice is crystal clear.

'We need to leave the country. We can't wait for Daniel any-more; the fighting has started. What's your plan?' Bewildered, Daniel stares at the laptop. Then he whispers as if his wife is not kilometres away from him: 'Michelle, what are you doing? Have you lost your mind?'

VII. Shadow Agreement

45

On the day of the attacks, right after the dating ultrasound at the private clinic, Michelle stood opposite Harper in the living room of the presidential wing. She agreed with her American sister-in-law. 'We need to leave the country. We can't wait for Daniel anymore; the fighting has started. What's your plan?'

But Harper wouldn't give her any details. It was better if Michelle knew as little as possible for as long as possible, she said. She promised they could leave within a few days. But first, she needed to pick something up, and for their safety, it was better not to see each other until then.

Michelle agreed. What else could she do? But the waiting was tough on her. It took three long days before Harper finally made it to her door.

'I did it, we can go.'

Michelle starts packing two small backpacks. She only takes her and Alexa's passport, some clothes and Alexa's stuffed dog.

'What's your plan?'

'It's not my plan,' Harper says, 'but Vigo's.' She brought out an old-fashioned phone and a laptop. 'Vigo called this computer our life insurance. Nobody alive knows it exists, except for you and me.'

'Hasn't that thing been hacked, like all the other phones and computers?'

Harper shakes her head. 'There is no network card or Bluetooth receiver in it.'

She says the computer and phone were hidden at a friend of Vigo's in Stolia.

'There's a phone number stored on the computer. By calling, we launch the operation. No one will pick up the call, but two hours later, someone will be waiting for us at a secret meeting place. Someone from MIT, the Turkish intelligence agency.'

'And then?'

Harper says MIT will take them across the Black Sea to the Turkish coast. From there, they will be taken to Ankara by helicopter. In the capital, Michelle can call the Dutch embassy, and Harper the American.

'Good news, right?' she says. 'Our governments need to protect and repatriate us. And until we make it to the embassies, the Turkish government will protect us.'

Michelle looks through the high window. Dusk has arrived early. Now that she hears what the plan is, she starts feeling afraid. 'How do we know it's safe for Alexa to cross the sea? And for me? I'm pregnant, and it's freezing out.'

'It's safe because we have this assurance,' Harper says and holds up a USB stick. 'I have no idea what is on it, and I don't want to know, but the Turks want to have it.'

Michelle asks why she doesn't want to know what is on the USB stick.

'What if it's a arms deal or something else that could cause suffering? Maybe I will start having doubts when I see what it is. I don't want that. I want to go home. But feel free to read the documents if that makes you more comfortable.'

Michelle takes the laptop, sticks the USB stick into the port, and opens the file. She sees a PDF of hundreds of pages. They look like transcripts of conversations. Most of it she can't read because it is in Russian or Kazichian, but then she finds a few passages in English. She reads a conversation between a Russian and a Kazichian – probably two diplomats or other important civil servants – discussing trade with Turkey. This is price fixing. No, it's something more systematic: secret trade agreements. Michelle concludes that Moscow is making deals with all the former Soviet states to push prices of imported Turkish goods down in the entire region. In this specific conversation, they are discussing the import of Turkish pharmaceutical products.

She keeps scrolling and realises every transcript is another conversation the Turkish government is not supposed to know about. Every conversation is another part of a giant shadow agreement.

'No,' Michelle says. 'This is too risky, Harper. This is too big. This could cause a conflict between Russia and Turkey.'

When she looks up, she sees her sister-in-law talking on the old phone.

'What are you doing?'

'I already gave them the signal.'

'Couldn't you have discussed that with me?'

Harper takes the USB out of the laptop and shuts it. 'We've been talking for weeks. It's now or never. I'm going home and you can come.'

Michelle looks at Alexa, who is whispering to herself while playing with a doll.

Two hours later, a red Porsche Cayenne drives down the Chair of God. Harper is behind the wheel and Michelle lies next to her daughter, hidden under a moving blanket. She feels the car brake and puts her finger on Alexa's lips. The girl looks at her mother with big eyes. They are at the gate at the foot of the hill, and Michelle can hear her friend talking to the soldiers. For the first time in her life, she feels the urge to ask a higher power for help. Not because she wants to surrender, but just to do something. To have some sense of control. 'Please,' she whispers with her nose to Alexa's head. 'Protect us.'

There is laughter and the squeaky gate opens. Slowly the car starts moving again.

'We're free!' Harper says a minute later, and she hits the wheel. 'We did it.'

Michelle throws the blanket off and lifts Alexa onto her lap.

'What are we doing?' the girl asks for the umpteenth time.

'We're going on a trip,' Michelle says. She doesn't dare promise they are going home anymore.

They drive out of Stolia and enter a modern suburb. Harper stops at an industrial site and points across the street. 'That's where the meeting is. In that mall.'

'What will we do if someone follows us?' Michelle asks, checking in the mirrors if someone is there.

'Then they will see us shopping.'

Alexa diligently puts her own little backpack on and walks with her mother. Michelle can hardly look at her. She feels too guilty.

As they enter the deserted mall, Harper says they have to find a carpet shop on the third floor. They take the escalator and quickly see a fluorescent-lit space with Persian carpets on the walls. Behind the till sits an old Turkish man with a newspaper.

Harper hesitantly walks towards him. 'I'm here for the meeting,' she says quietly.

The man mumbles something and points to the back.

They walk to a door with a Kazichian warning. Harper knocks twice and waits. After a few seconds, the door opens and a woman with emerald-green eyes and pitch-black hair appears. She is wearing so much foundation, red lipstick, and eyeshadow, that it makes her face look like a mask.

'I need to ask for the code word,' Harper says quietly to the woman. Michelle sees red stress marks on her neck.

'Atlantis,' the woman answers and she gestures for them to come in quickly.

Behind the forbidden door is the storage room. It smells strongly of chemicals and Michelle holds the collar of her jacket in front of her mouth and nose to focus on the conversation. The woman asks for the USB stick. Harper explains it contains two documents. For the first part, the password is 'Atlantis'; the password for the second part she will give when they get to Ankara. The woman puts the USB stick in the inner pocket of her suede jacket.

'It takes about an hour to prepare for the boat ride to Rize. Hopefully, during that time we can get a helicopter to come to the coast, otherwise, we will have to drive all the way to Ankara.

We hadn't counted on a child. It will be a long, uncomfortable journey.'

'And you'll make sure we get to the embassies?' Michelle asks. She has folded her collar back to speak clearly. The woman looks at her and is startled. 'Madam Lechkova? What are you doing here?'

Michelle is surprised the spy knows who she is. 'It's not my government,' she stammers. 'I just want to go home.'

'This deal was for you,' the woman says to Harper, 'and in some situations for your husband, Vigo Lechkov. But only if he wouldn't have control over the High House anymore. I don't want to cause a conflict between my government and yours.'

'They've only been in the country for a few weeks,' Harper says. 'They have nothing to do with the Mardoe Khador. They don't even speak the language.'

The Turkish woman brings out the USB stick again. 'No,' she says. 'I'm sorry, it's one passenger or none. I'm only willing to take you, that is a great risk already.'

Michelle takes a step toward the Turkish spy. 'Please, I need to get my child out of here. Away from the attacks. There are things on that USB your government wants to know about. Price agreements for the import of . . .'

'No.' The woman holds her hands up in the air. 'Please, Madam Lechkova. You are pushing me into a life-threatening corner. Do you even know who you are? Do you know what will happen when someone in your position trades secrets with someone like me? You are the wife of the incoming president. And that is his child. In this storage room wars could break out.'

The Turkish woman walks back into the store. The squeaky door closer shuts the door and the three of them are standing in the tiny closet.

'Are we going now?' Alexa asks. 'Mummy, are we going on a trip now?'

Michelle looks at her daughter, who is pulling on the straps of her little backpack – ready to leave on a trip, as her mother explained – and gets angry. She opens the door and calls for the

Turkish agent. The woman pretends she doesn't hear her and walks faster.

'You are taking me!' Michelle yells across the store. 'Or I tell my husband about the deal that almost took place here.'

The woman stops.

'I'm serious,' she says. 'You ensure we get to Ankara safely, or I tell the High House about you, and the documents you tried to steal from the Lechkov family.'

The spy takes them to the parking lot behind of the mall, where a Turkish man is waiting for them by an old Citroën. The woman gets inside the car with him and says to follow them in their own car; if someone stops them, they can say they are going shopping. They follow the Citroën out of the city and reach a narrow, badly maintained coastal road. Michelle looks out of the window and thinks of Vigo's accident. Is this the road where he got murdered? The road where it all started? Or ended.

After half an hour, they stop at a small port and Michelle sees a few fishing boats and an abandoned sailing yacht. She smells sewer and salty water. At the end of a pier a black speedboat docks; the big, shiny outboard motors look like two white teeth in a row of rotten ones. The buzzing they produce is so loud that it echoes around the harbour.

'Not exactly a quiet escape,' she says to the Turkish woman as they walk onto the pier.

'We're playing with fire,' the woman says and looks at her reproachfully. 'The most important thing is we get out as soon as possible. And those boats are fast.'

Michelle sees how scared the woman is and starts feeling doubts again. Maybe she pushed too hard. She has been warned a few times that the risk is too great and maybe she is letting her flight instinct lead her too much. Maybe she should return to the capital to talk to Daniel, to try and find a solution together one last time, as they have always done. But before Michelle can say anything, Harper points behind her. She turns round and sees three SUVs quickly drive onto the deserted parking lot.

'Run!' the Turk yells. 'We've been ratted out!'

The spy throws her smartphone in the water and runs to the boats. Harper drops her suitcase and sprints after her. Michelle, who needs to pick up Alexa, wants to run after them, but the cars hit the gate and race onto the pier.

Michelle has nowhere to go.

With Alexa in her arms, edge. But before she has to jump into the ice-cold water, the cars come to a screeching halt. The wooden pier creaks under the weight. Armed men jump from the two cars in the back and sprint towards her. She yells that she is unarmed, but the men pass her by and run down the pier. When she turns round, she sees the Turkish woman jump onto one of the boats. The pilot takes off at full speed and with a roar and waves of white foam, the boat leaves the pier, heading to the harbour mouth. Harper, who was right behind the Turk, jumps too, but misses the boat by a hair and falls into the cold water. Michelle sees her friend disappear in the foam.

And then she hears her name. The door of the first car opens, and Daniel gets out.

'Michelle, stop! Stay away from that boat!' He takes a few big steps towards her and grabs her arm. 'What the hell are you doing? Are you trying to kill us all?'

'I need to protect my babies,' she hears herself say. Then the tears come and drown out the rest of her defence. She feels so many emotions that she can't communicate anything except for confused desperation.

Daniel pulls her to the car. She says that he is hurting her, but he ignores her.

'Talking to Turkey? Have you lost your mind? Do you under-stand how irresponsible that is? You might have caused a giant diplomatic crisis, or worse.'

The words slowly get through to her. Daniel knows about the plan. He knows they were talking to Turkey. But how? Who told him that?

He opens the car door and gestures to the back seat. 'What did you think would happen in Ankara? What did you think the Netherlands would do? That they would yell "shame!" at the Kremlin and everything would be all right? You would have got stuck there too, just like here. But over there I wouldn't be able to protect you.'

Suddenly the truth hits her. 'You listened in on me,' she whispers.

'And for good reason,' he admits immediately. 'If I hadn't done that, you would be on the run without protection. And I would have Erdoğan coming for me. As if I don't have enough enemies already.'

But our phones were off, she thinks. *Where did he hide the microphones? And when? While I was sleeping?*

A shot is fired.

She turns round and sees the Citroën drive off. The Turkish accomplice is trying to escape but two of the soldiers are in the car park. They shoot and puncture the tyres. The small car zigzags and comes to a halt against a concrete wall.

'Make them stop,' she says, pulling Alexa, who also started crying out of sheer confusion, closer to her.

But Daniel doesn't do anything. He stands next to the car and looks at the spy getting pulled from the Citroën. One of the soldiers holds the Turk and the other punches his stomach twice, hard. Shocked by the violence, Michelle covers Alexa's eyes.

'Daniel, say something!'

'You don't leave me any other choice,' he says. 'I can't let these people go anymore. That would be too dangerous, for all of us. For you too.'

With a thundering roar, a helicopter flies low over the harbour. A soldier with a rifle hangs halfway out and one of the soldiers on the ground points towards the speedboat on the horizon, after which the helicopter flies on.

The Turkish woman will get arrested too, Michelle thinks, *and it's all my fault*. She hears someone splutter and sees the soldiers have fished Harper out of the water. They walk with the dripping-wet American between them and pass the car with Michelle and Daniel.

Michelle is reminded of the night of Nia's arrest. Harper looks up at her with a black eye and a burst lip, her eyes filled with fear.

'Let her go,' she says. 'Daniel? What are you doing? Let Harper go.'

'How could I let her go? She committed treason. She provoked conflict with another country and put everything on the line. Do you think I want to do this?'

'That's your brother's wife. She is family.'

Daniel sits next to her in the car but doesn't say anything.

'Daniel! What are you doing to her?'

'I don't have a choice. You're forcing me to do this.'

She looks at Daniel, but it is like he is sitting behind a milky glass wall. All she can see are the contours of a man.

46

During their first holiday together, Michelle and Daniel drove across Italy for two weeks. The trip consisted of private drivers, private flights, private dinners in top restaurants, and even a private island off the Italian coast. They celebrated life, and obscenely so. But Michelle got to know Daniel more intimately on that trip, too. The conflicting puzzle pieces of his life – being a scientist in Europe and a billionaire's son from Kazichia – started to fit together more and more. She saw sides of him she didn't know how to relate to. Especially the way he spoke of his birth country; he was more opinionated than she'd thought.

Their trip ended in Florence. There, he started telling her about one of the important men in his life: Grandpa Petar. They were sitting on the balcony of their suite overlooking the Duomo, waiting for their guide. Michelle asked about Petar's story and the origin of Kazichia. Daniel was holding his coffee cup, facing the sunny city, and talked about the way Petar's mother, his great-grandmother, got kidnapped during the Great Terror.

Petar was nine years old when his mother, a simple farmer's wife, kissed him on his forehead, crossed the fields to the market, and never returned. There was no official report on why she got arrested. What became clear over time was that she tried to sell a basket of early-ripened citrus fruits. When she walked over to a group of soldiers with her merchandise, she got punched and pushed to the floor. Two soldiers dragged her through the mud and took her. Later that day, Petar and his father found the basket his mother had woven between the market stalls. No one in the village dared to tell them what happened. No one dared speak to the little boy looking for his mother.

Petar's father was ostracised from the kolkhoz because his wife was said to be ideologically corrupt, and he got depressed. Little Petar tried his best to run the farm, but without his father's help, that was impossible. Moreover, the threat of a looming arrest hung over the little house like a circling vulture.

After two years of struggling, Petar found his father's body hanging from the citrus tree that grew early-ripened fruits every year.

'Just imagine your life starting that way,' Daniel said, facing the Italian square. 'That little boy was ostracised from his village, left behind by his parents, without a cent to his name. The world portrays him as some megalomaniac or a money-grubber, but as a young boy, my grandpa saw what the world can do to the people you love. He saw that anyone can end up in the mud, or hanging from a fruit tree, however good or bad you are. And so, he started to work his way up. He wanted to rise above men like Stalin so he could protect his own family and loved ones from all those maniacs.'

He tried to hide his emotions, but Michelle could tell that he was close to tears.

'What a beautiful way to look at it,' she said.

He drank his last sip of coffee and shook his head. 'It's the only way to look at it. Because that's how it happened.'

She asked about the labour camps where torture was said to take place. Where even children were put to work. Michelle said she found it wry to see that Petar had turned into the oppressor. He seemed more like an abused person turning to abuse than a protector.

'You don't get it,' Daniel snapped. 'Those are prisons. In America, prisoners work too, right? People like your father look at Kazichia, and all they see is corruption. But that country was born from the love of a nine-year-old boy for his father and mother. Petar knew he would never leave his own children by that basket in the mud. Whatever it took, he wasn't going to let that happen. He was going to protect them. And guess what? If you fight out

225

of love, you can make anything happen. You can shape the world map to your heart's desire.'

Power and love are connected for Daniel and Petar, she thought. You protect love by becoming more powerful than your enemies. But the price Petar Lechkov had been willing to pay for his power was high. Higher than she found morally acceptable. And she was not sure if Daniel agreed with her.

After their trip to Italy, Michelle read a biography of Petar Lechkov by American journalist Anderson Holt. The author wrote about inhumane conditions in the Kazichian labour camps and the horrific ways in which the OMRA suppressed every form of rebellion. It was nothing short of a totalitarian regime that violated human rights in every possible way, the book said. Most of the discoveries the author had made didn't surprise Michelle, but still, seeing them all in one place was confronting.

And then the last chapter. The story she had never heard before. The story she had never wanted to hear. Holt wrote about an island in the Central Lakes that was not in the atlas: you couldn't even find it on Google Maps. It was a secret island on which the Lechkov family had built a holiday home. Petar went there for a week every year during Christmas to go ice fishing. The only days in the year he took off. According to Holt, a dark secret was hidden under that ice. According to him, there used to be a fourth group of oligarchs in Kazichia, the Tsaada family. Melano Tsaada was the head of Samto Minarit, a mining company similar to Lechkov Industria that was mostly active near the Russian border. The rumour was that Melano had proposed to Petar that they merge their companies. When Petar refused, the Tsaadas kept growing their imperium, sometimes at the expense of Petar's possibilities for expansion. The two families got into a conflict and the High House was distressed; for the first time, Petar Lechkov's authority was being questioned.

In December 1997, the entire Tsaada clan was invited to the yearly Christmas celebration on Lechkov Island. Grandfathers, grandmothers, fathers, mothers, children, and grandchildren, even the two dogs were invited. It seemed like a peace offering from Petar to keep the region stable, but since that holiday, no one has ever heard from the fourth family again. Their family crest disappeared from the High House, Samto was taken over by Lechkov Industria, and when someone mentioned the name 'Tsaada' to Petar's face, they got fired immediately – or worse. What happened exactly, Holt couldn't prove. But he had seen the giant, frozen waters surrounding the island: the perfect place to bury a bloodline. And he had found a private security guard who worked on the Lechkov island.

I can't name my source, but according to eyewitness reports, women, children and young dogs are at the bottom of that lake. An entire family was slaughtered and tucked away under the ice. Why? Because Petar Lechkov always wants more. More power, more influence, more money. The year after the disappearance, the Karzarov family and the Yanev family built their own vacation homes on their own islands. From then on, they were probably too afraid to celebrate Christmas on Lechkov Island. Even they fear Petar, a man who sacrifices children to keep his crown.

47

'*Il treva var*,' Daniel says.

The driver nods and starts the engine. They leave the port, but the car with Harper in it doesn't follow them. Michelle stopped asking what would happen to her. She is not getting an answer, anyway.

The rest of the drive is quiet. She thinks about the morning they drove to Schiphol a few weeks earlier; their last moments in the Netherlands, not knowing what was coming. It was quiet then too, as if they could all feel they were heading for chaos. As if the future was written on the flags waving by the airplane hangar – in the rising storm. *At which point should I have said stop?* she thinks as they enter the capital city again. *At which moment should I have walked away to remain a good person? After our first kiss? Or when we heard that Vigo was dead?*

Whatever that moment was, it has passed now. The damage has been done.

She thinks about Harper. She is scared for her. And that means she is scared of her own husband – her Daniel. She is scared of him because she doesn't understand him anymore. Or maybe she never did. She is scared for Alexa, too. Michelle wants to be alone with her daughter so she can explain what happened. Or rather, lie to reassure her. It feels like she has to catch up on hundreds of hours of motherly tasks, and every day, hundreds more get added. No, not just motherly tasks; the girl needs both her parents.

*

Even when the Lechkov family enters the presidential wing again, still nobody speaks. Their shoes tap the wooden floor, the door squeaks while Daniel opens it for his wife, and Michelle's breathing sounds mechanical and unnaturally loud.

She closes the door and asks Daniel what will happen.

'Not now,' he whispers in English. 'First, we need to calm down our girl, then we can talk.'

He sits on his knees and rests his hand on Alexa's little shoulder. Michelle stands with them while Daniel lies about the violence at the fishing port. Standing in that exact position – Daniel on his knees, Alexa with her arms along her body and her backpack still on, and Michelle hanging over them with the suitcase next to her – they talk for almost thirty minutes until the worst anxiety leaves the child's face. All that time, the girl is quiet. Daniel picks her up and stands up. His knees crack. The three of them walk over to the couch, and together they answer the muddled questions that finally come. Daniel turns his phone off, and when someone knocks on the door, he yells something in Kazichian to chase them away. The only thing he focuses on is showing his daughter she can still trust her parents. When Michelle looks at him, she sees Alexa's father again. Her husband, so empathetic and patient, who always takes time to comfort his wife and child when needed. She recognises him. But when he puts his hand on her back, she shudders. It was an illusion. This man is not Daniel. Not anymore, at least.

That night, it takes hours to get Alexa to fall asleep. Michelle and Daniel take turns sitting by her, explaining everything that happened again and again. At ten-thirty, she finally falls asleep. Michelle stands by the bed and looks at the sleeping girl. Finally, she looks like a kid, worried about a fight on the playground or scraped knees after a fall. But that is an illusion, too. She is not that kid anymore.

As Michelle sneaks back to the living room, she takes a few deep breaths to prepare for the talk. Daniel is waiting on the big Chesterfield, holding a glass of red wine. She knows that frown, those careful eyes, those fingers, searching for something at the foot of the glass. They look like the frown and the fingers of her lover.

'And now?' she asks and sits next to him. 'What happens now?'

'All I ask of you, all I have been asking of you since we got here, is to trust me. That's all. Trust me while I try and save our family. But today you showed me you not only distrust me, you're trying to sabotage me. You're trying to make it harder for me. Why?'

She sees he is emotional and for some reason that comforts her. 'Explain to me what you're doing,' she says. 'Make me a part of your plan.'

He takes a sip and puts the glass on the wooden side table.

'How can I trust you, Michelle? You are a danger to everything I am trying to do. You are a danger to yourself and your children. I can't tell you my plan anymore, because I don't know what you are capable of.'

His words are so hurtful that she needs to stop herself from smashing the wine bottle against the new TV. 'How can you trust *me*? I don't even know who you are anymore. What will happen to Harper? Will she disappear, just like Nia? Think about her American family! They will never know what happened to their daughter and sister. Isn't that unfair? She is an innocent woman just trying to get home. Like me. Let her go, Daniel. Give her a ticket to New York.'

He stands up and buttons his blazer. 'I don't understand how you could ask something like that. Do you think I *want* this? Arrest my own family? Harper can't go home, and neither can you. Together you've made it impossible.'

She gets up and wants to grab his arm, but he walks away.

'I don't know who you are,' he says. 'I don't know you anymore, this woman collaborating with Turkey. But I assume the fear got to you. I assume you will come to your senses as soon as we're safe. So, until then, you're staying here, in this wing. You and Alexa.'

She feels a knot in her stomach. 'What? Are you locking me up?'

Daniel opens the door. Two guards come in. He instructs them in Kazichian and sees how the guards look at each other; they feel awkward. The president is telling them to keep his own wife, an important member of the High House, captive.

'This is unnecessary.' She tries to sound calm. 'We'll stay in the High House, I swear. You don't need to lock me up. I'll listen to you, I'll lie low.'

He says he is sorry. There is no other way. He says it seems she is too scared to see he is doing all of this for her. For her and Alexa. But Michelle doesn't believe him. She doesn't believe him, and she can't believe this is happening. She grabs his arm and wants to pull him back to the couch. They need to keep talking, and everything will be all right. But he pulls away and closes the door.

VIII. ERIS

48

In the war room on the closed-off third floor of the OMRA head-quarters, Daniel is showing Radko and Yanev what he has been working on. They are in front of a big screen with a map of Kazichia. Across the map, red dots blink. Radko points to a cluster of dots and asks what they are. Daniel explains that it is a rebel camp belonging to the Jada, hidden in the forests. It has been there for years.

Yanev taps his unlit cigar against the screen. 'All these dots are rebels? How did you find them?'

In simple terms, Daniel explains that he copied and improved the reverse image search technology from Google. His algorithm searches on social media and forums for everyone using the symbol of the Man with a Thousand Faces, and those users get saved and indexed in a database – including the location of their computer or phone. 'We use the symbol of their leader, the logo of the Man with a Thousand Faces, as a Trojan horse.'

But that is just the beginning.

He says he added code to the Google technology to find rebels in the physical world too. He turned the logo of the Man with a Thousand Faces into a QR code: a physical hyperlink. Everyone who uses their mobile to take a photo of a protest sign with the symbol or takes a selfie while wearing the symbol on a T-shirt, clicks on Daniel's link. All those devices then show an automatic notification: a generic pop-up. But when someone clicks to close the pop-up, the intelligence service gains complete access to that device. Because most Jada or Neza use cheap Android phones and don't know how to secure their even cheaper computers, the database extracts not just their location but their name and social media activity, too.

'Everyone that gets close to the rebel symbol exposes themselves to us,' Daniel says. 'And they appear as a dot on this map.'

Yanev smiles. 'So, we know exactly who our opponents are and where they reside? We can even see them before they pick up their first weapon?'

Daniel nods. 'The programme just started, and profiles get added every day. The longer the uprising lasts, the better we can see which mining villages are about to rebel. Or which parts of the city are filled with rebels. The more popular the Man with a Thousand Faces gets, the more we know about our enemies.'

'Enough to beat them?' Radko asks.

Daniel looks at Yanev. 'If I get complete access to all government databases, we will find out much more about them. When we link these data to the database on the sixth floor, with all the citizen data, then we will know where all of these dots live and who they work for. We will know the names of their children, and where those children go to school. We will know everything about every enemy soldier.'

The head of the infamous OMRA slowly turns round. He looks dejected. 'You are a dangerous man when you have your back against the wall. Maybe just as dangerous as your grandfather.'

'You said yourself that there is another bomb – maybe two. I don't want them to explode.' Daniel puts his finger on the map. 'And I don't want these camps to mobilise and start to storm Kazichian villages.'

'I will make sure you get full access,' Yanev says. 'Stop this madness, please. But be careful. If you connect those two databases, we will turn into a surveillance state. We will break more privacy laws than exist.'

Radko clenches his fist. 'Enough with the talking! Time to firebomb those villages. Time to avenge my son!'

Yanev shoots Radko a startled look. 'What do you mean? Your son wasn't hurt, right?'

'But he could have been! The attack on the base was an attack on his life. Time to strike back. Maika agrees with me. The Jada have forgotten who's in charge here.'

Daniel says they should ignore his mother's orders. Everything is going according to plan. His second, secret operation too.

'What secret operation?'

'We are kidnapping Nairi from the Jada,' Daniel says, and he gestures at Leonid, who is standing by a whiteboard.

Igor Yanev drops his cigar in shock. 'You're *what*? We might as well attack them right away.'

'No one will know that we're kidnapping her. She won't even know herself.'

Leonid turns the whiteboard round and seven photos of serious-looking men appear.

'Uncle Radko, would you please clarify the operation?'

Radko explains to Yanev that they secretly flew in seven specialists. Daniel had asked him to find the best mercenaries in the world willing to do anything for money, no questions asked. He points at one of the specialists. 'This is specialist number four, a Dutchman. He is on his way to Nairi's headquarters in the Akhlos to take her to the Lechkov Island.'

'And you think the Jada will let that happen?' Yanev asks, picking his cigar up off the floor and lighting it again.

Daniel explains that Nairi will go with her kidnappers because she thinks she is speaking to a journalist from CNN and an American soldier. She was sent CNN coverage of the civil war, in which a correspondent travels through Jada territory. That item is real, and the reporter really travelled through the Akhlos, but the face of the journalist was changed into the face of a Kazichian spy. 'It is a deepfake,' Daniel says, 'made with my artificial intelligence – ERIS. We sent the video to Nairi so that she thinks the spy works for CNN.'

'The Jada can't pass up on the opportunity to pitch themselves to America,' Radko adds. 'Even if they aren't sure about the intentions of the strangers in their village, they will take the risk.'

'This operation has started already?' Yanev asks, and he looks from Radko to Daniel and back to Leonid. 'This is way too risky.

And for what? To question her? I need to get consulted for decisions like these.'

'You're right,' Daniel says. 'It won't happen again, but we didn't have much time. We needed to seize the opportunity.'

'You need to hear his p-plan,' Leonid says – clearly taken aback that his own boss didn't get informed. 'It's b-brilliant. What we are doing to Nairi may seem like an interrogation, but it's something else entirely. The world has never seen anything like it.'

Yanev takes a few short drags to relight his cigar and looks around the room. 'Fine, let me hear it. What are you doing with Nairi? What's the plan?'

49

Two weeks after the bombings, the Man with a Thousand Faces uploads a video. It is the second message from the rebel leader. The figure sits in front of the same grey wall, wearing the same balaclava. But this time, the voice is not distorted, it is a woman's voice. And that woman is not just addressing the Jada; she is asking all minorities to make peace and focus on the true enemy. Side by side. She tells Jada and Neza to ask themselves: what are they willing to do to give their children a better future? What if it means they need to forgive their Neza or Jada brothers? Isn't that hardly a sacrifice?

'You need to become one of the thousand faces,' the woman says, 'because I am simply one of those faces, too. I am nothing without all of you by my side.'

And then she pulls the balaclava off.

Nairi of the Jada appears.

'I am showing you my face because this is not about me. It's about all of us as a united front. As one soldier with thousands of faces, a soldier of the Jada and the Neza, against the Mardoe Khador.'

While the YouTube servers process and publish the video, an army of bots gets to work. A protocol is ready to send the video to the whole world without any human hand needing to click a button or press a key. The video is spread amongst thousands of Twitter accounts, Instagram, and Facebook profiles and shared on all kinds of political forums. Once the video gets traction, the work of the bots gets made invisible by all the real users sharing it and commenting on it. After a few hours, all the bot accounts get deleted automatically except for one. A bot-controlled email address sends Nairi's video to all major newspapers and news platforms from Eastern Europe and America. And then that email address also disappears, and there is no trace left of the bot army.

Within a day, the internet gets flooded with the revelation: Nairi of the Jada is the Man with a Thousand Faces. She has radicalised. She is the rebel leader who lets bombs explode throughout the country. And that truth is accepted immediately; of course, it's her – who else?

Now that the rebel leader has a face, her follower number grows exponentially. The mystery of the faceless figure made the uprising magnetic, but with Nairi's face, it turned legitimate. She is a tough but peaceful person. She always works restoratively. So, if even Nairi doesn't see any other way to make progress except with violence, it is time to take up arms.

In her video, Nairi says she doesn't expect violence from everyone. There are other ways to join the uprising: by showing your support on social media for example. In response, more and more people around the world change their profile photo to the symbol of the Man with a Thousand Faces. In Kazichia, T-shirts get printed, more banners get painted and the symbol gets spray painted on the walls of Kazichian cities. The protest on the round-about by the parliament grows busier – Jada and Neza chant side by side against the inert, grey parliament, staring at the rebels, motionless, like an indifferent, sleepy old man.

The Kremlin, represented by Yuri Andropov, tries to contact Daniel but can't get hold of him. The Russians want the High House to make a statement and for Daniel to get elected as president as soon as possible so he can launch the counterattack. Andropov lets the minister of foreign affairs know that Kazichia can count on military support.

'Coincidentally, four divisions have just been brought to a state of preparedness for military drills near the border,' he says. 'So supplies of weapons or manpower don't need to take long.'

The CIA also watches the video, and Jonathan Rye gets to work immediately. Finally, the Americans know whom they need to make contact with. Rye sends an insurgency team to the Akhlos to find Nairi. He has an arsenal of weapons and resources they can offer the Jada rebels to dethrone Daniel Lechkov. But something bothers him. Something is off. The Man with a Thousand Faces was not just a mystery because he was nameless, but also due to the complexity of the attacks. Synchronised bombings on extremely secured locations. A cyber attack so advanced it shut down a whole government. And this Nairi is supposedly responsible for that? How did she do that? How did she find the resources to do that? The American is mystified.

The political leaders of Kazichia are confused, too. The High House wants to defend itself against the growing terrorist movement but is not allowed to act. The intelligence service and the Department of Military Strategy is explicitly instructed to wait – no reports, no analyses. The diplomats and the Ministry of Foreign Affairs are told that any meetings with America and Russia are to be suspended. The premier doesn't receive briefings from the High House and needs to go on pretending the Man with a Thousand Faces doesn't exist, while the members of parliament drive through a growing group of protesters to get to the parliament building. The uncertainty scares people and strengthens the call to action. Yanev wants to deploy the riot police to squash the protests, but Daniel stops him. Radko and Maika want to start military action against the rebel camps, but don't get permission.

All that time, no one knows what Daniel Lechkov is planning. At the new department of the intelligence service, he sits at the head of the table, behind him the digital map of Kazichia, showing more and more blinking lights. He looks tired but sounds firm. 'We need to wait. Just a little bit longer. The stronger the Man with a Thousand Faces gets, the stronger we get. When our time comes to attack, we use the Man with a Thousand Faces to pit everyone against each other. Until then we need to be patient.'

While his team starts to voice its concerns, Daniel sits at the head of the table unperturbed. The map on the wall behind him has now been filled with so many dots that they look like red, blinking wings growing from his shoulders.

241

50

In the quiet house in Oregon, Sophie walks over to the big white closet in the living room. The closet filled with photo albums, photos of Sophie with her parents. On holidays, on family outings, during Christmas. Smiling faces. Photos of Sophie, her mother, and the man supposed to be her father. The man who supposedly died of cancer.

Could *that* even be a lie? His illness?

With two hands, she pulls the albums off the shelves. The books fly across the wooden floor. When the closet is empty, Sophie sits on her knees and checks all the photos. She goes through every page of every album and eventually finds one loose photo of her squished red face right after she was born. Apart from that, there is no photo of her from before she was three. No photo from before 2019, the year she went to Kazichia. She takes her phone and opens the family cloud server. She opens the folder with home videos and filters by date. The oldest file is a recording of her fourth birthday. Life before then has been erased. Hidden. Stashed away. Like Sophie's memories of that time are stashed away. Memories that resurface now and then, and then disappear again. *A chase. Shootings. A house on a hill getting stormed by an angry mob.* Memories that make her feel like she is stepping outside of herself, that her life is something she reads about in the third person singular. But this is *her* story, and she has a right to it. And for maybe the hundredth time that week, she calls her mother, the woman who should have told her that story years ago. But she is gone. She disappeared almost two weeks ago, and the house is empty. Only Sophie haunts the place like a ghost exorcising the past.

She walks to the marble kitchen island and pours herself a glass of red wine. She wants to keep searching, but without help, it is proving to be very difficult. Only one option remains. In her notes are two names. The first one is the professor researching deepfakes with Daniel: Tim Stewart. Sophie finds his details in an old university database and calls the listed phone number, but nobody picks up. The second name is Anderson Holt, the American journalist who wrote a book on the unrest and attacks in Kazichia in 2019. *The Uprising*, it was called. She finds a phone number, but it's not in use.

Frustrated, Sophie looks at the dark kitchen windows. Her childhood home seems to be detaching itself from America. Behind those windows is nothing: no phone lines to call, no people to show her the truth. She finishes the wine and finds the book by the American journalist. It is about the Jada rebels who attacked the High House. Literally. The journalist describes their leader, the Man with a Thousand Faces, as a hero. Someone who was unfairly deemed a terrorist. According to the journalist, there was only one source of evil in that battle, and that was Daniel Lechkov.

Sophie gets a strange feeling in her stomach when she sees her father's name and quickly reads on. The journalist writes relatively little about him. The first half of the book is about the minorities. In most of the second half, Holt speculates on the identity of their leader. According to the articles Sophie found, Nairi of the Jada was the Man with a Thousand Faces. But the journalist doesn't believe that.

In Jada circles, Nairi has been elevated to legendary status. She has unprecedented influence in the Akhlos, so it seems plausible that she is the Man with a Thousand Faces. She could get the men of her people to pick up their weapons and follow her to Kazichia City. But there is enough reason for doubt.

According to researchers of two renowned think tanks, an organisation of specialists must have worked together with the rebels. It was confirmed that they were not receiving help from America at the time of the attacks. So, who did help them? On top of that, Nairi has not been seen in public since the uprising, not even in her own village. Locals claim she went with American journalists and never returned. I traveled to Inima to interview her family, and her uncle is convinced something is off.

Finally, a team of forensic data analysts analysed the video wherein the Man with a Thousand Faces claims responsibility for the attacks. They argue that the face under the balaclava does not have the same shape as Nairi's face. A man is said to be hidden under the mask. So, while the Jada keep honoring Nairi like a goddess, and the press has recorded and archived her story, this journalist keeps asking himself: who is the Man with a Thousand Faces?

Sophie's phone rings. In the quiet house, the ringtone sounds much shriller than it normally does. She picks up and uses her voice for the first time in weeks. 'Hello?'

Someone breathes shallowly. Grating.

'Hello? Who is this?'

The breathing gets louder, and she hears clicking and smacking. The voice that starts speaking is low, it speaks English with an accent. 'Is this who I think it is?'

'This is Sophie Joubert, who is this?'

The man on the other end gulps. Again, that strange clicking sound – probably dentures.

'Am I speaking to Professor Stewart? From the Netherlands?'

'You can call me Tim,' the old man says.

'I am looking for someone who can tell me more about Daniel Lechkov.'

'Miss Joubert, I can tell you everything about Daniel. Probably more than he could tell you about himself.'

51

Sophie lies. She lies to the old professor that she is a journalist writing about the history of Kazichia. Her lie gets more complicated than she had planned; she brings in an editor who was unhappy with her first draft and talks about how frustrating the writing process is because of her lack of sources. She hears herself lying, and for the first time, she wonders if her search is dangerous. Did her father or mother do something criminal, and is that why they are hiding in America? For the first time, Sophie isn't wondering what she might find during this search, but what she might lose.

The man on the other end of the line believes her story about the article. He doesn't even ask how she got his details. 'You are trying to find your way through the shards of information warfare,' he says. 'For a long time, Daniel Lechkov was engaged in battle with a rebel leader of the Jada. Those two fought each other in the physical world with bombs and treaties, as people have been doing for centuries. But also in the digital world, with cyber attacks, lies, and media manipulation. That makes it very hard to recover the truth.'

'When did you get to know Daniel?' she asks.

The old man says he studied at a British boarding school – Hewton public school. After he graduated, he went to London to study artificial intelligence. He was still involved in the boarding school, working as the assistant to the housemaster.

'I'm not sure if you are aware, but a boarding school is divided into houses,' he says. 'It was my job to care for the new boys of

Chester House. One of those boys was Daniel. The first days at Hewton are difficult for everyone. You just left your parents and, in Daniel's case, find yourself in a different country. And on top of all of that, the older boys bully the younger ones, as a form of hazing. They soak them in water or urine while they're asleep.' The professor clicks his teeth. 'Are you still there, Miss Joubert?'

'Yes, I am,' she says. 'I'm listening and taking notes.'

The professor says that Daniel struggled a lot when he arrived in England. Despite his extraordinary talent for maths and special attention from the headmaster, he couldn't get settled. The boy wanted to return home, but that wasn't an option; he wasn't allowed to enter his birth country because the two heirs needed to stay apart. And so, he was a thirteen-year-old boy stuck between East and West.

Tim offered to talk to him.

'I just wanted to help out,' the professor says, and he clicks his dentures again. 'No one could have predicted, myself included, that I would give Daniel's career and life direction and meaning for decades to come.'

'Can you tell me about the day you first met Daniel?' Sophie asks.

'The first time I met Daniel, I saw a charming boy standing in front of Chester House. He was pretty short but had an athletic build. Broad shoulders and strong arms. Daniel is a handsome boy with deep eyes if you know what I mean – eyes that make you wonder what he is thinking. I suspect he was suffering from depression back then. He never would have admitted that, but I strongly suspect he fantasised about suicide at some point.

'To try and help him, I did the same thing a maths professor did for me once: I showed Daniel that people with a talent for maths equations hold the future in their hands. The digital age was about to begin and Hewton had a Power Mac 6100 – at that time an advanced computer. I don't know how old you are, Miss Joubert, but we are talking about 1995, long before the quantum revolution. Anyway, I showed Daniel how to apply mathematics in the digital world. He grasped the possibilities unbelievably quickly. The word "genius" is overused, but Daniel is undoubtedly a genius. Within a few days, he wrote simple programs on that Mac with HyperCard, and after a few weeks, we started using real code languages. We saw each other once a week, and Daniel started doing better. His scores got better, too.'

Sophie gets goosebumps on her arms. Little by little, she starts seeing the outline of her father. 'And after your time in England, you started doing research together?' she asks, her pen ready.

The professor coughs. 'Daniel helped me with scientific research for years. I obtained my doctorate in Amsterdam and asked him if he wanted to come work for the university too.'

'What did you work on?'

'It's very technical, Miss Joubert, so it is hard to go into details without using esoteric terms. But in broad strokes, our first experiments and research were on so-called auto-encoders. Through the years, our research became more complex, and we started focusing on generative antagonist networks that could make deepfakes and generate synthetic voices. Our field developed at lightning speed. It was a great time. You know what a deepfake is, I assume?'

She gets a hunch and starts leafing back in her notes. 'How can a network make a deepfake? How do you copy the right face? What kind of data is needed for that?'

The professor explains you need to show a network a massive amount of images of a face before you can generate an undetectable deepfake. You need to feed the network hours of material, preferably high resolution. 'The more sophisticated the networks are,' he says, 'the less data you need to make a deepfake.'

'Do you have a name for those images?'

'Training data,' he says. 'That's what you call the data you give the network to teach it to generate a face.'

Sophie circles a word on the first page of her notes. A word she wrote down when she had just found her mother's old laptop. 'Approximately how much training data could that have been, in those days?'

'Now, a network sees someone's face and can reproduce it immediately. Back then, we could make a perfect deepfake with our antagonist network using about ten hours of data. With a hundred hours, we could make a mask indistinguishable from the real thing. By no one. Even today.'

The pen in her hand stops. She stares at her notes with an open mouth.

'A hundred hours of training data for the antagonist network,' she tells herself.

On the notepad, it says the strange code from the interrogation video: ANTD 100. Under the code, Sophie writes:

Antagonist Network Training Data 100.

The professor is still talking, but she isn't listening anymore. She sees the woman with one arm tied to the chair. The woman who needed to keep talking, to repeat words until the code had gone from 100 to 0. She realises why that woman was being detained. And why she didn't understand what the goal of the interrogation she found on her mother's laptop was. The men in that video didn't ask questions because they wanted information, they needed training data. They were training a network to make deepfakes of Nairi's face. That is why she needed to repeat certain words and look straight into the camera again and again. And apparently, they needed the deepfake as fast as possible, turning the conversation into torture.

'Someone kidnapped her and made a deepfake of her,' Sophie says quietly.

'What did you say?'

'Nairi of the Jada. Daniel Lechkov kidnapped her and made a deepfake of her. It looked like she said she was the Man with a Thousand Faces, but it was Daniel, using her face.'

The other end of the line is quiet now, apart from the raspy breathing.

'It wasn't her,' Sophie argues. 'Maybe Nairi never was the Man with a Thousand Faces. Maybe the High House just kidnapped the most likely candidate. That way, they controlled both sides of the uprising. They were the establishment and the rebels at the same time. But why?'

'To have more power,' the other end of the line says. 'It's that simple.'

'You knew this?'

'I recognised ERIS, the code I built with Daniel. But I had no proof. And every time I explained to someone that Nairi was a digital illusion, I got called a conspiracist. A madman.'

Sophie starts understanding what happened. While she and her parents were stuck in Kazichia, the rebels attacked. Her father needed to think of a way to protect them without letting the war escalate, so he made a deepfake of Nairi. That way, he could confuse and control the rebel army.

'I know who you are,' the old man says suddenly. 'I know this conversation is not for journalistic research.'

It takes a few seconds for his words to get through to her. Then she doesn't ask what he means, but how he knew.

'Because I have been waiting for this call for sixteen years, dear girl. I don't know where you are and why you got called Sophie there. I don't know how much you remember from your time in Kazichia, but it's a great relief to hear you're alive. I was so scared you and your mother had got killed when the Man with a Thousand Faces attacked. But there you finally are, Alexa. Because that is your real name, did you know that? Your name is Alexa Lechkova.'

Sophie starts shaking, and Alexa with her. The phone taps softly against her ear. She tries to regain control by grabbing the kitchen counter and focusing on one point. But it doesn't help. All she can hear and see is that name: Alexa. Her name. And the world around that name is falling apart before her eyes.

52

Sitting in a meeting room with Radko, Daniel suddenly takes action. The mysterious waiting has ended.

'It's time,' he says. 'Let's begin the second phase.'

'Are we finally mobilising?' Radko asks.

'No, we're going to Baghsenka.'

Radko knows they are expected at the head office of Karzarov Transport that afternoon because Daniel wants to appoint a successor for Lev Karzarov. He wants to prevent the transport sector from becoming even more unsettled. But he didn't know the visit was part of Daniel's plan to keep Russia and the Man with a Thousand Faces out of the capital.

As they leave the room, Maika exits her office, her body swaying. 'There you are!' she yells across the house. 'We need to talk.'

Daniel tells Radko to wait by the helicopter platform and walks to his mother. Maika is holding a crystal whisky glass and asks why she isn't a part of the crisis team. Why Daniel is avoiding her. He says she should go inside, and closes the door of his mother's office behind them.

'I want to know how Nia is,' she says, her words slurred. She squints and plops down on her desk chair. 'And why did you lock your family up? I wanted to talk to Michelle today but wasn't allowed to see her. Have you lost your mind, boy? You had your wife and little daughter locked up in Vigo's wing. Your pregnant wife.'

'In *my* wing. And it's for their own safety. You have no idea what went down. What Michelle tried. She didn't leave me any other choice.' Daniel sighs. 'We need to talk, mother. You keep advising Radko about a more aggressive approach to the Jada uprising. Stop doing that. There is a plan, a good plan, and I am implementing it. You wanted me to take the lead and I am. And you keep trying to contact Nia. I understand you miss her, but it's dangerous.'

'You don't get it at all, my boy! What are you babbling about, "advice"? I didn't advise Radko, I *ordered* him: burn the rebels. That Man with a Thousand Faces turned into a living legend within a few months. We need to get ahead of this, and the only way to do that is by intimidation.' Deep crow's feet run to her ears like cables. 'Or do you think there is a friendlier way to calm the Jada down?'

'Mother, enough.'

Maika slowly swirls the tumbler of Yamazaki, making the two ice cubes tap against the crystal. 'Maybe it was a mistake to give you the Mardoe Khador.'

Daniel sighs and rubs his face with his hands. 'This isn't working,' he says from behind his palms. 'I don't know how to say this, mother, so I'm just going to say it: you need to retire. I'm taking over.'

'What?!' Her eyes get smaller, the cables tighten. 'Look at me when you talk to me. I can't hear you like this.'

He drops his hands but looks at his lap. 'I need to do this, mother. You are retiring. Right now.'

Maika swings her glass and smashes it to the floor. The Japanese whisky and French crystal splash around the room. Daniel protects his face from the flying shards.

'Who do you think you are?!' the old woman shrieks. 'No one, not even your grandpa, has led this country longer than I have. When he lost his mind, I took over. When your father dropped dead, I got those old men under control within two hours. I've had to take care of your brother. And then you came, with your computer jargon and your vague ambitions. A troublemaker is what you are, and *I* kept the peace. I led the High House because it's my house!'

'No, mother. Not anymore. I am up against the Man with a Thousand Faces, and I will make sure it works out, believe me. And you need to grieve your son's death. You need to take some rest.'

'How dare you involve him in this? You need me, you don't have any experience.'

'I will ask for advice, but from now on, you won't have access to parliament. You won't be able to contact the OMRA.'

'What is this? Is this revenge for the past? I know you didn't want to move to England. You were young, and I'm sure it was hard, but don't pretend that the most expensive boarding school in Europe was a war zone. Please don't pretend it was traumatic for you. It seems like you're too afraid to see it, but I'm doing all this for you. For all of you.'

Daniel says nothing.

'What do you want to hear? Sorry? Is that what this is about? I'm sorry?'

'That would be nice, but that has nothing to do with what is happening here. I'm making a political decision, and a business one. It's not personal.' Daniel walks round the desk and crouches beside her. 'Dear Mother, you have been fighting for so long, and you've lost so many people. If I think how much I . . .' His voice breaks, and his face looks drawn. 'I miss Vigo every day.'

Maika puts her hand on his cheek. 'I want to stand beside you while you're doing this, my boy. You can't do this by yourself. You're not a leader. But we can make you one. Together.'

'Help me by stepping aside. You will see I have everything under control. In about eight hours, the entire Karzarov empire will be ours, and Uncle Lev will cross the border voluntarily so we can arrest him. Within a week Russia will stop spying, and they will withdraw some of their troops from the border.'

His mother looks at him, her eyes filled with contempt. 'Do you really think so? How is that even possible?'

'By nightfall, they will all fear me and do exactly as I say. Just watch what happens in the next couple of hours.' And then, before she thinks of another way to make him feel dependent on her, he turns his back on his mother and leaves the office.

53

The Karzarov empire is managed from a head office near the edge of the town of Baghsenka – near the factory that was blown up by the rebels. The main entrance is a restored train station, with the modern glass head office standing over it like an enemy spaceship. The general assemblies are held in a large room on the top floor. All the major shareholders and the board of directors wait for Daniel Lechkov there. They don't know what he will tell them, but aren't allowed to refuse his request to address them. All members of the High House have that right. The chair, Lev Karzarov, obviously couldn't make it, but minister Ivanov does his honours.

Despite his three-piece English-tailored suit, the old minister looks bad. His purple skin hangs on his skull like a wet washcloth, and he has deep yellow fissures in the corners of his mouth. Ivanov has a bad feeling about Daniel coming. For the past few weeks, he has done everything he could to keep the Karzarov empire out of the wind. Don't attract attention and just wait patiently was his strategy. The Kremlin can seize power in Kazichia at any moment, which would still make Lev Karzarov one of the most important men in the country. And then he, Vadim Ivanov, will be the one to have guarded the throne for him.

The tall doors open, and Daniel enters. Ivanov welcomes him dryly and wants to start an introduction round, but the presidential candidate rudely interrupts him.

'Is everybody here? Or are there at least enough to initiate a vote?'

Ivanov feels slightly unnerved and wants to say something, but

Daniel doesn't give him the chance. 'Great, I would like to cut to the chase. Due to the attacks and increasing unrest in the country, the premier has signed an emergency order. With Nairi leading the uprising, the unrest will only increase. The government and the Mardoe Khador need to do everything to guarantee the safety of their citizens. This means we will intervene wherever we see fit.' He brings out a stack of papers. 'I am here to explain what we plan on doing with Karzarov Transport.'

'This is impossible!' one of the Karzarov brothers yells out.

'This is unheard of!' an uncle shouts.

Ivanov is unsure what to do except wait and hear Daniel's plan.

'These are unprecedented times,' Daniel continues. 'We don't know how Nairi got access to our networks and most secure locations. To protect the economy of Kazichia, the High House needs to ensure that our country's transport sector and infrastructure remain as stable as possible.'

'I am here to guarantee that stability, Mr Lechkov. It's unnecessary to intervene,' Ivanov interjects. He tries very hard to stay polite. 'What would benefit Karzarov Transport is stability. The less change, the better, and that is my policy.'

Daniel puts his fists on the big glass table, held together by two old railway tracks. 'That's not enough, Minister. I'm here to take over.'

The room goes dead silent for a split second. Then the Karzarovs object loudly. The government intervention gets called unlawful, criminal even. The chaos gets worse, and though it's technically Ivanov's job to keep order as vice-president, he lets it happen.

'At this very moment, fifteen per cent of this meeting consists of representatives of Gazprom or the Russian state,' the presidential candidate shouts over the men. 'I propose to increase the number of Russia-backed members to thirty per cent.'

The room gets quiet instantly.

Daniel sticks three fingers in the air. 'We will give Russia thirty per cent of control, but I will replace Lev Karzarov as head of this board and name a new vice-president. Ivanov will immediately be relieved of his position within the company. Karzarov Transport becomes part of Lechkov Industria. That takeover will happen gradually, until it's all one conglomerate under the Lechkov name. It will take about four to five years.'

Ivanov gets up and wants to adjourn the meeting but doesn't get the chance.

'I'm not done,' Daniel says. 'The second condition for this order is that all members of the Karzarov family will be bought out. All power needs to go to the stockholders and the board of directors.'

Ivanov is still standing but doesn't say anything. Suddenly, he sees it: Daniel's plan. Somehow, the OMRA found out that the Russian interests in Karzarov Transport are much higher than the official fifteen per cent. Almost half of the people present have secret ties to Russia, and a proposal to increase the official interest will definitely get approved. Especially after Lev Karzarov, the CEO, lost face and had to flee the country. But how did Daniel find out about the ties to Russia? Is the company bugged?

The new networks, Ivanov thinks. *That's it. Daniel used the cyber attack to spy on the other families.*

The cousins and uncles don't see Daniel's plan for what it is and keep protesting loudly. But not for long, because the noisemakers are outnumbered. Almost no one supports the Karzarov men. One by one, they get quiet and sit down. They look at their board members and stockholders and realise they are being betrayed. The silent majority will cast them aside.

'This can't be happening,' one of the Karzarovs grumbles. He looks at Ivanov. 'There must be a way to stop this. Right? Vadim?'

'I have one last condition,' Daniel says, before the minister can respond, 'and then we will hold a vote.'

The room goes dead quiet; some wonder if this is too good to be true, while others helplessly await their fate.

'Russia will extradite Lev Karzarov to the Kazichian government. Within twelve hours, I want to look him in the eyes, on Kazichian territory.'

Ivanov bursts into a sarcastic chuckle and looks around. 'We can't tolerate this. This man has gone mad. This company was *built* by Lev Karzarov and his father.'

The Karzarovs are encouraged by his words, and Ivanov kicks it up a notch by ordering security to come and escort Daniel from the building. But it's all for show. He knows what will happen: Daniel Lechkov will erase the Karzarov family as his grandfather did the Tsaada. The High House will go from three to two families, and there is nothing they can do to stop him.

Ivanov looks at the high grey walls of the meeting room. Behind the angry Karzarovs seated at the long glass table hang photos of their prominent family members. At the entrance hangs pater familias Sergej Karzarov, and next to him his heir Lev and his brothers, and next to them cousins: the bloodline that built and managed the empire. Thanks to their relationship with Gazprom, they were untouchable in the region. But precisely that opening to Russia, Daniel is using now to sideline them in one single blow.

'We're voting now,' Daniel says. 'If my proposal gets approved, no one leaves this room until the Kremlin is informed. Contact with the outside world is forbidden until after the vote. Whoever tries to warn Lev Karzarov will immediately get detained and convicted of treason. A special military unit is waiting for my orders downstairs.'

'You're creating an enemy you can't handle,' Ivanov says. 'You will get me out of this building today, but you will never remove me from the parliament. I am one of the Twenty, and we will come for your crown.'

The parliament is the last place where he can defend his position. He will need to convince the other ministers to turn their backs on the High House. If he can't, the Lechkovs will arrest him as soon as they have taken over Karzarov Transport.

You need to fight, he tells himself. *This is not over yet.*

But when he looks at the other side of the table, at the young Lechkov son waiting while members of the general assembly cast their votes, he doubts his chances. Ivanov hardly wants to admit it to himself, but when he looks at Daniel Lechkov, he fears the next great leader of Kazichia has risen.

When Daniel walks out of the head office of Karzarov Transport a few hours later, Radko is waiting by the cars with a few soldiers from the Circle. His shallow breathing clouds the yellow beams of the headlights.

'Did it work?'

Daniel nods as he gets in the car. 'We have hold of Karzarov Transport. Lev is getting extradited today.'

'What do you want to do once you've arrested him?' Radko asks as they drive off.

Daniel looks through the window at the dark, empty ring road of Baghsenka. 'We will show him as much mercy as he showed us: none. And none to his family. None to his wife, his children, his brothers and sisters.'

It gets quiet.

'Are you not letting your emotions rule you, Daniel? You've already won.'

'Emotions? This is the pragmatic approach. I need to turn off my emotions to do this. We will make sure everyone knows the head of the Karzarov family died in an interrogation room of the intelligence service. And we will make sure everyone knows his family will suffer because of his lapse of judgement. However powerful you are, anyone can get arrested.'

'So, no one dares to betray you,' Radko says.

'It's the only way to keep our families and all families of Kazichia safe. And that end justifies any means.'

54

Lev Karzarov sits on the snow-covered natural stone terrace of his Kazichian country house overlooking the villages in the Tumani valley near the Russian border. His hunched shoulders make his neck disappear in his thick blue winter coat. He is smoking a cigarette. Next to him sits a tall, thin man with his feet on the table, whistling a happy staccato melody. Yuri Andropov has been the middleman between the Mardoe Khador and the Kremlin for years, and Karzarov now considers him a friend.

He is feeling tense because he would rather not set foot in Kazichia; it feels like an unnecessary risk. But Andropov received word from Ivanov – the minister wants to speak to him as soon as possible – and Russia guarantees his safety. And so, Karzarov crossed the border to see his mentor and old friend. But as soon as the door to the terrace opens and Karzarov turns round, he realises he made the biggest mistake of his life. The biggest mistake he will ever make.

He has been betrayed.

'Uncle Lev,' Daniel says as he walks to the table with four guards and Radko at his side.

Karzarov jerks his head to Andropov, who still has his feet on the table. 'Is the Kremlin betraying me? After everything I risked for you?'

The Russian shakes his head. 'Lev, I promised you Moscow would do everything to save Karzarov Transport. I'm a man of my word, always have been.'

Karzarov jumps up and runs to the stone wall that fences his terrace. Over the edge waits a free fall of many metres.

'Just sit down, Uncle Lev,' Daniel says. 'Death will come soon enough.'

He looks into the abyss. He wants to jump but doesn't dare.

'I had to, Daniel,' he says. 'We were going to lose everything if I hadn't intervened. Your brother was distracted. He was a cocaine junkie. Just like his wife.'

With his fists clenched Daniel walks up to him. 'You killed him. And you wanted to use his funeral to ruin me and my family. That seems like overblown punishment for bad leadership.'

'I didn't know they were going to kill him.' He places a foot on the wall. 'If I had known, I would have warned you.'

Andropov laughs and swings his feet off the table. 'Listen to him! Lev Karzarov, the good Samaritan.'

Daniel stands next to Lev and looks over the edge. 'Ivanov didn't betray you. I gave the Russians a third of Karzarov Transport in exchange for control and your extradition. Everything you've built, everything your family built, belongs to me now. Your cousins and uncles will get arrested, and their families, too. I will destroy all of them.'

Lev cries out. His voice echoes in the valley. Two black birds soar up from between the boulders.

'You're a simple, emotional man, Daniel Lechkov,' he says, trembling with anger. 'You gave the Kremlin a third of the entire transport sector? Why? For *this* moment. For this very moment, in which you can take everything from me. But what will happen after? After this, you will have lost everything. Your grandfather curses you, boy. You surrendered the country to the Russians.' He shakes his head.

'You're right. I want to see you on your knees from desperation. Jump over the edge, even better. But this is all a bonus.' Daniel looks over at Andropov, who is still seated at the table, and continues in a whisper. 'You think it is all about borders and industry, but that time has passed. It's about information now. Whoever controls the most information wins. Always. Russia was already part of Karzarov Transport. They have been for years, and you knew that because you allowed it. I just pulled them to the surface and made them visible. Everything the Russians do or discuss from your companies, I can see now.'

Karzarov looks at the young Lechkov beside him. He terribly underestimated him.

Daniel gets closer to his uncle. 'I have complete control over the two largest industries of the country and our government's entire IT infrastructure. I might be short-sighted or emotional, Uncle Lev, but I'm also the most powerful man since Petar Lechkov.'

Karzarov doesn't feel anger or envy anymore, just emptiness. Just exhaustion and hollow defeat. 'What will happen to me?' he asks.

'You will come with these gentlemen from the security service.'

He sighs deep and long, as if letting his soul fall down the cliff in preparation for what's to come. 'Can I see my wife one last time?' he asks. 'Your aunt? Can I at least know how she is?'

'No. All you may know is that Nia won't get special treatment for being a woman.'

Again, he considers jumping. He leans forward, and Daniel does nothing to stop him, but then he thinks of something. 'My little daughter, Katja, she is still in Moscow. She can't take care of herself. Will you send someone to care for her? Or have her come to Kazichia?'

Daniel looks at him unmoved. 'When I was in that car, sedated by your drugs, I begged for my wife and child's life. But you wouldn't give me anything. So that's what I will give you now in return. Nothing.'

'But how is this a little girl's fault? I'm begging you; her life is hard enough as it is.'

Daniel shrugs.

Karzarov leaps at him. He tries to hit him, but Radko grabs his hood and pulls him off the balcony. The soldier drags him through his own house, and Karzarov screams at Daniel that this is just the beginning of their battle. He will do everything to make the High House fall. He will never stop. Never! But as they walk through the front door, Karzarov sees a black car on the driveway and falls silent. He has seen plenty of people disappear in cars like that. He has often given orders to pick someone up in a car like that. And he knows that after getting in, there is no coming back.

After Karzarov is taken away, Daniel walks to the Russian still sitting at the table.

'Andropov, I presume?'

The man nods and gives Daniel a smirk.

'You threatened my daughter on the phone. My three-year-old daughter.'

'Absolutely!' The Russian sticks out his hand over the table. 'How wonderful to finally meet you.'

Daniel ignores his hand. 'Do you have anything to do with the Jada uprising? *Asch-Iljada-Lica*, are you helping her?'

'Absolutely not. That wouldn't benefit us. In fact, the Kremlin would like the uprising to disappear because they fear the CIA will work with the Jada. We want to help you stop Nairi.'

Daniel nods. 'That's not a problem. We have a plan. I will make the uprising disappear, and I will bring stability. That is what you wanted, and that is what I'll do. All I ask is you let my family go home.'

'You know we can't do that.'

'What can you do?'

'That depends. What do you want?'

'Stop the espionage,' Daniel says. 'Stop tapping our lines, stop the shadow politics, and stop meddling with our parliament. And withdraw your troops from the border region. At least the tank divisions. I want an open line to Moscow. I have shown that I'm a friend, so treat me like a friend.'

'Those do seem like reasonable demands, Mr Lechkov.'

Andropov rubs his hands together and pulls a black leather briefcase from under his chair. 'Moscow sends me to neighbouring countries to start partnerships. That is what I do. And as far as I can see, you have become a partner of ours.' He places the briefcase on the table and starts turning the combination locks. 'I will make sure the Kremlin takes a few steps back. The pressure will no longer be dialled up.' The combination locks click open.

'But if I can't see you anymore, I won't know who you are, Mr Lechkov. That's why I'm leaving you this official reminder of the conditions of our partnership.' He opens the briefcase and walks away. 'Have a wonderful day and give my best to your mother.'

As the Russian, whistling a tune, leaves the terrace, Daniel turns the briefcase to see what is inside. The case is filled with glass shards – thick glass, like from a car window. He takes the biggest shard. It is bright red. Red with dried blood. And the edge of the shard has brown hairs plastered to it. Brown like his own hair. Brown, like his twin brother's hair. Slowly, he puts the shard back and closes the briefcase carefully, as if he could disturb Vigo in his sleep. He gently lays his hand on the black leather, and he keeps standing there, all alone, on the terrace of the Karzarov country house, overlooking the valley of Kazichian villages that cautiously gossip about the family that lives on the hill – about the things that those people are willing to do to stay rich like that. He stands there with his hand on the briefcase and cries without making a sound.

Then he dries his tears and calls Leonid. While the phone rings, he walks through Karzarov's house to the front door.

'I want you to make Nairi and all the European specialists disappear,' he says. 'Forever.'

Leonid objects. He says they divided the operation among several different specialists, so no one understands what their goal is. It is unnecessary to make this many victims. No one has an overview of the whole operation.

'This plan will only work if no one knows what ERIS is,' Daniel says. 'We can't afford to take any risks. The soldiers need to disappear. Definitely the specialist we sent to Nairi. I want everyone executed, and I want their bodies to disappear. Clear?'

Leonid sighs but says he'll make it happen.

Daniel hangs up and takes a look at the living room. It looks like the Karzarovs could come home at any minute. He looks at the dining table for a moment, with a special chair for Katja, and then walks outside.

IX. The Mass Grave

55

We are flying over the island in a small plane. It looks like a rectangular rock between dozens of small pools of water, all connected by a giant dark green lake. I have never seen anything like it. Nairi is very nervous. She has been playing with an empty water bottle for the entire two-hour flight. Occasionally, the village elder puts her hand on Nairi's shoulder. I am also feeling tense, because I still don't know where we will end up, at Nairi's downfall or her salvation. I look at Sasha, sitting opposite me in silence. I can't read her face.

We land on a plain strip between the pools, where a few snow scooters are waiting for us. The only way to get to the island is by crossing the frozen lake. From the snow scooter, I see a long, stone stairway leading from the ice to a large building over the rock. The building looks like an exclusive resort, and as we climb the stairs, I start feeling more relaxed, this isn't a black site or a Kazichian prison. This looks like a warm welcome.

When we enter the reception hall, a doctor is waiting for us. The man asks the village elder if she wants to get her check-up right away or if she wants to rest from the trip first. While the old woman shuffles behind Sasha and the doctor, Nairi gets invited to the recording studio. I walk with her to the basement. We end up in a space of twenty-by-twenty metres, with cameras and all sorts of other equipment. It all looks professional. Three or four seemingly non-threatening people walk about the room. They don't look like they're in the military, I think, more like camera people or technicians. That's good news. These people don't want to hurt her. They want to talk to her.

One of the cameramen taps my arm and asks me to go back up. He says there are no outsiders allowed at the recording. I hesitate, but then he explains I'm a guest on the island, just like she is. A room has been prepared for me where I can freshen up and rest. Meanwhile, Nairi has sat down and doesn't seem aware of my presence anymore. Intensely focused, she listens to the instructions given to her by one of the men – she has one goal here and will let nothing and no one distract her from that.

I lie down on the soft bed and allow myself to relax. Nairi is safe here. And I am safe here. I close my eyes and see hers – those brown, sometimes green eyes. I think of yesterday, when she took off her sweater and revealed that the scars ran down to her left breast. With anyone else, that would have repulsed me, but not with her. It was like she was showing me who she was. Like the scars told her story, as mine would tell my story – the ones I got in Yemen, and before that Palestine, and before that Central Africa, and before that another hell on earth. And the scars I gave myself: the red lines from cutting and the black ones from tattoos. My body is filled with lines. On my back is an hourglass with high waves and dark, foamy water behind the glass instead of sand. On my arms, rows of ink lines – one for every successful operation. And on my stomach and thighs, a jumble of predators running through a misty forest. Someone once didn't want to have sex with me anymore after taking off my shirt. She said I look like someone who needs pain. But that isn't what it is. That's not my story.

Last night, I was with Nairi, and she didn't say anything about it. She helped me take off my T-shirt and rested her warm hand on the hourglass.

56

I jolt awake and jump out of bed. With my fists clenched, I step forward, ready to attack, but no one is there. The room is empty. All I hear is the whistling of the wind over the moonlit lakes outside my window. It looks like the sun has just set, but it doesn't feel like I slept for only an hour. My eyes are swollen, and my body feels lethargic. I turn on the light and see two plates on the table by the door. A piece of meat with steamed vegetables, and a fried egg on two pieces of bread: dinner from last night and breakfast from this morning. The food is cold and dry. I slept all day and the next day. I never fall asleep easily, and definitely not this long and this deep. Someone opened that door and put the food there, and even that did not wake me up. This isn't like me at all. Maybe my body is preparing itself for a life of herding goats in the mountains.

I freshen up and leave the room, looking for Nairi.

The building is minimalistic, with natural stone and large windows that allow an extraordinary view of snow-covered rocks in green waters. The landscape is almost alien. When I get to the hall, I see two soldiers standing by the stairs to the basement. I tell them I'm here for Nairi, but they refuse to let me through. One has a Russian accent, and the other one is French. They are mercenaries, but not like me. These are simple foot soldiers hired by the dozen. When I ask them who they work for, they pretend not to understand me.

'What time does she finish?' I ask.

'That will be a while,' someone behind me says.

I turn round and see Sasha standing on the railing. 'They just started and will keep going all night.'

'Why did they start filming at night?'

'The first day went very well. It went so well that she has a live connection to Atlanta now. It's early in the day there.'

'Can we see the broadcast somewhere?'

'No. It's not a live broadcast. They record the interviews for later. Just wait a little bit, soldier. One, two days at most, then she's done.'

The next day, I want to explore the house, but most of it is off limits. Almost all the doors are locked or guarded by soldiers who pretend they don't understand me. I can see they have a pass that opens every door, but I don't get an opportunity to steal one without getting into trouble. All I can do is walk from my room to the hall or take the stairs to a large living room. On one of the leather couches, the village elder sits drinking a cup of tea or coffee. She is wearing her black robe and stares at the snow falling outside. I ask if she is feeling better, and she says she is delighted with the doctor. He told her there is still hope. The day after tomorrow, she will get picked up to travel to a clinic where they can cure her.

'Cure? That is good news.'

'It's some kind of infection, I think.'

'You're not sure? I can talk to the doctor.'

She shakes her head. 'No need. Our ancestors brought me here. It's not my time yet. I knew it. I could feel I still have work to do in the mountains.'

I ask if she has spoken to Nairi.

She shakes her head again and coughs. It still sounds deep and painful. 'She is busy,' she mutters and takes a sip.

'Doesn't that seem strange to you? Why can't we speak to her?'

'Trust these people, soldier with no name. They are helping us. They are helping me to get better, and they are helping Nairi to write history. Don't be impatient. We want them to honour their promises.'

'I would love to see her for a few minutes, that's all. I want to make sure she's all right.'

She smiles, and her beady eyes disappear into her wrinkled skin. 'I understand, but you need to lie low. Promise me that? Don't thwart us. Big things are about to happen. I can feel it.'

I promise her and go back to my room. The day crawls by. I do some burpees and extensive stretching, and I eat well. I clean my gear and check my weapons. I think about the Jada. About Nairi, and what makes someone exceptional – what makes someone a leader. Right before nightfall, I walk over to the hall again, just to see if I can find her, but instead of Nairi, I see the village elder again. She is about to enter her room but stands still when she sees me. 'Patience,' she says quietly, and she gestures for me to turn round.

The morning after, a knock on the door wakes me up. I think of Nairi knocking on my door in Inima. But this time a short Kazichian man walks in. A weird little guy. He stutters and his head jolts back and forth as if someone else controls his movements. I have read about people developing tics and speech impediments after experiencing trauma. It looks like he went through something that became part of him.

'The c-c-client is very content,' he says, without introducing himself. 'The last phase of the operation will commence now. Get ready, you leave right away.'

I tell him I want to see Nairi. The short man stares at me in silence. He has a lazy left eye – he didn't exactly win the genetic lottery.

'I-I heard from Sasha that you feel connected t-to the Jada woman,' he says. 'Those people captured your imagination.' He chuckles. 'You're not the only one.'

'Who are you?' I blurt out. 'Why are you working with CNN?'

He walks up to me. 'Th-this nice room and tasty food are g-giving you an attitude, I notice. W-what is it to you who I am? You're here to fulfil an assignment. You signed a contract.'

I stand up and repeat that I want to see Nairi. My impatience surprises me.

'Listen here, s-s-soldier. I-I am here to make the interview with Nairi a success, that's all. You c-can either help us with that or resign and take the first flight back to Europe. Th-that will be the last time you ever cross the Kazichian border.'

I can't contain myself anymore. 'You're a Kazichian,' I say. 'Why are you helping Nairi? Why do you work with CNN? You're not American.'

He hangs his head and sighs. 'A-a-at this very moment, a group of soldiers is gathering not far from here. They want to stop the interview with Nairi. Will you help us to neutralise that camp, or are you returning to Germany?'

I ask why the soldiers want to stop the interview and how they found out about the interview in the first place.

The Kazichian turns round. 'Okay, f-f-fine. This was your last day in Kazichia. See you never.'

I follow him. 'No, wait. I want to finish the assignment. I'll help you with the soldiers. I won't ask any questions from now on.'

Annoyed, he nods and walks off. 'Get ready, you leave in five.'

A young soldier comes to collect me. We walk a narrow path to the other, flatter end of the island. A Russian Hind helicopter is waiting for us there, on a concrete platform. Seven armed soldiers are in it.

'Where are we going?' I ask after I've sat down, and the door has been closed.

One of the soldiers smirks. 'To the city of the red deer.'

57

We are on the top floor of the highest building. I think it is a factory from the Soviet era, but it's hard to see, only the outer walls and floors are still there. Through the openings that were once windows, we look out on a small city reclaimed by Mother Nature. The flats are surrounded by trees and shrubs, some walls are overgrown with thick roots. The roads and pavements are not visible; everything is green with plants or white with snow.

The buildings look like nests, not houses.

As we sneaked into town two red deer fled from a ruined petrol station. The biggest one was at least one and a half metres high, with the most impressive antlers I had ever seen. He stopped in front of the forecourt and looked at us as if we were unwelcome visitors. You can't blame the animal; we have come to bring death and destruction.

From the high rise, we look out on an encampment. At the end of a block of flats are a few containers and military tents against a row of low buildings. There are flags everywhere with a symbol I don't recognise. Is this the Kazichian army? Music is playing, and here and there, fires burn in empty barrels. Through the scope of my M4, I see armed men appear and disappear between the tents. From our observation post, I count a few dozen soldiers.

After assessing the situation, I turn to the commander lying next to me, looking through his scope.

'Okay, tell me, what is the plan here?'

'We got the order to eliminate everyone in this camp,' he says. 'No exception. No one can live to tell this.'

'Everyone? Because they want to stop the interview?'

'The Central Lakes need to remain a safe place.' It sounds blunt. He is not used to counter-questions. 'This entire region is off-limits. Those men down there know that. Clear?'

I nod, and the man looks through his scope again. He's not American, this commander, but Kazichian – by now, I recognise the accent immediately. The rest of the small combat unit is from the region. There are no Americans.

So, no CIA operation after all?

'Is your client the same as mine?' I ask. 'Who do you work for? America?'

The commander slowly turns round. 'Is there a problem, soldier? My assignment is to neutralise that camp and get all of us back to the island as soon as possible. Will you help me, or are you going home?'

I look at him. He is right. Why would it matter that I don't know who I'm fighting with, as long as we are on the same side? We are here to protect Nairi, and I will do everything in my power to help her.

I stand up and explain to the men how we will execute the coordinated attack on the camp. The tents are in between high buildings. That feels safe for the soldiers on the ground, but it creates a lot of blind spots we can use. Especially because no one in that camp is keeping watch; some men with weapons are shuffling around, but no one is really paying attention, and no one uses the height advantage in the empty flats.

'It's like they *want* to be attacked.'

Using a stick, I draw imaginary lines on the concrete floor and explain how we will split up into two teams: Team Alpha invades from the east side and Team Bravo from the west. Half of every team provides coverage; the other half invades the camp from different angles. The enemy has greater numbers, but we will use the element of surprise.

'Wait until you hear me fire. That is the sign to open your attack. Not a second earlier, not a second later. It all comes down to cooperation, precision and speed. Clear?'

The men nod, and the commander starts dividing the teams into two.

'Keep in contact with him through your radio,' he says, pointing at me. 'He is in charge.'

As I approach the camp, zigzagging from one building to the next, I hear in my earpiece that our watchmen in the flats are ready to cover us. They describe the positions of the enemy troops, and I draw a map in my head. When they are done, I remind everyone of their role.

'Focus on your own quadrant and trust the rest. I will move to the middle, you will move from outside to inside, as discussed.'

Four soft voices confirm. I whisper it is time to move in. Focused, I sneak in the direction of a white cloth that is hanging between two containers, like a makeshift entrance to the camp. I see that strange symbol on the cloth, like I saw on the flags. What kind of group is this? The cloth sways in the wind and someone in my earpiece says there are three men on the other side. I hold my M4 against my shoulder and tilt the weapon so I can use the offset red dot instead of the scope. Occasionally the bottom of the cloth folds up because of the wind. I spot three pairs of legs. The Kazichians have their backs to me. They are talking and laughing. I take another step closer. The cloth gets swept up by the wind and at that moment I pull the trigger three times, fast. The bullets pierce the symbol. Three loud shots echo in between the buildings, followed by a few dull thuds as the bodies hit the ground. I jerk the cloth to the side and see two soldiers lying there. The third one wears a helmet. He sits on his knees with convulsing muscles, like a short-circuiting robot. I pull out my SIG and shoot the back of his head, under his helmet.

The others open fire, just as we agreed. They are good soldiers. Around me, I hear screams and people running. Now I'm in the camp, I see the tents and containers form a circle around a stone building – it looks like a checkpoint or a toll booth. I check my flanks and shoot three soldiers trying to flee. Then I take out two on the other side, trying to hide behind a pile of sandbags. In my earpiece, someone says my flanks are clear. I walk to the building. I brought two flash grenades with me. I throw both of them through the thin window. The explosions are short but heavy. Dust clouds from the outside walls. When I hear moaning, I climb in through the window and step on a desk against the wall.

Five young men are on the ground, their hands against their ears. Two don't look older than sixteen, none of them older than twenty-one. Some of the weapons they carry don't have magazines and they are wearing bulletproof vests that look homemade and completely useless. I have to shoot them, these guys, but I need a moment to collect myself. These aren't soldiers, these are boys playing war. And I tower over them like an executioner at the gallows, wearing the best military gear in the world, with more experience than an entire American division altogether.

What am I doing here?

One of the boys tries to talk despite the sharp pain in his eardrums. I don't understand the language, but he is begging for his life. People always do, despite knowing there is no way to be saved. Sometimes they crawl away when the first shot wasn't fatal, as if I would spare them if they could leave the room. Every human tries. Just for one last breath, even if it is one excruciatingly painful last breath.

From the table, I eliminate the boys one by one by shooting the backs of their heads. One by one, they fall to the ground and stay there. The begging has stopped.

Killing people gives me no satisfaction at all. It's not some dark desire I'm fulfilling, it's just my job. Some people are good at sales and start working for a cigarette manufacturer. Not because they love lung cancer, but because they need to earn a living. I stay for a few seconds to make sure the bodies at my feet are dead. My smouldering gun points upwards, like a burning cigarette. In my earpiece, I get told that the other soldiers have the rest of the camp under control.

Under control means all of them have been eliminated.

Mission accomplished.

I can't help but wonder who we just slaughtered. Were these men – if you can even call them that – really a danger to the island? To Nairi?

58

Two of the soldiers in the camp have been kept alive and are being questioned by the commander and his second. The rest of us are collecting intel – paperwork, phones, computers – after which the camp and the jeeps will be lit on fire. The assignment is clear: don't leave any proof we were here. No proof of what has taken place.

We scour the camp and take everything we can find. It's not much, but eventually, I find a laptop in the stone house. I step over the bodies to pick the dusty thing up. Immediately, the screen turns on and Nairi appears onscreen. What is this? When I press play, Nairi starts talking, but I can't understand what she is saying. She is wearing a black sweater I don't recognise, and her voice sounds hollow. I scroll down and see images of her, and the symbol I saw in the camp. With some guesswork, I find the translate button in the browser, and the article turns into English text.

Nairi of the Jada is the Man with a Thousand Faces.

I don't understand. This can't be true. Nairi told me she never wanted to be a terrorist. That is why she was hoping the rumours were true, so someone else could do what she couldn't. Was all of that a lie? Had she been the Man with a Thousand Faces all along? I find it impossible to believe. And then something else: the strange symbol I didn't recognise, is part of the uprising, apparently. If that is true, who did we just kill?

I turn one of the bodies on its back and my stomach turns. This is clearly not a Kazichian man, but a Jada. I recognise the flatter nose and the round face, whereas Kazichians have sharp noses and straight, angular jaws. The people I slaughtered like animals less than an hour ago are the same people offering me a home in the Akhlos mountains.

I feel panicked and my thoughts get jumbled. Did Nairi get tricked? Was I working for the Kazichian government? But why did Nairi get welcomed on the island so warmly? Why were there cameras and other equipment ready for an interview? They could have just thrown her off the plane.

I hear something. Something drives towards us from the forest behind the deserted city. I hear a low hum and the hiss of a pneumatic braking system.

I run out and one of the other soldiers waves at me. 'Time to go!'

'Back to the island?' I ask.

The soldier nods and points. From the woods, four military trucks emerge. The convoy drives through the overgrown streets of the ghost city and stops right by us. Out of the first truck climbs the short stuttering man I met on the island. The commander walks up to him, and they talk for a bit. The man pulls out a black box with an antenna. I have no idea what it is. He presses a few buttons and looks at me.

'T-t-ime to go!' he shouts and points at the forest.

The camp and the cars have been lit, and the fire is spreading quickly.

The soldiers divide among the vehicles, but I just stand there like an idiot. Why were we here? Why did these men need to die? These boys? I still don't know what exactly took place here, or who gave us these orders, but the feeling I am fighting on the wrong side is getting stronger by the minute. And now? Do I eliminate these soldiers one by one to prevent more Jada from getting killed? That is a suicide mission. So, what then?

Back to Nairi. Back to the island.

If this army is the enemy, then Nairi, sitting in that beautiful house, is in danger. I don't know why she is being filmed and interviewed, but she needs to get out of there. I need to help her escape and return to her village. I promised her. I swore. And without a vehicle, I'm stuck in the wilderness.

I run to the last truck and climb in.

The trucks drive along a bumpy road into the forest. I am sitting on the wooden benches with two other soldiers, under the green cloth. Nobody says anything. Everyone is looking at their boots. And the deeper into the forest we get, the more nervous I feel. I want to get to Nairi as fast as I can. I never should have taken her to that island. I never should have left her there.

Again, I ask if we're going back, and the soldier opposite me mumbles not to worry. I see something in his eyes as he looks at me. Something that wasn't there a few hours ago. It looks like fear. Is he afraid? Of what? Of me? Maybe I'm imagining things. I try to control my breathing and calm my heart rate down.

The trucks turn into a side road, and I can tell by the sighing brakes that the first truck has stopped. Our vehicle joins the queue and slows down. The thick leafless treetops obscure the sky and engulf us in darkness. While the truck turns, I stand up to stick my head out of the opening. I want to see where we're going, but one of the soldiers grabs my legs.

'Stay in your seat.' He points at the bench. 'We're almost there.'

Now I'm sure of it; something is wrong. The soldier doesn't want me to see where we are going. He doesn't want me to know what happens when the trucks come to a standstill.

I pretend to sit down, but right before I hit the bench, I jump up and punch the soldier opposite me in his larynx. Panicked, he starts gasping for air and tries to pull out his gun. The soldier next to him wants to jump forward to grab me, but I'm too quick for them. In one smooth motion, I grab my K-bar blade while I hit the soldier opposite me a second time with my elbow. He lost all interest in his gun now and grips his throat with both hands. Still with the same motion, I thrust the blade into the other man's throat horizontally, until only the handle is visible. He stops in the middle of getting up as if I skewered him on the knife. I push him back down to the bench and retrieve the weapon from his neck. The other soldier is still catching his breath, but I pull his hands aside and cut through his carotid arteries and trachea. With my arms out, I keep the two soldiers in their place on the wooden bench. I let them drown in their own blood. Convulsing, they look at me, hitting my hands. They try to fight and yell, but nobody knows what just happened. The only sounds I hear are the humming engine block and my own nasal breathing.

The truck turns further and comes to a halt. I hear soldiers emerging from the front vehicles – the frozen forest floor cracks under their heavy boots. One of the soldiers opposite me is dead, the other one attempts to call out to his mates one last time. I pull his chin up, opening up the cut in his throat. Blood gusts from his arteries, covering my arms, and I see pent-up fear flowering and blooming in his eyes. It doesn't last long: soon, the leaves wither, leaving his face expressionless and empty.

59

I gently lay the two soldiers down and climb out of the back of the truck. From the corner of my eye, I see a group of people at a clearing in the forest, but there is no time to take in my surroundings. I slide under the truck and wait there on the cold ground. I am holding the M4, but in this situation, it's useless. Silence is my biggest friend now.

The driver gets out. He yells something in Kazichian and knocks on the side of the truck; he wants us to get out. I wait until he approaches and hold my knife out. My arms and hands are the same colour as the handle: blood-red. My sleeves are drenched and heavy as if I have been standing out in the rain. When the driver gets to the back of the car and looks inside, I plunge my knife into the back of his knee. He collapses like a sack of potatoes. I drag him under the truck, but I am a tad too slow, and he manages to cry out before I get to him.

I strangle him, but the damage has been done. From under the truck, I watch as two soldiers approach us: they heard the scream. I press even harder, and the driver's eyes bulge out of his sockets. When he stops moving, I pull him from under the truck. On his combat belt hangs a grenade that I confiscate. The two soldiers are close now, but I manage to sneak by the vehicle unseen and crouch among the trees.

From here, I can take in the situation.

I see a row of civilians being led forward. They look around skittishly. One of them is a woman I know. Sasha. She is wearing the same coat as when we were in the mountains, but she is tied up, and tears stream down her face. She keeps wailing something, a word I can't make out. Together with two large men, she is led forward. They walk towards the hole in the ground.

I know what this is. I know what is about to happen here. I know mercenaries who fought in Yugoslavia, or Bolivia, men who had to kill civilians. This is an execution. That hole in the ground will be turned into a mass grave today.

A shot sounds and the face of the CNN woman disappears behind her flowing hair while she falls backwards in the pit. Next up are two men. The one closest to me has a neck tattoo I recognise. They're mercenaries. Just like me.

Two shots sound and the men fall in the pit.

What did that short, stuttering man say again? *This is the last phase of the operation*. The phase where everyone who worked on the operation, gets cleaned up.

Someone cries out. I suspect the bodies by the truck have been found. They are talking about 'mercenary' and start looking around. I feared a coordinated search operation would start, but the men at the mass grave don't know what to focus on, the mercenaries, so they don't escape their executions, or the two soldiers calling out from the truck. The moment of indecisiveness allows me to create some distance. I start circling the clearing. As I sneak through the trees, I check my magazine and load my weapon.

What do I do?

I crouch in the bushes and stay very still, weighing my options. Two shots sound again. Another two specialists killed. Every soldier that was sitting beside me blindfolded in the back of that Hercules plane, is probably waiting by the pit to meet his end now. And there is nothing I can do to save these men, however hard that may be for me. If I give up my position, it's all over. I *need* to get away from here. I *need* to save Nairi from that island. That's my priority as a soldier of the Jada.

Just as I want to sneak deeper into the forest, I hear a scream. A piercing sound, like the cry of an angry panther. I glance towards the mass grave and see an old woman stepping forward. Long grey hair obscures her face. Is it the village elder? Then, that piercing scream sounds again and someone else joins the old woman. She appears as if it's the most normal thing, as if I could have expected her to be here. Maybe I should have.

It's Nairi.

Her hand is tied to her belt with a zip tie, and she looks like a shadow of herself. Her skin is grey, her eyes half-shut. But still, she fights. She tries to bite the soldiers and kicks them. One of them thumps her stomach with the back of his rifle and she collapses.

Before I realise what I'm doing, I get up from my hiding spot and walk towards her.

I see from the corner of my eye the soldiers by the truck are approaching me. Within a few seconds, they will see me, but I don't care. I keep walking and get my M4 ready. Nairi tries to run away but is grabbed and pulled next to the old woman again. Behind her, a soldier appears, his barrel pointed at her head.

I need to hit him.

Between his skull and my rifle is about seventy-five metres, and I estimate I can't shoot more than twice before I am taken down. Probably just once.

I sit on one knee.

'Nairi!' I yell to scare the gunmen and win some time. As she turns round, I breathe out calmly and pull the trigger.

Nothing.

Nothing happens.

My reflex is to tilt the weapon to find the malfunction quickly, but I don't have time for that. I hit the bottom of the magazine, hoping that will fix the problem, and try to fire again, but nothing happens.

The M4 jams.

I tilt the weapon but don't see a problem.

To the right of me, shots are fired. The soldiers have seen me. Bullets fly past me. I lie down and pull out my SIG. A bullet hurtles right past me, and I hear the bark of a tree bursting.

The village elder bends over from exhaustion or fear, giving me a second chance to shoot the executioners. I breathe out and apply pressure to the trigger.

Nothing. This one doesn't work either.

How is this possible?

I want to check the SIG, but then two shots are fired from the other side of the mass grave. Short, dry bangs, dulled by tree trunks and snow-covered dead leaves.

Nairi looks at me. She has turned round. Her eyes look brown, but I know they are dark green. Dark green as the water of the lakes where I left her, on the island of the enemy. Her head collapses and pulls her into the pit. A dull thump sounds when her body hits the frozen earth. She is gone. She fell, as the leaves from the trees surrounding us – as if it was natural, insignificant. As if it was supposed to go like that. And it's my fault.

X. Soldier of the Jada

60

I feel rage rushing through my fists. Like boiling water, it burns the insides of my knuckles. I used that pain for a while, to rise above my humanity. When I had to kill a woman or an old man, I pulled that rage up and let it blind me. It made it less difficult. But the rage got more intense each time, and it started taking less and less effort for it to return. And then I lost control. The feeling wouldn't go away. It got so bad that I started cutting myself. I'm not proud of that, but it was the only way to relieve the pressure. And I had to make it stop, or I might have transformed into someone else. Someone drowning in his rage. Someone like my father.

The first time I got arrested, I was thirteen. They signed me up for anger therapy. Compulsory. Three times a week I sat there and got told how to breathe and count to ten. It never helped. It felt like I had to fight a forest fire with a water gun. Everyone said it was my attitude, that I would never get anything accomplished this way. But I knew they were wrong. I knew they didn't understand what was happening inside of me. But I couldn't put words to it. I couldn't contain it.

Now I can.

For the first time in my life, I understand why my heart has a storm brewing inside it. That's not a curse but a blessing. And the point isn't to calm the storm: I need to weaponise it and point it in the right direction.

I am lying on my stomach on the cold forest floor, not far from the mass grave they dumped Nairi in as if she were a barrel of illegal chemical waste. My M4 stopped working, my SIG Sauer handgun stopped working, and so I had to watch her skull explode. That mysterious woman. That fighter. I had to watch them erase her, like a spelling mistake. And what I feel now, burning inside me, isn't simply rage. It is a force much older than me. Maybe as old as my bloodline. A primal form of violence that keeps echoing, generation after generation, like a remnant of the Big Bang.

That therapist said that anger blinds you, takes control away from you. If this is true, then whatever I felt all along wasn't anger. Because now that I'm letting it rage, now that I stop resisting, my entire being is focus and energy.

I see the executioners that just killed my one true love. They are pointing their weapons at me.

I see the other soldiers from the corner of my eye, the bullets already left their guns.

And I see the parked trucks to the left of me, along the edge of the forest.

Most people freeze when something unexpected happens. Most people wait until they're dead, or until they get saved. Not me. I don't freeze. I become a blaze.

I crawl backwards into the snowed-under bushes and roll onto my back. Bullets fly around me, but I am hard to spot because of my camouflage. I pull out the grenade that I stole from the soldier in the truck. The boots of my opponents are getting closer, but the group doesn't form flanks. They are making a rookie mistake; our target is by himself, so we're going straight in.

I pull the pin from the grenade, but don't throw it yet. I release the clamp, and, in my mind, I count to three, then I throw it over the bushes and roll onto my stomach, my hands covering my ears.

The grenade explodes mid-air, right in their faces. Perfectly timed.

With ringing ears and blurry vision, I get up and run along the clearing. There is no use in going deeper into the forest because I don't have weapons to defend myself with. The men will chase me, and they will find me. So, I run to the trucks. The engine of the front truck is being started; the brake lights turn on. That's where I need to go. That vehicle is my only way out.

The soldiers by the pit divided themselves; two stay with the prisoners, and three approach me, right through the grave. They open fire again and keep shooting until I disappear behind the truck. I run to the driver's side and open the door. Behind the wheel is, exactly as I'd hoped, the short stuttering man. As soon as he sees me, he climbs over the centre console to the passenger seat to escape. I let him climb through the car and take a seat on the now empty driver's seat, which I push back as far as possible. Then I pull the short Kazichian, who is trying to escape through the other door, back into the truck. I sit him on my lap like a toddler.

'N-n-no!' he yells, trying to hit me.

I press him against me and put my knife to his throat.

'Shift and drive away,' I whisper into his ear.

The short man struggles for too long, and the soldiers start circling the car.

'Tell your men I will cut your throat if they shoot the tyres.'

'There is n-no use. You will never make it out of the c-c-country alive.'

'That's why you better take me seriously, Mr Stutter. I've got nothing to lose.'

To the right, over by the pit, there is yelling and shooting I see from the side window one of the mercenaries took his chance and is trying to save himself. The soldiers have to divide their attention now. I take the hand of the short man and lay it on the gear stick. Then I take my pocketknife and stab it right through his hand into the stick.

'Shift and drive away,' I say.

To my surprise, he doesn't scream. Growling like an angry animal, he does as I say. While he shifts the vehicle into first gear, his body trembles with pain. But he doesn't scream. He is a fighter, just like me.

While we pull up slowly, the Kazichian shouts something at the soldiers through his window. Presumably, he told them to follow us, but I ignore it. First, we'll create as much distance as we can and then I'll come up with my next move.

The soldiers step aside hesitantly and let us go.

'W-w-where to?' he asks, his teeth clenched.

I tell him to drive down the road. I have no idea where it leads to, but if we tried to turn and go back to the city of the red deer, I would give the soldiers a second chance.

'P-pull the knife out,' he says. 'I'll do a-as you say.'

'That knife stays there until we lose everyone,' I say in his ear. He smells of cigarettes.

I search his coat pockets and take his smartphone. With one hand, I open the door and throw the mobile into the woods.

'W-w-what is your p-plan exactly?' he asks. 'What is your goal?'

'No need for you to know,' I say. 'You do as I say, and you don't ask questions.'

61

Rows of stems or stumps surround the farm, white with snow. I don't know much about agriculture, but I think it's corn. Behind the farm is a large barn with open doors next to two storage silos – a good place to hide the truck. I tell the short man to drive onto the property.

'W-what do you want to do here?' he asks. His head hangs slumped over the wheel; he looks pale. I ask him to shift gears to climb the hill, and he moans with pain. But he has stopped asking me to pull the knife from his hand. He probably realised that the bleeding would start.

The farm is old but well-kept. I lean forward to try and see if anyone is home.

The short man looks at me. 'Wherever we go. They will f-f-find us.'

I ignore him.

After the soldiers disappeared from the rearview mirror, I sat in the passenger seat. I gave the short man the chance to talk. I asked him about Nairi and the operation, but he kept insisting he didn't know anything. I asked why she was filmed. He said he was just following orders, like me. I don't know if he is telling the truth. I find it hard to read him, that weird little man with his strange eyes. And so, we drove through the woods in silence, looking for a way out of this mess.

'Keep driving,' I tell him.

The barn is spacious and the truck fits easily. Against the wall are a few barrels, an old distilling kettle, and three bathtubs covered with plastic slabs. When I get out of the car, my nostrils burn. This corn farmer brews his own whisky or vodka. Or tries to. That's why the doors need to be open, it smells flammable in here.

Before I get the Kazichian from the truck, I circle the farm. The house is quiet. There is no one home, but not for long; I see a big pot brewing on the stove. Still, I am sticking to my plan of hiding out here. This is the perfect spot: the truck is out of sight and the large fields around us prevent a surprise attack.

When I get back to the barn, I see the short Kazichian has laid his forehead on the wheel. He is almost unconscious. I pull both his hand and the knife from the gear stick, waking him up in a scream. He grabs his wrist and fights the urge to pull the knife from the wound. He hisses threats of ways he will kill me between his teeth. But when I grab him, he lets himself be carried like a feverish toddler.

I take him to the first floor of the house, from where I can watch the property through the windows. I put the short man in a chair in the hallway. He is weak and barely awake, so I give him some more water. When he finishes that, it's time for questioning.

Movies give a distorted idea of torture. You usually see a heroic man pursing his lips despite his gruesome pain – like it's a question of character. In reality, the human body is a simple system. It has buttons in different places, and when you press them, the mouth starts talking. No secret is great enough to offer resistance. On the contrary. Often, you don't even have to press the buttons. When you tell the person what you plan on doing, their imagination does all the work for you. In almost all interrogations I had to do in my life, I never touched anyone.

I pull the Kazichian's grey trousers down so that he sits on the wooden chair in his underwear. He looks at me as if he knows exactly what will happen next. Maybe he has been on my side of this exchange.

'Why did Nairi of the Jada have to die?' I ask.

'W-w-within twenty minutes the Circle will be here. M-maybe

they're here already. Those are the m-most skilled soldiers of the C-C-Caucasus.'

I take his underwear off and slowly pull my knife from its holster. I rest the red blade on his purplish scrotum. The Kazichian squints. I see the desperation in the way he frowns. He doesn't want to imagine what is about to happen, but he does. He knows what I'm doing, and why I'm doing it, but he can't resist me. It will be about five to ten minutes, then I will know everything he knows.

'What is the goal of this operation?' I ask calmly. 'Why was Nairi being filmed in that basement? Why didn't they execute her immediately?'

The short man shakes his head and says he has children.

Very slowly, I turn the knife. 'Then you won't miss these as much.' I slightly press the blade, causing a superficial cut. 'As soon as I cut your balls off, I will put an elastic band around your empty sack. I don't want you to bleed to death. I want you to feel it. I want you to know what happened.'

He shuts his eyes and tries not to turn my words into visuals. 'Th-they will find us. Y-y-your time is up.'

'No one followed us. Tell me about the island.' I press the knife harder into his skin. It starts bleeding in earnest now. He can feel the warm fluid running down his leg, he can smell it, and I see tears in his eyes. And that is the moment I know I broke him. 'Tell me what kind of a place that is, and I will make this stop.'

He mutters something. I tell him to speak up, and he tries again. 'It's the Lechkov family's holiday home,' he whispers. I can tell he is finally speaking the truth.

'Are they my client?' I ask. 'Did Lechkov orchestrate all of this?'

Before he can say anything, we hear a car approaching.

Through the window, I see an ancient Lada drive up the property and stop at the barn. A man in a black fleece gets out. He probably wonders what that giant truck is doing there.

I take the big Rolex from the Kazichian and get his wallet from his pocket. 'I am taking the farmer inside. If you speak a word of Kazichian, I will skin you, head to toe, with my knife. Understood?'

The man shakes his head. 'No worries. This is Neza territory. That farmer ha-hates me and my language. He won't he-help me.'

When I walk down the stairs, the farmer sees me through the window. He stands still. Under his arm he carries a big diving suit, and he has bottles over his shoulder. I open the front door, and he drops his ice diving equipment.

I wave and force a friendly smile. My sleeves are dark red with blood. 'Mr, is this your farm?' I ask.

I smell fresh fish.

He nods and looks over his shoulder at the car – does he have a harpoon in there? Or another weapon?

I walk up to him and show him the watch and the money. 'For you,' I say, and unfold the stack of bills. 'I just need some help.'

The farmer looks to his left. Right at that second, I see something shimmer in the corner of my eye. I thought it was the Rolex at first. I thought sunlight was reflecting in the sapphire. But if the farmer sees it too, the shimmer must be coming from further away.

I let myself fall backwards but still get hit in my shoulder.

The bullet came from the right.

It burns and my arm goes numb, which means I can't break my fall. I land on my chin on the frozen path. I bite my tongue and taste blood. I hear the whistling sound of the bullet flying past the farm, so it must have been a graze. I lie on my side and gaze across the fields. Behind the swirling banknotes, I see the reflection. A sniper sits hidden among the trees.

How did they find me this quickly? We drove over old tractor tracks, and I checked multiple times for helicopters. I threw that short man's mobile out right away.

How do they know where I am?

The farmer runs back to his car, and I dive for the porch. Another shot. Part of the wooden fencing shatters. After the second shot, I run inside and shut the door.

I turn round and see that the farmer can't get away; the tyres of his car are being punctured by bullets. A woman gets out, and the two of them run to the barn.

I get up and run upstairs, ignoring the pain in my shoulder. I feel the blood oozing under my clothes down my arm. It's a lot of blood; I don't have much time.

The short Kazichian is still sitting on his chair with his pants on his knees.

'How did they find me?' I ask.

He smirks. 'Your equipment is filled with t-t-trackers. W-why do you think your w-w-weapons malfunctioned? Lowlife. We control you like a ro-o-obot.'

The glass in one of the windows shatters, and a bullet impales the wall on the other side of the landing. I crouch and pull the pocketknife from the Kazichian's hand. He cries and tries to apply pressure on the wound but I grab his wrists so he can't. The blood shoots out like a geyser. An artery was hit. Without help, this man will die today.

Will I too?

'Why did Nairi of the Jada need to die?' I ask, holding his hands. 'Tell me the truth if you want me to apply pressure on that wound. Was she the Man with a Thousand Faces? Why did you film her?'

'Th-the soldiers outside.' He tries to smile again. 'You have no idea. That's the Ci-Circle. The deadliest unit we've ever trained. Even if I told you the truth, you would never make it out of here a-alive.'

Another shot through the top window. They are shooting too high on purpose because they don't know where their leader is. The salvos are meant to keep me inside the house, away from the windows. That means the rest of the team will come to the farm.

'Tell me the truth and I'll let go of your hands!' I yell and stab his shoulder with the small knife.

'ERIS!' he cries. 'We needed Nairi for ERIS.'

'What is that?' I ask, but before he can respond, another shot is fired through the window.

There is no time left; the team is on its way. I push the man back in his chair and walk downstairs. In the kitchen, I sit crouched next to the pot of potatoes to catch my breath.

What can I do? Is this the end? How can I stop these men without weapons? Should I go look in the farmer's car, and see if there is a harpoon in there?

I look through the kitchen window for a split second, then duck behind the stove. I didn't see anyone running across the fields, so there is still time. But they are coming, no doubt. They will most likely attack the house from all sides at the same time.

What can I do?

Above my head, the pot is on the stove. The spluttering water sounds out of place, as if it's just another lazy Sunday. I look up and see the blue flame get pulled towards one of the shot-up windows. The window that gives me a clear view of the barn, where it smelled like moonshine whisky.

That's it. That's my way out.

I get up and run through the front door. I run before I have time to get scared of the sniper pointing his scope at me. I need to take this risk. Because if I survive those few metres to the barn, where the farmer and his wife are hiding, I still have a shot. If I make it to the barn, I can beat them all.

62

Thatia Lazarova lies on her stomach between two tree trunks, waiting for her target to show himself again. Because of her white and dark green camouflage, she almost disappears into the vegetation; only the black rifle scope of her AW Covert bolt action rifle stands out in the snowy forest.

'One more time,' she whispers to herself. 'Show me that cute face one more time.'

He should have been dead, her target. She heard the farmer's car and pointed her scope at the front of the house. The man walked outside to reassure the farmer, just as she thought he would. She took her time, pointed and fired. But at the very last second, he ducked.

'Blondie? You got him?'

One of her fellow soldiers asks for a status update over the radio, but Thatia doesn't respond. She hates that nickname.

Then, the man gets up. Thatia tries to hit him again as he ducks across the porch, but she sees the door open and close. He is back inside.

'Blondie, you there? What happened?'

'I don't get it,' she says. 'How did he know I was going to shoot?'

'Sunshade, Blondie?'

That's it. She forgot to attach the sunshade to her scope. That lucky bastard saw the shimmering of the polished glass. How could she be so stupid?

Without losing sight of the house, she tries to feel her way to the rifle case. 'Don't call me that,' she hisses in the radio while grabbing the cap. 'I'm a brunette.'

'Blonde, brunette, it's all the same to me, girl.'

A deep male voice interjects. 'Enough chitchat. Focus.' Major Zichy, their commander, is fed up.

They still can't handle it, Thatia thinks while she attaches the shade on her scope. *They feel threatened. If I make a mistake, they enjoy it. So unprofessional.*

She keeps watching the house, applying pressure by firing at the windows. After a few minutes the target reappears. The man casually runs out the front door and crosses the porch. Does he want to die? Thatia points the crosshairs just in front of his body to lead her target and moves with him, breathing calmly, applying pressure to the trigger. But then he suddenly stops, takes a step back and runs on. She tries to move with him again, but he disappears in the wooden barn.

Shit!

'Did he bring Torelli?' The major sounds tense.

'Target was alone, Torelli must still be in the house,' Thatia says. 'Maybe he's trying to escape with the truck.'

Now that the target is in a different building from the hostage, they can reposition. The unit is split into two: team Alpha approaches the barn, team Bravo the farm.

'Alpha and Bravo cover each other, sniper backs both.'

'Someone get Blondie on her back,' someone says. 'Best view all around.'

'Quit it! Leonid Torelli works directly for director Yanev. If he dies, we're in big trouble. Team Alpha, take your positions . . . now!'

Right and left of Thatia, bushes start moving. The men spread along the edge of the field. In the meantime, she watches the barn and the farm. Leonid Torelli doesn't show himself – he might be dead already.

She wonders what the target's plan is. He is supposed to be a trained soldier, so he must realise that escaping is impossible. Why did he run to the barn, then?

Major Zichy checks in through the radio. 'Team Alpha in position?'

While the team members confirm one by one, a low sound emerges from the barn. The truck appears.

'Sniper, is that the target? Confirm.'

Thatia shifts her body slightly, trying to see through the side window of the vehicle, but the truck bumpily crosses the field. 'Negative,' she says. 'Vehicle is too far away to identify driver.'

'Team Alpha – go,' the major says, and the men enter the field, their weapons ready to fire.

'We're counting on you, Blondie,' the joker says in her earpiece. He doesn't sound so tough anymore.

The truck doesn't drive off the property, but steers towards the farm. For a second, Thatia fears the target wants to pick up the hostage, but then the truck starts circling the house. The circles get bigger and bigger.

'What is he doing?' someone asks. 'He is driving in a spiral.'

'Focus on your job.' The commander sounds curt.

The truck starts speeding up, the circles are getting bigger.

'Sniper here: driver is not the target,' Thatia says. She sees an older man in a black sweater sitting behind the wheel. Probably the farmer. 'I repeat: driver is *not* the target. Target must still be in the barn.'

The truck stops in the middle of the field. The farmer gets out with his hands in the air. He is crying and yells something, but she can't hear him. His shoulders are shaking.

'What is he saying?'

'His wife,' one of the soldiers replies. 'He says his wife needs help in the barn.'

'Team Bravo in position?' The major is unperturbed. 'Target is most likely holding a civilian hostage. Elimination of target has priority. Sniper, watch both buildings.'

Again, everyone confirms quickly, and after a split second, the second team approaches the farm. The entire unit is on the field now, except for Thatia, she is still hidden in the forest. She sees the major crossing the field with team Bravo. The farmer has sunk to his knees, and she still sees his lips moving, but the men pass him and his truck, like he's invisible. One of the soldiers quickly checks if there is someone in the back of the truck, but says it just has empty barrels.

'Sniper,' the major's voice says in her earpiece, 'when we are thirty metres away, I want a few cover salvos through the roofs of both buildings.'

Thatia monitors the house and the barn at the same time, to cover both groups. During the admission test for the Circle, the instructor had sent her away because of her petite physique. Kazichian snipers use the big Russian SVDK rifle, firing munitions that can penetrate all types of bulletproof vests and armour, but the recoil of that calibre is gigantic, and Thatia couldn't get the weapon under control. For the instructor, that was reason enough to dismiss her. But Thatia didn't accept the rejection and decided to get her trusted AW Covert rifle from the barracks and return to the shooting range without permission. She lay down between two shooting ranges and took turns shooting the targets to her left and right. Her agility was unmatched for a sniper. Her barrel shifted back and forth with mechanical precision, like a robot in a car factory. The trainer and other snipers gathered around her, while she shot up the sandbags with unbelievable speed. And when her magazine was empty, she turned round to face the instructor and said: 'I can't shoot through every armour, but I can cover two flanks at once. Even three.'

She got accepted to the training programme on the spot – the first woman in the Circle. She felt proud but knew her battle with Kazichian sexism would soon begin. But on this day, among the dormant corn fields, she knows she can finally show them her worth. Her entire unit is in the open field and to cover them, she needs to watch two buildings at once. This could be the end of 'Blondie' and 'girl'.

'And now we wait,' she tells herself, sliding the barrel from left to right. 'Take a deep breath, it will happen soon.'

But then the yelling starts. First from the men in team Bravo, standing near the farm. Thatia immediately points her rifle in their direction but doesn't know what to do. She doesn't see a target or a fight happening. The soldiers standing around the porch start shouting and waving their arms. One of them hits his legs and takes off his helmet, as if insects are crawling under his skin.

'What is happening?' she asks, but no response.

Then the soldiers in team Alpha start shouting and waving their arms. Thatia looks at the empty, snowy field, filled with desperate men. They look like they have collectively lost their minds. Like they are bewitched.

'What is happening?' she repeats. 'What do I do?'

She looks past her rifle at the farm. Some men drop to the ground and start rolling. Others clutch their throats.

'Fire!' Major Zichy cries suddenly. His voice is so loud her earpiece crackles. 'It's burning!'

Thatia sees no fire and no smoke, but still their entire unit is on the ground. She gets up, hangs the AW Covert on her shoulder and takes her AK 12 assault rifle. Running down the hill, she hears shots fired from the barn.

'Target is here!' someone yells in the radio. 'He . . .'

A shot is fired. Silence. Another shot.

Thatia feels cold sweat on her back. The men in teams Alpha and Bravo are being eliminated, one by one. She runs faster and checks if her rifle is loaded. She wants to slam the magazine one extra time to be sure, but suddenly stands still. Something is off: her cheeks feel hot. She looks up and sees the air in front of her vibrating.

'Fire!' the farmer cries. He is still on his knees, waiting in front of the truck. 'Stop there! Invisible fire!'

Thatia looks at the man but doesn't know what he is talking about. Then she sees blue barrels sticking out of the truck and realises what happened. The target dumped a flammable chemical around the building, in the shape of a spiral.

The farmer looks at her and shouts something about his wife in the barn. 'Help us,' he says, 'help my wife.'

She asks why he can't walk to the farm.

'Ethanol,' the farmer says. 'Ethanol fire is invisible and has no smell, and snow spreads the flames. He lit the fire in the barn. My wife is there. Help her.'

Thatia sees a trail of melted snow between the corn stalks; the target waited until all the soldiers were in the spiral, then ignited the fire.

That dirty bastard.

She takes better hold of the AK 12 and runs along the edge of the invisible flames, towards the barn, using the truck for cover. The radio is eerily quiet. The shouting stopped. But the silence doesn't last long.

With a giant blow the barn explodes and transforms into a fireball that rises up in the air.

Thatia Lazarova's small body gets hurled to the cold ground with a thump. She feels a cutting pain running from her spine to her legs and wants to cry out, but the fall sucked the air out of her lungs.

Dead silent she lies there, staring up at the light blue sky.

First, she hears creaking footsteps, then his face appears. The face of the one-man army that just killed an entire combat unit of the Circle.

63

I am back at the farm and run to the sink. I must have spilt some ethanol on my hands because they are scorched. The pain mostly stings my underarms, not my hands, but I know that's where it's coming from. I smell the burning skin and see the red circles on my fingers. As the water runs on my hand, bits of skin fall off like layers of soap. Quickly I remove my hands from the water and fold them under my underarms until the burning stops. Where is my head? The water spreads the ethanol flames instead of putting them out. The pain is almost unbearable. These are serious burn marks that will get infected if I don't get them treated. Just like my shoulder.

Outside, I hear the farmer's wife running on the path. She is looking for her husband. These people didn't deserve this, they had nothing to do with this. I regret having to hold her hostage, but the only way this plan would work is if the farmer would do exactly as I said.

The stuttering Kazichian is not moaning anymore. The explosion in the barn tore the house up, so maybe the blast knocked him out. Maybe he bled to death. Walking up the stairs, I pull the area map from my pocket. At the top of the stairs, the Kazichian is on the floor. I turn him over and hit him in the face. No reaction. Then I get my black etui and grab the adrenaline injector. Mere seconds later, he sits up straight and mutters a word I don't know. I pull his hair and make him face the map.

'Show me Lechkov Island. How do I get there? Where is it?'

He turns his head with a dazed look.

'I have a tourniquet that will stop the bleeding. Do you want to live? Point out the island.'

His eyes move to the map.

I circle the Central Lakes. 'It must be here somewhere. I have antibiotics.'

'You w-will never leave that place a-alive,' he whispers.

'Then you might as well point it out,' I say, and I squeeze his hand.

With his index finger he creates a red circle of blood on the map. In the middle of a small lake. There is no island there. Not according to the cartographers. But it's exactly the same spot as the woman with the sniper rifle on her back pointed out. Before I cut her throat. This can't be a coincidence; it's the place. Someone there can tell me why Nairi had to die. What goal was so important that she needed to be sacrificed. And why she had to get strung along in a recording studio. On that island, I might win back my place with the Jada.

I put the short Kazichian down and stumble down the stairs. He tries to call out to me, probably for the help I promised him, but I don't have time. My shoulder hurts like hell and the nerves in my hand are still burning. I feel my strength fading away. If I don't act soon, I'll be dead before I reach that island.

I swipe the glass shards off the kitchen table and unroll my black etui. It's not much, but enough to save myself. I take out a parcel of pure amphetamine, mix it with caffeine and snort the thick powder. This isn't my favourite combination; in thirty minutes I'll be parched. But my strength comes back immediately, and my sight is focused again. The pain in my arms will fade in a couple of minutes. In the meantime, I take two packets with crystals and crush them to dust with the back of my knife. It's PCP, so I need to be careful. Slightly too much and it will turn me into a zombie, but just the right amount, and I will be an unstoppable fighting machine.

When the speed has dulled the pain, I take off my shirt and study the bullet wound on my shoulder. It's still bleeding, but there is no time to stitch it. I brought a cautery pen for small wounds which I use to sear the tips of the blood vessels. It's hard to keep the pen straight because of the pain in my burned fingers, but still, I manage to fuse the skin a little bit. Instead of my own clothes, I put on one of the soldiers' gear. The trousers have burn holes and the shoes are too small, but apparently, my own gear is bugged.

I listen at the bottom of the stairs for a second, but the man upstairs is quiet, so I leave the farm. On the property, I see the farmer's diving gear. I take the bottles and the thick ice diving suit; they might be useful for approaching the house undetected. I walk over to the sniper on the ground, staring at the sky in a puddle of her own blood, turn her round and take her AW Covert.

As I run through the corn fields filled with bodies and rubble, the diving suit and rifle over my shoulder, I see her face in my mind.

Nairi.

She saw me. And that allowed me to see myself.

XI. The Battle for Stolia

64

A black Volkswagen Passat is parked in the old centre of Stolia. At first sight, there is nothing suspicious about the car. The front bumper hangs loose, the passenger door is dented. But it is a rental car from 2009 which has seen all corners of the country, so some damage is expected. The car is parked on the edge of a centuries-old square, at the entrance of an underground bazaar, where it will get towed. That's notable. But a Western tourist could have mistaken the yellow markings for a parking space.

At first sight, it is just a car parked next to a square.

A Greek teenage girl places her foot on the front tyre of the parked Volkswagen to tie her shoelaces. While she pulls on the laces, a Canon camera dangles around her neck. The memory card contains hundreds of photos of the capital. And the laptop in her large backpack contains thousands more, of different cities and nature reserves in the region. She has a few months off before the academic year starts and wants to travel as much as she can. Taking photos gives her a reason to visit a place, or not. And it is a sort of armour she can wear when she is alone among strangers. Without that camera, she would be too shy to leave her hostel; with her camera, she is an adventurer exploring the Caucasus – even unstable countries like Kazichia.

After tying her laces, the girl mindlessly passes the black car. She is on her way to the underground bazaar but doesn't know it closes at six. As she enters the square, the market quickly clears out. More and more people walk up the tiled stairs and spread around the sand-coloured fountain like water. When she sees the sudden crowd, the girl stops. She grabs her camera and takes a few steps back. The dull autumn sun is low, the beams hit her lens directly. But still, the girl wants to record something. She quickly adjusts the shutter speed to very high, closes her aperture to almost a pinhole, sets the white balance to automatic, and starts shooting.

Like a paparazzo, she lets the camera go off, and the memory card fills up with dozens of images. Normally, she never takes photos as if it's a lottery draw, but she knows that somewhere on that tiny square there is a beautiful portrait series lurking in the backlight, which can only be captured by a barrage of images. And indeed, among the meaningless photos of an overexposed square, portraits appear on the memory card. Occasionally, one of the bazaar visitors stands between the sunbeam and the lens, revealing their face.

The face of a Kazichian man in a suit, rushing off.

The face of a Russian woman, puffy-eyed from last night.

The face of a teenage girl frowning into the camera. She was at the sulfur baths with her mother but doesn't want to go back there. She hated it, wearing a bikini with all those strangers. And she hated that her mother kept complaining about her father – as if they are girlfriends.

The face of an old man selling tins of tea at the bazaar every day. His joints hurt and his wife wants him to stay home, but the man likes being among people – it makes him feel like he is still part of this world.

And on the other side of the square, the face of a Neza man holding a phone. That is the most important photo in the series; he is the one who parked the Volkswagen Passat at the edge of the square.

The Neza man looks at his phone and talks to himself – he seems unsure of something. But after some hesitation, he presses the hash sign twice and walks off. His phone sends an empty text message. That message bounces against the nearest transmission tower, back to the square. Back to the black Volkswagen.

A Nokia 105 is hidden in the spare wheel compartment of the Passat. That Nokia receives the empty text message and starts buzzing, releasing a little over four volts – enough to make the small five-volt relay switch, which pulls twelve volts from the bundle of penlight batteries, sending it through the simple circuit. In the same trunk, taped to that circuit, is four kilos of C4. The RDX ignites and explodes. The trunk of the car rips open like a cardboard box. One millisecond later, the second explosion follows, the six kilos of C4 hidden under the front seats ignites too. First, the car jumps on its front wheels, then, it disappears in a sea of fire and black smoke.

The explosion thrusts the Greek girl with the backpack forward. The lens of her camera shatters against the pavement, and the viewfinder she was looking through crushes her eye and enters her skull. She is unconscious before hitting the ground and doesn't feel the wave of fire washing over her body and onto the square. As the blaze moves away, all that is left are her charred remains. The backpack has disappeared. The camera and memory card have been deformed into shapeless lumps. The portraits, all those pure expressions and contrasted lines, are ripped apart, like the souls that housed them. Erased from the square.

The shockwave of ten kilos of C4 rips the façades from the two-centuries-old houses on the square to pieces, smashes dozens of shop windows one street down, knocks down patio tables a second street down, knocks the dust from the bathhouses, then climbs the Chair of God. There, Michelle sits in her bathroom, massaging her belly. The windows in the living room start shaking. She drops the jar of oil and gets up. The towel slides from her lap, and she stands in the windows naked – unable to move, waiting for what will happen.

Alexa's cot is in one of the sleeping quarters, where a cabinet with porcelain trinkets rattles and rings. The girl starts tossing and turning, her breathing is irregular. She doesn't wake up, but her tiny body has been producing so much cortisol that it will affect her hormone balance for the rest of her life. Fifteen years later, she will wonder where her deep-rooted anxiety stems from.

She will try to find out why she was in Kazichia, while there was fighting. And why no one can know.

The shock wave rages on, out of the old town, onto the Abv'ar roundabout in front of the parliament building. The group of Jada and Neza protesting there has grown, transforming the roundabout into a square – traffic gets redirected, and the parliament building is almost impossible to reach. When the car explodes, the crowd quiets down. Banners with the symbol of the Man with a Thousand Faces are lowered, and people turn round to see the black smoke in the distance. After a few seconds, they start shouting.

'Nairi! Nairi! Nairi!' thousands of mouths cry out.

The security at parliament hear the explosion and close the gigantic steel ornamental doors, using them as barricades. Those doors are never used; they are meant to give the building an air of historicity. But after the explosion, the five men close them for the first time in case the protesting minorities decide to storm the government.

At the moment of the explosion, Vadim Ivanov is in the parliament building, talking to the Twenty. The old trickster is out for revenge. He wants to free Lev Karzarov from the clutches of the intelligence service, so the Karzarov family can still seize power. He explains to his audience that the chaos on the street is thanks to their new leader, Daniel Lechkov. They, the Twenty, must unite their powers and prevent Daniel from officially getting himself elected president.

When the explosion makes the windows of the parliament building rattle, Ivanov goes quiet at first. The blast shocked him, like the rest of the parliamentarians, but soon he realises that the ultimate reason to dismiss Daniel was just presented to him on a silver platter.

'This needs to stop,' the old man says as the other men look at each other in fear. 'Daniel Lechkov needs to disappear. Today.'

That same Daniel sits in the head office of the OMRA, a few hundred metres away. The bulletproof glass and reinforced concrete block the blow from the car bomb. He can't hear that the battle for Stolia has begun.

65

Radko and Daniel had just started deliberating with the army chiefs when the door to the war room slams open. Everyone goes quiet as Yanev, the OMRA's director, enters.

'Ivanov is in parliament, inciting his friends.' Igor Yanev sounds as cool as ever, but his forehead gleams with sweat. 'We need to take action. He is trying to convince them to abandon our side.'

'Are you sure?' Radko asks, and he tells one of his commanders to get extra army units in a state of readiness.

Yanev explains he has a direct line to premier Rosca. She doesn't want Ivanov to seize power, because her position depends on the Lechkov family.

'How does Ivanov expect to convince the parliamentarians?' Daniel asks.

Yanev wants to get a jug to pour himself a glass of water but stops midway and looks up. 'Let's be honest with ourselves, Daniel; there is not much needed to convince them. Protests are sweeping the city, they're blocking traffic. And we still have no idea how the Man with a Thousand Faces could have pulled off those attacks or shut down our entire IT infrastructure. Ivanov will tell them you lost control. And frankly, I think he's right.'

'That *I* lost control?' Daniel slams his hand on the table. 'We are waging information warfare against this uprising, that is more complex than the richest superpowers have ever done. Behind the scenes, I have more control than most . . .'

'But no one knows that,' Yanev interjects. 'You need to tell the parliament about ERIS and all your other plans. You need to call for elections as soon as possible, and as a new president, show them what you've done to get Nairi...'

'Everyone out.' Daniel's voice breaks. 'Everyone except you two.' He points at Yanev and Radko. 'What is wrong with you?' he whispers as the chiefs leave. 'No one is supposed to know.'

'Your uncle agrees,' Yanev says. 'The inner circle is too small. There are too many secrets.'

Alarmed, Radko looks up. 'I told you several times how much I worry,' he says quietly. 'The group that knows your strategy is too small. That makes us vulnerable.'

'Our plan will only work if it remains secret,' Daniel says. 'We can't tell them about ERIS. The country believes that Nairi is leading this riot *because* we have been this careful.'

'All the Twenty see is the chaos in front of the parliament building,' Yanev says. 'And they think you don't know where to start. Or worse, that you're too scared to do something. If Ivanov offers a solution, they will follow him. Daniel, we can't wait any longer.'

Daniel gives him a bewildered look. He explains that the first deepfake video needed to provoke, or no one was going to believe it. 'But after that, we made our move.'

'Igor is right,' Radko says. 'The protests will become uncontrollable, and Ivanov will remove us from power. You need to do something. Today.'

'The protests will not become uncontrollable,' Daniel says. 'We made Nairi say that people need to stay calm. Their leader forbade them to use violence.'

'You're overestimating the effect of your deepfakes,' Yanev says. 'People aren't software code. The behaviour of groups is not binary; it's unpredictable. The city could descend into chaos at any moment. We need to deploy the riot police before it's too late.'

Daniel shakes his head. 'Not yet. Leonid's team is monitoring the situation using our new camera network. It's all under control.'

'If you don't act today, the parliament will choose Ivanov's side. Dominoes will fall, one by one.'

Radko clears his throat. 'You're a genius, Daniel, but not a natural politician. You're in this room setting out innovative strategies, but that is only fifty per cent of your role, maybe even less.

You need to show them that you're in control. And that you're not one to mess with.'

The glass door opens again, and two commanders re-enter the room. 'A bomb just exploded,' one of them says, and points to the window.

Everyone turns round to watch the black smoke.

'A big one,' the soldier says to the silent room. 'In the middle of the city centre.'

Daniel leans towards Yanev. 'We'll make a deepfake right away, letting Nairi claim responsibility. I want ERIS ready for a new video.'

Radko and Yanev start shouting over each other. They tell him to stop uploading videos. They tell him he has given Nairi more than enough legitimacy. It is time to strengthen their own position. It's time to strike back.

Daniel sends the two commanders to the hallway. 'We'll use this attack for the last phase of the plan,' he says. 'Today, we're saving the High House from a years-long power struggle and my family from captivity in Kazichia. Today, I'm making everything right.'

'How?' Yanev asks wearily.

'By giving America a foothold in the Akhlos.'

66

Daniel had been trying to persuade the United States for weeks to cooperate with the Man with a Thousand Faces. Or rather, to cooperate with his deepfake. But there had been no progress yet. America initiated contact with Nairi a few times after her first video, but only indirectly, and it never led to anything. So, Daniel decided that the Man with a Thousand Faces would give a speech for an important American NGO.

Since the uprising, Nairi has been getting dozens of invitations to come and speak about her people. One of those invitations came from Voices of the Oppressed, an NGO that had been supporting the Jada and other minorities from the region for a long time. The Man with a Thousand Faces was invited to speak about her struggle on a video call. Her life-size image was projected during the main event of a congress, and on the screen, it seemed as though Nairi was talking about her people and her culture, and the inhumanities of the Lechkov regime. In reality, Daniel had recorded the video at the Kazichian intelligence service.

The performance was a great success, and the press ran with Nairi's story. The whole world was watching, and no one even considered the possibility that Nairi wasn't alive anymore.

Jonathan Rye noticed the support the movement had received, but still had his doubts about the Man with a Thousand Faces. His gut told him something was off. He kept monitoring the uprising but didn't approach them. The protests kept growing, and higher-ups at the CIA started pressuring Rye. They wanted him to seize the opportunity. Rye tried to keep his bosses at a distance. He explained he wasn't sure the Jada were powerful enough to be a real threat to the High House, even with help. But after the car bomb in the centre had gone off, no one could ignore the Man with a Thousand Faces. Even Jonathan Rye. Within ten minutes of the explosion, his boss messaged him, not with advice, but with an assignment.

Make a deal with Asch-Iljada-Lica. *Make sure America gains influence around the Akhlos mountains. The longer you wait, the greater the chance that Russia will attack. If you don't act fast, we'll need to replace you.*

An hour after the attack, Daniel's team intercepts an attempt from the CIA to contact Nairi. They want to discuss the future of Kazichia. Daniel's plan has finally worked, but now he needs to convince Radko and Yanev to give him one last chance.

'Please, Uncle Radko, Uncle Igor, this is the last step. After this, I'll reveal my plans. After this, we'll scare the protesters away and call for elections. After this, I will show myself as the leader of the country. But I can't accept the presidency until we control Russia, the internal unrest and the CIA. I can't take the position until I give my family what they want: freedom from the GRU. And to do all of that, I need to talk to America. So, give me another few hours of your trust or it was all for nothing. Take a walk with me, and I will show you.'

Without waiting for a response, Daniel walks to the other side of his new intelligence division at the OMRA. Reluctantly, Radko and Yanev follow him to a door, which opens as Daniel puts his finger on the screen. They step into a cramped room filled with patch cabinets and desks with monitors. Thick cables pile on the floor like tree roots. Three people look up from their computer screens, and one of them turns his monitor, so Radko and Yanev can watch. The screen is white, with the symbol of the Man with a Thousand Faces in the centre.

'In here, we've been working on ERIS 2.0 for the past few weeks. The most cutting-edge technology in the field of deepfakes.'

A chair stands against a green background, surrounded by cameras. Daniel sits down on the chair and puts on a thin cap. On the monitor Nairi's face appears, but the image is frozen. A white circle starts turning to indicate the processors need some time. Daniel sits very still and looks straight into the lens. The patch cabinets start blazing, everyone in the room is typing furiously. The turning circle disappears, and the frozen image of Nairi starts moving.

'ERIS 2.0 is online,' a woman says from behind her computer.

Yanev and Radko watch the monitor and see Nairi moving. She waves. The men look over at Daniel, who is waving too.

'Making deepfake videos was just the first step,' he says in unison with Nairi. 'ERIS 2.0 is the future. The synthetic voice and the deepfake get rendered almost in real time.'

On the screen, Nairi is speaking the same words as Daniel, but in her own voice and with a Jada accent. When Daniel blinks, she blinks too, but in her characteristic, slow way. He has taken over his enemy completely, as though wearing her skin.

'With ERIS 2.0, we can do video calls and live streams, disguised as anyone whom we have extracted enough training data from. In this case the Man with a Thousand Faces. There is some lag, but less than one and a half seconds.'

Daniel and Nairi take a sip of water, but Nairi's hand is empty: she is sipping air.

'ERIS 2.0 is so advanced,' they say, 'that even the GANS and auto encoders of the CIA can't detect the deepfake. The Americans will think they are phoning Nairi of the Jada.'

'This way, we can talk to Russia as the Lechkov family, and America as the rebels,' Yanev says proudly, as if he came up with the plan.

'Exactly. From now on, we're playing both teams. Just like I promised all this time. We'll be more influential than ever before.'

'But what if the true Man with a Thousand Faces exposes himself?' Radko asks. 'This is a dangerous game.'

'This is the new truth,' Daniel says. 'Too many people believe that Nairi is the Man with a Thousand Faces now. No one else can claim that position anymore. Especially now that we're talking to America about collaborating.'

'The line is open,' the woman says and points at the microphone by Daniel's chair.

The screen turns black, and a male voice emerges. He introduces himself as Jonathan Rye of the CIA. He says he is using an end-to-end encrypted connection which only allows audio. He asks if Nairi can turn her camera on so that they can make sure they are speaking with the Man with a Thousand Faces.

'Quite the honour,' Nairi says when her camera turns on.

'The pleasure is all mine.'

Rye introduces his team to her and starts a monologue about freedom. 'The reason we are speaking today is because we both want the world to be free from tyranny.'

Behind Daniel's monitor, Yanev and Radko purse their lips, trying not to respond to the hypocrisy.

'Absolutely,' Nairi says. 'A Kazichian government which is democratic and representative of all the communities of this beautiful country, would be better for everyone.'

'If we work together, we could make that dream a reality,' Rye says.

The American is probably stalling the meeting until his team gives him the green light. They check where the signal is coming from, if no one is listening in and if the image or sound was manipulated. After a few minutes, they feel confident that Nairi is legitimate, because suddenly, Rye gets straight to the point.

'We can donate weapons and expertise to the resistance if those resources will be used in ways that align with our objectives. By which I mean, a country not ruled by corruption.'

'Forgive me for my bluntness, Mr Rye,' Nairi says, 'but as you may have noticed, today is an eventful day for Kazichia. I will have to ask you to be brief, since we have lots of work to do. If the United States and my people join forces against corruption and tyranny, against what price would that be?'

The American starts listing his demands. From the way he wants to become part of every strategic decision the rebels take, to the influence the United States would want in a future Kazichian government. 'Evidently, without standing in the way of a healthy democracy,' he adds.

'Evidently,' Nairi mutters.

Daniel looks past the screen at Igor Yanev, who gives a thumbs up or thumbs down after every demand the CIA makes.

'I think we can figure this out, Mr Rye,' Nairi says. 'But I hope the CIA realises this will take years.'

'Of course. We play the long game.'

'Before we start our collaboration, I would like to request a favour from you.'

'Of course,' he repeats. 'A sign of trust.'

'I want to ask you to smuggle two people to America and take them to safety. Two Dutch people. A mother and child.'

Jonathan Rye agrees immediately. 'A mother and child? No problem. No father? Two or three doesn't make much difference for us.'

'The father would like to keep his wife and child in Kazichia, but they want to return home.' Daniel and Nairi's eyes darken, and they rub their faces as if trying to wipe the emotion. Daniel rubs with two hands, Nairi with one.

'Who are they?' a deep, unfamiliar voice asks.

'Two members of the High House who are effectively held hostage by the GRU. A pregnant mother and her three-year-old daughter. We're asking the CIA to place them in the witness protection programme. If Russia leaves them alone, they will want to return to Amsterdam. Their home.'

'Someone from the High House? Why do the Jada want to protect someone from the High House?'

'It concerns the wife and child of Daniel Lechkov.'

'Is this a joke?' Rye asks.

'The mother and child mean very much to me. I couldn't have orchestrated this resistance without their support and their sacrifices. And now, all they want is to go back home.'

The other end of the line is quiet.

'It wouldn't just mean the world to me personally,' Nairi continues, 'but also to the fight. We want to rattle Daniel Lechkov. If his family suddenly disappears, that would be yet another setback.'

'How are we supposed to smuggle these two out of the country without starting a war? We can't send a team to the Mardoe Khador, as you hopefully understand.'

'No need. We can get them to a deserted location in the east of the country within twenty-four hours. There, they can get picked up by helicopter without anyone knowing.'

The line is dead quiet. The Americans have pressed mute to deliberate.

Daniel sits in his chair with the cap on his head and watches the screen unblinkingly. As though he tries to control Rye with his mind.

The line reopens.

'If you send us the coordinates, we will send an extraction team there in exactly twenty-four hours. If the woman and child are there at the agreed time, and we can get away without being seen, we will take them and help them build a life in America. If we get the impression that you kidnapped them, we will abort the operation. And the collaboration. If you miss the time slot, there won't be a second attempt.'

'Then this is a historic moment, Mr Rye,' Nairi says, relieved. 'The beginning of a close bond between America and the true Kazichia.'

Yanev and Radko look at each other, Radko's nephew won't be there for the birth of his second child. Because without him, no Man with a Thousand Faces. And without the Man with a Thousand Faces, no extraction by the CIA. But at the same time, he has achieved a historic victory for the High House: a direct line to America and thus, the ultimate means to keep Russia outside the country's borders.

67

Michelle stands at the large windows of the Mardoe Khador over-looking the old town and waits. There is not much to see, but the black column of smoke that rose between the buildings at the foot of the hill lingers in her mind. She'd got dressed and put make-up on as if she were going to leave the house today – as if she is *allowed* to leave the house. But all she can do is stand by that window and wait for the second explosion or the first gunshot.

In the end, the silence is not interrupted by more violence, but by the front door to the apartment opening. She flinches. No one has been allowed in or out for days. The only interaction she has had, other than with her daughter, is with the security in the hallway. She knocks on the door, waits for it to open slightly, and tells the embarrassed man on the other side what groceries or things she needs.

Now, the door swings open and Daniel enters the living room. Funnily enough, she feels relief when she sees him, not anger.

'What happened?' she asks.

'You're safe,' he says, 'believe me.'

She hears the words coming from his mouth, but after every-thing that happened, they don't carry meaning. Or weight.

How does he know? How does he know if we're safe? He didn't know a bomb would explode, at walking distance from his wife and child. He has no control at all; no one has control. Daniel doesn't, and his enemies don't, either.

She saw the video of Nairi taking responsibility for the attack. The Jada terrorist addressed the protesting crowd in the capital again and asked them to remain peaceful. But Michelle doubts they will listen to her. That Nairi started something too powerful to keep under control. In the past few days, she has been seeing more profile photos with the symbol of the Man with a Thousand Faces. It reminded her of the response to the Charlie Hebdo attacks, but this time they are supporting the bad guys. She saw Western people use the symbol for their profiles – even the husband of a colleague changed his profile picture. She doesn't get it. The Man with a Thousand Faces coordinates terrorist attacks, what's sympathetic about that? How is it any different from the planes hitting the World Trade Center in New York, or the attack on the Bataclan in Paris? That Nairi is a terrorist. An extremist. Maybe the public feels differently because she is a woman. Or because her soldiers don't have beards or wear hijabs. But whatever they look like, the Jada are motivated by the same things as the Taliban; they want to dismantle a government and make their own culture dominant. They want to escape from poverty and oppression. And to do that, they use violence against civilians.

And still, people all over the world are rooting for the Jada to get their way.

The Man with a Thousand Faces has become a symbol against oppression. A symbol more powerful than Kazichia and Nairi. Definitely more powerful than Daniel. He can promise to protect her, but what can he really do? They're all stuck in a snowstorm, and no one can control the weather.

She doesn't tell him those things, though. There is no use.

'What do you want from me?' she says, trying to sound cold.

'You can leave here,' he says. 'If you still want to.'

She turns round and walks to him quickly as if trying to catch his words before they disappear. 'What did you just say?'

'I did it; there is a way to return to the West. But it won't be easy.'

She doesn't believe him. 'To Amsterdam? Home? What about the Russians?'

'The Americans can take you. You'll have to stay in America for a while using fake names – I don't know where exactly. If Russia stays calm for a while, there will be a meeting with the Dutch embassy.'

'Is this real?' she hears herself ask. She feels as though she is hovering over the conversation, looking down like she isn't part of it. 'Is it over? How did you manage to do that? Why now?'

'It will be a long journey. You can't simply leave for the Netherlands. And there is something else.'

She gestures at the Chesterfield by the door and sits down. He nods and sits down next to her.

'You want to become president,' she says. 'You'll stay here.'

'I can't come with you,' he says. 'I want to, but I can't. It's better if that's all you know. This was the only way.'

'Can you come later? In a while?'

'Maybe. I'll try my best. But I don't know how long it will take. Might be years.'

He gives her the same look as when Alexa was born; so exhausted that his defensive walls have collapsed, like wet cardboard. He passed the finish line he had been working towards for months. The marathon is over. All that is left is thirst and strained muscles.

'You did it. Whatever your plan was all that time, you did it,' she says, and she can tell he is about to break down. 'You kept your promise to us.'

'I need to ask you one more thing because I will never forgive myself if I don't. But promise me you won't get angry.'

She nods.

'Have you ever thought about what it would be like to stay? In Kazichia? You could be anything you want. You could have a career in politics, the industry, whatever you want. You can start an environmental department within Lechkov Industria – the possibilities are endless. And the possibilities for our children would be endless too. They would play a big part in the course of history. They would lead important, meaningful lives.'

'That's nepotism,' she says.

'It would be a big change, but is there a part of you that would consider staying here? With me, so our family can stay together.'

'It might seem like you can get everything under control here because you felt like your grandfather could too, but it doesn't work that way. Petar kept up the illusion of being a puppet master, but no one controls the future, Daniel. It will always be a struggle, however many plans you think of. In this house, you will always have to keep fighting. It will never be safe. And your work is never done. The only way to stop this misery is by coming with us to America.'

'If there was a way to come with you, I would. What am I supposed to do here, without you? But there isn't. So, if you want to go home, I will make it happen. It's my fault you're stuck here, so I will help you get away.'

Michelle feels relief and sadness – it's like those two emotions are inextricably linked. 'This isn't your fault,' she says, and she doesn't mean it.

'So, you want to leave?'

She nods. 'Our children need to go home.'

He holds her hands and tells her he understands. 'Pack a small suitcase. Just the essentials.'

'Will it happen that fast? Where are we going?'

'In a few hours, we'll take the helicopter from the airport. It will take us to another smaller airport, and from there we'll fly to the Central Lakes. I'll say goodbye to you on Lechkov Island. And without me, you'll travel to the agreed location.'

She stands up and holds him again. 'Can't you stay for a bit? Let's wake Alexa up. She misses her daddy.'

Daniel shakes his head. 'I have to go. We'll see each other outside by the cars. Wear something warm, it might snow later.'

68

Daniel enters his mother's office to call Leonid. He wants a status update before flying to the Central Lakes. They agreed he would report on the unrest in the city every few hours – Leonid's team is monitoring the situation surrounding the parliament building day and night – but he hasn't heard from his friend since he told him to make Nairi and the mercenaries disappear.

The phone rings but no one answers, so he calls one of Leonid's analysts. The phone barely rings before a panicked voice answers. 'Mr Lechkov, the protests are getting violent. The crowd is starting to spread throughout the city centre, Kazichians have been attacked on the street. We strongly advise you to step in.'

'Why didn't Leonid tell me about this?'

'We haven't seen Mr Torelli for days, sir.'

Daniel freezes. 'Why don't I know this?'

'Because you forbade us from ever talking to anyone else. You said our work for ERIS was so important that no one ever ...'

Before the man can finish his sentence, Radko and Yanev enter, with a group of soldiers and spies trailing behind them. Through his own network, Radko just found out that Leonid has disappeared. 'They're saying he was kidnapped by one of the mercenaries.'

Stunned, Daniel looks up. 'A mercenary?' he asks unconvinced. 'Why would he turn against us?'

'As I keep repeating,' Yanev says, 'people aren't software code. You can't predict their behaviour based on your input.'

'We will find Leonid, and save him,' Radko says. 'One of the Circle units is on its way to the area where Leonid was kidnapped. That mercenary is alone, and his gear is bugged, so we know exactly where he is.'

'And we're wiping the capital,' Yanev says. 'I just saw the riots with my own eyes, the city is in disarray. Enough is enough.'

'The crowd is too big for riot police,' one of the soldiers says. 'There is a division on its way that can control the city faster.'

Daniel nods and says he understands the decision. 'How long until the soldiers get there?'

'One and a half hours, maybe longer.'

'We waited too long,' Yanev says as he lights a cigar. 'A lot can happen in one and a half hours. A strong wind could turn into a storm.'

Michelle stands on the driveway of the High House with Alexa, waiting for Daniel. It's very cold out and the air has turned grey. *We haven't made it out of the snowstorm yet*, she thinks, zipping up Alexa's coat.

Behind her, a voice calls out. Maika walks out with a teacup in her hand. 'Did my son finally set you free?'

'We're waiting for him,' Michelle says curtly. 'We're about to leave.'

'I heard you packed your bags,' her mother-in-law says. 'Are you trying to escape again?'

She turns round. 'How did you know?'

The old woman gestures for a servant and hands him the porcelain cup. 'I know everything that goes on in this country, especially if it concerns the future leaders of the Mardoe Khador.'

Michelle sees the smug gleam in her eyes and is dying to tell her that packing her bag is part of Daniel's plan. She is tired of her threats. But Michelle knows that would jeopardise her escape, so she holds her tongue.

'Come, Alexa. Let's play in the garden until your father gets here.'

Without saying another word, she takes her daughter's hand and walks to the orchard, behind the house. Petar had that orchard planted to commemorate his parents. The garden was named after their tiny farm in old Kazichia: Malen'kitzch. Alexa lets go of her mother's hand and runs around the dormant citrus trees.

With her back facing the driveway, Michelle watches her daughter. She hopes Maika has gone back inside.

What is taking Daniel so long? she thinks. *We can't miss our rendezvous.*

Daniel is about to join his wife when premier Rosca enters the office. She looks terrible; her long plait has turned into a bunch of knots, and she has a red scar across her cheek. She needs to catch her breath before she can speak.

'Ivanov hijacked the general sitting,' she says. 'And he convinced the Twenty to vote on the presidency. It is happening *now*. If he gets the majority vote, they will free Karzarov from the OMRA building and appoint him president.'

Igor Yanev stands up but says nothing. He is dumbstruck: his worst fear has come true.

'Are the Twenty still in the parliament?' Radko asks.

'They're stuck in there,' the premier explains. 'The crowd of protesters on the Abv'ar roundabout grew so big, that now, no one can leave. It's a miracle I could get out.'

'I need to go there,' Daniel says. 'I need to show them I'm in control.'

'But how?' Yanev asks. 'You lost control. The house of cards will collapse today.'

Alexa suddenly stops running. She stands still between the fruit trees and looks down from the hill.

'What is it?' Michelle asks.

'Men,' she says. 'Men are coming.'

Michelle walks towards her and sees something moving at the foot of the hill. She walks a bit further and watches from between the trees. Outside the gates of the High House, a crowd has gathered. Hundreds of people, and the crowd is still growing. She hears their voices. A brooding, ominous sound, not unlike a beehive.

This is trouble.

She grabs Alexa, crouches down to her knees and wants to sneak to the other side, then sees a man there. He is by himself and passes the orchard, walking towards the High House. He is wearing an old tracksuit under his big coat, and a cigarette hangs between his lips. The man looks around as if he is unsure of what to do. Michelle doesn't know how the stranger got in, but she can feel something is about to happen.

She sneaks around the trees and sees more intruders walking along the edge of the garden. All normal people, dressed in work clothes or casual outfits. They're surprised to be standing on the Chair of God, and look at each other, waiting for someone to be brave enough to enter the Mardoe Khador.

'There are men and women,' Alexa concludes drily.

Michelle is quiet. She crouches down further and waves at the security men waiting for Daniel in the driveway. But they don't see her.

And then, the first brick hits one of the big windows of the High House.

'What was that?' Yanev opens the door to Maika's office.

Two security guards run into the hallway.

Radko walks to a window. Dismayed, he points outside. 'They got in! The Jada climbed the gates.' He starts shouting orders to his adjutants, who grab their phones immediately.

'Where is my family?' Daniel asks the head of security. 'They need to get to the airport. Now!'

'It's over,' Yanev says quietly. 'Escape with your family, Daniel. The Mardoe Khador will fall. You aimed too high.'

'No,' he says and takes out his phone. 'There is a way to save everything.'

Before anyone can ask what he is planning this time, Daniel starts instructing the team monitoring the camera system. He says something about auto-encoders and database crawlers but no one in Maika's office understands what he is doing.

'My people are on it,' he says as he hangs up the phone. 'If this works, the chaos will stop within an hour. Meanwhile, I have to get to the parliament. I know it's risky, but I don't have a choice. If we can't stop Ivanov, the Russians will come and that would be the end of all of us.

'Let me go to the parliament,' Radko proposes. 'I'll relay your message. Go to the airport with your family. Say goodbye to them.'

'No,' Daniel says. 'You're right; I need to become a politician. I need to put up a show to secure my presidency. So, I will. I will show them exactly what I can do.'

'Then I will go with you,' Radko says. 'We'll take my car.'

Everyone in the office tries to stop the men from leaving. 'The crowd will rip you to pieces.' The premier holds up her ripped coat.

'Help my family get out of here,' Daniel tells the head of security as he exits the room, 'and Radko and I will save the Mardoe Khador.'

69

Eighteen-year-old Sophie – Alexa – stands in her mother's office looking at a timeline. She has taped a row of papers against the inside of the slanted roof; everything that happened, from Vigo Lechkov's funeral to her first childhood photos in Portland. Somewhere around the time that Alexa disappeared, and Sophie appeared, she drew a red question mark.

She had filled most of the timeline in over the past few days. But to her right is a sheet with dozens of Post-its on it with all the events she hasn't been able to give context to or a place in time yet. Like the memory of a frozen lake. Alexa walking on green-blue ice, something black swimming under her feet. She doesn't know where or when that was. But she knows it's important.

She wrote some remaining questions on the big sheet: *Why isn't my father in America? Why aren't we in the Netherlands? Why am I not allowed to know what happened?*

She decides to call Professor Stewart again.

'Just to paint a picture, I was never married,' the old man mutters on the phone. 'In fact, I never had a relationship; that just isn't for me. But I loved being a kind of extension to your family, dear Alexa. I worked with your father, I was a friend of your mother, and I saw you more often than your grandparents. You were very important in my life. And then, one day, all three of you disappeared. Vanished into thin air. For sixteen years.

'For the first days after you left, I assumed you were lying by the pool in that awful desert resort your mother liked visiting. But then I saw reports about the coup in Kazichia. I did some

329

research and found out that Vigo Lechkov had died, and you never arrived in Dubai. My hypothesis was that you went to Kazichia to bury Daniel's brother and then couldn't get out anymore. As you understand, I was very worried.

'I went to the police, but they had no idea what to do with my story. And the Dutch embassy didn't, either. I went to Michelle's parents, but they didn't have the intellectual capacity to fathom what was happening – forgive my bluntness – let alone come to a solution. They were mostly panicking. So, when it turned out I was the only one who could do something, I bought a ticket to Stolia.'

'You could still travel there?'

'A travel warning went out, but the airport had reopened a few days after the failed coup. I booked a hotel in the old centre, overlooking the Mardoe Khador. If you were still alive, you must have been in that building. I spent days worrying and wondering in my hotel room. Multiple times, I walked around the High House as closely as I could to observe it, to see how I might contact you. Meanwhile, the capital got more restless. I don't know how much you read about the attacks, but during my stay a car bomb went off less than a kilometre from my hotel. It was extremely dangerous, and I was worried the airport would close again.'

Sitting on the attic floor, Alexa listens to him breathlessly and stares at the timeline. She follows Tim's story from left to right, day after day. 'Was my mother in danger?' she asks. 'Did you talk to her? Was I there too?'

'Well, that's the thing; I never found you. It got so dangerous there that I had to leave you, your mother and your brother or sister. That was very difficult, but what could I do?'

Alexa looks up.

'Brother or sister? There was another child?'

'Of course,' the professor says. 'Don't you have a brother or sister there, in America? Michelle was pregnant.'

Alexa shakes her head as though the old man can see her. She takes a Post-it and writes a new question on her sheet filled with question marks: *Do I have a brother or sister?*

330

'But as I said,' the old man continues, 'it got so dangerous in Stolia that I fled. I didn't have a choice.'

'Why? What happened?' Alexa asks, her pen ready.

The professor clicks his dentures. 'What happened, dear Alexa, is very hard to describe. Let me put it this way: the city turned into a warzone. And the High House turned into a sea of flames.'

70

The Abv'ar roundabout is crawling with people. White banners and flags are raised above the crowd. Jada and Neza, but also members of the Maraniari, Pasāru-var and Chit'i chant the name of their new communal leader, the first person to unite the different tribes of Kazichia.

Nairi! Nairi! Nairi!

Accompanied by four SUVs, Radko's armoured car drives onto the roundabout. The heavy vehicles are there to keep everyone at a distance, but the convoy gets surrounded almost immediately. The soldier behind the wheel mutters something and shakes his head.

'Can we drive through this?' Daniel asks.

A carton of milk is smashed against the windscreen. The driver turns the wipers on to clean the white stain.

'That Jada woman of yours turns those people into wild animals,' Radko says. He gets a handgun from a compartment in the door and shows him how the safety catch works. Daniel puts the weapon in his belt.

A rock hits the roof of the car. Then another one.

The crowd becomes denser, and they drive on very slowly.

'Do we need to go back?' Daniel asks, looking from one window to the next. 'If we go back, we'll lose the parliament, but if we die here, we lose it too.'

'We're too far in now,' Radko says. 'Turning here with all these people is too dangerous.'

Daniel grabs his phone and calls Leonid's team again. He wants to make sure everything is ready for his plan to win back the capital. But the crowd outside the car is so big, that the connection falters.

After Daniel hangs up, Radko wants to ask what the plan is, when a face appears at the side window. A boy has run past the outer cars and presses his nose against the darkened glass. 'Lechkov!' he yells. 'It's Lechkov, I saw him!' He starts hitting the window with his fists.

A soldier in the rear car opens his window slightly and points his gun. The boy takes a step back and stops following the car.

'Are we going to make it, do you think?' Daniel asks for the umpteenth time.

Four or five men push past the cars and start hitting the windows. One of them is holding a rock. The windows are made of bulletproof glass, but after six hits, a white circle appears. The rebel cries out with anger as he waves the rock around. His eyes are red.

'We need to hit the gas,' the driver says, 'or we'll get stuck.'

Daniel agrees and the five cars accelerate at the same time. The daredevils that were hitting the windows have disappeared. People jump aside or get dragged. There is yelling and people hitting the hood of the car, but then a path emerges. Close to the parliament, the first car bumps into something. Daniel turns round and sees a man lying on his side, he isn't moving, and his arm hangs from his shoulder at an impossible angle.

'Mr Lechkov, General Lechkov, you're getting out from the right side,' the soldier says, and he yanks the wheel.

The car comes to a screeching halt by the stairs of the parliament building. The other cars form a wall in front of the presidential car. The soldiers jump out to hold the crowd at gunpoint. Daniel gets out and runs up the stairs two steps at a time. Rocks fly right by him. Miraculously, he makes it to the entrance unscathed, but there it seems his luck has run out. The metres-high ornamental door is closed. Groaning, people are pushing, but the door is heavy, and the hinges are rusty. Daniel looks back at the roundabout. The crowd is moving. The civilians are coming towards the building. They are coming to get him.

'Hurry up!' he shouts when there is a slight opening. He pushes his fingers in the crack and wants to pull, but it doesn't do much.

The soldiers at the foot of the stairs are under immense pressure. Radko sees the situation is getting risky and gives the order to shoot over the heads of the protesters. But the riled-up men and women have been protesting for days, and the gunshots don't impress them anymore. They keep coming closer. A boy gets stuck in the pushy crowd and climbs onto the car in front of him. One of the soldiers sees him and fires a warning shot, which startles the boy, and he jumps on top of him. Very quickly, the soldier is overpowered by two protesters coming to the boy's rescue. The soldier furiously kicks in every direction and frees himself from their grip but gets hit in the face with a piece of metal – a female protester has grabbed the soldier's rifle and is using the barrel as a melee weapon. Blood streams from his nose. The soldier tries to get away, but the woman hits him again and again until his face is nothing but a bloody mess and his arms fall weakly. The woman expertly removes the safety catch from the semi-automatic weapon and climbs onto the roof of the car.

'Nairi!' she shouts and shoots the air a few times.

Hundreds of voices respond to her. 'Nairi! Nairi!'

Then, the dam bursts. The crowd streams between the cars to the stairs. The remaining soldiers shoot at the protesters and hit dozens, but it's too late – the crowd is too big. A few soldiers jump into the cars to get themselves to safety, but most are caught off guard by the sudden charge and, crying out, get trampled.

Radko runs up the stairs, barely staying ahead of the flood of people.

'What are you still doing here?! Go inside!' With both hands, he grabs the door and shouts through the crack. 'We pull on three!'

He counts down and roars as he pulls. With his giant hands, he manages to move the door. In the opening two staff members appear, they push from inside.

'Squeeze yourself through the opening!' Radko orders.

Daniel pushes himself as hard as he can and is pulled inside by the staff members. Just in time, because outside, the protesters have reached the door. Three young men run up to Radko. One of them has a metal bar that he threateningly swings from side to side. Daniel sees it happen and pulls his gun out. He tries to aim at the man, but the crack in the door is too small to get an angle. Radko turns round swiftly and kicks the man between his legs, but one of the other men attacks him from behind. He circles Radko's neck with his arm. For a second the Kazichian giant is surprised, then he bends forward, launching the man onto the stairs and into the crowd. The third attacker stares at the enormous soldier, unable to move. Radko Lechkov walks up to him and hits his fists together.

'Get over here, goatherder, I'll crush your skull.'

Terrified, the man looks behind him, to the group coming up the stairs. Radko uses that moment of doubt and ducks for the door.

'Pull him in!' Daniel shouts.

Many hands grab the heavy man by his coat and pull him through the narrow crack, but there he gets stuck.

A gunshot. Radko cries, and he grimaces in pain. 'Pull!' he groans.

More gunshots, but this time the bullet misses him and hits the stone wall beside the doors.

With a last shove, the giant pushes himself inside the building and drops onto the marble floor. The staff members start pulling the door shut. The hinges creak and screech. Two Jada men try to squeeze in through the shrinking opening but have to give up to keep their arms from being crushed. The door falls shut. Someone opens fire with an automatic rifle less than a second later, but the bullets bounce off the steel door, back to the roundabout.

Daniel lets himself drop to the ground next to Radko and tries to catch his breath. They hear muffled pounding and screaming from the other side of the big door. A rock flies through one of the windows further in the hallway, caught by the bars behind the glass. The sound of the square floods in through the broken window. 'Nairi! Nairi!' the crowd shouts – they smell Lechkov blood.

The walkie-talkie of one of the staff members beeps. 'The Mardoe Khador has fallen,' it says. 'Is someone with Mr Lechkov? The High House has fallen.'

Radko, moaning in pain, takes his phone and looks at the incoming stream of messages. 'They're in,' he says.

'Is my family safe?' Daniel asks, panting.

'I don't know,' Radko says, while trying to take off his jacket to find the wound. 'Is this the end, Daniel?'

Daniel looks up at the austere ceiling.

71

The rioters force their way into the High House. It happens suddenly, and all of them barge in at the same time, as if they are all part of one hive mind. More rocks hit the big windows, and men and women climb inside over the windowsills.

Michelle picks Alexa up and runs past the citrus trees, back to the front of the house, where Daniel is waiting for them. Hopefully. She needs to get to the cars so they can drive to the airport. When she leaves the orchard and looks at the gate at the foot of the hill, she sees it's crawling with people. Those dozens of intruders at the house are the vanguard, the scouts for the ant colony. Standing by the gate are hundreds more men, women and children, deciding if they will make the climb, too.

She starts running again. Her hips are painful because they are getting weaker, and her pregnant belly hurts because she is pressing Alexa against it. But seeing that group gives her enough strength to make it to the driveway. The gravel crunches under her trainers. At the front door, she sees two men. She ducks behind a stone vase and covers Alexa's mouth with her hand. By the fountain, there are cardboard protest signs with the rebel symbol drawn on them.

'Madam Lechkova, we were looking for you.'

Startled, she looks behind her. A group of security guards exits the garden with Maika. Some men run to the house immediately to follow the intruders with their weapons drawn.

'What is happening?'

'We're taking you to the bunker.'

'Where is my husband? We need to get to the airport. There is a helicopter waiting for us.'

'Mr Lechkov is on his way to the parliament.'

'What?'

'He has just left. I am the head of security of the Mardoe Khador, Madam Lechkova. And I was personally instructed by Mr Lechkov to escort you to the bunker. There we can wait until a helicopter can come.'

'Back inside?' Michelle gets up. 'No way. We are leaving for the airport now.' She picks Alexa up and walks to the cars waiting for her.

'It's not safe, Michelle!' Maika shouts. 'Look at all those people!'

The old woman starts shouting orders at the men and while Michelle can't understand a word she says, she can guess what she is saying. Her mother-in-law wants Alexa to be taken from Michelle and brought back to the High House. She wants the men to secure the Lechkov bloodline. But Michelle walks to the cars as if Maika no longer exists. Despite the chaos, despite the fear-filled city, she feels a certain determination and courage she has never felt before; she is not going back into that house. She fled down the hill twice, but every time someone told her to turn round. Every time, someone said it was too dangerous. That she needed to wait. The longer she waits though, the more dangerous it gets. So now, she will listen to no one but herself. The third time is the charm, and this time, she will head straight to the airport. With or without Daniel.

A short man gets out of the first car. He is wearing an oversized suit; she recognises him from her last ride to the airport. The driver gestures for her to go back. With two hands he points at the people at the foot of the hill, then at Alexa. Michelle smiles like she doesn't understand and puts her daughter in the back seat. Right before she shuts the door, she tells her everything will be all right. She has promised that many times since arriving in Kazichia, but now, it feels different. Alexa feels it, too. She doesn't cry or hyperventilate, she looks Michelle straight in the eye and nods.

The driver shakes his head furiously and calls for the guards at the top of the hill. He tries to stop Michelle, but she grabs the keys from his hand and pushes him aside. When she sits in the driver's seat and starts the car, she hears men in the driveway running up to her.

'Madam Lechkova! Stop!'

'There we go,' she tells Alexa calmly and sends her a smile through the rearview mirror like they are going off to spend a day at the park. 'Hold on.'

The car skids in the gravel and shoots down the hill. She has no idea what to do when she reaches the gate, but as the car accelerates, her desperation dwindles. For the first time in weeks, the paralysing hands of perceived powerlessness are starting to lose their grip on her.

At the gate are four soldiers, as usual. As Michelle approaches them, they gesture for her to drive back up the mountain.

Could I drive through the gate? she wonders. *That would be an appropriate way to say goodbye.*

But she slows down the car and opens the window.

'We need to get out of here,' she says in Dutch as if the Kazichian young man can understand her. 'Let me go, I am the president's wife. Let me through *now!*' Her voice gets louder and angrier. She points at the gate.

The boy gives the other soldier a bewildered look, who then shrugs and presses the button.

'Thanks,' she says and rushes down the Chair of God.

72

Standing on the driveway of the High House, Maika furiously berates everyone. A few guards run down the hill in a futile attempt to catch up with the car. Maika says the soldiers by the gate need to be warned. She grabs the walkie-talkie from one of the guards and opens her mouth but is startled by a noise in the garden. Close to the driveway, people are walking around. Intruders.

The guards immediately form a circle around her and escort her inside. 'We are taking Madam Lechkova to the bunker,' one of them says in the walkie-talkie.

No response.

When the group enters the foyer, they encounter five intruders pulling oil paintings from the walls. The men almost seem surprised when they see seven guns pointed at them, as if they weren't expecting any resistance. Three guards stay behind to keep the men at a distance while the rest take Maika up the stairs to the first floor. There are about ten high-ranking civil servants and members of the three families there, including Petar in his wheelchair.

Maika kisses Petar's forehead and stands behind the wheelchair.

'Bunker entrance, as fast as possible,' one of the guards says. 'Be very quiet.'

They sneak over the mezzanine and carefully watch the ground floor. Then, through a doorway leading to a hallway, leading to another hallway. Left. Right. Another door. Behind her, Maika hears screaming, but she doesn't look back. All she has eyes for is Petar. The great Petar Lechkov, the founder of the country, now sneaking around in his own Mardoe Khador, because the Jada and Neza are hunting him.

Finally, they reach the hall in the back of the High House where they can take the stairs down to the office with the bunker entrance. But it turns out they made a mistake. From the other side of the hallway, a mob of intruders comes running up the stairs – men and women dressed as if it's just another day of work, but with eyes full of rage.

'Watch out!' Maika shouts, pulling Petar's wheelchair back. 'Do something! What are you waiting for? Shoot!'

One of the guards shoots the ceiling and the group on the stairs stops, stunned.

'Lechkov!' an older man yells, and he points at Petar.

'There they are!' someone from downstairs shouts, pointing at Maika.

The Jada and Neza on the stairs start to move again, and from under the mezzanine, more people appear. More intruders stream into the hallway like water from a burst pipe, looking for a member of the family.

'We need to leave,' Maika says. She turns round but sees another group approaching from the other side. 'Shoot!' she repeats. 'We're stuck. Do something or give me the gun.'

Someone shoots at the group on the stairs, and a few rioters jump over the banister to dodge the bullets. The people in the middle have nowhere to go. A woman is shot in her back and rolls down the stairs like a rag doll. She pulls a few protesters down with her.

'Keep shooting!' Maika yells. 'We need to get down those stairs! We need to get to the bunker!'

Something flies over the wooden railing of the mezzanine, and a bottle shatters on the wall behind Maika and Petar. Everyone ducks. A sea of flames engulfs the panelling. A black cloud shrouds the group. There is screaming and crying. But not from Maika. She gets up to take Petar's wheelchair and almost gets hit with a second Molotov cocktail. Just in time, she drops to the ground. She sees the bottle explode in the face of the minister of finance, who is standing right next to her, and watches in horror as the fire covers his wailing body. His arms thrash about, then he drops to the ground. The flames spread to the wheelchair, lighting Petar's hair up. The old, trembling man tries to stand up but isn't strong enough to get away from the fire.

Maika jumps up and takes her jacket off. She drapes it on Petar and passes the still-burning body of the minister of finance to squeeze behind the wheelchair. She makes a run for it, still pushing the wheelchair. The guards shout after her that she is running towards the intruders but to no avail. She is in shock and her instinct to flee has completely taken over. Her body wants to get away from the flames for good reason because a third Molotov cocktail engulfs the mezzanine behind her in roaring flames.

Two Jada men watch in disbelief as Maika Lechkova, the ice queen of Kazichia, emerges from the smoke. She runs straight at them. And not just that, she has the mythical Petar Lechkov with her. It is like she is presenting the founder of the country to them for a blood sacrifice. When she has almost made it to the stairs, the Jada stop her. Other protesters join them, and together, they lift the old man from his wheelchair. Suddenly, Maika returns to herself. She starts punching their arms, telling them they don't belong here. That they need to leave her family alone. But the men ignore her. They look at Petar. They are holding their greatest enemy – the founder of everything evil and unattainable, the architect of their oppression. He hangs slouched in their arms, in the shape of an old, helpless man, but they don't know what to do. The moment has too much weight; there is too much meaning being compressed into one instance.

Then, a tall Neza man appears who seems to have less trouble navigating himself into history books. With two hands, he picks Petar up and lifts him above his head. The other men help him. They are grateful for someone taking charge. Petar is lifted over the heads of the intruders to the edge of the banister. It looks like a tribute for him, and the group one floor down cheers as if their team has won the cup. But then the men hurl the body over the edge.

Petar hits the stone floor with a dull thump, and the hallway falls silent. Everyone stands rigid as if stuck between terror and hope. Smoke crawls across the ceiling towards the chandeliers. A small cloud of smouldering paint flakes descends towards the main hall, like an unassuming sparkle of fireflies.

Then Maika lets out a cry, and everything begins moving again.

The guards shoot through the smoke, trying to hit the intruders. The tall Neza man ducks, then sees Maika try to run back. He grabs hold of her and puts her against the wall. The guards manage to extinguish some of the flames with their jackets but are then attacked from the back by a new group of intruders that entered via the main entrance. They are pushed onto the ground while the rest of the ministers and other elite watch, frozen in fear.

Maika is pushed and shoved by different men and women. Her two-piece suit is ripped, and someone pulls her hair. Hollow-eyed, she looks around. When the mob stops for a moment, she stands with her arms by her sides and waits. She knows there is nothing she can say to sway the crowd. All she can hope for is that it will stop before she is dead.

The tall Neza man steps forward and kicks Maika in her stomach. The old woman falls to her knees and people jostle for a part in the lynching. Punches and kicks come from all sides, and Maika screeches like an animal, but not for long. Soon, it is quiet.

Two Jada men run towards the group and pull people off Maika. 'You should be ashamed!' they shout. 'Are you the new monsters of the High House?'

More Jada and Neza join, who find the violence went too far. One by one, the brutes step aside until Maika appears – curled up in a foetal position. Her shoulders are still moving, and she is still breathing, but she is in terrible shape.

One floor down, on the stone floor in the hall, lies Petar. He isn't moving anymore. His breathing stopped. His pale face lies turned to the first window that was smashed. The window overlooking the Malen'kitzch. In his glassy old eyes is the reflection of a citrus tree, behind a simple Kazichian farm. He sees that tree for the first time in eighty years. It's a small but healthy tree, with sweet fragrant flowers. Every year, the fruits ripened a little earlier than the rest of the orchard, and the farmers in the village couldn't understand why. 'Stubborn,' his mother called the tree. Just like her son. She braided a basket to put the fruit in, to sell on the market.

'*Avaly*,' Petar Lechkov's lifeless lips want to say. Mum.

And then, life lets him go.

73

Smoke from the burning cars hovers over the monumental houses in the old city centre. There is shouting and honking. Someone yells through a megaphone, fireworks explode. The Man with a Thousand Faces towers over the chaos as if guarding the uprising. Michelle doesn't know the way to the airport but uses the statue as a lighthouse in the storm. The city gate is right under the faceless soldier, so if she can get to him, she will have made it out of the old town at least. Then she needs to find a main road. She hangs over the steering wheel to see the statue and tries to drive closely along the city wall, so she won't get lost in the alleys.

Suddenly, a group of men with scarves over their faces runs into the road. She hits the brakes to avoid hitting them, but the men don't seem to see her. They run towards a shop. Michelle sees the owner anxiously trying to close his blinds, but the men kick in the glass and climb in. Desperately, the man searches for help with his eyes. When he sees Michelle, he waves.

What am I supposed to do? she thinks, then changes direction.

She drives under the statue. The city gate isn't barricaded, and she can get to the main road without problems. The wideness of the road calms her down.

Alexa asks where her daddy is.

'He had to go and do something,' Michelle says and smiles in the rearview mirror.

The girl stares out the window. She is tired. How could she not be? Once they get to America, they will spend a week lying in bed. Talking and sleeping, that's all.

While more and more big government buildings appear, Michelle realises she should avoid the parliament building and the roundabout full of protesters. But she has no idea where it is. Maybe she is driving right into the heart of the unrest. With one hand, she tries to open Google Maps, but the network is still congested. She can only text or call.

Shit.

Illegible traffic signs appear. She tries to decipher the Kazichian signs but can't make sense of them. She does see a sign with E117 on it. Hoping that means highway, she takes the turn.

While she drives past buildings that look like embassies, she sees a group of people burning a giant Kazichian flag. A young girl films the flag burning with her phone. In one of the buildings, she sees curtains rustle and realises that Kazichian civilians are probably hiding everywhere. Terrified that their houses will get burnt to the ground, or their children will get hurt.

Where are the riot police? Or the army? Was the High House really that arrogant, that they didn't see this coming?

She finds it incomprehensible that Daniel didn't come with her. This genie is out of the bottle; Kazichia will never be the same after today. The people walking around the capital for the first time, have seen how many they are. And they have seen that the seemingly untouchable palaces of the oligarchs are just buildings, constructed of stone, wood and glass. You can break the glass, you can burn the wood, you can tear down the stone walls.

The E117 turns out to be a highway. It is so quiet that she can stop the car on the ramp to study the different traffic signs. She finds a white plane on one of the signs and turns onto the empty ring road around Stolia. Hopefully for the last time. Going a hundred on the slowly ascending highway, Michelle looks out over the city. She sees the parliament building in the distance. At first, the roundabout seems quiet. But then she sees it is an optical illusion – there are so many people out protesting that, from afar, they have merged into an even, dark colour.

What are you doing there? she thinks, mentally questioning Daniel. *There is nothing here for us anymore.*

She hits the accelerator even harder and sees the airport appear on the horizon. For some reason, she starts laughing. She laughs hysterically. She looks at that white building with its ugly grey control tower, and she bursts out laughing. And Alexa laughs, too. First forced, because her mother does, then sincerely. Harder and harder. For a few minutes, they laugh for no reason, until tears roll down their cheeks. Only when they pass the sign for Vorta Airport do they go quiet.

Michelle parks the car right by the sliding doors in the middle of the pavement. As she picks Alexa up from the back seat, two women approach her. One of them explains there is a helicopter ready that will take them to a small private airport. There, a plane awaits, going to Lechkov Island.

'Great,' Michelle says. 'Let's go.'

Behind the doors, a man is on the phone. When he sees Michelle, he hangs up and tells her he is the pilot. The High House just let him know that he should fly to the centre.

'I don't care, we're leaving now. Do you know who I am?'

'That's exactly it, Madam Lechkova,' the man says. 'I have received confirmation that I should pick up your husband from the parliament building. But your husband didn't give orders, he just made a request.'

'I don't understand.'

'Your husband wants to be picked up so you can travel to the Central Lakes together. But he gave you the final say; if you deem the situation too risky, we leave the city immediately. The army is under way and once they have disbanded the riots, cars can get to Mr Lechkov. But until then, this helicopter is the only way for him to get out.'

Distressed, Michelle looks up at the suspended ceiling. What now?

'Where is Daddy?' Alexa asks again. The girl senses that the conversation is about her father.

'The choice is yours, Madam Lechkova. Do we leave for the Central Lakes, or do we fly to the city first?'

Michelle looks from the pilot to Alexa. This is their only chance to escape. Her only chance to get her daughter to safety. She pictures the dark blur of people protesting in front of the parliament building. That crowd is against Daniel and everything they think he stands for.

'Madam Lechkova? What do you want to do?'

74

The Chamber is a modern white space with a big pulpit, surrounded by two hundred seats in semicircles. The members of the Chamber stand in groups on the floor between the pulpit and the seats. The meeting is over: jackets are slung over chairs, sleeves are rolled up, and everyone is smoking as if their life depends on it. The tension is palpable. No one can go outside, and no one knows what will happen if the intruders come in.

When Daniel enters the Chamber, everyone falls silent. Everyone except Ivanov. The minister of agriculture hands his cigarette to a colleague and approaches the presidential candidate. 'I'm afraid you are too late. The Lechkov dynasty is over.'

'Sit down and shut up,' Daniel says.

Ivanov smiles. 'The vote has been validated. Karzarov will be your successor.'

Daniel points at the registrar's seat. 'Sit.'

Radko stands next to Ivanov and puts a hand on his shoulder. Grumbling, the old man falls into the chair.

Daniel coughs as he walks to the pulpit. 'The members of parliament seem to have forgotten why they live in this country,' he says.

The eyes of all members fix on Daniel – the man they just sentenced to death – as he walks up the steps and sits in the pulpit.

Outside, something explodes, and cheering erupts.

Daniel turns on the microphone. 'Why do you live in Kazichia? Why is this the place where you and your families could build empires, where you earned billions of *ivot*? Why is Kazichia the place where you are free?' He leans over the pulpit like a priest and looks down at his parish of robber barons. 'Because *my* family guarantees that freedom – and has, for decades. We keep America out, we keep the United Nations out, we ensure this remains *our* country. And I am here to guarantee that freedom in the digital age. I can keep out the new digital enemy.'

Behind the building, shots are fired, and there is loud singing.

'Outside of these walls, I don't hear a digital enemy. I hear a real one,' Ivanov says, and he tries to stand up, but Radko pushes him down with one hand.

'You don't understand anything about these times, old man,' Daniel says.

Disgruntled mumbling.

'I hadn't expected the protests to become uncontrollable. But my systems at the intelligence service are working as they should. The situation is under control. It's a matter of waiting now.'

'Under control?' Ivanov chuckles and looks at Radko. 'Gather your soldiers, General Lechkov, because the only way to end this is with old-fashioned fighting.'

'The army is already on its way,' Daniel says. 'And we can definitely wait for them. They will shoot a few people and scare the rest of them back to the mountains. But what will we gain from that? More outrage. And more protests. More attention from the international community. And you don't want that, do you?' He looks around the room, but no one dares to respond. 'Gentlemen, whether you like it or not, we need the Jada and the Neza. So, I don't want to knock them down, I want to control them.'

Daniel wants to say something else but is interrupted by a few dull thuds. It sounds as though the rioters are banging on the doors with sledgehammers. Everyone looks to where the sound is coming from, Radko too.

A few ministers start whispering to each other, shaking their heads.

'You have lost your grip on reality,' one of them finally dares to utter.

Daniel leans into the microphone. 'Gentlemen, I can try and explain to you how we are using cutting-edge technology to wipe this city clean, but I'm afraid that would go right over your head. My proposal is simple: if the streets go quiet in twenty minutes without a single gunshot, then you will support me. I will have proven to you that the Lechkov family still guarantees your freedom like we always did. But if it turns out I have lost control, as was suggested here, if the army needs to come and save us, I will give up my title to Lev Karzarov voluntarily. I swear on my daughter.'

'What?' Ivanov says. 'You want us to wait here for twenty minutes to see if the rioters will go home on their own?'

Radko turns round. He seems sceptical of that promise, too.

'Not on their own,' Daniel says, 'but thanks to my strategy. Thanks to my digital weapons. Within twenty minutes, we can step outside safely. If it turns out I'm wrong, I will step down.'

Ivanov frowns at the almost president and says nothing. And the rest of the Twenty, and the other parliament members, are quiet too. But outside on the streets of Stolia, the people aren't quiet anymore. They are singing an old Neza song. A song about giants stomping and celebrating after chasing away evil spirits, and accidentally splitting open the earth.

Seven kilometres away, in the basement of the intelligence service, a giant server cabinet is soaking up data like a thirsty camel. A database puts together profiles of Jada and Neza rebels; people who proudly use the symbol of their rebel leader as an emblem of solidarity. But that symbol is the Trojan horse that grants the database access to their lives. And because Daniel can use the government databases, he indexes not just their location, but all their personal information. And their families', too.

On the day of the riots, when the protesters try to force entry into the parliament building, the database gets to work. The AI camera system Daniel had installed around the important buildings, scans the crowd and finds the aggressors — the small group of agitators forming the heart of every riot or protest. Their faces are scanned, and the database tells the intelligence service who they are. Where they live. The names of their children.

While Daniel addresses the parliament, cars stop at a hundred-and-thirty different addresses throughout the city and surrounding villages. Doorbells ring, and mothers, brothers and sisters open the door. They are taken to the kitchen or the bedroom and forced to call their family member or send them a text. On the phone, they beg them to come back home, as soon as possible. If they don't, something terrible will happen.

'Someone is in my house,' a mother tells her son, who is in the High House and just hurled Molotov cocktails at the founder of the country. 'I'm begging you, come back.'

One by one, the most dedicated rebels race down the stairs of the parliament building, and from the Chair of God. They run home, where black cars await them. And with the disappearance of the hardcore rebels, the resistance falls apart like a flower without water. In the High House, Maika is in the arms of a guard, who looks around stunned. 'I don't understand what happened. It seems like they all just decided to leave.'

Fifteen minutes after Daniel addressed his parliament, he raises his finger. 'Gentlemen, do you hear that? It is quiet in the streets.'

Astonished, the parliament members all stare at Daniel because, to them, he just performed magic.

'This is a coincidence!' Ivanov tries, as the sounds of violence subside. But the old minister knows the game is over.

'This is a digital war,' Daniel says. 'A war you can only win with manipulation and data. And *that*, gentlemen, is the future of Kazichia.'

Daniel steps down from the pulpit and joins his uncle. The chairman announces a new vote, and when the last minister has cast his vote, and Daniel officially remains in power, Radko collapses next to the registrar's seat. Daniel grabs hold of his uncle and feels the uniform wet with blood.

'Hang in there,' he says. 'We're calling for an ambulance.'

'You won,' Radko says quietly.

Daniel stands amidst the remnants of the battle for Stolia. At the foot of the stairs lie the bodies of soldiers and protesters who were shot or trampled. Slowly, he walks down the granite steps. His face shows the painful contradiction between his unbelievable victory and the unbelievable price he has had to pay for it. The city is quiet, the parliament is convinced he is the only man to protect them, Russia is placed at a distance, and America has entered his sphere of influence. He, Daniel Lechkov, has succeeded as a politician. But his mother has been taken to the hospital in a critical condition. Just like Radko. His wife and daughter have narrowly escaped. The High House is on fire, his oldest friend was kidnapped, and Petar Lechkov is dead.

He walks down the stairs towards the empty roundabout.

The riot police form two walls from the parliament building, over the Abv'ar roundabout to a helicopter that hovers above the asphalt in the middle of the circle. He passes the policemen with his head down. His hair blows into his eyes. The helicopter blades swirl the remnants of the protest in the air. A cloth with the symbol of the Man with a Thousand Faces hits a policeman's helmet right after he salutes his leader.

As he waits for the pilot to land the helicopter, Daniel tucks Radko's gun into his belt. Then he looks up and sees his wife. Michelle looks out the window down at him, but the reflection of the glass makes it impossible to read her expression.

XII. The Frozen Lake

75

The helicopter flies away from the parliament building and climbs higher and higher. From up high, the city looks like the same place that Michelle saw from the window of their private jet a few months ago. A soaked-up ink blot. Something unchangeable. Opposite from her sits Daniel with a lifeless look in his eyes. She has never seen him like this. His mouth hangs slightly ajar, and he stares out the window without blinking, like someone just pulled him from a car wreck.

'It's over,' she says.

He doesn't react.

'Daniel? Do you hear me?'

Maybe he is in shock. That would be understandable; she doesn't know where her own emotions have gone. How is she still functioning?

'Daniel, it's over. It's done. The Lechkovs lost, and we're free now. We can go home together, start over. There is no Mardoe Khador anymore, and no more money. And what does it matter, anyway? We can make money ourselves.'

He looks at her as though she's speaking gibberish. 'What are you talking about?' he asks slowly. 'I won.'

'The Man with a Thousand Faces won,' she says.

Daniel rests a hand on her leg. 'I am the Man with a Thousand Faces. *I* won.'

Did he lose his mind? she thinks.

'I know it doesn't seem like I won. I lost control of the protests and because of that, my grandfather was killed and my mother almost beaten to death . . .'

'This isn't your fault, Daniel. None of this is your fault.'

'It is. And I will have to live with that. But you don't. What matters for you, is that I'm in control now. And that means you can go home. I will make sure, by staying here and keeping Russia content.' He looks at her just as she looks at him; the way you only look at the one closest to you. 'This is all for you.'

A few hours later, they are sitting in a small plane flying over the Akhlos. The plane climbs up along a mountainside and shoots out above an endless plateau. Countless bright turquoise lakes come into view, connected by winding rivers to a dark green body of water nestled against the mountains.

Michelle holds her stomach with two hands as she gazes out the window. It feels taut as a balloon and hurts a little. 'Are these the Central Lakes?' she asks to distract herself. 'The water has a strange colour.'

'It's because of the silt from the melting glaciers,' Daniel says. He still sounds absent.

The plane veers off and starts descending. Michelle sees an elongated rock in the middle of a frozen lake. A long stairway rises up from the ice and climbs against the rocks, leading to a dark grey house with a tall broadcasting tower next to it. It reminds her of a Frank Lloyd Wright design: lots of glass, long straight lines and a balcony that stretches across the front of the house, suspended over the rock. It's a stylish house; she's impressed. Still, she thinks about the rumours she has heard. Rumours about a fourth family, buried under the ice.

76

Among the trees, at the edge of the turquoise lake, lies a nameless
soldier. The soldier is wounded, malnourished and hypothermic,
but he feels as though Nairi is reaching out from the afterlife to
keep him safe, and that gives him strength. In reality, his strength
mostly comes from the PCP crystals that he snorted to numb his
nerves and block the pain from his wounds. He observes the house
from between the branches until he knows how many people
are on guard. The outer security ring of the island, the first he
encounters, consists of three soldiers patrolling on the ice. Their
job is probably to guard the island and its surroundings, but the
men don't seem very motivated. They are smoking cigarette after
cigarette, stomping their feet against the cold and chitchatting
without paying attention.

Across the icy lake, someone has drilled holes and set up fishing
rods to catch fish. The soldier estimates the holes are about two
metres wide, big enough for a man to climb through. He puts on
the diving suit and straps the tanks to his back. Then, with his
knife, he breaks the ice on the bank and slips into the water. Right
before his face disappears, he holds still. He hesitates. The cold,
the pain, the immense job he has tasked himself with; everything
is closing in on him. And he prefers not to be underwater. 'It
doesn't matter what is about to happen,' he whispers to himself.
'Darkness never lasts.'

Then, he puts in his mouthpiece and pulls himself under the
ice.

He swims for about two hundred metres before he passes underneath the soldiers, appearing behind the men suddenly as a ghost. No one sees anything, no one hears anything, and ten seconds later the three men lie dead on the icy lake. He drags the bodies to the hole and buries them under the ice.

With his knife in his hand, he sneaks to the staircase that leads all the way up the rocks. At the entrance of the house are two guards holding machine guns. He approaches them from behind. They have no time to respond. He hides the bodies under some bushes and quietly slips into the mansion. He is back in the reception area. There is no one there. He opens a door on the left side of the hallway, which leads to the waiting room for the guards, but that is empty, too. Suddenly, he hears footsteps. A single person. Heavy footsteps, he must be big. Dead silent, he waits behind the door, and as soon as the man steps inside he pulls him in by his arm, covers his mouth with his hand and drives the knife into his throat. The man collapses and because of the smooth fabric of the diving suit, he can't stop the body weighing at least one hundred and fifty kilograms from falling. It hits the ground with a thud. The weapon the man was holding, clatters on the tiles. The soldier listens intently, someone might have heard, but it remains quiet. No yelling, no running footsteps. For a minute, he stands like this, then grabs the keycard from the guard's neck. He recognises the card from his last visit to the house. That time when he wasn't allowed inside anywhere.

With the card he checks every part of the house, until he hears voices.

In the kitchen, a chef is preparing a fish. When he sees the soldier enter, he drops the intestines on the cutting board and raises his hands in the air. The soldier asks him who the dinner is for, and the old Asian man says that Mr and Madam Lechkov are on their way to the island. The soldier grins when he hears the name. Jackpot! He locks the chef and the maids in a pantry and walks on to the basement, where he abandoned Nairi. The walls in the basement are green and there is a chair surrounded by four cameras. At first, it looks like a recording studio, but as he enters, he sees there are braces with locks hanging from the chair backs.

The wood has deep scratches. He traces the nail marks with his fingers – the right armrest has a lot more than the left one.

'I'm sorry,' the nameless soldier whispers, and he looks beside him, as if she is there with him. 'They will pay.'

Then he looks around the room. The cables of the four cameras run across the floor to the other side of the basement. He follows them through a door, to a dark space. There, he sees a wall filled with blinking green lights. When he turns on the light, a cramped room appears with a few desks and computers. Against the back wall are cabinets full of cables. He walks over to one of the desks and sees a pile of hard disks. 'ERIS' the labels say. He tries to turn a few computers on, but they all require a password. The waterproof pocket on the inside of his suit allows for one drive, so he grabs a random one and stuffs it in there.

'What did they do to you?' he whispers. 'They made it seem like you were the Man with a Thousand Faces. But why? Why would the Lechkovs want that?'

When the soldier returns back upstairs, he hears a plane. He runs to the balcony that overlooks the lake and sees the high-profile visitors land on the private airstrip across the water. One of the dead guard's walkie-talkies crackles. The soldier picks it up, turns up the volume to hear a voice saying something in Kazichian. Probably someone travelling with the president and his wife. The soldier doesn't understand Kazichian, but the voice mentions 'Lechkov' a few times.

He pulls the hood of the diving suit over his head, takes the sniper rifle he stole from the female soldier, and walks back down to the lake.

It is time to demand the truth. He feels the burns on his hands, the PCP is losing its effect. There is not much time before he goes into shock. He needs to be fast and merciless.

77

Carefully, Michelle steps onto the frozen lake. She is scared of slipping, and rests one hand on her stomach. Daniel holds her, but the ice has some grip. Alexa runs onto it confidently and sits on her knees to look at the frozen methane bubbles. Michelle is relieved that the girl can still be carefree.

Two snow scooters are ready to drive them across the lake to the island. In summer, the family can land in front of the water dock with a seaplane, Daniel told her once, but in winter, they have to drive from the private airstrip across the ice. She climbs on the back of a scooter and lets Alexa squeeze in between her stomach and the back of the soldier that is driving them. She gazes at the island. The modern house with its tall, shiny windows looks photoshopped amidst the rugged nature. The long staircase winds from the dock to the terrace like a crack in the rocky cliff. There is no one in sight.

Time to leave this strange place, she thinks.

The soldier says something in his walkie-talkie to let them know they are coming. He waits for a response, but it's quiet. She sees that he hesitates and asks if everything is all right.

'They can't get in touch with the island,' Daniel says. 'Don't worry, this place is well secured. You can't reach it without a plane.'

The snow scooters take off, and the icy cold wind forces her eyes shut. She turns her face to the snow-covered forests along the lake and sees an animal scurry away – maybe a deer. She wants to tap Alexa's shoulder, but when she looks down, something flashes by under the green-blue ice. Something black. Alexa looks up; she saw it, too.

It looked like someone was under the ice.

I'm imagining things, she thinks. *The stress is driving me crazy.*

She takes a deep breath to get rid of that thought and looks ahead – towards the encroaching island that is almost hanging over them like a crouching giant. Her eyes shoot down to the pier at the bottom of the cliffs.

Something moves again.

Another deer?

A black figure appears on the ice. The figure climbs up from the frozen lake as if emerging from a cellar door. Or from a hole in the ice. She thinks she is imagining it and squints. But when she looks again, she is sure, there is a man with a rifle standing there.

She points forward and shouts, but the soldier has seen it already. He steers away from the house, and Daniel's driver does the same. The scooters pull up hard. Snowflakes hit Michelle's cheeks like hail.

Because of the roaring scooter engines, she doesn't hear the first shot. But she sees the soldier on Daniel's scooter getting hit and falling. As he slides over the ice, Daniel tries to grab hold of the steering wheel, but the second bullet smashes the glass window of the scooter, making the vehicle spin until it finally topples. Daniel is launched forward, hitting his face against the ice and slides dozens of metres towards the island.

Michelle cries out.

'When we get to the forest, we need to run!' the soldier in front of her yells. He sits hunched over and steers their snow scooter towards the dark row of trees, two hundred metres away.

She doesn't respond. They will never make it, she can tell. The lake is too big, and whoever that black figure is, he can hit moving targets.

She holds Alexa tight and waits for the impact. For the end.

The third shot hits their scooter. One of the rubber tracks is shredded and the engine starts spitting sparks, and jams with a rattling sound. She lifts her leg and yells at the soldier to do something.

But what can he do?

The scooter slowly comes to a standstill, in the middle of the lake. She sits with her daughter in a giant open plain, like a duck floating to a decoy whistle. Again, she squeezes her eyes shut, waiting for the bullet to hit her, but nothing happens. She looks to her side and the black figure has disappeared.

No one says anything. All she hears is the wind, softly whistling over the lake, whirling clouds of snow up in the air like dust. Thirty metres away, Daniel lies on his stomach. He isn't moving.

The soldier pulls her down, she needs to hide behind the snow scooter. He gets his rifle and shouts into his walkie-talkie: no response.

All the guards are in the lake, she thinks, as she pictures the black shadow under the ice again.

Behind them, someone starts calling out, it's the second soldier. He is still alive and tries to stand back up. His right arm hangs beside his body like a severed cable. With his other hand, he pulls out his gun and tries to aim. But another shot sounds, and his throat bursts open, blood streaming down his bulletproof vest. Choking on his blood, he sways like a tightrope walker for a moment then collapses.

Michelle wants to look away, but she can't. The growing pool of blood looks strange on the green ice. *This isn't real*, she thinks, looking at the red and green. *This is a dream about an invisible sniper.*

'Where is he?' the soldier asks. He has laid his rifle on the seat and searches for his opponent from behind the scooter. Or opponents. The wind rises and a snow fog emerges above the lake. 'Do you see something, Madam Lechkova?'

She is too scared to move or speak. She sits crouched on the ice as if the sniper can't see her if she stays very still. The turquoise lake is vast and empty, but along the shore lies a dense forest. Maybe there are more people in there? Maybe they are surrounded by the Jada rebel army? The third shot came from a different angle than the first two, so multiple people could be hunting them.

Water swashes. Somewhere behind them, towards the island, she hears sloshing, then cracking ice. As she turns round, she realises what has happened.

It's not an army. It's one man, swimming from one ice hole to another.

The black figure is suddenly near, but he still doesn't seem to have a distinguishable face. All she sees is a dark human silhouette. He aims his rifle and before she can speak, he shoots. The bullet hits the soldier in his chest, and he can't breathe. With two hands he tries to rip off his bulletproof vest because the bent armour plates press against his lungs.

She wants to get up and run off, when she hears a raspy voice. 'Stay down.'

The choking soldier gazes up at the black figure, his eyes wide open. Michelle does the same. The man is wearing a black diving suit. The diver stands over the kneeling soldier and gets out a gun. Reflexively, she covers Alexa's face with her coat. The gunshot roars like a fighter jet across the frozen lake.

She watches the man in front of her. The man holding their lives in his hands. But he doesn't shoot. He doesn't do anything.

'What do you want?' she asks. 'Who are you?'

'I'm here on behalf of Nairi of the Jada. And I want the truth.'

78

The man is wearing a diving suit and mask. The glass is covered in red marks; streaks of blood from the soldier he just executed. As he comes closer, he takes off his gloves. His hands are terribly burned; patches of skin hang from his fingers like wet shreds of paper. A big patch gets stuck to the inside of the fabric, and the man groans in pain.

Michelle feels Alexa trying to look up and holds her more tightly.

'Is that Daniel Lechkov?' the man asks after he takes off his gloves. His voice is distorted by the thick fabric covering his mouth.

She doesn't know what to say. He points his gun at Daniel's body. 'Is that the presidential candidate?'

'No, please,' she says. 'Leave him alone. We're not like the other Lechkovs. We're trying to get out of here. We're good people.'

The diving mask turns to face her. 'Good? You're the ones I've had to slaughter young Jada men for. For you, I kidnapped the innocent leader of an oppressed people. You murdered the purest woman in the world.'

She doesn't understand what he means. Is he with or against the rebels? Does he work for the Lechkovs? He doesn't have a Jada accent, it sounds European – maybe even Dutch.

'What is ERIS?' he asks.

She is taken aback. How did he find out about Daniel's company?

'I don't know anything,' she says. 'I am trapped in this country. All I want is to return home.'

'You're Daniel Lechkov's wife, of course you know what is going on. I know your kind of people; you look down on soldiers like me, you think I'm easy to manipulate. But I'm not leaving without answers. Your husband made me do terrible things.'

'I just know him as the father of my children,' she says. 'And my husband.'

'Your husband is the devil. And if you genuinely don't know that, you're blind.'

Michelle hears a deep, cutting rage in his voice. He hates Daniel. She thinks about Harper, fished from the Black Sea. And Nia, who was taken to the OMRA.

'Who is the Man with a Thousand Faces?' the diver asks. He fires a bullet beside her into the ice. Shards scatter everywhere and she feels Alexa cling to her.

'Nairi!' she cries. 'It's Nairi!'

'You're lying! What's ERIS?' He fires again.

'Stop! My daughter!'

She breathes as calmly as she can, but the oxygen can't reach her lungs. Her fingers start tingling and the lake seems to sway like a raft. She is scared she will faint. Her sight gets foggy, but she sees he is approaching her. She feels the gun against her head. The barrel is like the axle of a spinning top: the lake starts rotating around her, faster and faster. She wants to say she needs help, but the world is turning too fast, and all she can do is wait. She rests her hands on the ice and lies down on her back. The cold helps. She can orient herself. But now she can feel the pain in her lower back.

'I'm pregnant,' she says. 'You need to help me. Something isn't right.'

'I don't believe you. You're all liars.'

She can feel Alexa getting closer and opens her eyes. She gazes at her daughter's face, and the pain jerks to her abdomen, changing to cramps. She knows what is about to happen; she suspected it during the flight from the High House when her stomach turned hard. She looks at the diver – the faceless figure – and wonders if there is a human behind the mask. Someone capable of mercy.

'I think I'm having a miscarriage. If you don't help me, my baby will die.'

She feels something running down her leg. It's warm. Michelle puts a hand in her trousers, and the diver points his gun at her. There is blood on the fingers of her bright green glove – red on green.

'Help me, my baby doesn't have much time.'

'Is this real?' He looks at Alexa. 'Is your mother pregnant?'

'I don't have time,' she moans. 'Do you want to kill a child? Is it worth it?'

'Is there a hospital nearby?'

'I don't know, but there is a plane.' She tries to smile. 'Please. Disappear into the woods and let me save my child. No one knows who you are. No one will find you.'

He looks to his side and mumbles something as if someone is there. Then he walks over to Daniel, pulls him by his arms to the scooter and turns him on his back.

'What are you doing? Help me.'

He checks Daniel's heart rate and starts tapping his face to wake him up.

'I'm sorry,' he says as Daniel opens his eyes. 'But I'm not leaving before I get answers. If you can get this man to tell me everything I want to know, I will help you get to the plane. No sooner than that.'

79

Daniel's face is unrecognisable. Thick red streaks cover his swollen nose and mouth, and the whole left side is purple. Forcefully, the soldier sits him upright. Michelle wants to tell him to be gentle. She wants to tell him Daniel might have a concussion or worse. But she can barely speak, the pain in her abdomen cripples her.

Alexa sits close to her. She sees the girl whisper something and wants to rest a hand on her tiny leg, but even that is too much effort. It starts snowing again, and she sees flakes on her daughter's purple gloves.

'Who are you?' Daniel asks, slowly waking up. Carefully, he touches his painful face.

'I ask the questions, Mr President,' the diver says, and he places his gun against Daniel's head. The snow is getting heavier, painting the man's black mask white. The soldiers lying in a puddle of their own blood to the left of Michelle slowly disappear, as if being buried.

'Why did you bring Nairi here and film her?' he asks. 'What is ERIS?'

Daniel gazes at him as if he doesn't understand, but Michelle can tell he knows exactly what this is about. He seems startled that the diver knows about ERIS.

'Talk to him, Daniel,' she says, breathless with her last strength. 'Please, I think I'm having a miscarriage.'

His eyes shoot to her as if he is just now aware of her presence. He notices the blood on her glove and nods.

'Yes, tell me everything, and fast,' the diver says. 'Why did Nairi need to die?'

'You kidnapped Leonid Torelli,' Daniel suddenly says in Dutch. 'What did you do to him?'

The diver is taken aback for a moment. He looks at Daniel as though he has discovered something new, something unexpected. 'Is that the stuttering man? He's dead. The soldiers that were with him are dead too.'

Daniel stares at the diver in disbelief. 'You killed all of them by yourself?' he asks quietly.

'How did you make Nairi say those things in the videos?' the diver asks. 'Did you threaten to torture the village elder? Is that it? What does ERIS have to do with that?'

Suddenly, Michelle understands what Daniel did. She understands why he said he was the Man with a Thousand Faces in the helicopter. Nairi was kidnapped by the High House and Daniel made a deepfake of her. The videos of the Man with a Thousand Faces that Michelle watched on her phone are ERIS renders. Daniel is waging war with himself. That's how he closed a deal with the CIA.

But if Nairi isn't the Man with a Thousand Faces, who is? And where did they go? Why haven't they shown themselves?

'Daniel,' she groans, 'tell him everything. Tell him about the deepfakes.'

He gets up abruptly and tells her to shut up. His anger startles her, and the pain gets even worse.

The diver turns round. 'What do you mean? What is a deepfake?'

She wants to tell him, but Daniel shouts for her to be quiet, that everything will be lost if she doesn't shut up.

Alexa gets scared of her father's voice, and he crouches down to hold her and whispers she doesn't need to worry. Michelle notices a gun in his waistband.

Where did he get that?

The diver aims his gun at Daniel. 'No sudden movements.'

'I need to comfort my daughter.'

He grabs Alexa to hug her, but then shoves her onto the ice.

Michelle is startled by the fall, and by the ease with which Daniel pushes her aside. As though she were a cardboard box sitting in his way.

With a jerk, he turns round and draws his gun. The diver is so surprised by Daniel shoving his own daughter, that he responds too late. Daniel fires a shot, then another one. The diver jumps behind the snowmobile and slides over the ice, like a soccer player on a wet field, followed by Daniel who keeps shooting at him. The big gun almost smashes against his nose because of the recoil. Michelle hears the bullets slam into the ice until the gun clicks.

When she looks up, she sees Daniel standing over the ice hole. He stares at it as if trying to command the black water.

But nothing happens.

The diver has disappeared.

'Why didn't you tell him the truth? Why were you buying time?'

'It will be okay,' Daniel says. He supports Michelle as they stumble across the ice, Alexa next to them.

'Why were you buying time?' she repeats. 'I needed your help.'

She moans in pain and grinds her teeth.

'The plane is still here. We'll go to the snow scooter and find a hospital; it will all be okay. It's over, this mess is over. The CIA will wait for us.'

Michelle can barely keep her eyes open; she wavers on the edge of consciousness. 'This is because of you,' she says quietly. 'You say you have a plan to protect us, but all you want to protect is the plan itself. You want to protect your own influence, just like the rest of your family. You are literally shoving your daughter aside for it.'

He shakes his head.

It starts snowing harder, and she can feel Daniel is about to slip on the smooth soles of his dress shoes with every step he takes.

'This is all for you, Michelle,' he says breathlessly, and he looks behind him to see if Alexa can keep up. 'For our family. The Man with a Thousand Faces exists to protect you.'

'Don't lie to yourself.'

'It's the truth,' he says, his voice raspy from the cold.

She opens her eyes and lifts her head a little. 'Daniel...'

Her legs collapse and she sinks to her knees, but he manages to catch her and holds her in his arms. He starts running. Across the lake, to the snow scooter. The snow is getting heavier, and Michelle feels his arms and legs tremble from the cold, but he keeps running. Despite everything, Daniel keeps going. Over his shoulder, she sees the island. His grandfather's house towers over them, perched on the rock, like an unwavering onlooker with dark, mirrored eyes.

XIII. The Truth

80

Michelle turns off the TV, but she doesn't get up. She sits on the couch in her living room and looks at the dark windows. For some reason she feels as though she is being watched.

That can't be true, she tells herself and takes a last sip of wine.

The American government made her disappear. Michelle doesn't exist anymore. She is Noëlla now, a French expat living in a Portland suburb. And that life hasn't been disturbed for two years, so why would someone be hiding in the bushes outside her house now?

The psychiatrist warned you about feelings like these, she reminds herself. *This is part of your trauma. There is no one in the house.*

She gets up and places the empty wine glass on the marble kitchen counter. Then she drinks a few sips of water, goes to the bathroom, closes the curtains, turns the lights off and walks up the stairs.

While going upstairs she wonders if her daughter has thoughts like these. In the past year, her daughter's resilience has surprised her. From the day their new life in America started, she didn't notice anything off with Alexa.

Sophie, she reminds herself. *Her name is Sophie now.*

Even after two years, she hasn't got used to that name. Sometimes she misspeaks. She forgets her own name too, sometimes. When she called the hairdresser three months ago to move an appointment, she called herself 'Michelle'. The hairdresser couldn't find her in the system, and Michelle got annoyed, telling her to look again. Only when the hairdresser looked for the third time did she realise she was using the wrong name. She hung up the phone and has never been back to that place.

At the top of the stairs, Michelle opens her daughter's bedroom door. The girl is asleep.

She has a number saved on her phone that she messages every morning and every evening, so the Americans know she is safe. Those strict precautions will disappear after a year and a half, and Michelle is not looking forward to that. She likes knowing that someone is waiting for her message. It feels good to check if Sophie is safe in bed every night and then give the CIA, or whoever it is, a sign.

But that night, after closing Sophie's bedroom door and crossing the creaky wooden floor to her room, something stops her. Her finger hovers over the send button, but for some reason, she doesn't press it.

'Get a grip,' she whispers to herself. 'There is no one in the house.'

She presses send anyway and enters her bedroom.

The moment she sees the man standing by her bed, she freezes. The shock paralyses her, as if it's electric. She can't even scream, though she wants to very badly.

'Who are you?' she hears herself ask.

The man takes a step towards her. He is wearing a balaclava. 'Take a seat on the chair behind you,' he says.

Michelle hears the words but can't put them into action. All she can think about is the frozen lake. She pictures the diver with his black mask and the blood on her glove. Red on green. After the man insists she sits a few times, Michelle escapes the frozen lake, and returns to the bedroom. She sits down and notices she is still holding her phone. The phone she just used to tell her protectors that everything is all right. That she is safe. Now, she needs to try and call the emergency number, or security won't find out that she is in danger until tomorrow. By then, the damage is done. Whatever that damage may be.

Does he want money? flashes through her mind. *Or sex?*

The man tells her to put her phone on the floor.

She hears herself say that she has a daughter. And that she can go and withdraw money for him.

The man says he just wants to talk, and that he won't hurt her. He closes the door to the hallway. The bedroom is enveloped in darkness. All she can see is his moon-coloured silhouette sitting on the edge of the bed.

This is an assassin, she thinks. *Sent by the Russians.*

The man starts questioning her about her past life. He knows she has a fake name.

As he is asking questions, she notices he has a Dutch accent.

'Are you the man who emerged from the ice?' she asks in Dutch and looks at his hands. She looks for burn scars, but he is wearing gloves.

'All I want is answers to my questions,' he says. 'When I have those, I will leave forever.'

That makes her feel hopeful. *He wants information, that's all. He wants to know what happened.*

She admits her name is Michelle Lechkova, and her whole life is a fiction. He starts to ramble, asking all kinds of questions about Nairi. He holds a gun to her head. She feels the cold, icy lake against her back, and the cramp in her stomach. She sees the agony in her daughter's eyes, and it evokes rage in her.

You need to charm this intruder, she tells herself. *You can smell his sweat. His cold sweat. He is just as scared as you. And just as lost. Become his friend and lure him away from Alexa.*

'We want the same thing,' she says and forces a smile at him. 'People who want the same thing don't need to point guns at each other. I have an open bottle of wine downstairs. But you might know that already.' She is surprised by her own voice; it's not shaky anymore. 'Let's go and sit at the kitchen table. I'll tell my story, and you'll tell yours. We'll discuss everything that happened in Kazichia, from beginning to end. Together, we can find out the truth. Together, we can expose the Man with a Thousand Faces.'

And then she gets up and walks to the door. She gestures to him as an old friend. 'Come on, we can talk. But be quiet in the hallway.'

The black figure nods and follows her.

Michelle takes the bottle of wine from the counter. The man with the balaclava sits at the dining table. In the lamplight, he is more than a ghostly figure. He is a tall, muscular man dressed in black, a gun in his hand. Michelle feels her fear returning. But when he starts talking, she can hear how lost he sounds, like that day out on the ice. She reminds herself he has been searching for answers for two years, maybe even more. And he needs her to get them. She is in control.

'You want to understand what you were a part of,' she says, pouring the wine and immediately belting down her own glass.

'I want to understand why Nairi had to die,' he says. The balaclava dulls his voice. 'I want to understand why she was being filmed on that island. I want to understand what my client gained by making all those other people lose.' He places a hard disk on the table, with 'ERIS' written on it. 'I found this in the house on the Lechkov island. It's related to the videos they took of Nairi. Maybe together we can . . .'

Michelle interrupts him. 'There is only one way to put the pieces of this puzzle together, and to do that, we need to start from the beginning. You tell me exactly what happened to you in Kazichia, and I will do the same.'

'That could take all night,' the man says.

She nods.

He thinks for a moment, then starts talking.

'The first thing I remember of my operation in Kazichia is darkness. I was sitting in a transport plane blindfolded, and we landed at a military airport outside of Stolia. Then, I got an assignment from a voice on a telephone. I had to question people about the Man with a Thousand Faces.'

His monologue is long and meandering. As he talks, the intruder exposes a lot about the man behind the balaclava. Michelle learns he was a traumatised boy. A boy with many talents, which were exploited by the Amsterdam underworld, the Dutch army, and finally, every multinational and government that would pay for them. The man executed assignments without asking questions, even though she suspects he has a critical nature. He tells her

376

about the civilian executions and the violent interrogations in Kazichia – things that get people a one-way trip to the ICC in the Hague. Things that Daniel wanted to happen.

He tells her about his only love: Nairi of the Jada. How she was abducted right in front of him and executed.

'All I wanted was to return to the mountains with Nairi,' he says finally.

Then he is quiet, staring at his untouched glass of wine.

'For me, it started with a holiday,' Michelle starts. 'We were supposed to go to Dubai, but Vigo crashed his car – no, he was killed.' While she shares the whole story for the first time, more comes out than she had expected. She tells him about the death of her second child, the end of her life in the Netherlands, and the end of her marriage.

Daniel promised he would do everything to reunite with his wife and daughter in America, but since then, he has been elected president, overtaking all the public tasks that came with the presidency. And he has a new wife.

Why can't he leave his new position? Because this is the only way to keep protecting his family? Or because he can't give up power? Maybe for him, there is no simple answer to that question. Maybe love and power can't exist one without the other anymore, like paints that have been mixed into a new colour.

Michelle tells the intruder how she was smuggled out of the country by two CIA agents right after her miscarriage, and how she was forced to start a new life in America. The Dutch government promised they would initiate contact after a few months. That was two years ago. And she has the feeling that the third year will pass by even faster. Michelle and Alexa are starting to become enmeshed with Noëlla and Sophie. Maybe it's better this way; maybe she doesn't want to go back. And maybe it's better to go on without Daniel. If he doesn't play a role in Alexa's life, his war crimes won't, either.

She is honest with the stranger. About everything. About Daniel's plan, too. That he hijacked the uprising of the Jada to serve his own interests. She tells him everything she knows about

ERIS and what you can do with that technology. The man sits very still and listens – he doesn't even seem to be breathing.

As she finishes her story, morning light enters the living room.

The man rolls his balaclava up above his mouth. After all those hours, the damp fabric has coloured his skin red.

'Now I understand what Nairi was used for,' he says quietly. 'And why your ex-husband wanted to get rid of her. But if she wasn't the Man with a Thousand Faces, who was?'

Michelle shrugs. Her eyes feel puffy, and they sting. 'To be honest, I don't really care about Kazichia. I am trying to build a life for my daughter here.'

The man sits up straight. 'Was the operation I worked on to get Daniel Lechkov to power? Or to get you and your child out of the country?'

She shrugs again. 'If you asked Daniel, he would tell you it was all for his family. He would say the rebel attack was a chance to get us home. Nothing else.'

'But you're not so sure.'

'I don't know what the truth is anymore. People are good at lying, especially to themselves. He told himself that it was all for us. But who invents such a complicated plan to get his family out of the country? Who lets that many people suffer? There must be more behind it.'

The man looks at her. Now that it's light out, Michelle sees he has brown eyes. 'Did you have a simpler plan?' he asks. He doesn't sound judgemental; he sounds genuinely curious. 'Did you have a simpler plan, without victims or deepfakes? A plan that was safe for your children?'

Michelle is quiet.

'Maybe it was the only way,' he says. He sounds stunned at his own words. 'Maybe he sacrificed Nairi and fuelled the uprising to save you.'

'He didn't save our second child.'

His brown eyes harden. 'He wasn't counting on my resistance. Just like he hadn't counted on yours.'

Suddenly, Michelle starts crying – quietly but without holding back.

'You helped me finally understand,' the man consoles her. 'This will give me peace.'

She looks up. Tears have turned the intruder into a blurry figure. 'What do you mean?'

'I know now there is not much difference between me and my powerful clients. I may never know why I execute assignments. I may never know what the plan is or the goal. And still, I do everything exactly as I am told. But my clients don't know where their decisions come from either. No one knows exactly why they do things. Why, in a split second, they make a specific choice. Who controls those decisions? Where do they come from? Nobody knows, and that's why we think of stories afterwards, to justify who we are. We make up stories about who we want to be.'

Michelle watches the blurry figure rise to his feet.

'I'm leaving now,' he says, 'and you don't need to worry about me coming back. We will never see each other again.' He disappears behind the white curtains, through the glass swing doors, into the backyard.

Michelle dries her tears and walks to the bedroom to find her phone. Without double-checking if the man actually left, she sends a code to an encrypted number, confirming she is safe. Then she walks upstairs to get Sophie out of bed.

On the kitchen table lies the scratched-up, dented hard drive filled with ERIS training data.

81

Daniel Lechkov enters the empty presidential wing and sinks into the new calf-leather couch in the living room. It is so new that it squeaks as he sits down. After the invasion and the fire four years ago, everything in this part of the house was renovated and redecorated. As he loosens his tie, he looks at one of the few things that still needs to be replaced: the television. Against the wall hangs the smart TV he had put up for his daughter. In the middle of the screen is a big crack.

Daniel watches his own face in the television screen. The crack divides it into tiny puzzle pieces. Those pieces make up a stranger. A grey man, with thick pink scars covering his nose. The man on that screen looks nothing like the academic from the Netherlands. He has turned into a Kazichian president, married to a young Kazichian woman with whom he had a baby. He doesn't see them often and he isn't proud of that. But that's the price for a peaceful and calm country. He turned Kazichia into a place where hundreds of thousands of families no longer need to worry. Daniel is very proud of that.

He wants to get up to get dressed when he sees something move in the reflection of the screen.

'Sit down,' a deep voice says.

Surprised, he falls back onto the couch. The leather squeaks.

In the black reflection, something moves. In the corner of the room, someone emerges from the shadow. He hears rubber soles on the wooden floor and wants to turn round.

'Keep looking ahead,' a voice says in Dutch.

In the screen he sees a man appear right behind him, pointing a gun with a long silencer at his head.

'Who are you?' he asks. 'And how did you get through security?'

The man crouches behind the couch, pressing the cold gun against the back of Daniel's head. 'I know where your wife and child live,' he whispers in his ear. 'I paid them a visit in Oregon. Nice neighbourhood. Good schools for your daughter.'

'Are you the man who waited for us on the frozen lake?' he asks. 'The mercenary. The man who ruined everything. Was that you? What do you want from me?'

'We're here to answer *my* questions, not yours. If you don't answer, your family dies. If you do, I swear I will leave them alone.'

Daniel says he understands.

'Who is the Man with a Thousand Faces?'

He wants to say something, but the man presses the gun hard into his head, and he cowers.

'Don't you dare say "Nairi". This conversation will end with a gunshot if you do. I know about the deepfake. I know all about ERIS.'

Daniel sits up straight. 'Then why are you asking me who he is?'

'Because I have a theory, and if it's correct, you know the answer to my question.'

'What is your theory?'

'That it was always you,' the man says. 'The Man with a Thousand Faces. From the beginning. You pretended there was an uprising and that you responded with a deepfake. But there never was a Jada uprising. There was just a Daniel Lechkov uprising. You had messages placed on internet forums to incite violence. You had me interview Jada leaders about the Man with a Thousand Faces, so they would hear his name, thinking he was someone who mattered.

'You sent that first video of the rebel leader with the balaclava to the High House. You were behind those bombings; you gathered a rebel army. You had me kidnap Nairi, so your uprising had a face. You were the uprising. You were the face behind the mask. The Jada never could have done this without you. Never mind the Neza. You had the networks of the High House get attacked by agents of the OMRA, you had a Lechkov mine blown up by members of the Circle. You killed your own civilians to legitimise the Man with a Thousand Faces.'

The men are quiet. On the other side of the door a staff member walks by on the old wooden mezzanine. Daniel's eyes are fixed on the TV. Behind his eyes, thoughts shoot past like a string of computer code. After a few seconds, the code stops.

'If I tell you the truth, will you leave me and my family at peace?'

'I swear.'

'Okay, you are right,' he says quietly and nods. The nod is dry and curt, as if signalling to someone.

The man lowers his gun. 'What does that mean?'

Daniel shrugs. 'It means "yes". It means "you're right". What do you want to hear? Congratulations: you're smart. You solved the riddle; you exposed the Man with a Thousand Faces. I am the rebel leader.'

The gun stays lowered.

'Was this how you imagined this moment?' Daniel continues. 'I'm sorry, this is the end of your search. You found the truth, and now there is nothing left for you here. You asked a question, and I answered it. Will you leave my wife and child at peace?'

'I told you I would,' the man mumbles.

'And me?'

'I can't let you go.' The gun rises again. 'Not after what you did to Nairi and her people. Not after what you did to *my* people.'

Daniel raises his hands in the air. 'Before you shoot, think about what I just told you.'

The man removes the safety from his gun. 'Your next words will be your last.'

'Now that you know I'm the Man with a Thousand Faces,' Daniel says, his voice tense, 'you know I can't die. The uprising was shut down four years ago, but the Man with a Thousand Faces is still alive. Nairi hid in the mountains and wins a battle for her people now and then. She wins enough of them to keep America interested and to keep her followers loyal. The conditions in the mining villages and on the farms get better every year, and the OMRA is less and less active in the Akhlos. Life is good for the minorities. But I let the Mardoe Khador win sometimes, to keep Russia and other Kazichian oligarchs at bay. Everyone thinks that Nairi and I are in conflict with each other and both sides are content with how things are going. Things are balanced, every country benefits from balance. But when I die, that illusion disappears. The Twenty will grab power, and they will go back to oppressing the Jada. Everything would go back to the way things were.'

The man says nothing.

'Besides, you promised me you would spare my family,' he continues. 'If I die, Michelle's deal with America will be void because the rebel army will implode. Pull that trigger and you don't just shoot me, but also the Man with a Thousand Faces, an innocent woman and an endlessly innocent young girl.'

The intruder makes a sound as if swallowing something disgusting. He stands very still for a long time, then slowly removes the gun. In the television screen, Daniel sees him walking backwards.

'The operation is over,' he tells the reflection. 'Go home.'

'This isn't an operation for me anymore,' the intruder says, turning round. 'I am a Jada returning to the mountains, where I belong. There I will wait for a chance to strike, together with my people.'

Daniel turns round and as the man dissolves into darkness, he mumbles to himself, 'If you think I'm afraid of a Jada uprising, you still don't understand how I came into power.'

82

As Michelle unlocks her front door, she looks at her daughter's red Ford parked in the driveway. She opens the door and wants to call out her name, but sees the living room has been torn apart. Without closing the door behind her or removing her long grey raincoat, she walks in. Family photo albums are everywhere. Someone emptied the tall white cabinet and slung the albums through the room. A picture of her daughter, taken shortly after she was born, lies on the small glass table. She picks it up and stares at the girl's face – the girl that could still be called 'Alexa'.

She enters the kitchen and sees leftovers on the kitchen island and an impressive collection of empty wine bottles by the back door. Fruit flies swirl in the sunlight.

'Sophie?' she calls upstairs, but there is no answer. She walks up to the bedrooms, but there it is quiet, too. Walking to the bathroom, she hears music coming from the attic. From her office. Is Alexa in the attic? In her mother's office?

She found the secret laptop! flashes through her mind.

First, she can feel her stomach tighten, but then, immediate relief, as if she had been holding her breath all these years. The only reason she never told her daughter anything, was because the girl seemed fine not knowing. She was living her life as a regular American girl called Sophie. Alexa didn't exist anymore. Why would Michelle turn that life upside down?

But that would all change now.

How fitting, she thinks, *that this week it's time for the truth.*

She had just come back from a meeting with Daniel. For the first time in fourteen years, they saw each other. He was on holiday in California with his new Kazichian family, and Michelle had pretended to be at a conference. Daniel hadn't been in touch for years, but he'd requested to see her a few months earlier. First, she declined because she didn't want to face him. From the moment he was elected president and appeared on television with his new girlfriend, she avoided all news articles about Kazichia. It was too alienating to see him in front of that crowd of people, waving and smiling like every politician does. But then Alexa moved out, and Michelle was alone for the first time in years. Suddenly, the past started haunting her. The questions crept back up. She agreed to meet him, and two months later, she walked into a hotel suite in Los Angeles where he was waiting for her.

It was everything she had feared, but everything she had hoped for, too.

They had become strangers to each other. She and Daniel had been apart for so long that their shared memories had become fiction. For fourteen years, they had each replayed and reshaped everything that had happened; there was no longer one story in which they both played a part. The truth had been turned into two completely different narratives. But after two days of difficult and demanding conversations about Kazichia and the uprising, they finally discussed Sophie – or Alexa. And that brought them together. From that moment on, she was with the Daniel she knew from before Vigo's funeral. And with an aching heart, she got on the plane back home. The home where she would have to face the past one last time.

'Mom?' Alexa stands at the top of the stairs. 'Where were you?'

At the sight of her daughter, tears well up in her eyes.

And at the sight of the attic, her tears dry up in surprise.

Sheets of paper are pasted to the walls, filled with notes and Post-its. On the floor lie piles of books and photos. It looks like the office of a maniac. On Michelle's desk is her old laptop – her secret laptop.

'How did you access those files?' she asks.

'I know everything, Mom,' Alexa says.

Michelle's adolescent daughter looks exhausted, like she hasn't slept in days. But the look in her eyes is one of bright determination.

'Please be honest with me,' she says, 'because I know everything. Finally, I understand.'

Michelle nods and sits at the desk chair, while Alexa starts talking. She talks about the suppressed memories and her search for Kazichia City. About the things she discovered the past few days and the conversations with Tim.

'Please, Mom. The lies need to stop. You need to tell me who I am.' She points at the sheets on the wall. 'I know Daniel is my father, and I know what he did to save us. I know he was behind those attacks to get us to America. And I'm not angry with you guys, Mom. Not at all. I get it now. So please, stop lying.'

'Attacks?' Michelle asks. She doesn't follow.

Alexa nods and points at a part of the timeline. 'Yes, I know everything. I understand his whole plan. How he invented the Man with a Thousand Faces and incited a riot. I know why he thought it would be justified to have those bombs explode.'

Michelle doesn't understand what she means.

'You didn't know?' Sophie asks.

'No, Sophie, that's not right. Daniel made a deepfake to take control of the uprising. To take control of the situation.'

Alexa starts explaining what she has just discovered. Her theory of Daniel inventing the uprising and the Man with a Thousand Faces: it was all one giant digital illusion.

'But . . . if he was the Man with a Thousand Faces, why didn't he tell me anything?'

'He probably didn't want to make you complicit in war crimes.'

Michelle shakes her head. 'Dozens of civilians died in those attacks, we almost died during those protests. If he did all that, then he is a . . . a monster.'

The girl starts manically leafing through her notes, talking faster and faster. 'He wanted the protesters to cause enough chaos for the CIA to take the rebels seriously. But it went too far, he lost control. I thought you knew all this. He made a few big mistakes, but it was an extremely complex plan.'

386

'And the bomb in the centre of Stolia?'

'I'm still looking into that,' Alexa says, taking another pile of paper. 'I haven't figured out exactly how that attack was planned and executed. He probably used OMRA agents, but I'm too scared to really get into all that. It's not easy finding out your own father killed innocent people.'

As her daughter rambles on about the bizarre lie Daniel would have constructed, Michelle sees how passionate she is. Sophie's theory couldn't be the truth; Michelle would never have married a man capable of bombing civilians. But she sees the existential urgency her daughter feels in finding answers to her questions. And from the answers Alexa has found, a man emerges with a genius plan. A plan to save his family, whatever it took. Michelle sees that her daughter discovered a father who fights for her. She can now accept why she never saw him. It wasn't because he disowned or abandoned her, it was because he wanted to protect her – as every daughter hopes. Michelle sees a girl who has got her life in order amid chaos, by creating a story about Daniel Lechkov.

Alexa crouches next to her mother. 'Just admit it, Noëlla or Michelle, or whatever your name is.' She flashes a teasing smile, but her eyes are wet. 'I know what you had to go through, and I know why you hid this many secrets from me. But now it is time for the truth: Daniel Lechkov is my father. And he became the Man with a Thousand Faces, to protect us.'

Michelle kisses her daughter's forehead and gets up. 'Sweetheart, you're too smart for your own good. You got that from your father.' She looks at a printed-out press photo of a young Daniel and Tim, right after they started ERIS. 'Your *real* father,' she says, and she covers the two men with her hand.

As they walk downstairs, Alexa wonders if Daniel gave her those grey-blue eyes, and Michelle thinks about a conversation at her dining table with a masked man twelve years ago. A conversation about Daniel Lechkov and his ascension to the throne. A conversation about the stories we tell ourselves to give the truth a friendly face.

Acknowledgements

This book could not have come into existence without the guidance of my publisher and editor Steven Maat. Steven believed in my idea from the very first pitch and challenged me to turn Kazichia into a three-dimensional place – a country with a story. Thank you for your trust.

Pedro Cattori tried his best to teach an amateur something about machine learning and AI. Jonathan Tham told me everything about his time at a British boarding school. Jeroen Dobber gave me a crash course in international treaties, and Vincent Noteboom inspired me to write the scene with the ethanol fire and the sequence about Michelle's deal with Turkey. Thank you all. The details you contributed make up a book.

Thank you to everyone who read the manuscript and offered feedback. Especially my parents and Laura Noteboom, who reads everything I write – even when it still consists of experiments on scraps of paper.

Most of all, I want to thank my wife Desi. You give me space to write and keep me grounded at the same time. That's why you can be found between all the lines.

Credits

Lex Noteboom and Orion Fiction would like to thank everyone at Orion who worked on the publication of *The Man with a Thousand Faces* in the UK.

Editorial
Sam Eades
Brittany Golob

Copy editor
Francine Brody

Proofreader
Kate Shearman

Audio
Paul Stark
Louise Richardson

Contracts
Dan Herron
Ellie Bowker
Oliver Chacón

Design
Jet Purdie

Editorial Management
Anshuman Yadav
Charlie Panayiotou
Jane Hughes
Bartley Shaw

Finance
Jasdip Nandra
Nick Gibson
Sue Baker

Marketing
Lucy Cameron

Production
Ruth Sharvell

Publicity
Ellen Turner

Operations
Group Sales Operations team

Sales
Catherine Worsley
Esther Waters
Victoria Laws
Rachael Hum
Ellie Kyrke-Smith
Frances Doyle
Georgina Cutler

Rights
Rebecca Folland
Tara Hiatt
Ben Fowler
Alice Cottrell
Ruth Blakemore
Marie Henckel

Credits

Lex Noteboom and Orion Fiction would like to thank everyone at Orion who worked on the publication of *The Man with a Thousand Faces* in the UK.

Editorial
Sam Eades
Brittany Golob

Copy editor
Francine Brody

Proofreader
Kate Shearman

Audio
Paul Stark
Louise Richardson

Contracts
Dan Herron
Ellie Bowker
Oliver Chacón

Design
Jet Purdie

Editorial Management
Anshuman Yadav
Charlie Panayiotou
Jane Hughes
Bartley Shaw

Finance
Jasdip Nandra
Nick Gibson
Sue Baker

Marketing
Lucy Cameron

Production
Ruth Sharvell

Publicity
Ellen Turner

Operations
Group Sales Operations team

Sales
Catherine Worsley
Esther Waters
Victoria Laws
Rachael Hum
Ellie Kyrke-Smith
Frances Doyle
Georgina Cutler

Rights
Rebecca Folland
Tara Hiatt
Ben Fowler
Alice Cottrell
Ruth Blakemore
Marie Henckel